Reviews for previous

Limbo

'A hugely enjoyable, dimension-hopping,
time-travelling hybrid of comedy, SF and fantasy'
South Wales Evening Post

'A very satisfying and hilarious romp . . .
Terry Pratchett, beware'
The Argus

'Anarchic farce . . . unpredictable originality'
Dreamwatch

Limbo II: The Final Chapter

'Secombe occupies his ground with confidence
and never lets logic get in the way of his plot'
Guardian

'He's carving himself a niche as reliable comic fantasist . . .
The juxtaposition of the different worlds is deftly done'
SFX

'Gallops all over the place . . . funny and fast paced'
Dreamwatch

The Last House in the Galaxy

Andy Secombe acquired his love of fantasy at an early age, but he had to overcome a natural talent for prevarication, and an acting bug that lasted thirty years (including appearances in two of the 'Star Wars' films), before he was able to settle down to writing his first novel, *Limbo*. He now lives with his wife and two sons on a farm in rural Devon, and this is his third novel.

Also by Andy Secombe

Limbo

Limbo II

ANDY SECOMBE

The Last House in the Galaxy

TOR

First published 2005 by Tor
an imprint of Pan Macmillan Ltd
Pan Macmillan, 20 New Wharf Road, London N1 9RR
Basingstoke and Oxford
Associated companies throughout the world
www.panmacmillan.com
www.toruk.com

ISBN 1 4050 4618 X

Typeset by Intype London Ltd.
Printed and bound in Great Britain by
Mackays of Chatham plc, Chatham, Kent

To Mum

Acknowledgements

Thanks once again to all at Macmillan, chiefly Peter Lavery and Rebecca Saunders for being entertaining lunchtime companions. Also, love and thanks to my inspirational family.

The Last House in the Galaxy

The game had lasted all night. Now, with the sun beginning to stream through the windows of the close, cramped study, the two men faced each other across the green-baize-covered card table. Everything depended on this one, final hand. The solicitor, dressed in a Pierrot costume and dripping wet, placed the document he had hastily drawn up in the middle of the table.

'Gentlemen,' he said, 'do you agree to be bound by the terms of this contract, as witnessed by those here present?' He indicated the others in the room, including a man in a dressing-gown and wellington boots, a tall figure in a tailcoat and a fat man dressed all in black wearing a Balaclava and holding a pack of cards.

Mortimer Trenchard, clear-eyed, determined, signalled his agreement with a confident, 'Aye!'

The man facing him, red-faced and sweating profusely, called for another bottle of port only to be informed that his cellar was empty. Laughing grimly at the news and with a heavy heart, Elgin Huxley muttered his agreement to the terms, and the fat man dealt four cards . . .

Chapter 1

Matt would have to be quick. The Crusaders' ships were already approaching from the Nemotid Quadrant – he'd seen them as he'd set down – and soon Argus's rocky tunnels would be echoing to the sound of iron-studded boots. They may even know he was here – since the war had begun their tracking devices had improved beyond recognition. One thing was for certain, if he didn't grab the merchandise and get out of there soon, he was going to end up fighting hump-backed stelions in the arena on Cullorum.

Parking his ship in a small gully that he hoped would be out of sight of the incoming Crusader circus, Matt Fripp set the engines to stand-by and opened the door. He looked up at the towering rocks of the fortress and the unremitting grey sky above. 'Well, this is pleasant,' he remarked, shivering in the biting wind.

'Wrap up warm now,' came a well-modulated female voice.

'Thank you for your concern, Computer.'

'Are you going to be long? You know how I hate you being away.'

'Don't start,' Matt muttered under his breath. 'I'll be as quick as I can,' he said a little louder, making a mental note to turn down the computer's emotional sensitivity circuits when he had a moment. 'Oh well, here we go.' Pulling up the hood of his rain-cape, he left the relative security of the ship and strode out into the thin greasy drizzle. Making his way over the jagged and slippery rocks, he cursed the superstition that had led him to wear his ancient 'lucky' suede boots; the soles were worn almost smooth – hardly ideal for this difficult terrain.

Although barely thirty, Major Matt Fripp looked older than his years. Under his white-streaked hair was a face that was tired and lined, his grey eyes weary from witnessing the everyday horror of war.

Arriving at the foot of the fortress's monstrous black granite walls, he knelt and swept aside a drift of damp grey sand to reveal a tiny silver keypad. 'Bingo!' Tapping in the code that Glaak Raffin had confided to him, he was relieved to see a small doorway hiss open in the featureless rock. 'OK, Glaak, so far so good.' The space beyond was pitch-black and smelt unpleasantly of rotting seaweed. 'Welcome to Paradise Hotel.' Removing his rain-cape and taking a last breath of fresh air, he dived inside. The door closed behind him.

He was in total blackness. Feeling his way along the wall with his fingertips, his head collided with something solid – 'Ouch!' Reluctantly he pulled out his night-vision goggles. Anything that covered his face made him feel claustrophobic, but he couldn't waste time groping around in the dark. Putting them on, the surrounding gloom was immediately transformed into a ghostly grey-green landscape. He was in a small vestibule with several corridors leading off. 'One, two, three . . .' he counted the dark openings from the left. '*Four* is what the man said.' Matt started along it. After about twenty yards the corridor began to narrow and slope upwards. There were steps, but they had been made for feet far smaller than his, and he had to walk on tiptoe, bracing himself against the walls with his hands. His progress was slow and laboured and he was soon drenched with sweat.

'They could at least have put in a handrail,' he muttered as he clambered slowly upwards.

The corridor at last opened on to a wide landing. The ceiling was low and there was barely space for Matt to crawl, but there *was* light here, spilling dimly down a long ventilation shaft punched through the roof. It had been clumsily done, the edges were rough and unfinished, and the floor was strewn with rubble; but then no one was ever meant to see it – this part of the fortress had been closed for years. With relief Matt took off his goggles and pulled himself towards the round patch of light on the floor, rolling on to his back to look up the long, shiny-black chimney at the grey sky far above. It was a mistake. The glimpse of sky it afforded merely served to heighten the closeness of his surroundings.

'Let's get this thing done.' Heaving himself back on to his front, he made his way towards a louvred steel plate set into one of the walls. Taking out a small electric screwdriver, he loosened the four screws one by one. The plate came away and he was bathed in warm, fetid air from deep within the fortress. 'I love the smell of rats in the morning,' he grumbled, putting his night-vision goggles back on and pushing himself reluctantly through the narrow opening.

The ventilation ducting was barely big enough to take him. There was no room to turn, and Matt tried not to think about what would happen if he got stuck. Crawling slowly along he kept his mind focused on the job and the sequence of turns and bends in the ducting that Glaak had taught him. *One . . . two . . . three . . . four . . .* He counted the openings leading off on either side. *OK, now a left.* Manoeuvring himself around the bend with difficulty, he paused for a moment to catch his breath. *Easy now.* He set off again, once more counting the dark openings that he passed. *One . . . two . . . three . . . now right . . .* He was just about to ease himself around yet another bend when he stopped suddenly at the sound of voices.

'Honoured Ambassador,' came a thin, reedy treble.

It was answered by a bass deep enough to set the walls trembling, 'Gulgus Filch sends you greetings.'

Shit! Matt thought. *They're here already.* He had no idea through which room this particular piece of ducting passed, but reckoned it must be one of the large, formal state salons, which meant he was near his goal. Pulling himself around the tight right-angled bend, he edged along as quickly as he dared, trying not to make a sound. *Just concentrate. Count the sections of ducting*. Feeling with his fingertips, he searched for the rivets holding the sections together. *One . . . two . . . three . . . four . . . five . . . Yes!* In the bottom of the duct was a large inspection hatch secured by eight tiny screws, just as Glaak had said. After laboriously removing the screws with the electric screwdriver, he gently lifted the steel plate and eased himself through the hole.

The dimly lit room he dropped into was barely big enough for him to crouch in, but palatial compared with the confines of the duct. It was almost totally featureless except for a heavy steel door and what, at first glance, looked like a blank granite plaque set into the opposite wall. But closer inspection revealed that this 'plaque' was in fact made up of an intricate pattern of interlocking pieces, each one fitting its neighbour so perfectly as to be almost invisible.

Pulling off the night-vision goggles, Matt fixed a small hypersensitive microphone to the door and screwed the remote earpiece into his ear. So far, all was quiet. 'Let's hope it stays that way,' he muttered. Taking a rolled-up sheet of clear Perspex out of an inside pocket, he opened it out against the plaque and was delighted to find that it lined up exactly with the edges. Imprinted on the sheet was a series of angular white shapes numbered randomly from one to twenty, corresponding to the sections of which the plaque was made up. Matt pressed number one on the Perspex 'key' lightly with his index finger. The stone underneath gave slightly and, with a small hiss, receded into the wall. Matt carried on in the numbered sequence, each small stone hissing into the wall with every touch. When he hit number twenty the plaque, in a complicated series of movements, rearranged itself into a representation of the Argusian coat of arms – a rat rampant on a black field – before swinging back to reveal a hole just big enough for a small rodent to squeeze through. In the vault beyond was what Matt had come for – the Helian Cartogram.

The small black rectangle lay on a purple cushion surrounded by a 'cage' of orange light – a complex system of beams which, once broken, would trigger the quantum mechanics-based security system and send anyone in the room zinging simultaneously out across deep space and down into the planet's core: killing them and driving them mad at the same time. From now on, Matt would have to be extremely careful – one false move and he'd end up with a terminal case of split personality.

What didn't help his nerves was the sound he now heard through his earpiece: tiny scurrying feet followed by the heavy tramp of iron-clad boots – they were heading towards the vault. 'Fuck, fuck, fuck!' He removed his watch and aimed its tiny laser at a spot near the bottom of the cushion. There was a puff of smoke and a hole appeared in the purple material. Clamping it to the wall to keep it steady, he grasped one of the watch's three timing buttons and spooled out a thin wire probe, on the end of which was a miniature plasma-field generator and a video camera linked to a TV monitor on the watch face. Taking a deep breath, he fed the probe gently through the maze of orange beams and into the hole in the cushion. Staring intently at the image on the watch face, Matt manoeuvred the end of the probe with the watch bezel, navigating it up through the cushion's ancient Gasorian goose-down stuffing, guiding it gingerly around the weight sensors, and bringing it to rest right underneath the Cartogram itself. Matt locked off the probe and breathed again. 'Now for the difficult bit.'

Ripping open one of his thigh pockets, he extracted two identical brushed-steel rectangles and, unwinding the thin flex wrapped around them, laid them on the floor. Then he took out a black slab of solid plastic, exactly the same size and weight as the Cartogram and placed it on one of these rectangles. Plugging the lead from the rectangles into a socket on his watch, he was about to begin the transfer procedure when, through the earpiece, he heard the Gologon ambassador's party arrive outside the door.

Don't panic. Don't panic, he told himself.

Wiping the sweat from his brow, he started up the watch's tiny warp-generator, then watched closely as the Helian Cartogram became engulfed in the plasma field glowing at the other end of the probe. It was going to be a two-way transfer and the timing was paramount; if he acted too soon, the plastic dummy and the Cartogram itself would become fused. Too late and the alarm system would sense its loss and quantum physics would take over . . .

Outside the door the rats were keying in the opening sequence – he had less than half a minute. Matt's heart was thumping. *Steady, steady*. The dummy Cartogram was now also glowing in its own plasma field, signifying that all systems were go. One by one, the steel bolts on the door were being withdrawn. It was now or never.

Matt touched another of the timing buttons on his watch and the dark image of the Cartogram on the cushion began to dissolve. Immediately he hit the other button, and for a long second both real and dummy Cartograms appeared in three places at the same time: the cushion and each of the two steel rectangles. Matt held his breath.

Outside, the Gologon ambassador waited as the Argusian deputy custodian, a large black rat with grey-tipped fur, attended to the complicated lock on the massive door of the Cartogram chamber. As the last of the steel bolts slid smoothly back, the rat looked up at the big, grey Gologon.

'Soon it will be in your hands, Ambassador.'

'And not before time, if I may say so, Deputy Custodian.'

'Quite so. If you will permit me, Ambassador?'

'Hurry up,' the Gologon growled.

The deputy custodian clapped his hands and the officers of the watch slowly heaved open the heavy steel door to reveal the empty chamber.

Before entering, the deputy custodian bowed reverentially, as if entering a holy place, then stepped over the threshold and began keying in the combination on the complicated lock of the vault itself. In a matter of moments the Cartogram was revealed, safe and secure in its cage of orange light. Crouching low outside the door, the Gologon ambassador peered into the vault. There it was – the most powerful piece of kit in the universe, and it was almost within his grasp.

The deputy custodian turned back to the officers of the watch. 'On my signal!' he commanded. The two officers produced keys from around their necks and scurried off in opposite directions to insert their keys simultaneously into two identical keyholes at either end of the corridor. 'Quantum field – off!' the deputy custodian bellowed. The officers turned their keys and the orange light surrounding the Cartogram snapped off.

Reaching inside the vault the deputy custodian tenderly lifted the Cartogram from its cushion. He was about to hand it over to the ambassador when he noticed something odd. It didn't feel quite *right*. Puzzled, he turned it over, searching in vain the faint impressions of the many curious symbols with which one accessed the wealth of information within the Cartogram. The ambassador, waiting with his hand outstretched, was becoming impatient.

'What is it? Hand it over. What's wrong?'

The deputy custodian looked up at him, confusion and disbelief in his eyes. 'Honoured Ambassador. This is not the Cartogram. It seems that it has been stolen.'

Matt was almost at the outer door of the fortress before he heard the patter of tiny feet behind him. Stumbling through the green-tinged darkness, he hit the wall and groped around for the door button. *Where the fuck is it? Come on, come on!* At last he found it and the door slid open. Ripping off his night-vision goggles gratefully, Matt dashed out into the damp greyness of the Argusian day.

Slipping and sliding over the smooth rocks in his haste, he called ahead to his waiting ship. 'Open starboard hatch!' Nothing happened. A burst of white-hot energy seared past his head, singeing his left ear. 'Shit!' Diving behind a low granite outcrop he pulled out his proton pistol and returned fire. The officers of the watch, standing in the open doorway through which Matt had just exited, ducked back out of sight.

'Open starboard hatch!' Matt called again.

'What time do you call this?' the ship replied.

'Just open the fucking door!'

'Language!'

More proton pulses zinged over Matt's head. Now there were rats above him, too, raining down fire from openings in the fortress walls.

'Open the door or I'll blast it open!'

'You don't mean that.'

From high above him came the deep *thrum* of a maser cannon, and a second later the rock behind which Matt was sheltering exploded in a cloud of dust. Picking himself up and dodging the hail of fire, Matt weaved and stumbled over the slippery ground the short distance to his ship. He levelled his gun at the door. 'You've got just three seconds. One . . . two . . .'

'Welcome home.' With a *tchuck*, the lock slid back and the door hummed open.

Matt dived inside. 'Full power! We're leaving!'

The engines remained silent.

'Please!'

The engines suddenly burst into life and wound themselves up to a scream as, all too slowly for Matt, the slim silver craft lifted into the air. Pulling clear of the tall granite cliffs, Matt spotted two . . . three . . . four Crusader battleships appear from beyond the fortress. Strapping himself securely into the pilot's seat, he reached for the auto-pilot control toggle switch.

'What are you doing?' the computer asked suspiciously.

'I'm not going to argue with you,' said Matt, 'I'm taking us out of here.' He flicked the switch over to manual. Immediately the steering yoke came alive in his hands. Easing back on the stick to point the ship's nose skywards, he pushed the thruster sliders all the way to max and was answered by a roar from the engines. 'Here we go!' he yelled. Pinned to his seat by the extraordinary gush of power, Matt was above the clouds in moments and rocketing towards the concealing darkness of space. But the Crusader ships were right behind him.

A warning klaxon sounded above his head.

'Incoming hadron shell,' the computer informed him.

Matt threw the ship to port and the shell zipped past, disappearing into the void. 'OK, Computer, I need the coordinates for the Vagus wormhole in the Dark Quadrant!'

'And how do I calculate that with no data?' the computer sniffed.

Extracting the Helian Cartogram from a thigh pocket, Matt inserted it into the universal applications aperture in the instrument binnacle. 'This should have all the data you need.'

After uttering a muted 'wow', the computer went quiet while it analysed what it had been given.

The klaxon sounded again. One of the Crusaders' ships had somehow got ahead of him. Through the forward view-port Matt could see the blue flare of its weapons as it let go a salvo of hadron ordnance.

'Shit!' Matt pushed the stick forward and dived. He could almost feel the electric crackle of the shells as they passed overhead, inches from the hull. If one found its target it would short out the electrics and immobilize the ship. 'Anytime you're ready, Computer!'

It remained silent.

Now two of the battleships had slipped around behind while the other two were above, trying to force him back down on to the planet. Matt flipped his ship over and, pointing its nose heavenwards, released two muon torpedoes. They didn't hit either battleship but the manoeuvre had the desired effect: the Crusaders got out of the way, leaving him just enough room to power through the gap.

At last the computer spoke. 'I suppose you think that was clever?'

'You're just embarrassed because you can't figure out the Cartogram. That's it, isn't it?'

'It's an incredibly complex and elegant device, granted, but do you really think that a vast intellect like mine can't decipher it?'

'OK, so, the Vagus wormhole. Where do I go?'

Matt saw from his instrument readings that not only had the four pursuing ships now turned around and were thundering after him, but he also had a heat-seeking torpedo on his tail. 'Release chaff!'

Matt pulled back on the control yoke to put the ship into a climbing turn. At the same time the computer opened a hatch at the rear of the ship, releasing a white-hot plasma field designed to confuse the torpedo's heat sensors. As soon as the weapon flew into the field it detonated harmlessly.

'The wormhole?' Matt asked desperately.

'Take a right and head for Gweeb.'

'Could you be a little more precise, please?'

'Heading three zero one point five.'

'Thank you.' Matt changed course to the new heading. 'How long to Gweeb?'

'Two minutes and seven seconds at present speed.'

'And how long before the Crusader ships catch up with us?'

'Two minutes.'

'Great.'

'We have more incoming,' the computer warned. 'Five hundred kilometres and closing fast.'

'I see them,' Matt replied. This time there were three blips on his radar. 'Release chaff!'

The computer released another confusing burst of plasma while Matt threw the ship into a spiralling dive. Two of the torpedoes disappeared in angry red explosions, but the third kept on coming.

'You missed one,' the computer announced.

'So what do you suggest?'

'I've got an idea.' Before them a small green rainforest-clad planet hove into view. 'Welcome to Gweeb. Oxygen-rich atmosphere, plentiful liquid water and lush plant growth abundant in vitamins and minerals consistent with humanoid requirements.'

'And crawling with invisible demons, or so the story goes.' Matt glanced at the radar – the torpedo was closing rapidly. 'You said you had an idea?'

'The Vagus wormhole is beyond the planet, zero point six six parsecs into the Dark Quadrant. If we slingshot round Gweeb we should gain enough speed to outrun both the torpedo and the enemy ships.'

'*Should?*'

'Do you have a better idea?'

'No.' Matt flipped the auto-pilot switch and took his hands off the controls. 'Computer, you have the conn.'

'Aye-aye, Cap'n.' Making minute adjustments to the craft's trim, the computer aimed the ship at the very centre of the planet to take full advantage of Gweeb's gravitational pull.

The sudden increase in speed pushed Matt firmly back into his seat. He looked at the radar and for several agreeable moments watched as the ship began to pull away from the doggedly following torpedo, but it wasn't long before it began to catch up again.

'Thirty seconds to atmosphere . . .' the computer announced, 'altitude change and booster burn in five seconds . . . three . . . two . . .' An explosion rocked the ship: the torpedo had detonated right underneath it.

'Computer, damage report!'

'Ngraack . . . tharrghhh,' came the reply.

'Oh shit! Computer, I'm taking control – give me exact coordinates for the wormhole!' Matt flicked the auto-pilot switch back to manual, but the controls were impossibly heavy. Gweeb's green jungle canopy was coming up terrifyingly fast and Matt couldn't get the nose to lift. 'Computer, speak to me. What got damaged?'

The computer's voice was oddly distorted: low and strange. 'I've been hit. It's bad, Matt. I . . . Main stabilizer failure imminent.' The ship began to vibrate violently. 'Sorry . . .' the computer gasped.

A big red light began to flash over Matt's head. The craft was supposed to have skipped across the top of the planet's atmosphere like a pebble across a pond – instead it was plunging through it like a meteor; flames licked greedily around the overheating fuselage. 'Shit, shit, shit!' Pulling for all he was worth on the control yoke, Matt tried in vain to get the ship to respond. The planet's surface was looming larger, a vast sea of green stretching as far as the eye could see. It had certain death written all over it. Bracing his feet against the control panel, Matt strained with all his might and gradually, gradually, the nose began to rise. But it was too little . . . too late. The ship lurched violently as it ploughed through the tops of the trees and the stick was wrenched from Matt's grasp.

'Fuselage integrity compromised . . .' the computer whispered.

The ship careened off the jungle canopy.

'Hull breach imminent . . . Goodbye, Matt . . . We were a good team.' The computer uttered a long, drawn-out sigh, and went silent.

The ship slammed into the treetops once more. The impact caused the heat-weakened fuselage to break in two. The forward section, containing the bridge and the sweating and wide-eyed Matt, rose into the air once more. As he watched the green canopy come up to meet him one last time, a gigantic tree wider and taller than all the rest loomed large through the forward port.

Matt clicked on the intercom. 'Gulgus!' he yelled over the noise of the disintegrating ship. 'If you're wondering where your fiancée is, she's with Glaak, telling him all your little secrets. Hey, buddy, how does it feel to be shafted?'

What was left of the ship slammed into the big tree and, in slow-motion, Matt watched the forward port disintegrate and fly away in front of him, just before the bolts securing his seat to the floor of the cockpit let go and he too found himself sailing through the air.

Chapter 2

'I, er . . . urge you mo . . . most strongly to accept my client Mr Huxley's . . . latest, and ve . . . ve . . . very generous offer.' The small man in the dark suit didn't usually stutter but he was extremely nervous. Perched on an elegant but none-too-safe, wormeaten salon chair in the library of Hambledon Hall, Albert Smythe was sweating profusely. He hated coming here. Most of all he hated Lady Trenchard opposite whom he was now seated. Imperious and raptor-like, she looked down her long nose disdainfully at the shabby, sweaty little man. Albert mopped his forehead and continued, 'He . . . ha . . . has asked me to stress that this is definitely his fi . . . er, final offer.' Pulling a sheet of paper from the sheaf balanced on his lap, he handed it to Lady Trenchard.

She took it, glanced at it briefly, then passed it to the starched butler stationed behind her chair. Clasping her hands in her lap she smiled. It was not a good sign. She had the kind of smile that could reduce strong men to the consistency of vintage marmalade left too near the Aga. 'My dear mister Smith,' she began, deliberately mispronouncing his name. 'Convey our respects to Mr Huxley and thank him for his kind offer. However, we cannot possibly accept. We feel that his plans to turn the estate into a "leadership development centre" – hiring it out to businesses for the purpose of inspiring their jaded employees on "motivational" weekends – is not in keeping with Hambledon's illustrious past. I do not believe that the Hall's reputation would be enhanced by swarms of overweight, red-faced executives running about the lawns pretending to be soldiers and playing gun-balls.'

'Er, I think you mean paint-ball,' Albert corrected – it was a mistake.

Lady Trenchard glared at the hapless accountant, and Albert had the feeling that unseen hands were rearranging his internal organs. 'Frankly,' she continued, sitting up even straighter in her chair, 'to use an image that Mr Huxley will understand: he can take his offer and insert it where no sun shines. Whipple, show the gentleman out.' Lady Trenchard waved a hand in Albert's direction, as if wafting away a bad smell.

'Very good, ma'am.' Advancing across the threadbare Persian carpet, the tall cadaverous butler bore down on the small man like a well-bred Rottweiler. Albert leapt to his feet and, scattering paper like confetti, fled the room. Whipple followed him into the entrance hall and the little man was seen off the premises with all the ceremony of a clod of mud being removed from a wellington boot.

As Whipple shut the door after Albert, a portion of the plaster cornice above, decorated with apples and wheat sheaves, dislodged itself and fell on to the doormat with a *thunk*, missing Whipple's head by inches. The butler sighed and went to fetch a dustpan and brush.

Hambledon Hall, a rather sombre mansion set amidst rolling Devon countryside, and surrounded by fields where, for the moment at least, sheep may safely graze, was in a poor state of repair. The paint was peeling, the castellated facade was crumbling, and occasionally a decayed gargoyle would part company with the stone guttering and thump into the flower beds below. Even the once-grand entrance hall was now split down the middle by a large plasterboard partition which, for safety's sake, blocked access to the derelict ballroom and the precarious West Staircase. Over the years a vast amount of the family fortune had been poured into the Hall to prevent it from simply rotting away, and now the current occupiers, Sir Percival and Lady

Trenchard, most of their money gone, had been forced to retire to the modest but comfortable apartments in the East Wing – the only habitable part of the house.

During the great country-house boom years, the income from visitors had been not inconsiderable, and had enabled the Trenchards to open a small zoo in the grounds, which had been run by their only child, Tom. But now the public's enthusiasm for the opulence of the past had cooled, Tom had gone back to teaching, and the Trenchards weren't so much treading water as drowning.

They'd tried just about everything. English Heritage had turned them down, stating that the house was of insufficient architectural merit, and the National Trust, after doing their sums, reckoned it wouldn't bring in enough money to cover their maintenance costs. Most people agreed that the Trenchards would be forced to bow to the inevitable and sell up to property developers in the shape of Harry Huxley. But they reckoned without the steely determination of Pamela Trenchard.

After sweeping up the bits of plaster cornice in the entrance hall, Whipple made his way back to the library. 'Will there be anything else, ma'am?' he enquired. Lady Trenchard sat deathly pale and clutching at her chest in some distress. Reaching for the small vial of purple pills he always kept in his pocket, Whipple was at her side immediately. 'If I may, ma'am?' She opened her mouth obediently and Whipple placed one of the pills under her tongue.

After a few moments she regained her colour, and her breathing settled back into its regular rhythm.

'Thank you, Whipple. It's all this unpleasantness.'

'Dr Carmody's advice was to avoid unnecessary stress and confrontation.'

Lady Trenchard's face hardened. 'I'm damned if I'm going to be bullied into giving up the estate to that dreadful man. Who else is going to stand up to him? Not Percy. He simply collapses under pressure.'

'Very good, ma'am.' But as the butler turned to go, a troubled Lady Trenchard called him back.

'Whipple.'

He stopped in the doorway. 'Ma'am?'

'How much do we owe you now?'

'Four thousand, two hundred and fifty-seven pounds and forty-two pence, ma'am.'

Lady Trenchard looked down at her hands clasped in her lap. 'Thank you for staying with us,' she said in a faint voice. 'I don't know what we'd do without you.'

'Where would I go, ma'am?' Whipple replied, reassuringly. 'I have been in your service for forty years. Hambledon Hall is as much my home as it is yours. Rest assured I have no desire to live anywhere else.'

'Thank you, Whipple.' Lady Trenchard's eyes were glistening.

'Would you care for a cup of tea, ma'am? Or perhaps something a little stronger?'

Lady Trenchard produced a small lace-trimmed handkerchief from the sleeve of her cardigan and blew her nose before replying. 'It's rather early, Whipple, but perhaps just a small amontillado? For medicinal purposes, you understand.'

'Certainly, ma'am.'

Opening a drinks cabinet in the corner of the room, Whipple selected a cut-glass crystal schooner from one of its shelves and placed it on a small silver salver. Pulling the cork from the lone bottle of sherry nestling in the cabinet's interior, he filled the glass and, balancing the salver on one hand, glided back across the carpet with a smooth gait.

'Your sherry, ma'am.'

Lady Trenchard had got up and moved over to the window, and was now looking out over the rolling lawns. She turned to her servant and picked up the sherry glass in an elegant hand. 'Thank you, Whipple, most kind.' Taking a small sip, she closed her eyes to enjoy the feeling of warm relief as the fortified wine slipped affably down her throat. Then she up-ended the glass to her lips and downed the rest in one.

Whipple waited attentively at her side, bottle poised: he knew the routine well. Lady Trenchard feigned surprise to see him still standing there.

'Oh well, just another half a glass then, if you insist – to take away the taste of that awful man's visit.'

Whipple refilled the glass to the brim.

'You're a bad influence.' She clicked her tongue in mock admonition. She was just getting her lips into shape for her second glass when she thought she saw something resembling a man strapped into a chair suddenly shoot out of the large rhododendron at the bottom of the croquet lawn and disappear down into the ha-ha.

'Whipple, did you . . .?' she began but, turning to him, noticed that Whipple himself was preoccupied, staring intently at the salver in his hand which was crackling with electric-blue fire. Quickly downing her sherry, Lady Trenchard glanced back towards the view outside the window. The gardens looked as they always did: calm, leafy and utterly English. *Steady on, Pamela old girl*, she thought, *you can't afford to fall apart now*.

Without a word, Lady Trenchard held out her glass to Whipple once more. He arched a disapproving eyebrow. 'Dr Carmody said—'

'I'm well aware what that quack Carmody said,' she snapped. 'But I'm having a bit of a day.'

Whipple half-filled her glass.

'To the brim, man, to the brim!' she ordered. Whipple did as he was told, then walked directly back to the drinks cupboard, placed the bottle of sherry inside and closed the door.

'Will that be all, ma'am?' he said, once the bottle was safely out of sight.

'All? Oh yes, I suppose so,' Pamela Trenchard said vaguely. 'What time is luncheon?'

'One o'clock, ma'am, as always.'

'Of course.' She knew exactly what time luncheon was. It had been served at precisely one o'clock for as long as anyone could remember. But at that particular moment talking about familiar things was somehow strangely comforting. 'Thank you, Whipple.'

Whipple bowed and left the room, leaving his employer staring pensively out at the lush and verdant lawns.

Chapter 3

Gulgus Filch replayed the vid-screen clip of Major Fripp's last moments, as recorded by one of the pursuing Crusader battle-ships. A smile played around his lips as the ship dived, out of control, towards Gweeb. The Crusaders had been monitoring Matt's transmissions, so the Major's last words had been recorded for posterity: 'Gulgus! If you're wondering where your fiancée is, she's with Glaak, telling him all your little secrets. Hey, buddy, how does it feel to be shafted?' The signal went to white noise as Matt's ship broke up in the Gweebian rainforest. An evil gleam came into Gulgus's eye.

'Goodbye, Major Fripp.' Filch clicked off the vid-screen and looked up at the lieutenant standing to attention in front of his desk. 'Praise Valohem that he has seen fit to destroy another of our enemies.'

'Alleluia!' replied the lieutenant dutifully.

'Yes indeed.' Gulgus bared his teeth in a wide smile. 'Where is it?'

The lieutenant licked his lips nervously. 'Sir?'

Gulgus pushed back his chair and rose slowly. Even for a Gologon he was big, the width of his shoulders emphasized by the grand epaulettes of his black leather uniform. With a large head and a well-defined nose, he was quite handsome for his race. His mouth, set above a strong jaw, was mobile but cruel, and it was there one looked for any tell-tale signs of emotion; his piercing green eyes, enhanced by his shiny grey skin, gave nothing away. 'The Cartogram, Lieutenant. You did *look* for it, didn't you?'

'Well, sir, we scanned the entire planet—'

'That's not what I asked,' Filch said quietly, moving round the desk to stand menacingly over his subordinate. 'Did you land and search for it?'

The lieutenant swallowed. 'We, er . . . well, sir, in the circumstances, we decided that, erm . . . we'd break off and call in the sweepers . . . to do a really thorough job.'

Gulgus nodded. 'So, even though you were under direct orders to retrieve the Cartogram from the thief Fripp, you did not land and search for it,' he said. 'OK, we all make mistakes.' A smile spread across Gulgus's face, and the lieutenant relaxed. Then, in a sudden lunge, Gulgus grabbed him by the collar and marched him over to the large picture window at the far end of his air-conditioned office. 'You see that?' he whispered, pushing the lieutenant's face against the glass.

The window overlooked the gladiatorial arena that Gulgus had built for the amusement of the citizens and the 'purification' of sinners. Prisoners of war and convicted criminals from all over the universe were brought here and forced into life and death contests against each other, or pitted against hideous beasts like the dreaded hump-backed stelion, which had claws a foot long and teeth like steak knives. At the moment the arena was being cleared of the remains of the afternoon's entertainment; an army of cleaners was sprinkling sawdust on pools of darkly clotting blood, and heads and limbs were being collected and unceremoniously dumped into bin-bags.

'What do you see?' Gulgus asked.

'Nngthh,' the lieutenant replied, his mouth pressed firmly against the glass.

'I'll tell you,' Gulgus continued. 'You see the remains of those who have offended Valohem by displeasing me.' Gripping him firmly around the throat, Gulgus pulled the man away from the window and, holding him close, spoke into his terrified face. 'We're not just pissing in the wind, Lieutenant. We are on a real-life fucking crusade here, to spread the good news to the darkest recesses of the galaxy. For that we need the Cartogram. Do *you* believe?'

'Arrngh.'

'A little louder. Do you believe?'

'Yaarrgh.'

'Alleluia!' Gulgus said softly, forcing the man to his knees. 'I suggest you pray hard and listen closely for the reply, son. Listen – you hear that?' All the poor man could hear was a ringing in his ears. 'The Lord has a message for you. You know what it is? I'll tell you: disobey another of my orders and your liver will be food for the stelions!'

The lieutenant, who was turning blue, tried to nod his head, which only made Gulgus grip him even tighter.

'This time, I forgive you. But don't do it again.' The lieutenant was on the point of collapse before Gulgus finally released his grip. 'Now go, assemble a search party and await further instructions.'

The lieutenant staggered to his feet, saluted rather limply and marched unsteadily out of the room.

Gulgus's iron-shod boots clattered on the polished-steel floor as he strolled back to his desk and hit the intercom button. 'Send in the girl,' he growled.

Straightening his uniform, Gulgus ran a hand over the smooth grey dome of his head and waited in front of the door. It opened and an attractive young woman entered, escorted by two Gologon guards. She had olive skin, dark brown eyes and pouting lips. Her auburn hair was trimmed into a businesslike bob which emphasized the graceful line of her neck, and the zip of her all-in-one black leather suit was open just enough to reveal a softly inviting cleavage.

'Mariella, my dear,' Gulgus smiled. 'So glad you could join me.'

'What is all this, Gulg? Why'd you send these two goons? If you wanted to talk to me, you could have just called me up.' Shaking herself free of the guards' grip she strode easily into the centre of the room. She moved with an animal grace and had curves that would make any man want to run his hands all over her.

Gulgus eyed her intently. 'My child, whatever did I do to deserve you?'

Mariella went over to him and kissed him on the cheek. 'You're sweet.'

Gulgus took hold of both her wrists and pulled her to him. 'Are you looking forward to the wedding? Have you picked out something pretty to wear?'

'It's beautiful, Gulg. All satin and lace.'

'And pure white, of course.'

'Of course.'

He looked deep into her eyes. 'Like the driven snow. Have you been to confession today, child? Come, let's open our hearts to Valohem together. Let's get down on our knees and confess our sins right now. Here, let me show you how it's done.' Squeezing her wrists a little too tightly, Gulgus knelt and pulled Mariella down with him.

'Oh, Great One, whose message was brought to us by the prophet Elron, forgive me for I have sinned. It's about . . .' Gulgus looked at his watch '. . . thirty minutes since my last confession. I lost my temper with a subordinate and I may have gone too far with his chastisement. I ask your absolution.' He turned to Mariella. 'Your turn. Go ahead and unburden your soul to the Lord, and in his bounteous mercy he will wash you clean.'

Mariella was used to Gulgus's weirdness but this was something else – group confession was not usually his style. 'Well . . .' she began, 'I did snap at Conchita this morning when she made my bath a little too hot.'

'There you go,' said Gulgus. 'What else?'

'I, er . . . I looked at myself a little too long in the mirror.'

'The sin of pride! Alleluia! See, it's easy once you start. What else?'

'That's it, I think.'

'You sure?'

'Um . . . Yes.'

'Kneeling here in the presence of the creator of the universe, Lord of Lords, God of gods, he who sees all things and knows the dark secrets in all hearts, you are absolutely sure that there is nothing else you want to confess.'

Mariella managed to arrange her features into a look of puzzled incomprehension. It was impossible that he could suspect anything – her cover was perfect. 'No, I don't think so.'

'OK.' Gulgus stood and reached over his desk to flick on the vid-screen, swivelling it round so that Mariella could see it. 'This is a little clip recorded earlier today above Gweeb. It's a short piece entitled: Matt Fripp's final moments.'

Mariella flinched inside at the name but she was a good enough agent not to let it show. She watched Matt's ship plunge into the Gweebian rainforest and listened impassively to his last words: 'Gulgus! If you're wondering where your fiancée is, she's with Glaak, telling him all your little secrets. Hey, buddy, how does it feel to be shafted?'

Gulgus clicked off the screen. 'Now, what do you think he meant by that?'

Mariella stood up. She didn't have to pretend that she was shocked and confused. She was also furious. 'I really have no idea.'

'You were apprehended at the spaceport perimeter. Where were you going?'

'I was taking a flyer to Zemboz. I had a fitting with Allyana for the wedding dress.'

Gulgus shook his head. 'I checked with Allyana. You weren't due for a fitting until next week. You see,' Gulgus stroked his shiny grey head, 'call me old fashioned, but I've always believed that a groom and his bride-to-be shouldn't have any secrets from each other. For instance, like her being about to run off with a rebel agent.'

'Run off with Matt Fripp! Are you crazy?'

Gulgus blew out his cheeks. 'No, it seems to me I'm only just coming to my senses.'

'That is *so* like a guy. Even though Fripp's your sworn enemy you'd still rather believe him than me because he used to be your buddy.'

Gulgus smacked her hard across the mouth and she flew backwards, landing on the hard metal floor with a clang. 'Don't lie to me. I want to know how much you know, and the names of every other agent that has managed to infiltrate my organization. Cooperate and I'll make your treatment as painless as possible.'

Mariella sat up and wiped away a thin trickle of blood from the corner of her mouth with the back of her hand. 'You haven't found it, have you?'

Gulgus turned and perched on the edge of his desk.

Mariella smiled. 'Matt took it away from right under your nose and now you're pissed off because you can't find it. I bet you couldn't even get your men to land and look for it. Ha! The great Crusader war machine. You've conquered half the galaxy and yet you piss your pants at the thought of visiting Gweeb. You know, Gulg, you may be big but Matt was twice the man you'll ever be.' Gulgus advanced on her furiously, fists clenched. She looked up at him calmly, 'My, my, are we the teensiest bit jealous?'

Gulgus stood over her, shaking with rage. Then, after a few calming breaths, he reached down and pulled her gently to her feet. 'You know, baby, I think what we need here is an expert.' He smiled, then turned his head and called in a low voice, 'Glitch!'

Immediately a small door in a far corner of the large office whispered open and a thin sliver of darkness moved silently into the room. Mariella had gasped at the mention of the name, and now stared in horror at the evil creature making its way towards her.

From a distance the thing you first noticed about him – if you were lucky enough to detect his presence before it was too late – was that one side of his face appeared to be heavily made-up with something shiny and metallic. But as he got closer it became apparent that the right side of his face – and indeed his head – was completely missing. In its place was a scaffold of tubular chromed steel, and it was this that caught the light. But that wasn't all. From the crown of the skull, where the scaffold was screwed into bone, there projected a small spigot from which pivoted a curved arm; at its end hung a monocle containing a living eye. This arrangement was powered by a small electric motor enabling the monocle to orbit his head, giving him 360-degree vision.

The strange apparition stopped and bowed before Gulgus. 'You called, sir?' he asked in a soft, high-pitched voice. Glitch's roving eye completed a circuit of his head before coming to rest above his left ear.

Commissioner Glitch McGilvray was a Dastorian, a race prized by the military for their ability to infiltrate enemy territory completely unseen. The son of a much-decorated Dastorian soldier, Glitch had always had a fascination with the machinery of death, and it was this obsession that had led to his appalling injuries.

A lonely child, Glitch had been playing hide-and-seek on his own one morning when he had found a chest in the back of his father's wardrobe. The chest contained trophies from his father's many military campaigns, including a cornucopia of captured weaponry. At random, little Glitch pulled out a pulsar grenade and started bouncing it off the wall and catching it, with inevitable results.

Not one to be held back by something so trivial as massively disfiguring injuries, Glitch himself designed the roving-eye arrangement, and also the black leather sheath that covered his damaged right arm. But the sheath was more than merely cosmetic, it contained synthetic muscles giving him the power to crush bone. It was clear he was destined for great things.

Having few friends to distract him, he worked hard at school, always coming top of the class no matter how gifted his class-mates. Besides, students who threatened to gain better grades than he had a strange habit of disappearing.

On graduating he joined the secret service, soon becoming, by default, its head. It wasn't long before someone with such obvious talents came to Gulgus's notice, and Glitch was appointed his Commissioner of Covert Operations. The arrangement worked well, Glitch preferring the anonymity of a behind-the-scenes role to the glare of the public spotlight, and taking on many of the more distasteful jobs with which Gulgus did not wish to dirty his hands. Indeed, Glitch took to the post with relish, and had proved a most loyal and willing personal assistant. If he did have a weakness it was a fondness for the gaming table – he could never resist a bet.

'What is your wish?' Glitch's left eye looked straight at Gulgus while his other whirred once around his head before fixing itself on Mariella. She shivered involuntarily.

Glitch seemingly had the ability to dissolve before your gaze as he was talking to you, reassembling himself somewhere else in the room almost before you'd noticed he was gone. So suc-cessful was he at blending in with his surroundings that the first and last most of his victims knew of his presence was the elec-tric whirring of the motor that powered his circling optic.

'I, er . . . need some information,' said Gulgus, taking a step backwards. The Gologon was frightened of no living thing, but Glitch didn't quite seem to fit into that category.

'Ah,' Glitch aspirated. 'The lady has a secret, yes?' Apparently without moving, Glitch had somehow managed to get round behind Mariella and was now breathing down her neck. She started at his cold, clammy breath.

'She has many secrets,' Gulgus agreed. 'Find out everything she knows.'

'Master,' Glitch said and bowed again. 'I may have to . . . how shall I put it . . .' He stroked her cheek with a black-gloved finger. 'Beauty is such a fragile thing. How far may I go?'

'Do what you have to do,' Gulgus said grimly, gesturing to the two guards who had entered with Mariella. They took hold of her firmly, one on either side.

Glitch continued to observe her closely, his orbiting eye forever on the move, noting everything.

'You'll never get anything out of me,' Mariella said unconvincingly.

'On the contrary, my dear,' said Glitch, suddenly appearing in front of her. 'We have many little tricks to jolt a recalcitrant memory. Are you familiar with homeopathy – treating like with like? It is a most effective method.'

Mariella inclined her head and tried to look Glitch in the eye. 'If you want me to talk all it takes is a couple of dry Martinis – I'm a cheap date. But then, you'd know all about being cheap.'

'Ah, she has an acid wit, as sharp as a needle. Needles and acid, a fine place to start, no?' He clapped his hands with glee, and his roving eye did a victory circuit of his head. 'Oh, this is all going to go splendidly!'

Mariella had turned white.

'My laboratory, gentlemen. Chop, chop!' Glitch ordered. The guards on either side of her tightened their grip, lifting her off her feet.

As she was hauled out of the room, Mariella looked back at Gulgus. 'I guess this means the wedding's off?' But her heart wasn't in the joke, and she fumbled the delivery.

The door closed, and Gulgus turned back to the room. Glitch, who had been flickering excitedly all over the place, suddenly appeared in front of him. 'Command is a hard and lonely place, no?'

Gulgus pursed his lips.

'Ah, when love turns sour . . .'

The Gologon looked down at the Dastorian with ill-disguised

revulsion. 'Don't make the mistake of thinking you are above my disapprobation,' he growled.

Glitch dissolved and was suddenly at the other end of the room. 'Do not fear, my master. She will tell me everything.' He twirled and seemed to vanish almost immediately.

Gulgus tracked McGilvray's progress across the large office from the sound of the electric motor that powered his roving eye. Then the door finally opened and closed, and he was gone.

Gulgus breathed a sigh of relief and strode across to the corner where a holographic model of the galaxy twinkled and shimmered, those territories newly conquered by his forces glowing red. This visual proof of his power soothed him: it put things in perspective. After all, what was a woman? Less than a speck of dust compared to the vastness of the galaxy, of which – as soon as he possessed the Cartogram – he would become absolute ruler.

Smiling now, he went to the window and looked out over the arena as banks of floodlights blinked on, starkly illuminating its pitiless expanse of sand. The stands were filling up with punters, all waiting with eager anticipation for the evening show to begin. The sight excited Gulgus and, without thinking, he was about to reach across to the intercom to summon the one person who could always be relied upon to satisfy his cravings, but then he remembered.

'Ah, Mimi,' he said sadly. Even after all these years, in his mind's eye the image of his first wife was crystal clear. He sighed and shook his head.

In the cockpit of the small blue spacecraft, which had been trailing the cluster of Crusader battleships, tiny claws skittered over the controls. The pilot was, like the Crusaders, scanning Gweeb for traces of Major Fripp. But he could find no sign of him.

'Matt, oh Matt, where have you gone?'

Pulling a small black distorted rectangle out of his dense fur, the rodent pilot laid it on the instrument console and touched several points on its edge. Strange lights began to glow around the black lozenge's rim and, finally, a holographic image of the planet materialized above it, labelled: *Gweeb – here be monsters*. On one side of the planet, exactly at the spot where Major Fripp had crashed, was a small yellow dot signifying the entrance to a wormhole and, underneath, the legend: *Earth – quite good for potted meats*.

'No, no, no!' the pilot wailed. 'Matt, you idiot, you've gone through the wrong wormhole!'

There was nothing else for it – he would have to follow.

Giving the Crusaders a wide berth, the rat steered his ship down towards the planet. Once he'd entered the coordinates for the wormhole into the computer all he had to do was hang on.

'Oh well,' he said, 'here goes nothing', and, closing his eyes, braced himself for the strange and disorienting journey through several billion miles of compressed space.

In one of the battleships, the systems officer scanning the planet saw something flash across his screen. He was just about to alert his commander, but when he looked again it was gone.

Chapter 4

The first thing Matt Fripp saw when he opened his eyes was the face of General Glaak Raffin, who was standing on his chest.

'Matt! You're back with us. Good to see you!' said the rat.

'General, is that you?' said Matt, groggily coming to.

'How are you feeling?' Glaak Raffin asked.

'A little shaken,' Matt groaned. Glaak helped him undo the flying harness, and Matt untangled himself from his seat and sat up.

'Well, it's your own fault. You went down the wrong wormhole. We're at least fifty billion miles from where we should be.'

'Wrong wormhole? Wait a minute.' Matt searched his brain, trying desperately to remember what had happened before the lights went out. 'The last thing I remember is ploughing into Gweeb. I never even got near a wormhole.'

'You never got near the *right* wormhole,' Glaak corrected. 'You must have hit this one by accident.'

'I blame the computer – it never liked me.' Matt struggled to his feet. 'So, where are we?'

'Earth.'

'Earth?'

'The far side of the galaxy.'

'Oh.' Matt suddenly felt dizzy and sat down heavily on the red brick steps that led up out of the ha-ha. 'Do you know anything about this planet?'

'A little. My ancestors used to come here before the Cartogram was locked away. My great-great-grandfather was a big fan of something called Fortnum and Mason's. But, thankfully, this planet's presence is not widely known in Crusader circles.'

Matt ran a hand through his hair. 'Good – besides, they'll never risk getting that close to Gweeb.'

'It's only a matter of time,' the general sighed. 'But for the moment, at least, it seems we're safe.'

Matt suddenly looked concerned. 'Where's Mariella?'

'Ah.' Glaak looked at the ground.

'What happened?'

'She wasn't at the rendezvous.'

'Wasn't at—?' Matt stood and began nervously pacing the ha-ha. 'Where's your ship? I've got to go back, she's in serious danger.'

'She knew the risks when she volunteered for the mission.'

'No, you don't understand. I thought she was safely with you, so . . .'

'So?'

Matt stopped pacing. 'I kind of . . . I've probably blown her cover.'

'You've done what!' The general exploded, all four of his feet leaving the ground at the same time. 'What did you do?'

'Didn't you hear me on the radio?'

Glaak shook his head. 'No, I've got one of those confounded new Quantum sets – it only works when you're not listening to it. Oh, Matt, why did you do a stupid thing like that?'

'I don't know, I thought I was going to die. I wanted to say something that would really piss Gulgus off. Look, if you didn't hear it, maybe they didn't either?'

'Oh, they'll have picked it up all right. Their monitoring equipment is a lot less sophisticated than ours, which means it works.'

'Then let me go back and get her!' Matt pleaded.

The general was adamant. 'There's nothing you can do about it now.'

'They'll kill her!'

General Raffin stared hard at Major Fripp. 'What you did was very foolish, Matt. However I'm not going to allow you to assuage your guilt by going back and putting yourself and the whole operation in jeopardy.'

'But—'

'No buts. Mariella's a professional agent, and a bloody good one at that. If there's a way out she'll find it. If not we should try to remember that there is more at stake here than the life of one operative.' The general's face softened and he looked up at the major. 'She'd understand, Matt. And she'd be glad to know that her sacrifice was not in vain and that the Cartogram was safe.'

The colour drained from Matt's face.

'Come on, let's have a look at it, then.'

Matt bowed his head and stared dumbly at the ground.

'Come on, Matt, give me the Cartogram.'

'I . . . haven't got it,' Matt said at last.

The general's whiskers twitched. 'You haven't—?'

'I put it into the computer to guide me to the Vagus wormhole. It's still in the ship, wherever that is.'

'You haven't got it?' the general repeated, incredulously. 'You fool!'

'Now hang on just a minute. I barely escaped with my life!'

'You—?' the general began, almost speechless with rage. '*You're* expendable!' he exploded. 'We all are! All that matters is keeping the Cartogram out of Gulgus Filch's hands.'

'It's on Gweeb!' Matt yelled. 'They'll never look there, they wouldn't dare. They think the place is haunted.'

'It *is* haunted,' the general replied. 'Anybody who's ever landed there has been driven stark-staring mad.'

'There you are then,' Matt said, triumphantly, 'it's safe!'

'But for how long? The Cartogram is too big a prize for Gulgus not to risk everything to get his hands on it.' Glaak shook his head. 'Oh, this is terrible, *terrible*. We have to go back.'

'That's what I've been saying all along.'

'Very well,' sighed the general. 'Come on.' He led the way along to the far end of the ha-ha where his ship had come to rest, its nose up against the trunk of a large horse-chestnut tree.

Matt crouched and examined the small craft, inspecting it for damage. 'OK,' he said, 'it seems to be intact. I think we should be able to—'

'This place is perfect!'

'What?' Matt turned.

General Raffin had clambered up the tree and was staring intently at something. Following his gaze, Matt's eyes lit upon Hambledon Hall.

'Look at the size of it!' the general enthused.

'It looks as if it could do with a lick of paint,' Matt said, dubiously.

'It must have at least . . .' he quickly counted the windows in the crumbling facade 'fifty rooms! We could fit them all!'

'All?' Matt asked. 'Who's all?'

The general glanced down at him. 'The delegates, of course.'

Matt looked blank.

'For the conference.'

'Eh?'

'The Galactic Alliance conference!'

'Oh,' said Matt, catching on at last. 'I thought that was supposed to take place on Beta-Dromo 7?'

'It was,' said the general, barely able to contain his excitement. 'But Beta-Dromo 7 is too hot during the day for the Grublins from the ice-moons of Cassiopeia, and too cold at night for the Blatooms from the deserts of Ttring. Not only that but the accommodation there is little more than a jumbled assortment of poorly insulated huts, so sleeping arrangements are always a diplomatic nightmare. This location not only offers a temperate climate but every delegation can also have its own room. It's ideal!'

'And it's occupied,' Matt observed, seeing a tall man in a tail-coat appear on the front steps with a sweeping brush.

'I'm going to do a recce,' said the general, his claws clatter-ing on the bark of the tree as he scampered down to the ground.

'What about the Cartogram?' Matt reminded him.

'Oh, that'll be safe for the time being – it's on Gweeb, after all! Now then, let's just hope they speak a language this thing understands.' He checked the small black voice decoder slung around his neck. 'Stay here.'

And without more ado, the large fat rat scurried across the lawns towards the great house.

Lady Trenchard was still gazing out of the library window when she first heard the commotion coming from the region of the morning-room.

'Rats! Rats!' someone was screaming.

'Oh, Percy,' she muttered, a spasm of pain flitting across her face. 'What are you up to now?'

Collecting Whipple from the scullery, Lady Trenchard urged him towards the door of the morning-room. 'Whatever he's doing, stop him,' she ordered.

'Certainly, ma'am.'

Shooting his cuffs, Whipple opened the door and threw it wide.

The room was a mess. An antique table was upturned, a wing chair lay on its side and curtains and cushions were scattered over the floor. In the midst of this chaos stood an excited and breathless Sir Percival, brandishing a silver-topped cane. 'Ah, Whipple! Just the man,' he said. 'Bloody great rat! Appeared on top of the bureau.' His eyes darted wildly around the room. 'There he goes! Tally-ho!'

'The chinoiserie!' screamed her ladyship as the end of the baronet's wildly flailing cane came perilously close to several fine examples of Victorian porcelain atop the mantelpiece.

'Ya ha!' yelled Sir Percival, raising his stick yet again and this time narrowly missing the crystal chandelier.

The rat broke cover and streaked across the carpet towards the door.

'Coming your way, Whipple!'

Coolly, Whipple removed his morning coat and held it out in front of him like a matador facing down a bull. Seeing its way barred by the elegant form of the Trenchards' manservant, the rodent paused for a moment and sniffed the air. It was one of the largest rats Whipple had ever seen, and it now stood before him opening and closing its mouth and making the strangest noises.

'Whacklub! Squeeaakkkarrgh! Chaarrungshplit!' it went, while wrestling with some small black object almost concealed in its fur. If Whipple hadn't known better he would have sworn it was trying to communicate with him. Then, all of a sudden, the rat looked down at the carpet, shook its head and made a break for the corridor between the butler's legs. In one smooth movement Whipple dropped his coat on to the fleeing creature and gathered it up.

'Bravo, Whipple!' Sir Percival cried.

'Thank you, sir,' said Whipple, wrapping his coat securely round the rat and tucking it under his arm. 'Now, if you'll excuse me, I shall go and dispose of our, ahem, little house guest.'

With the rodent still bundled securely under his arm, Whipple, having picked up a plastic bag from the kitchen, was now making his way purposefully across the lawns. Trying not to think too deeply about what the rat might be doing to the satin lining of his morning coat, he had fixed his mind on his next objective: transferring the verminous creature to the plastic bag, weighing it down with stones and hurling it as far as he could into the green and murky waters of the lake which lay beyond the small conifer plantation. But just as he was approaching the ha-ha he heard a voice.

'Wheeep!' it went. 'Wheeup! Wheepeel!' Whipple looked

around. Apart from the large rodent struggling under his armpit, he was completely alone. It was odd but not entirely surprising. The large topiary peacocks and gently erotic statuary in the Italian garden were notorious for their sound-distorting qualities. If the wind was in the right direction, it was possible to hear a conversation held at the other side of the house as clearly as if the participants were standing right in front of you.

Whipple therefore surmised that what he had heard was nothing more than the sound of sheep bleating in one of the fields at the back of the house. But then he heard it again.

'Wheepple! Far guid's seek, lit mee ooot!' The voice seemed to be coming from the depths of his morning coat. It really was most disconcerting.

'Wheeple! Whipp . . . Whipple! Ah, that's got it,' went the voice. 'For God's sake man, give a chap a break. My nose is stuck down an armhole and your deodorant leaves a lot to be desired.' This time there could be no doubt about it, the voice was coming from within the folds of his coat. Whipple dropped it like a hot brick.

After a flurry of movement, the rat's fat brown body appeared from one of the sleeves and reared up triumphantly on its back legs, its arms spread wide: 'Ta dah!' Whipple recoiled in horror as the rat saluted and introduced itself. 'General Glaak Raffin, Chief Custodian of the planet Argus, at your service.' The general extended a front foot.

Whipple's highly developed sense of etiquette momentarily overcoming his bewilderment, he bent down and took the rat's foot between finger and thumb, and they shook hands.

'That was a close call, Whipple old man,' said the rat, producing a small black box from the deep fur of its chest. 'Thought I wasn't going to get this working properly in time. Voice decoders, eh? A blessing and a curse – but I suppose they serve a purpose. With seven billion languages in the known universe, who's got the time to learn them all?'

Whipple was rooted to the spot, yet at the same time eager

to fly with the utmost speed. He stood stock-still, jaw open, eyes wide, a fine mist of perspiration bedewing his forehead.

The rat looked up at him. 'What's the matter, cat got your tongue?'

'Bu . . . bu . . . bu . . .' Whipple began.

'General, who's your friend?' A man in a flying suit was clambering out of the ha-ha behind the rat.

'Wha . . . wha . . . wha . . .?' Whipple continued.

'Oh, sorry,' said the general. 'Whipple, meet Major Matt Fripp.'

Matt came towards him and extended his hand. 'Hi, nice to meet you.' But what Whipple heard was something that sounded a bit like: 'Glash harvard spring ma knees.'

'Ninety-seven point three on your voicebox, old boy,' said the general. 'Poor chap won't have a clue what you're talking about.'

'Glannish,' Matt said and, unzipping the neck of his flying suit, pulled out a slightly larger version of the rat's black box, dangling from a chain around his neck. Matt turned a dial on its side, then tried again. 'Hi, Whipple, nice to meet you.'

The dazed and confused Whipple shook his hand too.

'Nice planet you've got here,' said Matt.

'Nice—?'

'Look, I won't beat about the bush,' the rat said, suddenly brisk and businesslike. 'In the name of the Galactic Alliance I am requisitioning this house.' From deep within his luxuriant fur he produced a scroll of parchment bearing a beribboned wax seal, and handed it to Whipple. 'Signed by all relevant parties as you can see.'

Whipple unfurled the parchment. It was covered with unde-cipherable symbols and hieroglyphs.

'I'm afraid I . . .'

'I know it specifies Beta-Dromo 7, but as you are probably aware, the seal of Gnelph gives me authority to change the location as and when I see fit. I've seen fit.' The general snatched back the parchment and rolled it up. 'It's not going to be thousands of rats if that's what you're worried about. We're talking all sorts of weird and wonderful life forms, most of them no bigger than a flea – you'll be able to accommodate them easily, big estate like this. Of course there are the Wuboobians, but I'm sure you'll manage.' The rat shoved the parchment back into his fur. 'Now then, before we get down to details, how about a little something to eat? My colleague and I have just traversed the galaxy and are understandably a little peckish. So, I don't know about Matt, but I fancy a sirloin steak, rare, with chips – don't worry about the garnish.'

'Sounds good to me,' said Matt.

'And I don't suppose you've a bottle of something half-decent in your cellar? Ever since the war began good wine has been in appallingly short supply.'

'Now look here,' said Whipple at last, recovering some of his composure. 'Firstly, this is the middle of the morning; Cook doesn't serve luncheon until one o'clock. Secondly, I don't care where you are from, you are both trespassing, and unless you both have a very good explanation for your presence here, I am calling Rentokil and the police: in that order.'

'Now, calm down, old feller,' soothed the general, gently stroking one of the agitated butler's highly polished Oxfords. 'I know it's all a bit sudden – talking rodents, spacemen appearing out of nowhere and the like, but we are in earnest.'

'We need your help,' Matt chipped in. 'You see, we're from a star system on the far side of the galaxy—'

'That's it,' said Whipple, throwing up his hands. 'I'm calling the police.' And he turned on his heel.

Glaak looked up at Matt. 'We're going to have to get him up to speed.'

'I'm afraid you're right.' Matt made a lunge for the tall butler, holding him in an armlock.

'Keep him steady, now,' said the general, running up Whipple's body and perching on his shoulder. Producing a small silver disc, Glaak tapped it once and with a soft *hiss* it opened out into what looked like a pair of pince-nez. 'This might hurt a bit, but it's imperative you know what's going on!'

Once the general had placed the pince-nez on the protesting Whipple's nose, little clamps shot out and anchored them securely to his nasal cartilage.

'Ouch!'

'Now just relax, old man. Everything will become clear in a few moments.'

Whipple couldn't actually see through the pince-nez. Where the lenses should have been were two opaque discs which suddenly began firing rapid, bright-white pulses into his eyes. Whipple recoiled. Even closing his lids didn't shut out the intensity of the light.

'Get them off!' he screamed, struggling so violently that both he and Matt slipped over the edge of the ha-ha and landed in a heap at the bottom.

The general ran to the edge of the ditch and looked over. 'Relax,' he shouted. 'They interface directly with your optic nerve. You get distortion-free images inside your head.'

'It's hurting!' Whipple yelled.

'Don't look *at* them – look *beyond* them,' Glaak instructed, while Matt tried to keep hold of the hysterically flapping man. 'It only hurts if you resist!' After a few more futile attempts at escape, Whipple, his last vestiges of dignity gone, gave himself up to the experience and Matt was able to release him.

Now strange things were happening inside Whipple's head. Images of exotic and distant worlds began to flood his brain. There were terrible scenes of war – an army of chain-mail-clad soldiers marched across death-strewn battlegrounds, their war machines rolling relentlessly over everything in their path. Vast spaceships blasted entire planets to smithereens while the screams of their inhabitants fell on deaf ears. There were scenes of Romanesque games: the vanquished pleading for mercy as they were hacked to pieces by gladiators, or eviscerated by wild beasts. All the while the lines of the lost and dispossessed lengthened outside the refugee camps. There was filth everywhere, disease was rampant. Finally came pitiful images of the young and malnourished wailing in incomprehension at the awful unfairness of it all.

Eventually, it was over. With an electric *fizz*, the little pince-nez closed and dropped off Whipple's nose. He lay in the bottom of the ha-ha for a long time, eyes wide open, hardly able to comprehend what he'd just seen. The general scurried down into the ditch to join him.

'All right, old man?' he asked. Whipple merely groaned. His mind was full of images of death and destruction. 'Tell you what,' said the general. 'How about something to cheer you up – lighten the mood a little after all that serious stuff, hmm? Let's see, what else have we got in here?' Retrieving the pince-nez, he pressed a tiny button. A menu popped up and the general began to scroll through the table of contents. 'Ah, here we are, just the thing – an amusing short film about two men and a piano.'

The general made as if to put them back on Whipple's nose, but he pushed them away angrily and sat up. 'Get those things away from me!'

'Sorry.'

But Whipple's ire was not aimed at the general. He was filled with a fierce anger at man's inhumanity to man – or to be more precise, thing's inhumanity to thing. 'What *was* that?' he said at last.

'A terrible, terrible war,' Glaak explained, 'at present taking place on the other side of the galaxy.'

'Do you mean to tell me that those appalling events are happening *now*?'

'As we speak, old man. Of course, viewed from Earth it won't begin for another hundred thousand years, but it's probably best not to think of it like that. The point is, unless we do something about it, sooner or later it's going to start heading this way.'

'This way?'

Glaak nodded.

Whipple was bewildered by the horror of it all. Then, taking a deep breath, he turned and looked at the general, a look of steely determination in his eyes. 'How can I help?' he said. In that instant Whipple, as steeped in tradition as the Tower of London, as English as a furled umbrella, became a rebel.

The general smiled. 'Good to have you on board,' he said.

Whipple got unsteadily to his feet. 'There's one thing I don't understand.'

'Only one?'

'If you really are from the other side of the galaxy, how did you manage to get *here*?'

'Ah, glad you asked – wormholes.'

'Wormholes?' Whipple enquired.

'Matt, show him the Cartogram.'

'Well, General, I'd love to, but . . .'

'Oh damn, I'd forgotten. Here.' The general produced a small, black lozenge. 'Strictly speaking, I shouldn't have this – not a word to a soul. Of course, this isn't the real thing, but it'll give you an idea.' He nodded his head in Matt's direction. 'He lost the real one.'

'I was being shot at!' Matt protested. 'Anyway it's safe – it's on Gweeb.'

'It's only a matter of time before the Crusaders overcome their reticence, especially as they now know the Cartogram's there.'

Whipple was following this conversation about as well as a newt might follow a game of three-dimensional chess.

'Um,' he said at last, 'Cartogram?'

'Sorry, let me explain,' said the general. 'The Helian Cartogram is an ancient device. No one knows who made it, or when. All we do know for sure is that it is extremely old, and extremely accurate.'

'But what does it do?'

'It's a map,' the general said, simply.

'A map?'

'Of the universe,' said Matt.

'The—?'

'It sounds incredible, I know,' the general continued, 'but there it is. It's a map of the universe detailing all the star systems and habitable planets. But even more importantly, it highlights a network of wormholes that connect up the whole thing. It's been called God's atlas. Look.' The general touched the small black lozenge he was holding, and it came alive. Tiny coloured lights flashed in sequence around its border, and a perfect three-dimensional hologram of an alien star system began to hover unsteadily above its surface.

'My God.'

'Yes,' said the general, 'quite useful if you're in the Gologon Sector.'

'But I thought you said you didn't have the Cartogram?'

The general sighed long-sufferingly. 'Do you have any idea how impossibly vast the universe is?'

'Obviously not.'

'This is my own personal pocket version, covering just one sector of our galaxy – a mere drop in the ocean. Using this to navigate around the infinite universe would be like trying to use a Plymouth A to Z to get to Gelbhart's Neutrino. No, the real one is vastly more detailed, and hence more useful to our enemies. You see, although we have spacecraft capable of travelling at twice light speed, it would still take many thousands of years to cross even our own galaxy by conventional means. However, using a wormhole one can zip across it in minutes.' The general clicked off the small black lozenge and shoved it back into his fur.

'But why—?'

'Gulgus Filch,' Matt interrupted.

'Gulgus Filch?'

'Chief Crusader,' Glaak explained. 'It's our own fault, of course, we should never have allowed it to happen.'

45

'It was going to happen sooner or later, General. Gulgus just happened to be in the right place at the right time.'

'Perhaps if the Galactic Alliance had actually managed to do something instead of simply arguing among themselves . . .' Glaak sighed. 'But it's too late now.'

Whipple was feeling even deeper out of his depth; in fact the shoreline seemed to have disappeared completely. 'Um, I'm afraid I don't understand.'

'It's like this,' Glaak explained. 'Filch is a Gologon, which, in the old galactic hierarchy, gave him a status somewhere between effluent and green slime. Couple that lowly social position with a stubborn pride and you have a recipe for disaster. The trouble was, he wanted to be a pilot. Now, although the Space Force has always prided itself on being an "equal opportunities employer", in reality the old system still holds sway so, although he graduated with honours, the only job he was offered on leaving Space Academy was ship's cook. He was mightily displeased.'

'Yeah,' Matt agreed. 'We were room-mates at the academy. Graduation day was the last time I saw him. He'd just heard about the job he'd been offered and he was wild – he started smashing up the place. I tried to calm him down but he just looked me in the eye and said, "You are not of my kind!" and marched out. That was it, he never even stayed for the ceremony.'

'Of course,' said Glaak, 'Filch, being Filch, immediately got down to planning his revenge. He collected a group of other disaffected young Gologons around him and they hijacked an army cruiser and began harrying the main trade routes out of Bwellburbia. But back then Gulgus wasn't deemed a serious threat – he was just a kid angry at the system. It was after he was arrested and thrown in jail that the real trouble started.'

'Real trouble?' Whipple enquired.

'Jail was where he met Angmar Blatch—'

'Otherwise known as "His Bigness",' Matt interrupted.

'Who's telling this story?' asked Glaak.

'Sorry.'

'Yes, Angmar Blatch,' Glaak continued. 'Cordon bleu pastry cook, murderer, mercenary and high priest of a sect called "Elron".'

'Elron?'

'A fanatical offshoot of one of the ancient Gologon religions, named after a barking mad self-styled holy man who, as far as I can make out, hated everybody. The Elron have strict rules about sex, diet and hygiene, and their core belief – that any heretic deserves to die – makes them a little scary—'

'Not to mention a public relations nightmare,' Matt chipped in.

Glaak stared at Matt long and hard before continuing. 'Blatch took Filch under his wing and taught him all he knew about the austere and self-disciplined ways of Elron and how to use them to get what you want. When Filch left prison he had focus; he was as sleek and deadly as a heat-seeking missile. But, unfortunately, the Galactic Alliance still didn't regard him as a serious threat. The next thing we know he's got his own daily programme on morning television. It was pretty amateurish: Filch sitting in front of a curtain ranting about the inequalities of society and calling on all oppressed peoples to follow the one true path to Valohem: Elron. None of us paid it much attention; after all, he was just another Gologon with a chip on his shoulder. Unfortunately we underestimated the show's popularity among the low-paid and unskilled.'

'Yeah,' said Matt, 'just think how many lavatory cleaners, shelf stackers and telephone sanitizers there are scattered across the galaxy. When Gulgus called on them to rise up against their oppressors the rest of us never stood a chance.'

'It happened very quickly; they struck right at the heart of government. The cleaners, waiters and security staff we employed in the Galactic Alliance parliament building on Cullorum outnumbered the delegates three to one – they simply turned on us and took over.'

'Then Gulgus breezes in like the Messiah. That was when this whole Crusade shit started.'

Glaak turned to Whipple and addressed him earnestly. 'After the coup, all the top jobs were given to Filch's closest associates. It was chaos; they just weren't qualified, and soon the system was on the verge of collapse. But Filch was clever. Seeing what was happening, he reinstated all *Infidels* who'd been in charge of vital services like power, transport and food production, until he'd trained up his own people. Then he showed his true colours. As each minister of the previous regime was replaced, he was executed. Thankfully, a few of us fled before the blood-bath began, and thus the Rebel Council of the Galactic Alliance was formed. We've been sneaking round the galaxy ever since, hiding out wherever we can and plotting Filch's overthrow, which is where you come in, Whipple.'

'Me?'

'The Council needs to find a safe house, a place where we can meet in secret to plan our next move. This location is ideal, since the planet is off the map as far as Filch is concerned.'

'As long as he doesn't get his hands on the Cartogram,' Matt added.

'Yes,' the general agreed. 'We ought to be getting back to Gweeb to look for it.' He turned to Whipple. 'Can you get Cook to rustle up a sandwich for the major? Wormhole trekking is seriously debilitating.'

'Er, I'm sure we can find something in the kitchen.' The truth was, Cook had left in a huff after yet another of her salary cheques bounced, and Whipple had been preparing all the Trenchards' meals for some time now. But he had managed to keep that distressing fact from Lady Trenchard herself.

'What about you?' Whipple asked the general.

'I'm staying here.' Producing a tiny and well-polished briar pipe from his fur, Glaak clenched it between his teeth. 'You and I have a lot of planning to do.'

*

48

A short time later, armed with a sandwich made from slightly stale white bread and blue-tinged Cheddar, Matt was sitting at the controls of the general's spaceship while the general himself perched on the instrument panel, filling his pipe with tobacco.

'Now look, Major,' he said, 'no funny business and no heroics. Just get the Cartogram and come straight back. I don't want you risking the safety of the Cartogram for any foolhardy rescue missions. Mariella is dead, or if she isn't she soon will be. Forget her – that's an order.'

'Yes, sir,' said Matt, his jaw set.

'I'm going to start preparing things here. Hopefully, by the time we have the Cartogram safely in our hands we'll be ready to start receiving visitors.' Glaak hopped off the instrument panel and moved to the door. 'It's an old cliché, Matt, but the safety of the universe is in your hands. Good luck, and please, bring my ship back in one piece!' His tiny claws pattered on the metallic floor of the spaceship as he hurried outside. Matt pressed a button on the console and the door closed with an electric *whirr*.

The general's spaceship was a bit of a tight squeeze for a humanoid, but at least it had been built with certain concessions to Matt and his ilk: the co-pilot's seat and controls were full-sized, and it also contained a flushing lavatory.

Matt wound up the engines of the small craft. 'OK,' he said, 'let's take this nice and easy. Computer online.'

'Good day. I recognize you from your voice-print, Major Fripp, nice to have you aboard,' came a warm and friendly voice.

'It's very nice to be here.'

'Can I be of assistance, major?'

'You most certainly can. We're going to be swinging right around and heading straight towards a bush about twenty feet in front of us, and I need you to keep her level at head height . . . that's *my* head height.'

'Aye-aye!' the computer responded. 'If I might make so bold, sir, this ship was not specifically designed to fly through shrubbery.'

'Thanks for the warning, but you leave the thinking to me and we'll get along just fine. Nice and steady now. Take her away.'

'Aye-aye, sir.'

The ship lifted off the ground, turned slowly round and moved gently back along the length of the ha-ha. Whipple, watching from the shade of the horse-chestnut, thought the brightly coloured ship looked rather like a gigantic butterfly. But just as the tip of its blue nose was about to come into contact with one of the rhododendron's bright red blooms, the strangest thing happened – the nose-cone disappeared. From his viewpoint in the cockpit, Matt was no longer looking at a member of the genus rhododendron, series *griersonianum*; he was instead staring down a long tunnel, its sides swirling with pulsating lights. 'On the button,' he said with satisfaction.

Then, as if caught by an invisible hand, the ship was pulled into the portal at terrifying speed.

Whipple watched this strange event with wonder. Even though he was beginning to come to terms with pipe-smoking alien rats, disappearing spaceships were still rather unsettling for him.

'Now then, old chap, to business,' said the general, lighting up. 'We haven't got much time, so how many rooms have you got?'

'Rooms? Um, thirty-seven, and twenty more in the west wing, but that hasn't been opened up for years.'

'Fifty-seven, good, good.' The general made a note of this on his paw-pilot.

'You said we haven't got much time,' said a concerned Whipple.

'That's right,' the general replied. 'They'll start arriving as soon as they get the signal.'

'Signal?'

'When Matt gets through to the other side a signal giving the coordinates of the wormhole will be beamed from my spaceship to all members of the council.'

Whipple's eyes widened. 'Isn't that a little dangerous? I mean won't that alert Filch and his, um, Crusaders?' A conflict hundreds of thousands of light years away was one thing, the thought of it arriving on the doorstep was quite another matter.

'No need to worry, Whipple, old man. We've got the latest quantum transmitting equipment fitted to our ships.'

Whipple knitted his brows.

The general put down his paw-pilot with a sigh. 'What that means is, if the Crusaders are monitoring our transmissions, they won't pick anything up.'

Whipple scratched his head. 'I'm just going to have to take your word for that.'

'Don't worry, bloodthirsty monsters aren't suddenly going to appear and start slaughtering the local population just yet.'

'That's very reassuring, General,' Whipple said thoughtfully. 'Before we get into all this, there is one thing upon which I must insist.'

'What's that, old man?'

'Lady Trenchard must remain completely unaware of the whole arrangement. She has a heart condition, so any extra stress could be extremely hazardous to her health.'

The general looked up suddenly and took the pipe out of his mouth. 'Could be tricky that. As I said earlier a lot of the delegates would fit quite happily in a plain brown envelope, but the Goran-B'tLamboo boys are well over seven feet, and then of course there are the Wuboobians.'

'Please,' Whipple implored.

'What do you expect the delegates to do, creep around pretending they aren't there? No, sorry, it's just not on.'

Drawing himself up to his full six foot three, Whipple glared down at the rodent. 'Now look here, Lady Trenchard is a kind, sensitive woman, and furthermore I have been in her employ for nigh on forty years. As her loyal servant it is my duty to safeguard her interests. Either she remains ignorant of this undertaking or the deal is off.'

'I see,' said the general, scratching his ear with the pipe stem. 'You do realize I have the authority to simply take this place over with no reference either to you or its other inhabitants?'

'I'm still not above calling out the pest control people.' Whipple regarded the general in a manner that made the rodent feel distinctly uneasy. 'Do I make myself clear?'

'Crystal, old feller,' the general sighed. He thought for a moment, drumming his claws on the ground. 'Presumably you do have cellars?' he said at last.

'Yes, why?'

'And stables?'

'Of course.'

'You know, Whipple, in spite of myself I like you. So I'm going to play along with your little bit of subterfuge. The Wuboobians will be perfectly happy somewhere dark and damp and, as for the others . . . well, they'll just have to put up with it.'

Whipple flushed slightly and began to regret his previously blunt manner. 'Thank you, General.'

'Now, next question: diet. The Narglutts are very fussy eaters . . .'

Whipple was beginning to realize that there was more to being a rebel than simply swearing allegiance to the cause.

Through the deepest, darkest recesses of space tumbled an ancient asteroid, its once rugged surface worn almost smooth by the passage of time. This ancient, crystalline rock was older than the sun, older than the moon and planets, older even than the universe itself. It was not in orbit around any star, nor did it seem to follow any predictable path and, although it was mostly to be found out in the darkness of space, far beyond the reaches of the cold, brilliant illumination of starlight, it glowed with its own internal enlightenment.

If you studied the asteroid closely for a time, it was possible to make out a comfortable single-storey dwelling surrounded by a pleasant garden and a flourishing vegetable plot. And, listening carefully, you might also hear a whistle – a tuneful, three-toned whistle . . .

'Ah, good, kettle's boiled.'

The hand that made the planets, that formed Adam from the unpromising dust of Earth; the very hand that fashioned Eve and separated night from day, took down a tea towel from the shelf and, wrapping it neatly around the metal handle, lifted the kettle off the stove.

God opened the cupboard above the fridge and surveyed the contents. 'Earl Grey or Traditional Afternoon? Which to choose . . . which to choose?' Sighing, He placed a hand over his eyes and, reaching blindly inside, His fist closed around one of the packets of tea. 'Ah!' He said, peeping through his fingers, 'Traditional Afternoon – perfect. Now then, Rich Tea or Digestive?'

Chapter 5

After only a few minutes, but what seemed to Matt like several hours of high-speed buffeting as the small ship hurtled through the wormhole, he eventually emerged above the bright-green canopy of Gweeb. Quickly cutting power and diving under the shielding foliage, Matt checked for Crusader warships. He could read three on his scanners: two were still circling the planet but the other was close by and had probably already landed. He didn't have much time, as the Crusaders would have already picked him up, and it wouldn't take them long to get an exact fix and blow him to pieces.

'Computer!'

'At your service.'

'Scan for ship debris.'

'There are the remains of several ships hereabouts. Could you be a little more specific? Sorry to be a pain.'

'You're looking for a Class 4 L'Ohn Kriffth ship, ident: K-LOW 3097.'

'Thank you. Scanning . . .'

While the computer looked for the wreckage of his ship, Matt kept his eyes on the instruments, nervously checking for any signs that the Crusaders were priming their weapons for an attack. One of the orbiting craft was beginning to glow red, signalling that it was warming up its hadron cannon.

'Computer, is this going to take much longer?'

'Sorry to keep you . . . I think I have something for you now.

K-LOW 3097 is lying in a small clearing about three thousand yards from here, due east.'

'Take us there, but stay low.'

'Aye-aye.'

As the ship moved off, a hadron shell exploded in the space the craft had previously occupied seconds before. The small vessel was picked up by the shockwave and almost thrown into one of the trees.

'Sorry,' the computer said.

'You're doing fine.'

Dodging and diving between tree trunks and falling shells, the ship sped towards the clearing.

'Major, there's something you should know.'

'Don't tell me – there's someone else?'

'I'm sorry?'

'Never mind. What is it?'

'There seem to be others interested in your wrecked ship. One of the Crusader craft has landed almost on top of it.'

'How many?'

'Ten individuals, and . . .'

'And?'

'It's odd, Major, but the whole place seems to be alive. It doesn't make sense.'

'How far to the clearing?'

'Three hundred yards.'

'OK, take us down, I'll go the rest of the way on foot.'

The ship slowed and came to a whispering halt on the jungle floor. As the door opened Matt leapt from his seat. Standing in the doorway, he turned and addressed the ship one final time, 'I'm afraid this is goodbye.'

'I know,' the computer sighed. 'Say so long to the general for me. And may I say what a pleasure it's been serving under you, Major?'

'The pleasure has been all mine.'

Matt ran out into the jungle as yet another hadron shell

careened down from above and this time found its target. Glaak Raffin's ship exploded with an almighty bang and Matt was hurled through the air by the blast, landing underneath a fallen tree. 'Sorry, General,' he muttered, staggering to his feet and dusting himself down.

Some of the Crusaders who'd been searching Matt's old ship had heard the explosion and were already heading in his direction – he could hear them crashing through the undergrowth. Matt checked his pistol. It was reading low; he'd have four shots left at best.

'Shit.'

Then a thought occurred to him, or rather, popped into his head unbidden. *Create a diversion*, the thought went. *Set your pistol to overload and throw it into the bushes there.* Matt looked towards where the thought seemed to be directing him: a tangle of low-growing poisonous razor-thorn. Once sliced by one of its vicious tendrils, even if you managed to survive the blood loss, you'd die from septicaemia within forty-eight hours.

'OK,' Matt said to no one in particular, and flicked a switch on his pistol, reversing the neutron flow through its miniature nuclear reactor. The pistol emitted a low whistle and began to vibrate in his hand. Hurling it into the tangle of thorns, Matt was directed by yet another thought: *Hide behind that boulder*. He turned his head and noticed, not ten yards away, a large rock he was almost certain hadn't been there a moment before. However, now was not the time to question his observational skills; the Crusaders were closing in and the note of the pistol was rising. He ran towards the rock and hid behind it.

Soon the Crusaders appeared and surrounded the thorn bush, trying to work out what was making the strange and piercing noise emanating from the tangled shrub. Unfortunately for them two things happened simultaneously: they figured out what it was, and the pistol exploded, sending a murderous hail of razor-sharp thorns slashing through the air and slicing most of them clean in half. The Crusaders all died with the exact same look of awful recognition on their faces.

See, went the thought in Matt's head, *don't I look after you?*

Matt felt a strange tingling the length of his spine and began to wonder if the legend about this planet being haunted wasn't just a silly story after all.

'Now look—' he began.

No, you look, went the thought. *And listen very carefully . . .*

Matt could hear the rest of the Crusader warship's crew blundering through the forest to find out what had happened to their colleagues.

They're looking for you. They know you're here. Oh, you're afraid.

With each new subtle shift of Matt's emotions the thought seemed to grow, becoming stronger and more distinct.

Look down.

At Matt's feet lay half a dead Crusader, his gun still in its holster.

Take it.

Matt didn't stop to think, he stooped and slid the pistol free.

Now watch this.

'Over here! I'm over here!' Matt realized with a shock that the voice was his. The last thing he wanted to do was draw attention to himself but he couldn't help it. 'Here I am! Over here!' What was going on? His instinct was to run but he saw with horror that he'd somehow managed to get himself into the middle of a dense thicket of razor-thorn. Now he could hear the excited voices of the Crusaders. They were very close.

I could save you, ran the thought in Matt's head.

'By trying to kill me?' he said.

Stay with me and I'll look after you.

'Stay with you?'

I get lonely.

'Who are you?'

Oh, you're so deliciously naïve, I could teach you so many things.

'Can we go back to the bit where you said you could save me?'

What you feel, I feel. Stay with me.

The Crusaders were almost on top of him. Matt had already run out of options.

Say yes, Matt.

'OK, OK, I'll stay with you.'

You will?

'Yeah, sure.'

You won't regret it.

Just before the four Crusaders finally broke cover, Matt tucked the pistol out of sight in an inside pocket. As the soldiers surrounded him, he raised his hands in surrender.

'Well, well, well,' said their captain, a green reptilian creature who lumbered out of the bushes behind them. 'Gentlemen, we are greatly honoured. Do you have any idea who this is?'

The four soldiers looked dumbly at each other.

The captain clicked a dial on his wrist-vid and hailed his ship. 'Captain Libidy to Red One, we have Matt Fripp. Repeat, Matt Fripp is alive – we're bringing him in.'

The Crusaders standing around Matt were obviously impressed. 'Wow, a real live rebel,' said one.

The smiling captain turned back to Matt. 'How goes the rebellion, Major? Come on, give me the package and we can all go home.'

Matt smiled and nodded. 'Good work, Captain. OK, I'll come quietly. I can see when I'm beaten. May I?' Matt indicated his inside breast pocket.

The captain nodded.

'Here it is!' Reaching into the pocket, Matt whipped out the pistol and fired, winging the captain. But before the other Crusaders could fire back, a large net suddenly whisked Matt up into the air. The soldiers, standing in a circle around the now vanished rebel, fired their guns at where he had just been and shot each other instead.

Their wounded captain was an easy target as he blundered away through the tangled undergrowth, and from his exalted position above the forest floor, Matt picked him off with a single shot.

Excellent. You see, I said I would look after you. I can tell you and I are going to be friends, Matt. Hold tight now – going down!

The net was lowered gently to the ground and Matt stepped out. But then he felt a new and unpleasant sensation, as if something were leafing though his memory-banks.

What's this, a woman? She's very pretty, and very dead it would appear . . . No, you think she's still alive. Ah, there's something else, let's see . . .

There was more uncomfortable rummaging through his thoughts.

Rescue? You have a plan.

Suddenly the probing became more aggressive.

A Crusader ship? You plan to steal a ship and go to her.

Now it was getting painful. Matt felt as if his mind was being rearranged; he had the distinct impression that if he didn't somehow stop it he'd never get his thoughts back in order again.

You never had any intention of staying here. You lied to me! YOU LIED!!!

The screaming inside his head was unbearable, but there was no way of shutting it out.

Matt dropped the pistol and fell to his knees. It was as if a small angry child was running riot inside his skull, ripping out all his memory files and tossing them into the air. It wouldn't be long before all that was left was a collection of nursery rhymes and faded images of sunny afternoons in the garden with his dog.

Just then, the little bit of Matt's brain that remained intact had an idea. Quickly picking up the Crusader's pistol, he held it to his forearm. '"What I feel, you feel" you said. Well, how do you like this?' He pulled the trigger and a pulse of pure energy ripped a chunk out of his flesh. The pain was intense, but had the desired effect of stopping the raging wind in his mind. His thoughts were once more his own. Getting to his feet, Matt ran towards the clearing where the Crusader ship was parked.

Matt, Matt, don't do this. We could be friends, you and I. The voice in his head was softer now, more cajoling.

Matt tried to construct a brick wall around that portion of his mind that was still in some sort of order as he ran, painfully nursing his wounded arm, through the dense undergrowth. Now and again a wall of razor-thorn would rear up in front of him but he simply blasted a way through with the pistol.

'Faster, Matt. Come on,' he urged himself. Now he could see the Crusader ship, its big fluorescent red cross glowing unnaturally amongst the gently dappled greenery. Right next to it lay what was left of his old ship.

An energy bolt thudded into the tree beside him. 'Shit!'

Matt hit the ground. Peering up through the dense vegetation, he could see a lone guard, patrolling the wreckage. The guard was armed with a boson arc – a sort of hi-tech crossbow that fired bolts of pure methanol maser energy, and had a much longer range than Matt's pistol.

Weren't expecting that, were you, Matt? He caught you by surprise there.

'Why don't you go and mess with *his* mind for a change and leave me alone?'

Oh, Crusaders' minds are so dull. They're full of rules and regulations: what they can and can't eat; how to pray and how often; what they can and can't wear. They even defecate in a prescribed manner . . . Dull, dull, dull. Whereas you: you're like an oasis. Your mind is a pleasure garden of sensual images. Crusaders don't understand sensuality, Matt, they're obsessed with pain – other people's, of course.

None of this was helping Matt's concentration as he tried to figure out how he was going to creep up on the guard, get to the ship and retrieve the Cartogram. 'Will you shut the fuck up!'

You don't mean that, Matt. Think about it, stay with me and you'll never be alone again – I'll be with you wherever you go. Isn't that what you want? Isn't that what all your kind want?

Matt could feel whatever it was beginning to regain control; slipping inexorably back into his mind like a rising fog. The situation called for some extreme violence.

Leaping to his feet, Matt ran screaming towards the lone guard. The guard swung round and started firing, but he was so unnerved by Matt's reckless charge that all his shots went wide. Unfortunately for him, Matt's aim was deadly. Once the guard was in range of the pistol, Matt squeezed the trigger and the Crusader fell to the ground and lay still.

Oh, I enjoyed that. See what fun you and I could have together? With the Cartogram here they'll keep coming back to look for it and you can keep bumping them off.

Matt's adrenalin level was now at an all-time high. 'What the fuck are you?'

Haven't you worked it out yet?

'Obviously not.'

I'm the planet.

'The planet?'

Yes.

'What do you want from me?'

Company. Planets have feelings too, you know. Do you have any idea how tedious it can be, tumbling through space day in, day out? I'M LONELY!!!

Matt winced. He had no time for this. The Crusader ships in orbit would probably have realized by now that something was wrong, and could decide at any minute to land and investigate.

'Fuck it!' he yelled, blasting another chunk out of his forearm. 'Shit! Shit! Fucking shit!' He clutched the raw, throbbing wound. At least he'd bought himself another few minutes' silence to think.

Dragging himself to his feet, he started searching through

the wreckage of his ship, and soon found the remains of the cockpit, half-buried in razor-thorn.

Shooting a way for himself through the malevolent creepers, he finally got to what he was looking for – the ship's instrument binnacle. It was badly damaged, and the universal applications aperture into which he'd slid the Cartogram was all bent up, but he didn't have time to fiddle with it now. Grabbing one of the binnacle fitment handles with his good arm, he lugged it across the jungle floor and into the open door of the Crusader warship.

But the moment he entered the ship he was presented with his next problem.

'Chip not recognized – voice ident, please,' the on-board computer demanded coldly.

'Oh fuck,' Matt sighed, out of breath and bleeding all over the ship's stainless steel floor.

'Voice incongruent with stored data. Intruder on board! Alert, alert!'

Not your day, is it?

Matt sighed and stepped back out into the jungle.

Ah, so you've decided to stay after all.

Without saying a word, Matt walked back to the dead Crusader. Activating his watch laser he aimed it at a point just below the left ear, opening up a small slit in the soldier's neck. Gritting his teeth, Matt pushed his fingers into the wound and fished around in the still-warm flesh until he found what he was looking for – the recognition chip. Every Crusader had one; it was inserted at the medical examination when they joined up.

Pulling a roll of tape from one of his pockets, Matt ripped off a small piece and taped the warm and sticky chip to his own neck. Then, feeling ever so slightly queasy, he walked back to the warship and tried again. This time the computer greeted him by name.

'Welcome back, Larrgh Thaarrss. Did the mission go well?' Knowing that if he spoke again he would give the game away,

Matt quickly moved over to the ship's instrument panel and tapped something into the keypad:

Code Orange: 77796.

Immediately the door closed and locked, and the ship's engines began to hum. Matt had initiated the extreme distress function built into all Crusader ships. Once the distress code was entered, the ship automatically returned to base. Matt reckoned that the two orbiting Crusader craft would be frozen with indecision: too scared to land on Gweeb to investigate what was going on, and too scared to return to face Gulgus Filch empty-handed. If Matt could just keep his mouth shut, the ship he'd commandeered would carry on believing he was a badly injured Crusader and take him straight back to Cullorum – and Mariella.

You're leaving? After all we've been through, you're leaving?

Matt pursed his lips and collapsed into one of the seats. In less than a minute the ship would be airborne and not long after that zipping through space, far beyond the reach of this planet's influence. But it wasn't going to let him go without a fight.

Matt felt the ship rock slightly as the boosters fired, lifting it off the ground. He also felt a throbbing in the centre of his head as the presence in his mind rifled malevolently through his memory. Then it stopped. After a small pause, Matt's mind was filled with an image from his childhood: a dog running out into the road. The scene was imbued with all its original horror, and so real that he wanted to call out, shout a warning.

Now the truck was coming round the corner, but Matt's dog Chippy hadn't seen it. 'Mmbmmm!' Matt tried desperately to keep his mouth shut, telling his mind that this was just a memory, nothing more.

Come on, come on! Open your mouth wide and sing it: Chippy!

Matt's little boy watched, helpless, as his pet dog ran straight under the wheels of the truck. 'Mmbmmnhh!' The agony of that moment was still so real that Matt found tears streaming down his cheeks.

'You sound in terrible pain, Larrgh,' the ship's computer remarked. 'Would you like a tranquillizer?'

'Mmhmm.' Matt nodded eagerly and, reaching forward, typed Y-E-S on the keypad.

No! No you shan't!

'Lie on the couch, Larrgh,' cooed the ship's computer.

Matt got up and staggered to the upholstered leather couch against the bulkhead at the rear of the cockpit.

You're not going to leave me, like all the others! the planet screamed. *Say it! Say it out loud!*

The image in Matt's mind grew in clarity and intensity: the lifeless dog lying in the road in a spreading pool of blood. With failing strength, Matt struggled against the power in his mind. 'Mmhmmbmmh,' he sobbed as he fell on to the couch.

'There, there,' soothed the computer, 'we'll soon have you comfortable.'

A drawer in the bulkhead opened and out of it snaked an articulated steel arm holding a hypodermic syringe. 'Now this won't hurt a bit,' said the computer, plunging the needle into his arm.

Immediately Matt felt a relaxing balm spread through his body, and the voice in his head began to recede.

No! No! No!

As the drug and the ship's altitude gradually eased Matt further away from its influence, the planet's strident voice grew softer and softer, eventually dying away altogether. Matt sighed with relief and fell into a deep and much-needed sleep.

Chapter 6

'It's a rare delight to have such a fragile and pretty visitor to this room.' Glitch smiled at Mariella who was strapped into a large chair that looked a bit like a dentist's but had a few shiny chrome additions that put it in an altogether different league. Mariella had by now gone way past any attempt at glib humour and sat, silent and terrified, as Glitch's two assistants removed her shoe and placed her right foot in a steel clamp which, as it was tightened, splayed her toes slightly to expose the delicate, sensitive areas between them.

'Hydrochloric? Sulphuric? Nitric?' Glitch ran his finger along a row of glass bottles which stood on a shelf above the stainless steel workbench occupying one entire side of the clinically sterile room. 'And what strength? 20 per cent? 50 . . . 90 . . . 100? Ah, so many choices . . . so little time,' he muttered happily to himself. 'I know.' As he closed the eye in his skull, the other circled round behind his head and fixed itself on the terrified Mariella. 'Eeny, meeny, miny . . . mo!' He picked out a bottle at random. 'I can't look, I can't look!' he said excitedly, holding it up. He was like a five-year-old about to open a present at Christmas. '*You* tell me!' The revolving eye toured his head once, then came to rest level with the label on the bottle of acid. 'Ah, Sulphuric, 90 per cent! What an excellent choice!'

'What are you going to do to me?' Mariella asked in a small voice.

Glitch was suddenly at her side. 'Oh, we're going to have a lot of fun, you and I. Do you like games?'

Mariella swallowed hard.

'Let's play a little game of "guess the function", shall we?' Glitch slipped back to the long steel workbench. Opening one of its drawers, he pulled something out and hid it behind his back. 'And the first object is . . .' With his leather-clad hand, he produced what looked like a fat hypodermic syringe, but where the single needle should have been was a small bar from which sprouted four shiny, surgical steel needles.

'Um . . .' whimpered Mariella.

'Come along, come along, it's not that difficult.' Glitch had somehow managed to slip round behind her and was now holding the terrifying instrument in front of her face. 'Have a good look,' he whispered, turning it in his hand so that the light danced on its highly polished metallic surfaces. 'It's a beauty, isn't it? Made to my own design you know.'

Mariella gasped and tried to shrink away from the awful-looking gadget, but the straps on the chair held her fast.

'Give up?' Glitch said at last. 'I'll give you a clue – it's not for administering anaesthetic!' He dissolved in fits of laughter. 'Sorry, my little joke. You see, it's sole purpose is to inflict pain. But I imagine you suspected that already. OK, as you're hopeless at this game, I'll tell you what it is. I call it my inter-toe-tickler. Rather clever, don't you think? What it does is introduce substances of my choosing – in this instance almost pure sulphuric acid – into the highly-sensitive areas between the toes.'

Mariella had begun to vibrate violently. 'Do . . . you . . . expect . . . me . . . to . . . talk?'

'Oh, let's not spoil the fun, eh?' Glitch removed the plunger of the fat syringe. 'The marvellous thing about this is that in conjunction with my patented horizontal-plane delivery device,' he dabbed a pedal on the chair's pedestal, and a gleaming chrome arrangement of cantilevered arms slid silently out of the footrest, 'I can determine the depth to which I place the needles with pin-point accuracy. Oh, I say – *pin-point*, that's rather good, isn't it?' Chuckling to himself, he removed the glass stopper from the bottle of acid and filled up the syringe. 'We can either just tickle the epithelium or go in deep: muscle tissue, cartilage, even bone. Ah, the wonders of modern science.'

Replacing the plunger of the now full syringe, Glitch secured it in a small cradle at the end of the complex cantilevered arrangement at the foot of the chair. 'Now then, we just need to adjust the height.' Turning a black, knurled nut, he levelled up the syringe with Mariella's tender, exposed foot. 'Good, nearly there. How are you feeling, my dear? You look a little . . . peaky.'

Mariella opened and closed her mouth in mute horror. Her breathing was fast and shallow; she was close to passing out, but Glitch was too practised in his art ever to allow that to happen.

'Would you like a glass of water or something? I know what . . .' He gestured to one of his assistants who immediately brought over a kidney bowl containing another syringe. Without warning, Glitch snatched it up and plunged it into her arm. She gasped with the shock. 'A little adrenalin to keep you going. Can't have you missing the show now can we?'

Mariella's system was immediately on full alert. She was wide awake and every nerve in her body was tuned to maximum sensitivity. 'You bastard! You'll never break me!' she screamed, regaining some of her old fighting spirit.

'That's more like it. Alrighty, let's begin!' Glitch made himself comfortable on a small stool at Mariella's feet. 'Music!' An assistant flicked a switch and the room was immediately filled with the sound of a violin sonata. 'Music while you work.' He looked up at Mariella. 'Or in your case, a sonata to scream by.'

Grasping the spigot of a tiny crank on the cantilever arrangement lightly between thumb and forefinger, he began to turn it, bringing the terrifyingly sharp needles ever closer to the tender tissues between Mariella's toes.

Chapter 7

Whipple was in the kitchen making a pot of tea.

'Do you take milk? he asked General Raffin.

'Please.'

Whipple was about to pour milk into the Spode 'Japanese Garden' pattern cup when he paused. Glancing at the general, he put down the jug and, opening the crockery cupboard, got down a blue-glazed ramekin. It wasn't just the fact that he had a problem juxtaposing rats with fine bone china, it was also a genuine belief that the general would find it easier to drink out of a shallower receptacle.

'So tell us about this place,' said Glaak.

'Hambledon Hall?'

Glaak nodded.

'Built in the late sixteenth century by Sir Henry Trenchard, it was lost to the Parliamentarians during the Civil War. A grateful Cromwell gave it to the general who captured it – one Nathaniel Huxley.'

Whipple poured a drop of milk into the ramekin.

'Sugar?'

'Just one.' The rat tapped his belly. 'I'm trying to lose weight.'

Placing a silver strainer over the ramekin, Whipple poured the tea and added a spoonful of sugar. The general, whiskers twitching, stuck his nose into the steaming dish and took a tentative sip.

'By God, that's good,' he said, smacking his lips. 'You certainly know how to make a cup of tea, Whipple. Please, continue your story.'

'Hambledon stayed in the Huxley family for many years, until the nineteenth century when Elgin Huxley – childless, unmarried and a drunkard, by all accounts a deeply unpleasant chap – lost the estate in a game of cards. They say he left debts of over twenty thousand pounds, a fortune in those days.' Pulling out one of the beechwood kitchen chairs, Whipple sat at the table, spooned sugar into his own cup and stirred. 'It's quite an interesting story, actually. You see, Elgin's lavish parties attracted all sorts of people, including the Prince of Wales himself.'

'He came here?' Glaak enquired.

Whipple nodded. 'Among the prince's entourage was Sir Mortimer Trenchard, the eighth baronet, who viewed Hambledon as his birthright—' He stopped suddenly and frowned. 'Forgive my ignorance, General,' he said, replacing his spoon thoughtfully in his saucer, 'but how is it that you know what constitutes a good cup of tea?'

General Raffin wiped his whiskers with his forepaws. 'You'd be surprised at how consistent life is throughout the universe, Whipple. Admittedly, there are some strange looking coves out there, and some of their habits leave a lot to be desired. But everyone everywhere worries about the same things: how to get enough food, how to care for and protect their young, and whether or not their endowment policy is going to realize enough to pay off their mortgage. The problems of existence are universal.' He took another sip of his tea. 'Please, do carry on.'

'Where was I?'

'The Prince of Wales had just arrived,' Glaak prompted.

'Oh yes. Things didn't go well from the start. Elgin transgressed royal protocol by allowing the revels to go forward before the prince had made his entrance. But then Elgin made an even more foolish mistake, by requesting that the prince join him for a hand or two at cards.'

'That was bad?'

'Oh yes. You see, it was right after the famous Royal Baccarat Scandal. The prince had been summoned to appear as a witness in a matter of cheating at cards. He wasn't himself accused of any wrongdoing, of course, but having her son appear in a court of law was deeply embarrassing for the queen, and she had given him strict instructions not to indulge further his passion for the cards.'

'Ah,' said Glaak, 'I see.'

'The prince was on the point of storming out of the party, but Mortimer, seeing an opportunity to get his hands on the Hall, suggested that he himself should take the prince's place at the card table, to teach Huxley a lesson.'

'And did he?'

'Very much so. Elgin was never a good card player at the best of times, and he drank heavily. By dawn he'd lost what little money he'd been able to borrow, and then Mortimer pulled his master stroke. He proposed a wager Elgin couldn't refuse: he suggested one further hand of cards. If Elgin won, Mortimer undertook to pay off all his debts. If he lost, Mortimer got Hambledon Hall. Needless to say, Huxley lost, and the Hall reverted to the Trenchards.'

'Fascinating,' said Glaak from the depths of his ramekin. 'What happened to Elgin?'

'A broken man, he made his way to Plymouth where, after enjoying a brief encounter with a chambermaid in a seedy hostelry, he boarded a boat bound for America. The ship sank in a violent storm in mid-Atlantic. The Huxley line should have ended there – and for the Trenchards it would have been better if it had – but nine months later the chambermaid gave birth to a son. Had it not been for the fact that she had relieved poor Elgin of the only thing of value he still possessed – a gold pocket watch inscribed with his name – she would never have known the identity of her lover. But one mystery remains to this day. The Prince of Wales's personal cook, one Mary Salthouse, completely disappeared. After his royal highness's visit to Hambledon she was never seen again.'

'Well, well, well,' said Glaak, cleaning his whiskers. 'I would never have known this place was so steeped in history.'

'Most old houses have a story to tell. It's amazing what you find if only you scratch the surface.' Whipple took another sip of his tea. 'So, what's it like where you come from?'

'Planet Argus? Rather barren compared to Earth. Very rocky – very difficult to grow anything there. But then, it wasn't chosen for its potential as a market garden, rather for its remoteness and defensibility. Fortress Argus it's sometimes called.'

'Chosen, you said?' Whipple asked.

'It's a long story. You see, my race originated on a planet called Helios, a beautiful world rather like Earth, with trees, grass, mountains, etc. But then came the Cartogram and we had to find a safe place to keep it . . .' Glaak broke off. 'Do you think I could have a top up?'

Harry Huxley was in a bad mood. As his usual demeanour was that of a rhino with piles; to say that he was in a bad mood is to indicate that he was in very bad humour indeed.

'So what exactly did she say?'

Albert Smythe squirmed in his chair and mopped his forehead with an already damp handkerchief. 'Please, Mr Huxley, I'd rather not . . .'

'What did she say?' Huxley insisted.

'Oh dear,' said Albert, still mopping furiously. 'She said . . . You can insert your offer where no sun shines.' He finished with a small, nervous laugh.

Huxley's big, square face turned pink, then scarlet, then puce. The hairs on his close-cropped head bristled like porcupine quills, and the tendons in his neck stood out like the steel cords on the Tamar suspension bridge. Albert half expected the top of his employer's head to lift off and for steam to shoot out of his ears.

'THE COW!' Huxley brought both fists down on his desk simultaneously, rattling his morning coffee cup and setting the Newton's cradle swinging. He rose in a fury, sending his leather office chair scurrying across the room to collide with the wood-effect filing cabinet. 'She's done it now!' he raged, stalking the faux-Persian carpet. 'She's gone too far! She doesn't know what a dangerous game she's playing. No one messes with Harry Huxley. She's going to pay big time for insulting me like that. I'm going to break her fucking legs!'

Albert ran a finger nervously around his collar. 'You, er . . . you don't mean that, Mr Huxley.'

Huxley was round the large walnut-veneered desk in a flash. 'Oh don't I?' he breathed, bending menacingly over the small accountant. 'Do you know how much I've got riding on Hambledon Hall?'

Albert shook his head.

'Millions – but that's not the only reason I want that building. It's mine!' He pulled a gold pocket-watch out of his waistcoat and, flicking it open, pushed it into Albert's face. On the inside of the lid, below an engraving of Hambledon Hall, was the inscription: *To Elgin Huxley, from mother*. 'You see that? My family were cheated out of that house all those years ago, and I want it back. That woman's got a bloody nerve! Well, she's seen the last of Nice Guy Harry. Now it's time for her to meet Mr Nasty,' he said, snapping the watch shut.

Albert swallowed. 'Mr, um . . . *Nasty?*'

Huxley was dribbling over Albert's lap. 'Yeah, she's made a mistake and now she must pay,' he growled. Leaving Albert to wipe the saliva off his trousers, Huxley moved back behind his desk and hit the intercom. 'Patsy, get me Armani Banks.'

Chapter 8

Matt awoke to the gentle chanting of a choir:

'Ooh, aahh, he is great, he is King, he is everything . . .'

The sound was coming from a small speaker just above his head. Matt was still lying on the couch up against the bulkhead in the Crusader ship, and while he'd slept the wounds in his arm had been cleaned and dressed. Physically, at least, he felt almost normal. The same could not be said of his mind – his thoughts were flapping around inside his cranium like a flock of bats.

'Hello, Larrgh,' the ship's computer said softly. 'Did you have a good sleep? We're nearly home now. We'll be landing on Cullorum in approximately fifteen minutes.'

Larrgh? Cullorum? The names were vaguely familiar and reminded Matt that he had to do something, but at the moment he couldn't remember what. The phrase *Be Quite* flashed up in his brain. *Be quite what?* Then the image of a finger in front of a pair of pursed lips came into his mind. *Oh – be quiet?* He was hopelessly confused, and the choir's sudden gear-change into a spirited, hand-clapping gospel song didn't help.

'Alleluia, praise the Lord!' they sang cheerily.

Slowly coming to, Matt tried to reach out and grab one of his thoughts as it fluttered past. But it was no good, even if he managed to catch one, the moment he opened his hand to find out what it was, it flew away again. One, however, circled a little closer than the rest and ended up smacking him between the eyes. *Mariella!* Then he saw the bent and twisted binnacle from his old ship lying on the floor of the cockpit.

The paper clip, he thought. *No, no, no. Cup holder, erm . . . staple gun . . . magneto* . . . but thinking in words was too confusing. He tried images instead. A rustic scene popped into his mind. Under a spotless blue sky a gang of peasants laboured in a field, their pitchforks glinting in the sun as they loaded up a hay wagon behind a patiently waiting shire horse. *Horse* . . . Matt thought. *Horse and . . . cart. Cart? Horse and Cart . . . ogram! Yes! The Cartogram!* He got up suddenly and regretted it immediately. His head throbbed and the cockpit started to spin. Closing his eyes, he held on to the edge of the couch for support.

'Now, now,' chided the computer, 'you've been through a lot. You just lie back on the couch again and when we land the medics will come and look after you.'

The medics will come and look after me. The phrase conjured up soothing images of nurses in clean white coats tending his wounds and tucking him up in crisp cotton sheets. There was, however, a part of Matt's mind that understood the implications of this statement, and which urged him to go over to the binnacle and extricate the Cartogram from it without delay.

'Praise the Lord! Let him shine his light on you!' sung the gospel singers.

What was I about to do? Let me think, let me think, Matt pleaded. *OK, I was going to do something to the* . . . He raised his eyes and looked at the binnacle. *That thing . . . the . . . cheese . . . tarpaulin . . . Oh, fuck it!* His sympathetic nervous system was the only thing that seemed to be working properly so, although he had no plan, he sensed that somehow, if he got out of the way, his body would know what to do. *Forget everything I said. Don't think, don't think* . . . He got up and moved towards the lump of twisted metal in the middle of the floor. His fingers automatically reached into one of the pockets of his flying suit and took out a small electric screwdriver. Then he watched as his hands carefully undid the four screws securing the bent cover plate and withdrew the universal applications mechanism. Inside lay the Cartogram – *intact*.

'Praise the Lor-or-or-or-or-or-or-ord!' the singers climaxed, then were silent for a moment.

Matt placed the Cartogram safely in an inner pocket and wondered what he would do next. He remembered the ship's computer saying something about landing on Cullorum and a whole series of jumbled thoughts suddenly dropped into place like a course of bricks.

We're about to land on Cullorum and the medics will come on board and then, when they find out who I am, take me straight into the arena. Fuck! Did I have a plan when I began this enterprise? He racked his brain, searching for the remnants of any ideas he might have had for surviving this mission. *Mariella* was the one word that kept coming to him.

The gospel singers started up again in earnest:

'The Lord has given me hope!'

The Lord has given me soap, Matt rhymed in his head.

'And told me I mustn't mope!'

Because it's soap on a rope . . .

'The Lord is on my wavelength!'

For he has slipped me a length . . .

'And he has given me strength! Alleluia!'

The unseen gospel singers carried on praising the Lord while, through the forward view-port, the big blue-grey bulk of Cullorum drew rapidly near. Matt had to formulate a plan, and quickly. Running his fingers through his hair, he felt the piece of tape with which he'd fixed the Crusader's chip to his own neck. *My name is Larrgh Thaarrss*, he thought. If he could get into the hospital wing without being rumbled, he'd stand a chance of finding Mariella – if she was still alive – and getting out in one piece. But his flying suit was a dead giveaway.

Leaving the bridge, he stepped through the bulkhead doorway and into the sleeping quarters beyond. Entering one of the cabins, he found what he was looking for – a Crusader's suit, complete with helmet and a full array of weaponry.

OK, now we're skating, er . . . potholing . . . whatever . . .

'And that's the word of the Lord!'

'Aaaaa-men!'

Glitch's thumb was on the plunger of the hypodermic syringe. Its needles were now deep in the cartilage and bone of Mariella's foot and he was about to pump it full of acid. Having screamed herself hoarse, Mariella could do no more than plead in a whisper with her tormentor.

'Please . . . please don't . . .'

'Do you know what the acid will do to your bones?' Glitch asked her.

'No . . . please . . .'

'Turn them to jelly. As for the soft tissues, they'll start fizzing away like bath salts. It'll take time, of course, and did I mention the fact that it will be extremely painful?' He smiled. 'Oh yes, I'm sure I did.'

'I'll tell you,' she sobbed. 'I'll tell you everything!'

Glitch was about to signal one of his assistants to turn up the music, but at that moment a distant roar from the arena echoed down the corridors of the hospital wing.

'Is it that time already?' Glitch looked at his watch, then up at Mariella, her face contorted with pain. 'I'm sorry, my dear, but I have a pressing engagement. I have rather a lot of money riding on a hump-backed stelion in the first bout. He's matched against a fine, courageous warrior from Goran-B'tLamboo. It should be quite a contest.' He flickered across to the door, his mobile eye revolving excitedly. 'We'll continue this later. You can tell me whatever it is that's on your mind then. It'll be something to look forward to. What fun, what delicious antici-pation!' Throwing a leather cape over his shoulders, his black-gloved hand lightly touched the door release and it opened with a *hiss*.

'No! I said I'll talk! You can't leave me like this!' Mariella rasped.

'Can't I?' And he was gone, disappearing through the door with an electronic whirr.

Hurrying along the corridor, Glitch had to stand aside for a trolley bearing a wounded Crusader, which was being pushed at some speed towards the emergency room. It was a common enough sight; during assimilation sorties, the corridors were sometimes clogged with dead and dying soldiers, and Glitch barely gave them second thought. Nevertheless, there was something that didn't seem quite right about this particular Crusader, something that made Glitch's revolving eye fix on him. But whatever it was, Glitch would not be diverted from his entertainment now, and he hastened to his private box.

In the emergency room, the doctor on call had just removed the Crusader's helmet when he felt something being pushed into his belly. Looking down he saw the barrel of a pistol sticking into the waistband of his trousers.

Matt looked up at him. 'One move and I'll blow a hole in your carafe . . . basket . . . er, spleen.'

The doctor raised his hands. One of the attendants made a move for the door, but Matt saw him. 'I wouldn't,' he warned, swinging the gun on him. 'Move away from the . . . the . . .' the word *onion* popped into Matt's mind, but he was almost sure it was wrong. 'Get back in here!' he ordered impatiently, getting up off the trolley. The man hesitated, then stepped back into the body of the room. 'Good, now then . . .'

Mariella wanted to die. The throbbing ache in her foot possessed her whole being. She was ready to tell everything she knew – how many agents had infiltrated the Crusaders, their code names, the frequencies they broadcast on, even their make of underwear, if only someone would remove the needles.

The door hissed open. A Crusader stood there, gun in hand.

Now what? Mariella thought. Then he raised his visor.

'Matt!'

He levelled his gun at Glitch's two attendants. 'OK, let's get your personnel where I can see them.' The attendants looked puzzled. 'No, your . . . your . . . Look, put up your lapels . . . no . . . Shit!'

'I think he means get your hands up,' Mariella gasped.

'Yeah, what she said.'

The two assistants dutifully obeyed.

Matt took in Mariella properly for the first time. She was grey with pain and fatigue, and her face was wet with tears.

'My foot, my foot,' she gasped.

Matt looked down. 'My God.' Unstrapping her wrists he handed her the gun and, while she kept the assistants covered, knelt and studied the chromed mechanism at her feet. He was both impressed and appalled by the stark simplicity of its design, and tried not to think about what he would like to do to the animal that had invented it, concentrating instead on getting Mariella free.

Grasping the small crank between finger and thumb, Matt paused. If he turned it the wrong way he would only succeed in pushing the needles deeper into her foot.

'Turn it!' Mariella croaked.

'But—'

'Just turn the fucking thing!'

'OK, OK.' He took a guess. Slowly winding the crank anti-clockwise he kept a close watch on Mariella's face. After a quarter turn, she convulsed in agony.

'THE OTHER WAY!'

With trembling fingers, Matt turned the crank back the other way and gradually the needles began to slide out of her flesh. After several long, painful moments, they came free, and Mariella almost fainted with relief.

Matt quickly released her foot from the 'press' and undid the straps around her ankles. 'Do you think you can walk?'

'I can probably hobble a little,' she whispered hoarsely.

Matt helped her out of the chair. One of Glitch's assistants, taking advantage of the moment, picked up a scalpel off the workbench, but Mariella had seen him. She ducked and the scalpel buried itself deep in the padding of the chair. Mariella fired once and the would-be assassin fell dead.

The other assistant had been about to pick up a long, pointed steel instrument nearby but, seeing his colleague lying dead on the floor, thought better of it. Matt called him over and made him sit in the chair.

'Now you sit there and keep . . . you keep omelette. Fuck! Just sit down!' Matt strapped the assistant into the chair while Mariella stuffed the man's tie into his mouth to keep him quiet.

Matt turned to her. 'Are you OK?'

Mariella smiled sweetly up at him and nodded silently, then she pulled back her arm and punched him hard on the jaw.

'Ow!' Matt hit the lino. 'What did you do that for?'

'You jerk! If we ever get out of here alive, Major, I'm going to see that you're stripped of your commission.'

'I'm sorry, I—'

'You idiot! Do you have any idea what I've been through? You could have had me killed!'

Matt picked himself up and counted his teeth. 'Look, I'm really sorry about what happened, but can we discuss it later? I think we should probably get out of here now.'

Mariella breathed deeply. 'Very well, what have you arranged?'

Matt looked blank. 'Arranged?'

'You haven't got a plan, have you?'

'I work better when I optimize . . . shampoo . . . Shit! When I . . . improvise!'

Mariella looked at him strangely. 'You're a mess,' she said, unhelpfully.

'I'm just a little mixed up, that's all.' He had an idea. 'I know – you're my . . . my . . .' He pointed to himself, then to her, then to the gun she was holding.

'I'm your what?'

'My . . . my . . .' once again he pointed at the large red cross on his Crusader's uniform, then at her.

'Now you want to play charades?'

'NO! You're my . . . thing.'

'Prisoner?'

'That's the word!'

Mariella shook her head slowly. 'This isn't going to work.'

'Look. We can stay here and die or we can try and get away. It's up to you.'

She looked at him levelly. 'OK. Help me on with my shoes.'

Mariella perched on a laboratory stool while Matt fetched her shoes. He had to slice a large chunk out of the right one with a scalpel to make it fit over her swollen foot.

'Do you know how much those cost?' Mariella snapped.

Matt looked up at her. 'Can we just stop this, please?' He gently eased the shoe on to her foot. It was painful, but at least it was on. 'There, let's go.'

'Wait. Take me over to the workbench.' Together they hobbled across the room. Handing Matt the gun, she searched through drawers and cupboards, eventually finding what she was looking for – a bottle of painkillers. Grabbing it gratefully, she opened it, threw back her head and poured the contents into her mouth. She would have swallowed the lot if Matt hadn't stopped her.

'Easy,' he said, relieving her of the pills and putting them in his pocket. 'You may need some for later. Come on.'

Helping Mariella over to the door, Matt opened it and looked up and down the long corridor. It was empty. 'Ready?'

Mariella nodded and held on to him tightly. Matt closed the visor of his helmet and, clinging to each other, they made their way slowly and painfully towards the spaceport, Mariella wincing with every step.

*

Slipping into his box at the arena, Glitch was just in time to catch the end of Gulgus Filch's customary address to the citizens who were still crowding excitedly into the tiered banks of seats.

'. . . We are here to witness the purification of sinners. For those who enter this arena today have offended the Lord! Let their punishment be a warning to those who would rise against Valohem. Their sins will find them out! Let us pray.' There was a shuffling as the audience pushed bags, coats and small children out of the way to get to their knees. Gulgus clasped his hands in front of him and closed his eyes. 'Lord, it is our fervent prayer that those whom you have chosen in your infinite wisdom to appear before us will not suffer in vain. We pray that the spilling of their blood will wash them clean this day and allow them to find eternal rest in your merciful arms. Thank you, Lord. Amen.'

After a solemn choral 'Amen', the crowd erupted into jeers and catcalls as the first contestant appeared. A tall, strong Goran-B'tLamboolian warrior was pushed through a door in the concrete wall of the arena and on to the vast, sand-covered killing field. A small shield and a long spear were thrown in after him, clattering to the ground at his heels. After the darkness of the subterranean backstage area, the brightness of the artificial illumination was dazzling and, as his eyes slowly became accustomed to the light, he looked around, taking in the dark damp patches in the sand and the audience screaming with hatred, their faces contorted in an ecstasy of violent expectation. The warrior, erect and proud, regarded them impassively, picked up the scanty shield and spear, then turned to face the big wooden gates through which his terrifying opponent would presently emerge. He didn't have to wait long.

The crash of the gates being thrown open instantly silenced the crowd, and they waited in tense stillness for the contest to begin. The warrior nervously gripped his inadequate weapon and stared into the black hole in the side of the arena, trying to catch a glimpse of the creature lurking in the darkness. Then, in a sudden, terrifying rush, the massive beast thundered into the ring, tossing its huge head and stamping its feet. The audience cheered. The warrior knew his best chance of making a strike was now, before the creature's eyes had become accustomed to the light. He leapt forwards and thrust the spear deep into the stelion's long neck. Blood gushed from the wound, and the enraged beast reared up on its hind legs, its forelegs slashing wildly. But the warrior had already sprinted round behind the animal and now pushed the spear into the tender area underneath the tail. The stelion screamed and twisted violently round to face its tormentor and the warrior got in another well-timed thrust, the spear point slicing through the soft skin of its underbelly. The audience booed their displeasure as the warrior sprinted away out of range of the stelion's terrifying natural weaponry.

Breathing hard, warrior and beast eyed each other for a while from a distance. Then, to a wild cheer, the stelion put its head down and charged. Just as it seemed inevitable that the warrior would get pierced by the creature's two-foot-long nose horn, he leapt up on to its neck and stabbed downwards with the spear. The beast screamed and shook its head and the warrior was thrown off, landing heavily on the sand – breaking his spear in half in the process. Now he would have to fight at close quarters. The crowd was ecstatic.

The stelion came to a standstill at the far end of the arena, shaking its head like a wounded dog. Turning, it looked back at the warrior and at the broken section of spear in his hand, dripping with its blood. Pawing the ground and snorting through its huge nostrils, it fixed the warrior with large, blood-shot eyes, lowered its head and charged again.

The beast thundered towards him, and the warrior felt the earth tremble beneath his feet, but he held his ground, every muscle tensed, waiting, waiting . . . As the stelion was almost upon him, he vaulted over the creature's horn and landed on its back, stabbing down again and again with the broken spear. The beast reared up, blood gushing from a dozen wounds, but the warrior clung to the row of spines sprouting from the large hump on its back, continuing to slash great chunks out of the stelion's flesh. It was clear the creature was weakening, and Glitch was beginning to feel a little uneasy. The Goran-B'tLamboolians were nimble and cunning fighters and, in two previous bouts, this particular warrior had already killed one stelion and seriously maimed another. Glitch hadn't been able to resist the odds that were being offered on the stelion in this contest, but now it seemed that greed was going to be his undoing. He watched grimly as the warrior thrust the spear deep into the creature's back yet again. But then, just as he was about to leap off, the warrior lost his footing on the beast's scaly skin, now slippery with blood, and fell backwards on to one of the small spines running along the stelion's side. The sharp point ripped a jagged wound in the fighter's shoulder, and he fell to the ground and rolled away, leaving a dark red trail in the sand. The crowd cheered with delight, throwing their seat cushions high into the air.

Glitch watched with renewed interest as the warrior slowly hauled himself to his feet, and the stelion came in yet again. This time, his fighting arm incapacitated by his wound, the warrior could do no more than dodge the beast's charge. Sensing victory, and cheered on by the rapturous crowd, the stelion turned and galloped in with fresh impetus. Again the warrior side-stepped, but he was losing a lot of blood and it was becoming clear that, short of a miracle, he was unlikely to be able to withstand the persistence of this two-ton mass of muscle and spikes for much longer. The animal lowered its head and thundered in one final time. The warrior was not quick enough. The stelion's horn pierced him through the chest, and the victorious animal threw back its head in triumph. It made a tour of the arena with the warrior dangling limply from its horn before throwing the poor man down on to the blood-soaked sand.

Glitch watched with satisfaction as his well-backed stelion began to devour its beaten opponent with steak-knife teeth.

Smiling contentedly, he left the cool airiness of his private box and stepped out into the sweaty press of eager punters moving as one down towards the betting floor to collect their winnings. Glitch was just calculating how much, after tax, he was going to take home when a disturbing image popped into his mind. It was of a Crusader on a trolley – the trolley he'd passed in the corridor on his way to the arena. What was disturbing about this mental picture was that the feet sticking out from under the Crusader's tunic were not regulation, iron-studded black boots, but casual, soft-soled suede ones.

Fripp!

Turning and scything his way invisibly and violently through the crowd, Glitch hurried back to his laboratory.

The spaceport was situated to the west of Cullorum City. Although its chief function was military, it also handled a lot of civilian traffic. The vast, domed atrium of its main building was full of cafes and restaurants, and stalls selling everything from silks to small tins of pressed eggs from the rare Nilvernian spurle. Usually it was a lively, bustling place but, today being a fight day, almost everyone was at the arena.

About the only activity there was centred around a newly arrived consignment of prisoners who were in the process of being 'graded': sorted into holding pens like cattle at auction. The fittest and strongest were separated into two groups – one destined for the army, the other for training at gladiatorial school to feed the arena's insatiable appetite for new flesh. Children and the elderly, being either too young or too old to be useful as slaves, were put in another pen for 'disposal', and all the young females were marched off immediately to be turned into Brides of Valohem: incarcerated in isolated convents lest their beauty corrupt the young Crusaders, turning their minds from death and glory to gentler thoughts of love.

Through this scene of desperation and sadness, a helmeted

Crusader and his limping prisoner made their way towards the departure gate.

'Larrgh Thaarrss,' Matt announced himself to the departure-gate guard, who was busy trying to separate a weeping mother from her young son.

The guard looked up. 'What do you want?' he demanded.

'I'm taking this pie, er . . .'

'Prisoner,' Mariella hissed.

'Prisoner,' Matt corrected himself. 'I'm taking this prisoner to . . .'

'I can't hear you. Open your helmet,' the guard ordered.

Matt attempted to bluff it out. 'Um . . .' he said, raising his voice, 'I'm taking this prisoner to . . .'

'Are you deaf? I said open your helmet!'

If Matt raised his visor the chances were that he'd be recognized instantly. If he didn't, this officious guard would probably do it for him. Either way he'd have to fight his way out, and the odds were not good – the place was crawling with Crusaders. Matt's fingers tightened nervously around the grip of his pistol.

But just then one of the newly arrived captives, a young Melgawan being held in the gladiator pen, saw his lover being marched away to begin her lonely life as a Bride of Valohem. The sight was too much for him. Pushing his guard aside and vaulting the gate of the pen, he ran after her, screaming her name, 'Elthera! Elthera!'

The guard Matt had been speaking to unshouldered his boson arc and let loose a bolt. The young Melgawan fell forward and his lifeless body slid across the shiny marble floor, coming to an abrupt halt at his lover's feet.

After a moment's silence, all hell broke loose. The women wailed, the men shouted and the guards began arguing with each other about how the Melgawan had managed to get free in the first place. In the confusion, Matt and Mariella slipped through the gate unnoticed.

The departure lounge was almost deserted, apart from a few

late passengers hurrying to their boarding gates, and an Octa-vian – a large orange blob with eight arms. The Octavia are a highly intelligent race with well-developed literary and musical talents, highly prized for their vocal skills. But when their planet was conquered by the Crusaders, Gulgus's warped sense of humour, coupled with a fear of anything that could be construed as 'cultural', had them all designated as cleaners. Mind you, there was a certain logic to it: having eight arms meant that one Octavian could wash the windows, sweep the floor, pre-pare dinner and rock the baby to sleep with a gentle lullaby all at the same time. But the Octavia's humiliating treatment had done little to endear Filch to them, and had made them hungry for revenge.

Matt went straight across to one of the big picture windows overlooking the spacefield. The large concreted expanse of run-ways and taxiways beyond was illuminated by the glare from a thousand floodlights. Directly below, several civilian spaceliners were parked, one of them just beginning its boarding procedure. Beyond that, at the end of the short southern runway, stood a cluster of battle cruisers. 'There,' he said, 'we'll take one of those babies. Come on.'

'Wait.' Mariella was watching two space pilots who had just emerged from behind a door marked: SPACEPORT STAFF ONLY. They were heading off towards one of the boarding gates. '*If* we manage to hijack a ship and get out of here, and that's a pretty big *if* with you calling the shots, they're going to be coming straight after us.'

'Well, yeah,' Matt agreed.

'So, why don't we take a liner?'

'A liner? We haven't got a ticket.'

'How the fuck did you ever make it to major? Give me the gun.'

The Octavian, who had been listening, sidled up to them and whispered, 'Excuse me for butting in, but I couldn't help overhearing. Do you need a hand . . . or eight?' she smiled.

Mariella smiled back. 'Do you happen to know "The Angels danced in Garmela Bay"?'

The Octavian winked and opened her mouth to sing. The sound was so beautiful that whoever heard it simply had to listen. The two pilots stopped and turned, beatific smiles on their faces, as the Octavian ravished their ears. Slowly, slowly the singer made her way towards them, arms outstretched, captivating the crew with the most exquisite sound imaginable. By the time they realized what was happening it was too late – the Octavian had them in its grip and they were looking down the barrel of Mariella's gun.

'OK, fellers, let's go somewhere quiet and get naked.'

Glitch raced back along the echoing corridor. Slipping back into his laboratory, he found one of his assistants dead and the other strapped into the chair. Yanking the man's tie out of his mouth, he slapped him hard around the face.

'Where are they?'

'He took her. He was a Crusader . . .'

'That was Fripp, you imbecile!'

'I'm sorry, sir. I couldn't stop them.'

Glitch had an irresistible urge to seriously damage this idiot. He looked around for something that would cause him extreme pain, and his roving eye lit upon the syringe nestling in the chrome cradle at the foot of the chair. His assistant followed the single orb's gaze.

'No, sir. Please!'

Glitch snatched up the syringe and without preamble plunged the four needles into the man's belly. The assistant stared in mute horror at the bulbous body of the syringe sticking out from the area of his gall bladder.

'That was for incompetence!' Glitch snarled. 'And this,' he added, an evil smile spreading across his face, 'is purely for pleasure.' He pushed the plunger home, delivering the syringe's contents straight into the man's liver. For a moment the assistant felt a warm sensation creep over his abdomen then, as the sulphuric acid began to turn his liver to soup, he started squealing like a pig.

Boarding on liner GOAB 9579 was almost complete when the flight crew finally arrived.

'Where the hell have you been?' the chief steward snapped as Matt and Mariella walked up the gangplank in their ill-fitting uniforms. Matt nearly tripped over his over-long trousers as he entered the craft.

'Problems with my tailor,' said Matt, pulling his hat low over his eyes.

'Sorry, we were held up by an incident in immigration,' Mariella added quickly.

Smiling and nodding, they went straight into the cockpit and closed the door.

'Have you ever flown one of these things before?' Matt asked, gazing at the unfamiliar array of dials and gauges.

'No.'

'Great, now who's thinking ahead?' he said, strapping himself into the captain's chair.

Mariella assumed the first officer's position in the other seat. 'It can't be that difficult. You're a major in the Space Force for heaven's sake, and this *is* a spacecraft if I'm not mistaken,' she hissed.

'OK, OK. Now then, let's see.'

'Golf Oscar Alpha Bravo 9579 you are clear to taxi.'

Matt started. 'Who the fuck said that?'

Mariella put a finger to her lips, then pointed to the set of headphones dangling from the arm of his chair.

'Ah,' said Matt, putting them on. 'Er, say again, tower?'

'You are clear to taxi.'

'Ah, right. Golf . . . er . . . Bravo 9 . . . um . . . thing . . . clear to taxi.'

'You're breaking up Golf Oscar Alpha Bravo 9579.'

'Roger that, tower. Golf Oscar Alpha Bravo 9579, clear to taxi,' Mariella replied crisply into her headset. Matt breathed a sigh of relief and gave her a thumbs up.

'Golf Oscar Alpha Bravo 9579, proceed runway 9, west.'

'Runway 9, west, aye . . . er . . . roger,' Matt replied

Finding a control that he recognized, he pulled it and the engines began to slowly wind themselves up. When manifold pressure read quarter power, the big craft started to move off. Matt flashed Mariella a self-satisfied grin.

'The passengers,' she said.

'What about them?'

'You're the captain – you have to talk to them.'

'Talk to them?'

'You know, welcome them on board, tell them to relax and enjoy the flight.'

'How do I do that?'

Mariella pointed to a small red button on the instrument panel that had *cabin intercom* picked out in white around its circumference.

'Oh, right. OK . . .' his finger hovered over the button. 'I just welcome them on board and tell them to enjoy the flight?'

Mariella nodded.

'OK, here we go.' He pressed the button. 'Good after . . . evening, ladies and gentlemen, this is your motorcade, er captain speaking. I'd just like to welcome you on board and hope you have an original enclave . . . um, enjoyable flight. We're taxiing out to our designated runway now, and we should be a luxury item . . . that's airborne, soon.'

Mariella waved at him and drew her finger across her throat indicating that she thought he'd probably said enough.

'Cabin doors to automatic.' Matt clicked off the intercom and smiled across at Mariella. 'How was I?'

'Cabin doors to automatic?'

'It's what they always say.'

Matt piloted the liner out across the acres of concrete. He had no idea where runway 9 actually was, but there was a huge Pan Galactic Leviathan trundling towards the far side of the space-port. Assuming they were both heading for the same location, Matt got in line behind it.

The Leviathan made a turn to port. Following the big craft, Matt spun the small control wheel on the instrument panel and the liner obediently turned to the left. He was beginning to feel at home. 'You know,' he said, beaming at Mariella, 'this isn't so hard.'

Matt's headset suddenly crackled into life, making him jump. 'Golf Oscar Alpha Bravo 9579.'

'Er, go ahead, tower.'

'You are clear for take-off after Pan Galactic flight 6504.'

'Roger that, tower, clear for take-off after Pan Galactic 6504.'

The Pan Galactic Leviathan reached the head of the runway, slowly turned and pointed its nose down the rubber-streaked ribbon of concrete. Matt pulled the liner up and watched as the huge ship wound up its engines. Five seconds after the pilot had let off the brakes the massive craft was a blur, soaring away across the night sky.

Matt manoeuvred his own liner to the position at the top of the runway that the Leviathan had just left.

He turned to Mariella. 'Here goes nothing.'

'You give a girl such confidence.'

Matt pulled the throttles all the way out, and the ship's engines began to scream. All that pent-up power caused the fuselage to buck and roll. When he let off the brakes the liner shot down the runway like a silver bullet, and minutes later was streaking through the emptiness of space.

*

Glitch appeared in front of the guard at the departure gate.

'Soldier!'

The guard jumped several feet in the air as the empty space in front of him was suddenly filled with the evil form of the commissioner. 'Wah! Oh, it's you, sir. How can I help?'

'Has a Crusader passed this way escorting a woman? She will have had a pronounced limp.'

'Sorry, sir, I don't recall . . . Wait a minute, yes, there was a Crusader here a while ago. I believe he had a prisoner with him – it could well have been a woman.'

'Where did they go?'

'I've no idea, sir. We were very busy at the time, and . . . oh.' The guard petered out as Glitch dissolved in front of him.

'You were saying?' came a voice in his ear.

The man jumped again. 'Ah! I didn't see where they went, sir!'

'Scour the place. Contact the tower and lock down the space-port – nothing leaves.'

'Yes, sir, straight away, sir!' The guard ran off to gather a search party while Glitch flickered to and fro on the marble floor of the spaceport building, wondering how he was going to break the news to Gulgus.

They found the space pilots locked in a broom cupboard. They'd been tied up, gagged and left with nothing but their underwear. There was no excuse for incompetence of course, and soon they would be making their first and final appearance in the arena.

By the time Glitch had worked out what had happened, Matt and Mariella were already several light years away. A cruiser was despatched on a search mission but had little hope of finding them.

This latest incident, coming on top of news of the disaster on Gweeb, sent Filch into a rage, and he called immediately for Glitch.

'If there's one thing I can't stand it's stupidity!' he said, his fury for once overriding his fear of the commissioner. 'It's bad enough that the imbeciles searching Gweeb let Fripp get away with the Cartogram for a second time! But *you*, who should have known better, went off to the arena in the middle of an interrogation!' Filch stopped – he appeared to be talking to thin air. 'Where have you gone?'

Glitch, who had been flickering all over the room, came to a standstill and reappeared before him. 'Sorry, Gulgus.'

'We could have got the whole network out of her!'

'She was a very tough nut, Gulgus,' Glitch lied. 'I doubt she'd have cracked.' He started flickering again.

'Will you stop that!'

'As you wish.' Glitch reappeared and this time remained both visible and stock-still, his bloodless eyes fixed on Filch.

Gulgus went cold and was reminded of how little he trusted McGilvray. 'So then . . .' he began, trying to put out of his mind what pitiless cruelty his commissioner was capable of. 'We need to find them; bring them back before they do any damage.'

'Sir, the rebellion is a spent force . . .'

'They just lifted the Cartogram from right under our noses – twice! No, don't underestimate the rebels. Glaak Raffin is a shrewd operator and I'm sure he's up to something. And if we still had the girl we'd probably know by now what that was!'

Chapter 9

In the kitchen of Hambledon Hall, Whipple refreshed Glaak Raffin's ramekin. 'So tell me more about this Cartogram,' he said.

Glaak took a sip of tea before replying. 'It was discovered back on Helios following a cliff fall, sitting on top of a layer of solid granite. It was very puzzling because it was obviously the product of an advanced civilization – tests determined that despite its rock-like appearance it was in fact Bakelite – but the stratum in which it was found was millions of years old, way before anything like intelligent life had evolved. This caused great controversy: some dismissed it as a fake, others argued that the dating techniques were at fault, and no one could even guess at its function.

'For years it languished in the Mystery Artefact section of the Helian Museum. Then, one day, one of the curators, who had a little more curiosity than the others, took it out and gave it a good clean. Underneath the accretions of millennia she discovered some ancient symbols impressed into its surface. As she was painstakingly cleaning these out with a cotton bud, a strange thing happened: a holographic, three-dimensional map of the Cosmos appeared and hovered above the artefact itself. After a little more investigation an even more remarkable thing was discovered: if the symbols were touched in just the right order, squiggly red lines appeared, criss-crossing the map. These, it later transpired, were wormholes connecting points in space billions of light years apart. With this information it suddenly became possible to traverse the universe in a matter of moments.

'It was dynamite! And extremely dangerous. Of course, Helians, being completely trustworthy and genetically incapable of perpetrating a falsehood, would never think of abusing such knowledge, so we took it upon ourselves to keep the Cartogram and its secrets safe for the good of all the peoples of the universe, and immediately set about looking for a suitable stronghold. Argus was perfect. Being little more than an asteroid, its small size meant that it was easily defensible, and its remoteness allowed our scanners to pick up any potential threat, like an invasion force, well in advance of its arrival. So, that's where it remained, perfectly safe, for centuries.' The general stuck his nose back in the ramekin and had a slurp of tea.

'And what about Helios?' Whipple enquired.

The general wiped his whiskers thoughtfully. 'A very sad story. Only a small civilian contingent, including the curator who first discovered the Cartogram's secrets and her family, was allowed to live on Argus – to care for the Cartogram and to carry out further research. Because it was important the fortress was well defended, by far the major part of the population consisted of a large garrison of Helios's best warriors. It was a terrible, terrible mistake . . .' The general paused and took another sip of tea.

'What happened?' asked Whipple.

'The Helians' inability to tell a lie was, sadly, their undoing. Unfortunately, word of the Cartogram soon got out, but for security's sake no one save those on Argus knew its precise location, not even those Helians left at home. The Cartogram was as safe as if it had been locked in the heart of the sun. The same could not be said for Helios. With all its best fighting men absent it became an easy target. A group of N'Tam mercenaries arrived and threatened to level the parliament building if the Cartogram was not handed over to them immediately. The security council refused their demands, explaining that they couldn't comply even if they wanted to. The N'Tam demolished the building, wiping out the planetary government at a stroke. When the Cartogram was still not forthcoming they went on a killing spree. By the time the N'Tam figured out that the Helians weren't bluffing, more than two-thirds of the population lay dead and the planet had been rendered uninhabitable due to the fallout from their weapons. Those that managed to survive the attack soon died, and Helios has been a dead planet ever since, the garrison guarding the Cartogram being all that remains of our once great civilization.' The general sighed. 'But all that happened a long time ago.' He sniffed and stuck his nose back into the ramekin.

'My God,' Whipple exclaimed. 'It seems that the universe is an extremely violent place.'

'If you want to see real violence you should come to a Galactic Alliance Council meeting.'

'But if the Cartogram was safe on Argus why didn't you just leave it there?'

'The Crusaders found out where it was – quite by accident. They were mapping the perimeter of the Dark Quadrant and *blip!* up Argus pops on their scanners. Filch threatened to blow the planet and the Cartogram to smithereens unless we handed it over, giving us twenty-four hours to make up our minds. And he meant it. You see, although possession of the Cartogram would enable him to dramatically accelerate and expand his territorial ambitions, Filch's arrogance couldn't countenance the fact of its ownership by anyone else but himself.

'I had already passed on the everyday running of Argus to my deputy as I was far too busy working with the Galactic Alliance Council, so I only found out about Filch's threat at the last moment. Rather than let Argus and the Cartogram be destroyed in a cataclysmic attack, I told them to accede to Filch's demands, while I secretly organized the Cartogram's theft. It had to be done without the other Helians' knowledge of course, otherwise, true to their scrupulously honest nature, they'd simply have owned up to the Crusaders about the whole plot. Then Matt has to go and crash.'

Whipple frowned. 'But if the Cartogram *had* been destroyed, wouldn't your wish to keep it out of the hands of an aggressor have been fulfilled? You said yourself that the Helians themselves have no intention of using it.'

'*Had* no intention of using it,' the general corrected, 'but Filch's aggression has made us think again. The only way we're going to beat this madman is by keeping one step ahead of him. With the Cartogram we can slip around the Galaxy without his knowing where we are. But, that apart, to us Helians the Cartogram is a symbol; it represents our civilization. To let it be destroyed would render meaningless the great sacrifice of our ancestors. Besides, I have a personal interest in its safety.'

'How so?'

'The curator who discovered its importance was my great-great-great-great-grandmother.' Glaak glanced up at the kitchen clock. 'Good lord, is that the time? Where the hell's Matt?'

Having set the coordinates into the liner's computer, all Matt and Mariella had to do was settle back in the cockpit and watch the gradually changing panorama of the sky as the ship sped them across the inky wastes of space towards their destination.

Balancing the plastic tray containing his in-flight meal awkwardly on his lap, Matt was browsing through a copy of the *Galactic Informer* he'd found in a pouch beneath his chair. There wasn't a lot of news, most of the tabloid being taken up with pictures of wanted rebels and statements from Gulgus and his henchmen about their 'glorious struggle'. The most interesting section was the page of comic strips, and soon Matt was chuckling over the adventures of a square-jawed space pilot hero. He glanced across at Mariella. 'You ever read this – the adventures of Captain Nemesis?'

She glared back at him. 'I'm glad you've finally found your level.'

Matt sighed and put the newspaper away. 'How's your foot?' he asked.

'It could be worse, but I'll never be able to wear heels again.' Mariella stared at the unappetizing mess of her space dinner. 'By the way, where are we were going? Or haven't you worked that out yet?' She took a tentative forkful.

'Gweeb,' Matt replied simply.

Mariella almost choked on her rehydrated boeuf provençal. 'Gweeb? Are you out of your mind?'

'I'm as thrilled to be going back there as you are, believe me. It didn't do an awful lot for my sanity the last time I visited.'

'Why Gweeb?'

'That's where the wormhole is.'

'The wormhole's on Gweeb?'

'Well, not exactly *on* it, more above it.' He looked at his watch. 'The general's not going to be happy – I'm way overdue.' Forking a glob of watery mashed potato into his mouth, Matt shook his head and smiled.

'What is it?' Mariella asked.

Matt swallowed. 'He's going to be mad as hell when he sees you.'

'Why?'

'He told me not to rescue you.'

Mariella turned to him, her face like thunder. 'You disobeyed a direct order, just to come and get me?'

Matt shrugged.

'How many regulations can one man break in the space of a day?'

Matt frowned. 'I don't understand you. First you're angry with me because I put you in a bad bidet, er . . . situation, now you're angry because I came back to get you out of it!'

'OK, OK, truce.' Mariella tried another forkful. 'You never told me how it went on Argus,' she continued after a pause. 'I

'OK, OK, just keep looking straight ahead.' Approaching cautiously from behind, Jaymal pressed the muzzle of his pistol into Matt's neck. 'Don't do anything stupid now.' Leaning over him, the big man started punching numbers into the computer.

Mariella glared at Matt. 'I told you we'd never get away with this!'

'Just take it easy now, lady,' said Jaymal, intent on the console.

But Mariella wouldn't shut up. 'Do you have any idea what's going to happen to us when we get back?'

The ship began a long, slow turn. Mariella got up suddenly and started yelling at Matt. 'You lunatic! Look at the trouble you've got us into now!' She made a move towards him and Jaymal swung the gun on her. Matt leapt up and grabbed the man's arm, yanking it behind his back and forcing his face into the console. Mariella twisted the gun out of Jaymal's hand and smacked him across the back of the head with it. Agent Flange slumped to the floor of the cockpit, out cold. The steward, watching nervously from the back of the cockpit, put his hand tentatively on the door handle.

Mariella pointed the gun at him. 'I wouldn't, bellboy. You heard what the man said about this gun.' She waved him away from the door and indicated her seat. 'Why don't you come up here and sit down?' He meekly obeyed.

Matt wrestled Jaymal into the other seat and Mariella secured both prisoners with the headphone cables. 'Now what?' she said.

Matt clicked on the cabin intercom. 'Can a member of cabin staff please come to the cockpit? Thank you.' He looked up at Mariella. 'We're going to have to scare them a little, and we don't want any heroics.'

A moment later there was a knock at the door. Mariella opened it to reveal a nervous young blonde. She pulled the woman inside.

'You ought to know,' said Matt, 'that this ship is now in the

103

hands of forces loyal to the Galactic Alliance. Do as we say and no one will get hurt.'

'If you or any of your colleagues tries anything stupid we'll start shooting people,' Mariella warned. 'Starting with these two.' She indicated Jaymal and the steward.

'Do as they say, please,' the steward said in a small voice.

'Go back to work,' Matt continued, 'and carry on as if nothing had happened.'

The girl nodded fearfully and Mariella let her out.

Once she was gone, Matt turned back to the main console and the navigational computer. 'We've got to get rid of the passengers,' he said, scrolling through star charts. 'Here – Alkan 5, we can let them off there.'

'Alkan 5's a penal colony,' Mariella protested.

'I know.'

Mariella looked over his shoulder at the charts on the computer screen. 'Loomis Land's nearer. Why not set them down there?'

'Believe me, they'll be safer on Alkan 5.'

'Among violent criminals? They won't last five minutes.'

'Trust me, they stand a better chance against murderers and rapists than they do in Zach Loomis's fun park.'

Matt was about to reset the coordinates when the ship slowed suddenly and lurched violently to port.

'What was that?' asked Mariella.

Matt checked the readings. 'I don't know.' Clicking the controls to manual, Matt leaned over the comatose Jaymal and tried to steer the ship, but everything was locked up. Then, as the craft began to be pulled sideways, a small asteroid with a sign stuck into the top of it floated past the view-port:

LOOMIS LAND® THIS WAY

ONLY 500,000 MILES TO ACRES OF FUN!

'Shit!'

'What's happened?'

'We've been caught in a tractor beam. We're going to Loomis Land whether we like it or not.'

A voice came over the speakers. 'Spaceliner, this is Loomis Land Central Control. We have you now, just hold on for the ride of your life!'

The computer screen flickered and the star charts were replaced with the image of a middle-aged man with twinkly eyes, well-groomed hair greying at the temples and a bushy moustache.

'Hi,' he said, 'my name's Zach E. Loomis and I'd like to welcome you to Loomis Land.'

'I thought he was dead,' murmured Mariella.

'He is. He died over three hundred years ago. This is just a sim.'

Zach E. Loomis's simulation carried on with his welcoming speech. 'Here, folks, you can enjoy one of the galaxy's largest activity parks, in over three hundred million square miles of landscaped gardens. Have a fun day out in the family parks area, where you'll find Kiddies Kingdom and the Water Fun Playground. Or, if adventure is what you crave, go on a wild Jungle Safari and pick your way through the prehistoric beauty of a simulated virgin rainforest, with real live animals brought in from all over the galaxy. For those adrenalin junkies among you, there's the Limits of Human Endurance Area where you can become a Zach Ranger, and shoot real aliens on Mother Ship One. Then there's the pulse-quickening Elevator of Doom, where you'll have the opportunity to enjoy an exciting near-death experience.'

Mariella laughed. 'Is he serious?'

'Deadly' said Matt.

'All we want you to do is have fun, so sit back and relax while we take you on the ride of a lifetime.' Zach's image was replaced by footage of families tumbling down waterslides, herds of wild animals moving across a simulated veldt and cute costumed characters posing with smiling children.

'We're in big trouble,' muttered Matt. 'How much power is there in laughing boy's gun?'

Mariella turned the weapon over. The gauge on the bottom of the grip showed five green lights. 'It's full,' she replied.

'Good.'

The ship, manipulated by invisible forces, began to turn towards Loomis Land, and through the forward view-port the huge bulk of the planet hove into view. Underneath wispy cloud cover, among a sea of lush green forest and parkland, a thousand fabricated deep-blue lakes, bordered by beaches of imported fine white sand, sparkled in the sunshine.

'But they can't just grab a passing ship and pull it down, can they?' Mariella asked.

'Rhinn Sloane can do anything he wants,' Matt replied.

'Rhinn Sloane?'

'I'll explain later.'

Mariella stared out of the view-port at the fast-approaching planet. 'Well, I finally get to go to Loomis Land: I've wanted to ever since I was a little girl.'

'I doubt you'll be so enthusiastic once we get there.'

'Why, what's the problem?'

Matt clicked on the intercom connecting to the main cabin. 'Ladies and gentlemen, you're probably aware by now that we've been forced to make a small diversion. This is due to a minor technical fault, so there's no need to panic. The good news is that we're headed for Loomis Land. So I hope you're all in holiday mood . . .' he clicked off the intercom, '. . . and have come fully armed,' he added, grimly.

'Will you tell me what's going on?' Mariella insisted.

'There's no time to explain.' He nodded towards the steward. 'Do you want to ask him if there's a way down to the hold from inside the ship?

She pushed the barrel of the gun into the man's neck. 'Well?'

'There's a hatch in the floor of the galley. It leads straight down into the baggage hold.'

'We're obliged.'

After gagging the steward with his own belt and making sure that Jaymal wasn't about to wake up, Matt turned to Mariella. 'Let's do this nice and easy,' he said, 'and try and keep everyone calm.'

Mariella frowned. 'Why are you looking at me?'

Opening the door, they slipped out of the cockpit and made their way casually through the main cabin towards the galley area, which lay between the airy privilege of first class and the cramped hell of space economy. The cabin staff, wide-eyed with fear, regarded them warily.

As they moved through the first-class compartment, smiling and nodding, one of the passengers, a large red-faced businessman from Arggon Alta, accosted Mariella, grabbing her sleeve as she passed.

'I might have known it,' he began, 'a bloody woman pilot. That's just typical of this third-rate spaceline. No wonder we've suffered a technical fault. What's the matter, dear, can't find reverse gear? Now, listen to me very carefully. I'll speak slowly so you can understand. In three hours I'm due to chair an important business meeting on Varggenne Schpllitt. What are you going to do about it?'

Mariella looked down at him. 'What am I going to do about it?' she said, coolly.

'Yes,' the man spluttered, going even redder in the face.

She pulled the gun out of her pocket and stuck it in his ear. 'If you don't let go of my sleeve right now, I'm going to blow your head off, that's what I'm going to do about it.'

The man started screaming like a baby and tried to hide under the seat. The other passengers, seeing the gun, also went into wild panic. Suddenly it seemed the whole spaceliner was erupting with hysteria.

'So much for keeping everyone calm,' hissed Matt.

Hurrying to the galley, they found a recessed handle in the floor beneath the small porthole. Twisting it, Matt pulled back the square hatch to reveal a dark opening. Fixed to one side was a small ladder. He looked up at Mariella.

'After you,' she said, firmly.

Lowering himself through the hatch, Matt clambered quickly down into the darkness. Mariella, waving the gun around, screamed, 'Anybody who tries to follow us is dead', and the faces that had begun to crowd round the entrance to the galley suddenly disappeared. With a defiant 'Long live the rebellion!' she too lowered herself through the hatch, locking it behind her.

Matt was waiting at the bottom of the stairs in the dark and freezing hold. 'Long live the rebellion?' he enquired as Mariella joined him.

'It seemed like the right thing to say. What happened to your arm?'

'I'm into self-mutilation.'

They felt the nose of the ship rise as the controllers on Loomis Land prepared the liner for landing.

'Hold on to something,' warned Matt. Feeling their way along the wall, they found a strap securing one of the luggage pods, and both clung on to it. Seconds later the liner hit Loomis Land's artificial atmosphere and the ship was tossed about like a cork on a stormy sea. Eventually the shuddering subsided, and the whirr of powerful electric motors announced that the landing gear was being deployed.

'We've got to find the external hatch,' Matt said.

'Oh, right, no problem,' Mariella replied out of the pitch-blackness.

Matt searched along the wall with his fingertips. 'If we can escape on the luggage carrier we've got a chance.'

'Would you mind telling me what's so awful about this planet?'

'I used to work here. I spent my gap year as a Loomis Land Plaidcoat.'

'Now there's a colourful piece of your history you've been keeping from me.'

There was the hiss of retro-rockets as the ship was lined up for its final approach.

'OK,' said Matt. 'I've found the hatch. Can you work your way towards me?'

'Keep talking, and I'll find you.'

'Once the hatch is opened it shouldn't be too hard to get down on to the luggage carrier without being seen. They always start unloading the luggage first, before they've let the passengers off, so that should buy us a few minutes. Security won't even know we're here until they've spoken to the crew.' Mariella groped her way along the wall and eventually found him. 'How's your foot?' he asked.

'The painkillers are wearing off.'

'You'd better take another handful. We're going to have to move in a hurry once we get down.'

'I don't remember you being this energetic back in training camp.'

'I'm just trying to impress you.'

Matt handed Mariella the bottle of pills and she popped a few into her mouth.

'Brace yourself, we're going to be landing any minute.'

The spaceliner hit the runway and immediately the reverse-thrusters cut in. These super-powerful engines could bring a fully laden spaceship to a standstill in less than a hundred yards, and Matt and Mariella had to cling tightly to the luggage strap to stop themselves from ending up spread all over the main bulkhead. Thankfully the experience was short-lived, and soon the ship was taxiing sedately towards the main spaceport building.

Even before the liner had pulled up in its parking bay a baggage carrier was racing towards it, and the moment it came to a standstill the baggage-droids had the luggage hold open and were securing the unloading ramp in place. The droids, programmed to react to anyone in a uniform, saluted smartly as

Matt and Mariella emerged out of the darkness of the hold and slid down the ramp on to the flat-bed carrier.

'I'm enjoying myself already,' Mariella said, after landing heavily on the solid metal floor of the carrier.

'How many painkillers have you had?'

Clambering down off the back of the truck, Matt yanked open the door of the cab. The droid behind the wheel saluted. 'Hello, sir, proud to be of service. Are you having fun yet?'

Matt turned to Mariella. 'Waste him.'

She pulled the trigger and a pulse of energy melted all the droid's circuits. He fell out of the cab, landing with a clatter on the concrete.

'Get in.'

Matt and Mariella drove away towards the terminal building, leaving the droids unloading the ship in turmoil. Without the truck there to collect the baggage pods, they fell straight out of the hold and smacked into the ground, bursting open and spilling their contents all over the concrete apron.

Matt pulled up alongside the loading dock where the carrier was greeted by another troop of eager-to-please droids, all saluting and wishing both him and Mariella well. Helping Mariella down out of the cab, Matt led her through a small door and into the droids' staffroom. The moment their two spaceline uniforms came into view the droids, reclining on benches, all leapt up and started saluting like crazy.

'A uniform does wonders for one's self-esteem,' Mariella observed.

'Through here,' Matt replied, leading her through the room and into a small holding area where unclaimed bags were stored. A door in the pressed-steel wall opened straight on to the spaceport concourse. Matt pushed it ajar and peeped out. 'There's no security that I can see,' he said. 'Come on.'

'You certainly know your way around,' said Mariella as they joined the throng in the bustling arrivals hall.

'Like I said, I used to work here.'

Moving out of the densely populated arrivals hall, they passed through the departure section – it was deserted.

Mariella was puzzled. 'What happened here?'

'It never gets used these days.'

'No one leaves?'

'No one survives.'

Mariella stopped and turned to him. 'No one *survives*?'

'Keep walking,' Matt urged.

'No, I want to know what's going on.'

'It's a long story,' Matt replied. 'Come on.'

But Mariella wouldn't budge. 'I've got plenty of time.'

They were beginning to draw the attention of a couple of spaceport security officers lounging behind a row of unused check-in desks.

'OK, OK, I'll tell you, but can we just keep moving?' He grabbed her arm and dragged her away from under the security men's sunglasses-shaded gaze. 'When Zach Loomis died they kept his brain alive.'

'So that wasn't just a rumour?'

'No. It's in a jar in a vault about four miles under our feet. During his lifetime he kept very tight control of this place. No one but Zach was allowed to make decisions or to think up new rides and attractions. So, when he found out that he was dying, he did what any megalomaniac would do and organized it so that not even a little thing like death would interfere with his running of the Park.'

Now they were at the far end of the spaceport building, the empty exchange booths and shuttered spaceline help-desks testifying to the fact that this area was hardly ever used. Matt looked over his shoulder to see the two spaceport security officers standing in the middle of the concourse watching them with interest.

'This way,' said Matt, opening one of the big glass doors to the outside. 'We've got to look like we know where we're going.'

'We don't?'

Matt grabbed Mariella and pulled her through the doorway.

The tropical warmth of the outside air was a pleasant shock after the air-conditioned interior of the spaceport. 'At least it's a beautiful day,' Mariella sighed.

'Yeah,' said Matt. 'It's always a perfect 28 degrees.'

Glancing back through the glass door, Matt saw the two security men responding to a message on their wrist-vids. Looking up, they both drew their guns and started briskly along the concourse towards them.

'They know who we are,' Matt said.

'So now what do we do?'

'We panic.'

Just then, a black and yellow scooter-cab came shooting around the corner. Matt stepped out into the roadway and waved his arms, trying to flag it down, but it was obvious that the driver of the cab didn't want to stop and, angrily hooting his horn, he accelerated towards him. Matt turned to Mariella and held out his hand. 'Gun!'

She threw him the pistol. Catching it, he levelled it at the driver. The cab came to a skidding halt, inches from Matt's kneecaps.

The two security men were now running towards them, speaking urgently into their wrist-vids.

'Get in!' Matt shouted. Mariella opened the back door and jumped inside. Matt followed.

'I'm not supposed to stop here! I'll lose my licence!' the driver yelled at him.

'I don't give a shit!' Matt replied. 'Get us out of here!'

The driver obligingly stepped on the gas and the cab hummed away, leaving the security officers standing, flat-footed, on the concrete walkway.

'They're not going to let us get away with that.' Matt looked nervously out of the back window. 'They're going to shut this place up tight.' He pressed the barrel of the gun to the back of the taxi driver's head. 'Now listen very carefully and do exactly as I say and you won't get hurt. Try anything clever and your brain's going to end up all over the dashboard – understand?' The driver nodded slowly.

'Do you have to be quite so graphic?' Mariella complained.

'At the next junction take a right,' Matt instructed.

'That leads backstage,' the driver panicked. 'We're not allowed to take punters backstage.'

Matt pressed the gun harder against the back of the man's head. 'I don't think you heard me. At the next junction take a right.'

'All right, all right, I'll do whatever you say. Please don't hurt me.'

'That's better.'

The scooter-cab left the main road and squealed around the corner along the narrow road leading to one of the 'backstage' areas, where maintenance vehicles were usually parked and where those who worked on this particular sector had their meals and spent their breaks. After a couple of hundred yards the cab slowed. Up ahead was a gravelled compound surrounded by a steel-mesh fence, the way in protected by a quaint, whitewashed security post with a movable barrier. As the cab approached, a guard appeared out of the little white hut and slowly lowered the barrier across the road.

'Don't slow down,' Matt instructed the driver.

'But—'

'Don't slow down!' Matt repeated, shoving the pistol so hard against the man's skull that he drew blood. The driver got the message: he floored the accelerator and the cab shot forwards. The guard waved at them to stop, but when it became apparent that this wasn't likely to happen, he drew his gun and aimed it at the windscreen.

'Get down!' Matt screamed as two neat holes appeared in the Plexiglas. The cab careered on, straight at the guard, who only just managed to get out of the way as the scooter-cab slammed through the barrier, reducing it to matchwood. Slowly raising his head above the level of the dashboard, Matt saw that they were heading, at full throttle, towards a large, square, concrete building. 'Er, anywhere around here will do,' Matt said.

But the driver didn't respond. His wild, staring eyes were fixed straight ahead.

'I said you can stop now!' Matt yelled.

Something clicked in the driver's brain. He slammed on the brakes and wrenched the wheel all the way to the left. The cab went into a slide, bouncing sideways along the uneven surface and throwing up clouds of dust and gravel, eventually coming to a stop right in front of a massive steel door with a sign that read: *Pass door. Beyond here you're on show, so smile!*

'How much do we owe you?' Mariella asked the stunned and terrified driver, his hands still clamped to the wheel.

Matt pulled her out of the cab and over to the entrance door, which had a coded lock operated by a small keypad.

'Stay where you are or I'll shoot!' The security guard from the gate was running towards them, waving his gun.

'I don't suppose you happen to know the code?' Mariella asked.

'They change it every day. It used to be an eight-letter ana-gram of Zach's name.' He tapped C.L.A.M.S.I.Z.E. on to the keypad. Nothing happened.

'Don't move!'

'Our friendly guard is getting closer,' Mariella reminded him. Matt handed her the meson pistol.

'Try not to kill him.'

Sheltering behind the taxi, Mariella fired off a few rounds in the guard's general direction. The bursts of energy from the pistol died long before they got anywhere near him, but never-theless he stopped and took refuge behind a parked refuse truck.

Matt tried another combination: C.H.E.M.L.O.O.S. Noth-ing again.

'Move away from the door and put your hands up!' the guard yelled.

Mariella fired another couple of bursts and he ducked back under cover, but not before firing off a few rounds himself. Two bolts thumped into the door above Matt's head; another ricocheted off the roof of the taxi, prompting the driver to get out and run, screaming, from the scene.

Mariella fired back. Every time the guard's head reappeared from behind the truck she loosed off a blast or two. But he was beginning to wonder why none of the bursts were hitting the refuse truck. It wouldn't take him much longer to work it out.

'Matt . . .' Mariella warned.

'One more.' He tapped in C.A.M.E.L.Z.O.O. and the lock clicked open. 'Zach hasn't lost his sense of humour after all,' Matt observed, diving through the open entrance. Mariella let off another shot before following him through, and slammed the door behind her.

When the guard eventually made it to the other side of the big steel door, he was met with the usual scene: crowds of people milling around, buying souvenirs from wandering vendors, posing for photographs with actors dressed up in cute character costumes, or simply queuing for fun rides. Matt and Mariella had melted away.

Chapter 10

Back at Hambledon Hall, General Raffin was anxiously pacing the ha-ha, growing more and more concerned about Matt's non-reappearance.

'Members of the Council are going to start arriving soon, and I'd like to be able to assure them of the Cartogram's safety. I'd like to be able to *show* it to them.' He stopped pacing for a moment and looked up at Whipple. 'It won't do a lot for morale if I have to tell them that Major Fripp has run off with it. It took a lot of persuading to get them to agree to my plan in the first place, and I'm the one they'll blame, you mark my words.' He ran to the far end of the ha-ha and stared up at the rhododendron, willing it to bring forth the missing major. 'Oh, Matt, Matt, where are you?'

'Um, you mentioned a Mariella, I believe?' Whipple tentatively enquired, walking softly up behind him.

'I know what you're thinking,' the general replied quickly, 'but Matt's a good soldier. If he were to go after Mariella it would be in contravention of a direct order. He can be a bit of a maverick at times, granted, but he's a fine agent, one of the best we've got.'

'Of course he is,' said Whipple encouragingly.

Glaak slumped back on his hindquarters with a heavy sigh. 'You're right, Whipple. That's just where he's gone,' he said sadly. Suddenly he smacked his forehead with a front foot. 'What a fool I've been! Why did I let him go off on his own? In my

116

heart of hearts I knew he'd do this. I just hoped that for once he'd follow orders.'

'Don't blame yourself, General. You weren't to know.'

'I got carried away. I saw this big house and got excited by its possibilities as a rebel HQ. You know, between you and me, Whipple, I've never been much of a one for combat and all that gung-ho stuff. For me the attraction of the military has always been the planning. Give me a logistical problem and a stack of charts and I'm a happy rat.' He sighed again and looked despondently up at the rhododendron. 'He's not coming back. At least not until he's rescued Mariella and put this whole enterprise in jeopardy.' He gazed grimly at the butler. 'I had hoped to protect you from any unpleasantness, Whipple. But the thing is, assuming Matt does have the Cartogram, there are going to be a lot of very unpleasant types out there intent on taking it from him. And if he's captured it'll put Hambledon Hall right in the front line.'

'Oh,' said Whipple.

'Oh, indeed.'

Right in the middle of quaint, cobble-stoned Loomis Square, from behind a large bronze figure of Zach Loomis, his arms spread wide in welcome, the two fugitives watched their pursuer running to and fro, desperately searching for them among the sea of visitors. Eventually the guard gave up and muttered something into his wrist-vid.

'He's calling for back-up,' said Matt.

Mariella took in her surroundings for the first time. 'You know, it's weird, but this place seems vaguely familiar.'

'It's supposed to look like every place you've ever been, or heard about. Right in front of us is a detailed copy of the famous shrine on Frithh Banchusa.'

'Oh yeah.'

'Over there are the fabled restaurants of Gallowan Aight. A

little to their left are the bazaars of Maccabar, and behind us the Deserts of Monnd. And that's just for starters. You can take a trip around the galaxy without ever leaving the Park. But now we've got to lose these clothes – every guard will already have a description of us.'

Leading the way through a faithful plaster reproduction of the narrow, crowded maze of alleyways of the bazaars of old Maccabar, Matt suddenly pulled Mariella behind a reed screen flanked by two fake Maccaban oil-jars.

'This is the cast members' green room and changing area,' Matt explained. 'We ought to find something to wear here.'

The screen concealed a large room with worn and faded armchairs and sofas, and a carpet that looked as though it had seen better days. In one corner stood a small refrigerator with a thermal stove perched on top of it, covered in empty Styrofoam cups and pizza boxes, and in another, balanced on a stool, was an ancient family vid-screen. In the wall ahead of them, two doorways led off into the cool and dark interior of the building, one labelled MALE, the other, FEMALE.

'Where is everyone?' Mariella asked.

Matt looked at the wavering green digits of the thermal stove clock. 'Eleven fifty-two,' he read. 'Everybody will be at the galaxy parade. They make a circuit of the Park dressed up as famous characters from history. It finishes at twelve, so we haven't got long.'

'Out of interest, when you worked here, who did you dress up as?'

'I was a Plaidcoat – strictly non-performing.'

'Shame.'

'Remember, ordinary clothes, OK?' Matt instructed. 'Don't choose anything that might draw attention to us.'

They disappeared into their respective doorways. Unfortunately for Matt, in the men's changing room all the hooks were bare. The only clothes he could find were in a large wicker skip: the show costumes of a troupe of Bwellburbian acrobats.

The Bwellburbians are a race whose tallest members never grow above three feet. They are also, in humanoid terms, rather misshapen, having large thighs and tiny torsos. Matt plunged his hand into the skip and pulled out a pair of wide, canary-yellow, satin trousers, and a tiny, shocking-pink, ruffled shirt.

Matt looked helplessly around the otherwise bare changing room. 'Shit!' He had no choice. Removing the pilot's uniform, he pulled on the yellow trousers. They ballooned out from the waist as if inflated with air bags, and had elasticated bottoms that gripped his knees, leaving him exposing an awful lot of calf. The bright pink shirt, which was covered in flounces, was extremely tight and he had to leave it open to the waist. Catching sight of his reflection in the mirror, he thought he looked like a fairy-cake.

'This isn't going to work,' he said, shaking his head. Putting his lucky suede boots back on and tucking the Cartogram down the crotch of the trousers, he slipped the gun into the waistband and joined Mariella in the green room.

'Well,' she said, 'no danger of you being spotted. You'll blend in nicely and no mistake. No, sir, no one's ever going to—'

'OK, OK,' Matt interrupted, 'it was all I could find.'

'You'd be less noticeable in drag.'

'No thanks.'

'You know what you look like? A Slaveenian circus performer. Lose the suede boots and you'd be quite sexy in a dim light.'

'We've got to get out of here.'

'You never told me how nice *I* look.' Mariella did a twirl. She was wearing a loose silk shirt over a pair of red cotton pedal-pushers. It was the first time Matt had seen her in anything that could be described as feminine. She looked breathtakingly beautiful, not that he would tell her that, of course.

'You look . . . delightful. Now can we go, please?'

'After you, Sergei.'

They stepped outside into the heaving crowds.

'Where are we going?' Mariella asked, as they were swept

along the narrow streets of the counterfeit Maccabar on a tide of people.

'There's a long-stay ship storage-facility over on the other side of Galaxy Park,' Matt replied. 'It's where people leave their private spaceships when they arrive here. If we can get there we'll have our pick of the latest in inter-galactic transport.'

Emerging out of the crush of the Maccabar area back into the relative calm of Loomis Square, they quickly became aware of Park security guards stationed on almost every corner. All of them now had an image of Matt and Mariella on their wrist-vids, and were scanning the faces of everyone who came within eyeshot.

'Now what, O leader of the troupe?'

Matt pulled out the gun furtively and checked its power. Two green lights were showing. 'This thing's nearly out. We're going to have to be *really* careful.'

'I can't help feeling that was directed solely at *me*.'

'Let's just keep moving. No one ever stands and stares in Loomis Land. How do you fancy Gallowan Aight?'

'I've never been.'

'Well, now's your chance.'

They strolled nonchalantly across Loomis Square, heads down, eyes fixed on the cobble-stones. Mariella walked straight into one of the outstretched hands of Zach's statute.

'Ow, ow, fucking ow!' she exclaimed, holding her head.

'Are you all right?'

'No, I am not all right. Look!' She held out her hand; there was blood on it. 'What a fucking stupid place to put a statue!' she yelled up at the bronze figure of Zach Loomis.

'Everything OK, folks?' An eager, acne-covered young man wearing a tartan jacket was suddenly standing in front of them.

'Er, yeah, thanks,' said Matt. 'Everything's fine.'

'Yeah,' mumbled Mariella. 'I'll live.'

Taking her arm, Matt started to lead Mariella away, but the young man wouldn't be put off. 'Are you sure I can't conduct you to the medical centre, ma'am? We don't want that getting infected and spoiling your day, now do we?'

'No, no, she'll be fine,' Matt insisted, smiling tensely and tugging Mariella towards the Gallowan Aight sector.

'No, no. I really must insist,' said the young man, grabbing Mariella's other arm.

'Let her go, she'll be fine,' said Matt, trying to remain calm.

'Just doing my job, sir. I'm here to help.'

'If we need help we'll ask for it!'

There followed a protracted tug-of-war between the two men, with Mariella bleeding and groaning between them.

'Is there a problem here?'

Matt looked up into the mirrored sunglasses of the security guard. For a moment, both men stared at each other. Then, as realization dawned and the guard reached for his pistol, Matt yanked Mariella free and pushed the Plaidcoat forcefully into the security man.

'Run!' Matt yelled. Mariella raced towards the tented entrance to the Deserts of Monnd. 'No! Not there!' he screamed. 'Anywhere but there!'

'Freeze!'

Matt turned slowly to see the guard, knees slightly bent, with both hands on his pistol, which was aimed straight at Matt's nose.

'Oh no,' Matt muttered.

'Put your hands up!' the guard shouted.

'OK, OK,' Matt said, wearily. But as he went to raise his hands, he dropped to his knees and pulled the gun out of his waistband in one movement, getting off three shots in quick succession before Jaymal's weapon finally ran out. The bursts of energy thumped into the guard's stomach with just enough power to throw him off balance, and he staggered back into the welcoming arms of Zach's statue. Throwing the empty gun at him, Matt turned and chased after Mariella.

The Deserts of Monnd was a large enclosure, containing rides and attractions built into fake sand-dunes. They had names like: *Winds of the Prophet*, *No Hiding Place* and *Attack of the Desert Warriors*.

'We've got to get out of here!' Matt yelled, catching up with her.

But, behind them, a posse of guards was now elbowing confused punters aside and pouring though the entrance to the enclosure. Mariella started to run towards the ride called *Winds of the Prophet*, but Matt stopped her.

'No! In here!' He grabbed her arm and led her towards *Attack of the Desert Warriors*.

Although queues elsewhere in Loomis Land were extremely long, that outside *Attack of the Desert Warriors* was almost non-existent. Charging to the front, ignoring the cries of the few disgruntled punters waiting patiently in line, Matt and Mariella reached a sort of miniature station platform where paying customers were each given a boson arc and then ushered on board a little car which moved on to disappear under an archway through a curtain of strips of heavy-duty polythene.

'Here.' Matt grabbed a couple of arcs from a pile on the platform and handed one to Mariella. 'And take a handful of these,' he added, grabbing a stack of meth clips.

'Excuse me, but can I see your tickets please?' said a girl with lank blonde hair and braces on her teeth.

'This ride's on Zach,' Matt said, pushing past her and jumping into one of the little sand-coloured cars. Mariella clambered in behind him and the car moved jerkily off along a single metal rail towards the curtained archway.

Looking back, Mariella saw the pursuing guards reach the platform, then stop and stare at each other as if they didn't know what to do.

'They're not coming after us.'

'No, they won't follow us in here.'

'Why not?'

'Load up.' He handed her two meth clips.

Mariella took them. She was about to clip one on to the front of her weapon when she realized something. 'This is a *real* boson arc.'

Matt smiled at her. 'Er, yeah.' The car moved through the polythene curtain and into a simulated desert landscape.

Mariella clipped the magazine in place, then wiped the sweat from her forehead. 'It's hot in here.'

It seemed that they were in the middle of a desert, with nothing but rolling dunes stretching for miles all around. The only thing that threatened to destroy the illusion was a sign sticking out of the sand which read:

KEEP HANDS AND FEET INSIDE THE CAR AT ALL TIMES.

IF THE CAR STOPS REMAIN SEATED AND WAIT FOR ASSISTANCE.

AT NO TIME LEAVE THE CAR.

ENJOY YOUR RIDE.

Zach Loomis

'You never finished telling me about Zach,' said Mariella.

'Er, no,' said Matt scanning the fake horizon. 'Keep your eyes open.'

'What am I looking for?'

'You'll know it when you see it.'

Mariella gazed from the startling blue of the simulated sky to the glaring yellow of the imitation desert. It was hard not to believe that it was all real.

'What's that?' Mariella pointed at something on the horizon.

'Brace yourself,' Matt warned.

At first it looked like nothing but a black shadow, but as it got nearer it became apparent that it was a group of four horsemen, swathed in black robes, and riding like the wind towards them.

'This *is* a game, right?' Mariella asked uncertainly.

'That depends on how seriously you take your sport. Safety off.' Matt flicked off the safety catch on his arc and Mariella did likewise. 'Don't waste your shots. They short-change the punters with ammunition. You've probably only got five rounds to a clip.'

'You're making me nervous.'

'At least in here you get a weapon; in the other rides you simply end up getting fried by the sun or being buried alive in a sandstorm.'

The leading rider raised his arc and loosed off a shot. It clanged against the metal exterior of the small car. 'Shit!' Mariella exclaimed. 'They're using live ammunition.'

'Don't shoot yet!' Matt warned. 'Their arcs have got a longer range.'

'Is there anything else you haven't told me?'

'Did I mention that they're trying to kill us?'

'I'd kind of assumed that already.'

Matt sank down as low as he could inside the small car and raised his arc, taking aim at the lead rider. The other horsemen were now also shooting, and the air was full of bolts of bright blue energy.

Mariella, huddled in the back of the car, primed her arc and rested her finger on the trigger.

'Not yet!' Matt said. 'I'll take the lead one. You take the one over on the left.'

The riders galloped closer. Just as it seemed the horsemen were almost on top of them, Matt screamed, 'Now!'

He and Mariella let loose their shots simultaneously. The front two riders exploded and fell off their horses, to lay smoking and fizzing on the simulated sand. The other riders didn't even pause. Shouldering their arcs, they drew long scimitars and charged on towards the small car. But Matt and Mariella took aim yet again and soon all four riders were rolling around on the sand, their circuits sparking, while their riderless mechanical horses stood frozen above them.

'They're robots,' observed Mariella.

'They're just the first wave,' Matt warned. 'Reload.'

He jumped out on to the sand and discarded his spent clip.

'I thought we weren't supposed to get out of the car,' Mariella said, herself stepping out and reloading. 'Now, my maths was never very good, but if they were the *first* wave, then presumably . . .'

Matt put a finger to his lips and started up a sand-dune, indicating that she should follow.

Nearing the top, Matt lay down on his stomach and inched up the incline to the brow of the dune. Mariella crawled up beside him. 'You see over there?' Matt whispered, nodding in the direction of what looked like an untidy stack of old brushwood. 'That's a Whazool encampment. They'll know we survived the first wave and will be waiting for our car around the next bend. Watch.'

Sure enough, from their exalted position, Matt and Mariella observed a party of six Whazools steal out from their camp and creep across the sand to position themselves for an ambush. The robes they were wearing matched the colour of the sand almost perfectly – they looked like ghosts moving across the parched landscape.

The little car, which Matt and Mariella had recently vacated, snaked and stuttered along its track through the desert and, as it appeared in the open from around the base of the dune, the Whazools leapt out of hiding. They were just about to attack when they noticed that the car was unoccupied. Puzzled, they had a brief conference to decide on their next course of action.

'They'll split up,' Matt whispered. 'Two back down the track, two that way, and two this.'

'Are they real Whazools?' Mariella asked.

'Oh yes, all the way from the arid wastes of Spave Magna, and professional killers all.'

'But this is Loomis Land!'

'They only get the best. Ssh!'

Two Whazools were heading their way. One, keeping low, was coming straight up the sand-dune towards them, the other was creeping around its foot. 'Keep out of sight until the last moment,' Matt whispered.

'Where are *you* going?'

Matt pointed down the dune. 'To surprise his friend.' He rolled silently away, and Mariella ducked down out of sight and checked her arc: the meth clip read full. She lay flat and wriggled her body into the sand. She wouldn't be able to see the Whazool until he was right on top of her, and he was getting nearer. Now she could hear the muffled *tchunk*, *tchunk* of his big desert boots as he waded through the sand towards her position. Her heart was thumping. She'd heard stories about what this race of assassins did to travellers who happened to stray into their territory, but she was trying not to think of them at the moment.

Stay calm, she thought, easing herself deeper into the sand. *Wait, just wait . . . and keep breathing*.

The Whazool reached the top of the dune. Mariella, almost completely covered in sand, was lying right underneath him, but he couldn't see her. Then, out of the corner of his eye he caught a movement at his feet, but too late. Before he could strike, Mariella let one go right into his groin. The bolt charged through him, for a second leaving a hole just big enough for Mariella to see the counterfeit sky. The Whazool shouted a brief warning to his colleagues, then slumped on to the sand – dead.

Below, his partner heard the cry. But as he turned and started to run up the steeply sloping dune, he found Matt barring his way. Soon, he too was lying, lifeless, on the sand.

Mariella, now equipped with the dead Whazool's full-power arc, scrambled down to join Matt.

'Now we're properly armed they'll be a little more careful,' he said, busily going through his own Whazool's pockets.

'What next?'

'There's a door to the outside through their encampment. If we're lucky they won't have left anyone on guard.'

Mariella pointed to the little car which was still weaving its lonely way across the desert landscape. 'Why don't we just follow the track?'

'That'll take us straight to the pit.'

'The . . .?'

'Don't ask.'

Matt led the way across the track towards the ramshackle encampment. Crouching behind a stack of old, burnt-out ride-cars, they listened carefully for any sound. All was quiet. 'They must all be out looking for us.' He stuck his head over the pile of wrecks and a bolt of energy scorched past his ear. He ducked quickly back down.

'They left someone on guard?' Mariella asked.

Matt nodded. 'OK,' he said, 'plan B.'

'There was a plan A?'

Two more bolts of energy thumped into the pile of blackened cars, just above their heads.

'Shit! They're behind us! Run!'

Crouching low, Matt and Mariella raced through the crackling blue hail.

'Where to now?' Mariella screamed.

'Now we follow the track!'

'But you said—'

'Never mind what I said! Just go!'

Matt turned and emptied his meth clip at the attacking Whazools. Mariella sprinted down the line of the metal rail that ran incongruously through the desolate landscape. Something whizzed past her head and stuck into the rail up ahead. As she passed she saw it was a Whazool who had thrown a knife that had buried itself in the metal of the rail almost up to the hilt. *Those things are sharp*, she observed.

'Don't touch it!' Matt warned, running up behind her. 'The rail's live.'

'How are we doing?' Mariella asked.

'I got one of them,' said Matt, changing his clip, 'but they're very determined; they won't give up. Come on!'

'Do you know where we're going?' Mariella shouted as Matt charged off ahead.

'I hope so!' he replied.

In the distance, beyond the little car which was still travelling merrily along its track, Mariella thought she could see something shimmering on the horizon. 'What's that?'

Two bolts of energy zipped past her, blowing large craters in the powdery sand. Mariella spun round and returned fire and the Whazools dived for cover, instantly blending invisibly into the landscape.

Discarding her spent clip, she turned back and started running after Matt. What she'd seen on the horizon was getting nearer now, and beginning to take form. It looked like a hole in the fabric of the desert, or the blind spot at the back of the eyeball where the nerves leave the retina, and it was coming closer faster than seemed possible.

'Nearly there!' Matt yelled.

It was only a holographic image generator that gave the 'desert' the illusion of size, and now the sky and the horizon seemed to be closing in, everything contracting down towards the narrow arch up ahead of them. Mariella could actually reach out and touch the 'sky', and the rolling sands of the desert suddenly gave way to a steel, V-shaped gully through which the small car was about to pass. Mariella watched as it was tipped sideways by one of the sloping sides of the gully, and then trundled on into the darkness beyond, on a loop back to the entrance.

Suddenly Matt stopped and looked earnestly into her face. 'Listen to me. Whatever you do, don't look down.'

'What's that terrible smell?' Mariella asked.

'Like I said, don't look down.'

A knife embedded itself in the steel wall of the gully and an energy bolt threw up sand at their feet. 'Follow me!' Matt instructed. 'Keep looking up, and don't touch the rail!' Leaning against the sloping steel wall, Matt placed his feet in the small channel beneath the live electric rail and crabbed slowly sideways.

Mariella did likewise, but after a few steps the smell got much worse. 'What *is* that?' A bolt of blue fire exploded above her head, and she nearly lost her footing. The painkillers were wearing off and her foot was beginning to throb. Inadvertently looking down to realign her feet in the narrow channel, she saw something move below. For a moment she didn't know what she was looking at. Then it all became sickeningly clear.

She was standing on a narrow ledge above a pit full of a wriggling mass of cockroaches. But these were not the small beasts of earthly nightmares; these creatures, known as Klaproths on their home planet of Glyff Spawn, were about the size of a small dog. 'Fuck! Fuck! Fuck!' Mariella wheezed, fighting the urge to throw up.

'Don't look!' Matt ordered. 'Keep coming towards me!'

She shut her eyes, but that was almost worse. The image of the scuttling creatures on her closed lids gave her the impression that they were crawling around inside her brain. Hysteria was slowly beginning to overwhelm her. Her legs turned to jelly and she began shaking uncontrollably. She was stuck; she couldn't have moved now if her life depended on it – which it did.

'Come on!' Matt urged from the other side. 'Look, if it helps, they won't harm you – they prefer dead meat.'

That doesn't really help, Mariella thought, still unable to budge.

'Anyway, they're already full up with dead punters!'

Don't, she thought.

'It's a very efficient system. The punters are tipped in and then the roaches eat them.'

Please don't talk any more, she thought.

'Nothing is left,' Matt insisted. 'Clothes, skin, hair. They eat everything – even bone!'

'Will you shut the fuck up!' she managed at last.

'That's more like it,' said Matt. 'Come on, let's move now!'

Gritting her teeth, Mariella slowly felt her way along the sloping steel wall until Matt was able to grab her from the other side of the roach pit. 'Can we get out of here, please?' she said, limply.

'They don't do a lot for me, either,' Matt replied. Putting an arm around her, he guided her away from the churning stench. 'If I remember rightly there's a way out just down here.' Leading her behind the big cyclorama running around the perimeter of the ride, he found it: a set of double doors marked EMERGENCY EXIT ONLY.

'I think this qualifies as an emergency.' Matt nudged the crash bar with his elbow. Falling through the door, they at last found themselves outside. Mariella gulped in the deodorized and artificially scented air. But their troubles were not over yet. There came the familiar sound of a volley of boson arcs being tensed.

'Matt, how nice to see you after all this time.'

Matt looked up into the face of Rhinn Sloane, head of Loomis Land security. He was standing in front of a small but heavily armed gang of his men.

'Oh, hi, Rhinn, how's tricks?' said Matt.

Rhinn raised one of his many eyebrows. 'You still play cards?'

Chapter 11

Drikk Digit was suffering. He had hoped that his performance today would gain him entry into a very select circle indeed, but the show had not gone well. Drikk blamed himself. Work was hard enough to come by in this sector of the galaxy since the war had started, without throwing away chances like this.

Digit the Clown (a smile, a song, an inflated pig's bladder) was not in the first flush of youth. He belonged to a gentler age: a vanished world where kids had respect for their elders and betters, and still retained a sense of wonder at 'magic'.

To his father's never-ending shame, Drikk had swapped the cut and thrust of property insurance for show business, and run away to join the circus. His ambition was to be a flyer but, after a near-fatal accident one evening when he tripped over his cape on entering the ring, it soon became apparent that his lack of physical coordination was more suited to clowning. With his ungainly appearance and lugubrious air, he became the butt of all the other clowns' jokes, and the chief recipient of custard pies. But he didn't mind. For the first time in his life, there in the musky, animal smell of the big top, Drikk felt he belonged.

Sadly, his circus career was short-lived. Waking one morning to discover that the circus had moved on without him, Drikk was left with nothing but his sleeping bag and curly wig. It was tough, but what Drikk lacked in imagination he more than made up for in resourcefulness, and he had soon reinvented himself as a children's entertainer.

In the early years he hadn't done badly but, since the war

began, bookings had dropped off dramatically: now he was barely scraping a living. What was galling about his most recent failure was that he'd been trying to break into this particular social set for some time. The children went to a rather posh school and the mothers all actively socialized. Once in with this lot he thought he'd never look back; his life would be an endless round of party bookings as mother after mother recommended him to her friends. It was not to be.

He went over in his mind where it had gone wrong. He had arrived at the Symbiotes' an hour before little Feeoona's party was to begin, in order to give himself plenty of time to set up. He needed to hide the micro-transmitters around the room for the animatronics used in his act, and erect the false wall through which the Thrringg wolf would appear.

It had all started rather well. There had been roars of approval for the flying Suture monster as it swooped down on the birthday girl and picked her up in its beak. But from then on it was all downhill. When Drikk had pulled out the balloons to make the Graggle hound the children had groaned 'Boring!' before he'd even got to the bit where he asked them if they knew what it was yet. Then, when he'd set the hound free and it was wandering about the room snarling and slavering, one of the little tykes had poked a pin into it and burst it, which had made the entrance of the Thrringg wolf completely redundant, ruining the grand finale where the wolf devours the hound with one snap of its monstrous jaws.

Admittedly it was old stuff, but it was an act that had served him well over the years.

Children have moved on, he thought sadly as he gathered up his props and laid them neatly back in his travelling trunk. *These days they think nothing of seeing real people being hacked to pieces on 'Live from the Arena'. How can a cute little balloon Graggle hound compete with a hump-backed stelion? Kids, nowadays, all they want is violence.* He sighed and looked up as Mrs Symbiote came in.

'How much do I owe you?' she asked without preamble.

'We agreed fifty, I believe,' Drikk replied, deferentially removing his wig.

'Fifty?' Mrs Symbiote sniffed as she opened her purse. 'I could get a real Graggle hound for that. Here.' She handed him a sheaf of notes. He took it gratefully. 'You'd better count it,' she instructed.

'No need, madam. I'm sure it's all there.'

'At least something is,' she muttered.

'Did little Feeoona enjoy herself?'

'Well she's enjoying herself now. She's outside playing Crusaders and Infidels. It's the most animated I've seen her all day.'

'That's kids for you,' Drikk smiled.

'Yes, they're not stupid. They know what they like.'

Under Mrs Symbiote's withering gaze, Drikk closed the lid of his trunk and trudged it outside to where his Drill-Scoter was waiting. It was a tiny craft – there was only room for one in the cockpit – and the boot was barely big enough to accommodate his large trunk. Drikk had to strap the lid closed with an old leather belt.

'Well, thanks again.' He turned back to Mrs Symbiote but she was no longer there. Sighing, he climbed into the cockpit. He had to slam the door twice to get it to shut.

Unusually, Drikk had two bookings that day. But the second was nothing to get excited about. It was a long-standing arrangement to appear at the annual tea party at 'Clunn's Home for Foundlings' on Alborg. Mrs Clunn was an old friend and the orphanage didn't have a lot of money, so he didn't have the heart to charge his normal fee – he just took his expenses. *Oh well, off to Alborg.*

He turned the ignition switch, and choking clouds of smoke emerged from the exhausts of the ancient Drill-Scoter. As he pulled out the throttles, the machine lifted ponderously into the air, shaking and rattling as it slowly gained speed. Then, lifting its nose heavenwards, with a supreme effort it heaved itself up through the atmosphere and out into space, leaving a hazy blue-black trail across the sky.

Whipple, meanwhile, was doing his best to cope with a sudden influx of alien visitors. After picking up the signal and coordinates sent by General Raffin's spaceship, strange creatures had begun to turn up at all hours of the day and night. Thankfully, most of the interstellar craft in which they arrived were fitted with cloaking devices, and therefore, other than a strange wind whistling through the greenery on an otherwise calm day, there was nothing to signify their presence. These ships were now all parked, invisibly, in the top field, the solitary clue to their existence being that the puzzled sheep now only grazed its very margins.

The real problem was the smaller craft which, for the most part, were not equipped with the cloaking option. These were a real test of Whipple's resourcefulness, especially considering that the rhododendron marking the opening of the wormhole was clearly visible from the west window in the library – the spot favoured by Lady Trenchard in which to enjoy her customary morning sherry. Whipple's cunning was fully employed in distracting his employer's attention.

'Unseasonably warm for the time of year, ma'am.'

Accustomed to absolute silence as she communed with Bacchus, Lady Trenchard nearly choked on her amontillado. She turned and frowned at her employee. 'What?' she said after a long pause.

'I was remarking on how hot the weather is, ma'am.'

'It's July, man. Of course it's hot.' Closing her eyes, she recomposed herself and brought the sherry glass once more to her lips.

'Is this view to your liking? In my opinion the view from the east window is far superior.'

Lady Trenchard regarded Whipple as if he were mad. 'All you

can see from the east window is the corner of the stable block and a cobbled yard. Now then . . .' Licking her lips she went back to her sherry.

'The pears on the step-over cordons are ripening nicely—'

'How can I enjoy my elevenses with you babbling away like a schoolgirl?' Lady Trenchard spluttered furiously. She fixed him with a steely glare. 'In all the years we've practised this ritual, not once have you so much as breathed. Now, all of a sudden, you're blathering about heat in July and the condition of bloody fruit. What is the matter with you, man?'

Out of the corner of his eye, Whipple saw a silver flash as yet another visitor shot through the wormhole and disappeared into the ha-ha. Lady Trenchard was too busy remonstrating with her servant to notice.

'Forgive me, ma'am. I was just passing the time,' Whipple explained.

'Well don't. Please allow me to enjoy the rest of my sherry in peace.' Sighing irritably, she contemplated her glass for a moment, then chucked it down her throat.

It was also becoming obvious that General Raffin had been rather economical with the truth regarding the size and number of the alien creatures requiring accommodation. There seemed to be hundreds of them, and most were a good deal larger than any flea.

Of course, Whipple had no trouble concealing the colony of tiny Grushkins, which resembled nothing so much as cheese mould – they were now happily encamped on a Stilton at the back of the larder. Likewise the Grublins from the ice-moons of Cassiopeia were quite at home on the dairy products shelf of the refrigerator. Certain of the guests, however, such as the statu-esque delegation from Goran-B'tLamboo, had been a little more tricky to disguise. But, kitting them out with swathes of mater-ial and strategically placed tassels, Whipple had managed to deploy them throughout the house as standard lamps and drapes.

Other guests included: a trio of multicoloured Florea from Tryst, small-brained, birdlike creatures who endlessly repeated themselves; crystalline spirit beings from Alohoma who could appear and disappear at will; a two-headed Duppy from Mealon that argued with itself constantly; and a host of floor-creepers and wall-crawlers. One of the strangest was the Mufflet: a blue life form with a globular body, long neck and small, removable head, which it pulled off now and then and played with like a rubber ball. It claimed that this helped it to think, but it was very disconcerting to watch.

However, it was the Wuboobians that stretched Whipple's ingenuity to the limit. Large, sack-like beings with long, horny outgrowths on their flippers, the females are highly intelligent creatures possessed of a mordant wit. The males, on the other hand, are smaller, have an IQ on average a good 30 per cent lower, and communicate by breaking wind and whistling. It's a mystery how the race has survived, especially as the phrase: 'Would you like to go to the pictures tonight?' translates as three farts and a whistle. A typical exchange would go something like this:

Male: Would you like to go to the pictures tonight?

Female: (*waving a flipper*) Good God what did you have for lunch – anchovy stuffed sea slug?

Male: (*flushing slightly*) Er . . . would you like to go to the pictures tonight?

Female: I can't, I'm varnishing my horny outgrowths.

Male: (*now beetroot red*) What about tomorrow night?

Female: I'm watching them dry.

The females, being far too intelligent to get themselves involved in anything so inconsequential, eschewed politics, a field which was left solely to the timid, dim-witted males of the species. Which was unfortunate – the Galactic Alliance Council was seriously lacking in wit.

For the time being, Whipple had secreted the Wuboobians in the cellar and, as long as Sir Percival didn't insist on going down himself to choose the dinner wine, that was perfectly safe. Any strange smells that seeped up through the floorboards could be blamed on Napoleon, Sir Percival's ancient springer spaniel.

On the whole, Whipple was rather successful in keeping the truth well hidden from his employers, but there were times when the deception came close to being discovered.

One evening, as Lady Trenchard was on her way to bed, she could have sworn she heard the tapestry wall hanging on the upper landing humming the Goran-B'tLamboo national anthem. And that wasn't all: as she opened her bedroom door she spotted something scuttling under her bedroom chair. *Oh dear*, she thought, *mice. I'll have to get Whipple to put more poison down*. But the creature sharing her bedroom was much more interesting than a mouse. It was in fact a shape-shifter from Q'tark which, rather like a chameleon, could take on the shape and texture of anything it stood next to. After closing the bedroom curtains, Pamela Trenchard sat on the bed and took off her shoes. She was about to put on her slippers when she noticed that, where before there had only been two, she now had three fur-lined sheepskin moccasins. She closed her eyes and shook her head. *Now, now, Pamela*. After several deep breaths, she opened her eyes and counted her slippers again. *One, two. There you are, silly girl*.

Clambering into bed she enjoyed one of her best night's sleep ever, the reason being that her 'pillow' was in fact a Mingley: a soft, squishy creature from Blaart. Unfortunately the poor Mingley didn't sleep a wink.

Glaak Raffin wasn't having an easy time of it either. The delegates, on the whole, were an argumentative bunch. Many were unhappy at the atmosphere of stealth in which they were being forced to conduct their business, and there were rumblings of discontent about the shabbiness of the attic room above the servants' quarters in the West Wing, which had been pressed into service as a council chamber.

Standing on the wallpaper trestle that was acting as a conference table, Glaak addressed the Council's first Earth assembly. 'Gentlemen, welcome to Hambledon Hall. Before we get down to business, first of all I need to lay down a few house rules. I have already spoken to you individually about the need for discretion when moving around the Hall in daylight – in order not to startle our hostess. But Whipple further informs me that, strange as it may seem, the inhabitants of this planet are totally unaware of there being any other life existing in the galaxy, let alone the universe; they think they are completely unique.'

There was assorted laughter from the delegates.

'I know, I know, but there we have it, and we must do all in our power not to disabuse the citizens of Earth of their erroneous belief. Unfortunately that means *no* visiting any nearby habitations and *no* fraternizing with the locals.'

There was immediate dark muttering from the delegates about this curtailment of their freedom, but when Glaak moved on to break the news about the Cartogram's uncertain whereabouts the chamber exploded into full-blown uproar.

'Gentlemen! Gentlemen, please!' Glaak implored. 'I have every faith in Major Fripp's ability to bring about a successful end to his mission.'

'You seem to be the only one who does!' shouted a furry green creature from the swamps of Namloom, which was clinging to the ceiling with its many-hooked feet.

'Fripp is unstable and prone to disobedience,' said a large, menacing Grimley. 'And the fact that he is a humanoid makes him untrustworthy!'

The humanoid delegate from Gallazion was on his feet in a flash. 'I find that remark deeply offensive! May I point out to my colleague that not all humanoids are Crusaders, just as not all Crusaders are humanoids. Indeed,' he pointed a finger accusingly at the Grimley, 'was it not a member of *his* race that first signed away mining rights to Allgothion-3, thereby ensuring Filch and his cronies an almost limitless supply of trithium?'

'There was never any treaty with Filch!' the Grimley retorted. 'The Crusaders invaded Allgothion-3, as the delegate from Gallazion knows full well!'

'Fellow delegates, please let us not fight among ourselves,' Glaak entreated.

'The fact is, your plan has been a catalogue of disasters from start to finish,' piped up a smug, fat-bodied Glubbus from Sleema. 'First you have the Cartogram stolen, then you lose it, then you lose Major Fripp! Why didn't you just hand over the Cartogram to Filch in the first place and have done with it?'

There was more angry shouting.

'I move a vote of no confidence in General Raffin!' shrilled one head of the Duppy.

'I have every confidence in the general!' said the other.

'Order! Order . . .' Glaak rapped the table angrily with his pipe. Gradually the hubbub in the room died down. 'Gentlemen, have we forgotten what we are doing here? Our sole purpose is the overthrow of Gulgus Filch and his evil empire. We *will* have the Cartogram in our hands before long, of that I am sure.' A dissenting murmur began to build, but the general continued talking over it. 'Meanwhile we must prepare. For too long now we have bowed under the yoke of oppression. But, the worm is turning, gentlemen; it is time to fight back.'

For once there was agreement around the table, many of the delegates responding with a 'Hear, hear!'

'Let me outline my plan to you.'

'Another one of his useless plans?' muttered the Glubbus in a sneering aside.

'Do you have a better idea?' said the Grimley.

'I move,' said the Duppy, 'that we implement the general's plan immediately!'

'I move,' said its other head, 'that Glaak Raffin's plan be struck from the record!'

'I move,' said an empty bench at the back of the room, 'that we should only debate General Raffin's plan once we are sure it can work!'

'May I once again remind the Alohoma Ambassador that the chair does not recognize any delegate it cannot see!' said Glaak.

The Mufflet, meanwhile, removed its head and started bouncing it round the room.

'Please!' Glaak implored.

'I demand a recount!' shouted one of the Florea.

'Hear, hear!' said the next.

'I demand a recount as well!' yelled the third.

'We haven't had the vote yet!' Glaak shouted.

'I move we debate General Raffin's plan only after we have debated the amount of time we should spend debating it!'

'I move that we debate the last motion!'

'I move that we move the debate!'

'Gentlemen, enough!' Glaak roared, furiously. 'Either you *listen* to my plan, or accept my resignation. It's up to you!'

The delegates fell into a sulky silence.

'Good, now please can we concentrate on the matter in hand!' Glaak produced a rolled-up star chart and spread it on the table. 'These planets . . .' his front paw described an arc across the chart, taking in several tiny highlighted dots strung across it like fairy lights '. . . represent the edge of the Meridiana Quarter – one of Filch's recently conquered territories. The main army has been withdrawn and has already embarked upon its next conquest, even before the small occupying force has had time to rebuild the infrastructure of the zone. But that is not a worry to the Crusaders; Filch does not fear insurrection. He rules by the twin weapons of terror and theology. His newly subjugated citizens, having seen the monstrous brutality of which his troops are capable, are regaled with tales about the never-ending tortures that await them in the afterlife should they have the temerity to step out of line. After that the Crusaders need no large garrison force to keep them under control. A few thousand men is usually more than enough to produce cringing dread across an entire planet. That is Gulgus Filch's masterstroke – it gives his main battle force the flexibility to strike from planet to planet quickly and at will. But it is also his weakness. Filch's empire is vastly overstretched; the only reason it's still holding together is that there is no organized opposition. Using the Cartogram, and with the combined forces that the Alliance can muster, it will be possible for us to slide in, inflict damage, then slide out again before the Crusaders know what's hit them. Harrying the fringes with small, lightning strikes will force Filch to move large numbers of his troops to defend the boundaries of his empire. Then we simply slip round behind and hit him where he's weakest. With this tactic, if we can win back just *one* planet, show the population that this monster is not invincible and demonstrate that there is a way to fight back, then we can start a tidal wave of rebellion that will roll all the way back to the centre – to Filch himself. It will take patience, planning and split-second timing. But I believe, if we work together, it will succeed.'

Glaak leaned forward on the table. 'Gentlemen, it *must* succeed.'

Chapter 12

'You got any more bright ideas?' Mariella glared at Matt through the gloom of the police holding cell.

'Excuse me, it was you who wanted wind chimes, er . . . fresh air,' Matt replied.

'You haven't done that in a while,' Mariella observed.

'It only happens when I'm dancing . . . Shit! When I'm agitated!' Something sticky dropped into his lap. He looked up. A family of slime foot Gna-Gnas were hanging from the ceiling, oozing all over his trousers. 'Do you mind?' he yelled at them. The Gna-Gnas regarded him a moment with their soft doe eyes before moving slowly off across the ceiling to huddle in a corner.

'You want to fill me in on what's happening here?' Mariella eyed him steadily.

Matt breathed deeply. 'After Zach died he continued to communicate with the park managers via probes wired into his frontal lobes. Zach, or rather his brain, kept coming up with ideas for new rides and attractions, and the managers put them into practice. It was business as usual, the Park continued to boom – so why change a winning formula? But then he seemed to lose his grip on reality.'

Mariella raised an eyebrow. 'I can't imagine why.'

'Yeah, but the system had worked without a hitch for years. We think his brain caught a virus or something. Afterwards it was as if he couldn't tell the difference between his conscious and subconscious thoughts, and ideas started coming straight out of his nightmares. The Deserts of Monnd was the first "assassin-ation park".'

'Why didn't anybody say anything?'

'Rhinn was more or less in control of things by then. Of course, if they'd looked a little more closely at his credentials when he first applied for the job of head of security, they might have discovered that he was a crime boss on the run from the Intergalactic Police. Once he'd replaced all Loomis Land's secur-ity guards with his own men, he took complete control. The managers and VPs were terrified of him – anybody who stood up to him just disappeared.'

'And *you* worked for him?'

'I wasn't the only one. I'll bet Gulgus never mentioned it to you, but in the old days, he and Rhinn used to be buddies.'

'Gulgus?'

Matt nodded. 'Back when he was attacking the trading routes into Bwellburbia he needed funds to buy armaments. Rhinn used to deal in all kinds of shit, mainly drugs and booze, and he saw an opportunity. In exchange for a piece of the action, Gulgus allowed Rhinn's trading ships to pass unmolested.'

'That's a relationship I think Gulgus would rather be kept a secret.'

'And then, of course, there's Rhinn's little disposal business.'

Mariella made a face. 'Disposal? Does that have anything to do with the cockroaches?'

'Anybody looking to get rid of someone neatly and con-veniently just gives him a call and, after the payment of a small fee, the "target" is sent free VIP tickets to Loomis Land. The tickets come in a package saying that they're an executive gift for using such-and-such a credit card, or for being so-and-so's millionth customer – and who can resist a free trip to Loomis Land? The guy turns up with his family, not suspecting any-thing, and is shown the sights.'

'Ending with a once-in-a-lifetime visit to the Deserts of Monnd.'

'Exactly.'

'But how could he keep all this secret for so long?'

'Who's left alive to tell?'

'Hence the empty departure lounge.'

Matt shook his head. 'Er . . . no, not exactly. The reason for that's kind of weird. The fact is nobody *wants* to leave.'

'I'm sorry?'

'They like it so much here they want to stay for ever. I remember when I first arrived. I was eighteen and I thought Loomis Land was just for kids and people with no imagination. I was going to wear the tartan coat for a year, make enough money to put myself through space school, then get out. I mean, it's all phoney. The food in all the restaurants tastes exactly the same; the buildings are made of plaster; the sand, the rocks – it's all fake, and yet . . .'

'And yet?'

'It . . . *has* something.'

Mariella looked at him sideways.

'Really. This place has got some kind of magic. After a few days I never wanted to leave.'

'You're kidding me.'

Matt shook his head. 'Just think, here you have no worries, the streets are clean, there's no crime, everybody's happy; everyone you meet has a smile on their face. After two weeks of "Hi, how are you? Do you need help with that? Have a nice day!" who wants to go back to: "Get out of my fucking face!"? In the old days, when your fourteen days were up, the Plaidcoats came to your hotel and made sure you got your flight home – it was a rule that was rigorously enforced. But when Rhinn took over, to maximize his profits, he introduced a 'stay as long as you like' policy. Now you can even get a refund on your return spaceline ticket. Of course, when the cash from that finally runs out you're in trouble. If you can't pay the hotel bill you're pushed out through the resort gates into Twilight World: a wasteland crawling with wild beasts that used to be people. They call themselves Spooks.'

'Twilight World?'

'This is Loomis Land. What else are they going to call it?'

'So how come *you* got away?'

'I *had* to get out. But believe me, I wouldn't have left if Rhinn hadn't been about to kill me.'

Mariella leaned back against the wall and folded her arms. 'Something tells me that if I'd known your past history I might have thought twice about embarking on this little jaunt with you.'

'Rhinn found out about my talking to Zach and he went crazy. It's amazing how the prospect of one's death can focus the mind, so I escaped on a food shuttle.'

'You talked to Zach?'

'Yeah – well, to his brain. I told him what Rhinn was up to: about people getting killed, and families spending all their money and getting trapped here. You know what he said?'

'What?'

'"Yes, but are they having fun?"'

The electronic latch hummed then *tchucked* open. Around the door appeared a man with a face seemingly carved out of stone. He was holding a pistol.

'Oh, Matt,' said Mariella, 'I do believe our table's ready.'

Matt closed his eyes and whispered, 'Don't.'

The guard's granite features remained unmoved. 'Shut the fuck up, lady, and come with me.'

'So that'll be Loomis Land's famous hospitality, will it?' Mariella fluttered her eyelashes.

Matt shook his head. 'Cut the crap and follow him,' he warned.

'Yeah, just do like your boyfriend says and you might save yourself a bruising.'

'Right,' Mariella said, thoughtfully. 'I am at your disposal.'

'And please, don't use that word,' Matt muttered.

Chapter 13

'Now look here, General, I have had about all I can stand. I've spent a very unpleasant morning relocating a party of flatulent sacks from their quarters down in the cellars to the last remaining free stall in the stable block because of the methane hazard they present!' Whipple was in the kitchen berating Glaak Raffin, who stood on the pine table in the middle of a mess of star charts, smoking his pipe. 'This house has been invaded by cheese mould, giant slugs and multi-limbed swamp creatures! The garages and stables are crammed with interstellar craft, and the fields are so full of them the sheep can't get near the grass! And, furthermore, I object most strongly to being treated like a servant by pink blobs resembling unset blancmange—'

'But that's what you are, isn't it?'

Whipple was momentarily fazed at being stopped in mid-flow. 'I beg your pardon?'

Glaak Raffin gazed up at him and took a leisurely puff on his pipe before replying. 'A servant. Isn't that how you'd describe yourself?'

'Yes, but . . .' Whipple spluttered.

'Walked straight into that one, old man.' Clenching the pipe between his teeth, General Raffin went back to his charts. 'Now, if you'll excuse me . . .'

Suddenly the door opened and footsteps began to descend the staircase leading to the basement kitchen. 'Hide!' Whipple hissed.

The large rat dived off the table and, finding itself at Whipple's feet, headed for the nearest hiding place, which happened to be up Whipple's trouser leg. But Whipple had no time to protest as Lady Trenchard swept down the stairs and into the kitchen, like a galleon in full sail, closely followed by her dinghy of a husband.

'Where's Cook? Or to be more precise, where's luncheon?' she demanded.

Whipple's eyes flicked to the big pine-cased kitchen clock. It read ten minutes past one. 'Oh, er, . . . I've given Cook the day off, ma'am.'

Lady Trenchard turned her steely eyes upon him. 'Whatever for?'

Whipple held her gaze. 'Compassionate grounds, ma'am. Her mother is not in the best of health.'

'I had no idea her mother was still alive.'

'She is barely clinging to life, ma'am.'

'Good God, Cook's hardly in the first flush of youth. Her mother must be ancient.'

'Quite so.'

Lady Trenchard pursed her crimson lips. 'Very well, *you'll* just have to make us something, Whipple.' She turned back to her husband. 'It seems that luncheon is somewhat delayed.'

Sir Percival, *Daily Telegraph* in hand, was still busy wrestling with the crossword. 'Sorry, my love?' he said, distractedly.

Lady Trenchard closed her eyes and inhaled noisily through her nostrils. 'Luncheon, dearest,' she enunciated carefully, 'is going to be a little late.'

The baronet simply shrugged. 'I'll have whatever you're having, my dear.'

His wife put a hand lightly to her chest and recomposed herself. 'No,' she said, 'Cook is . . . Oh never mind.'

Sir Percival, eyes glued to the paper, smiled and nodded.

'Do what you can, Whipple.' Lady Trenchard was on the point of leaving when the general lost his purchase on Whipple's Y-Fronts and started sliding down his leg. Scrabbling frantically, he dug his claws into Whipple's thigh to prevent himself from slipping any further, and the glowing end of his pipe came perilously close to Whipple's crotch. But apart from the butler's raised left eyebrow, the casual observer would never have suspected that anything was amiss in the trouser department. Lady Trenchard, however, didn't miss a trick.

'Whipple?'

'Ma'am?'

'Something appears to be moving in your trousers.'

Whipple smiled reassuringly. 'No, ma'am, I assure you, below the waist all is as quiet as the grave.'

'Know the feeling old man,' said Sir Percival, peeping out from behind his wife.

Lady Trenchard looked long and hard at her servant, but his mask was implacable. 'Will there be anything else, ma'am?' he enquired after a considerable pause. Thin wisps of smoke had begun to rise from the area of Whipple's groin, but Lady Trenchard thought it best not to pursue the matter.

'Er, no. I don't believe so.' Her eyes then went to the star charts on the table. 'What's all this?'

Fighting a strong urge to leap around the kitchen batting his trousers and screaming, Whipple calmly answered, 'A new hobby, ma'am – astronomy.'

'Well,' Lady Trenchard replied dubiously, 'don't let it get in the way of your duties.'

'No, ma'am.'

'It's a lovely day, so we'll take luncheon on the terrace.'

'Very good, ma'am.'

Lady Trenchard turned back to the stairs, leaving Sir Percival still studying his *Telegraph*. He looked up at Whipple. 'Got one for you, Whipple. Six letters: "Depression after two-thirds of scull makes pest".'

'Rodent,' Whipple replied immediately, beads of sweat beginning to break out on his forehead.

For a moment, Sir Percy looked confused, then understanding dawned. 'Ah, of course: Scull: *row*, knock off the W and you get *ro*, plus depression: *dent*. Excellent, knew I could rely on you.'

'Come along, Percival!' Lady Trenchard called impatiently from the top of the stairs.

'Oops, I'm in trouble! Better be off. Coming, dear!' and Sir Percival followed his wife out of the kitchen.

As he closed the kitchen door, Whipple gripped the edge of the table and gasped, 'Get out of my trousers – immediately!'

The general appeared sheepishly from beneath Whipple's immaculately ironed trouser cuff. 'Sorry, old man.'

'Never, *ever* do that again.'

For several days after this incident, Whipple walked with a slight limp.

But, sadly for the Trenchards' manservant, it seemed his troubles were just beginning. Taking his usual evening stroll around the grounds after spending several close and sweaty hours in the kitchen cooking, washing up and serving dinner to his employers, who remained in blissful ignorance of their dearth of staff, he heard the unmistakable sound of an orchestra coming from the vicinity of the West Wing.

Approaching the Italian garden, he was surprised to see a half-clothed woman cavorting in the fish pond with a man dressed as Pierrot. Whipple was just about to inform them that this was private property and that bathing was strictly forbidden, when he heard the sound of raised voices. Looking up, in the dim evening light, he saw several figures appear on the balcony immediately outside the ballroom. One of them was obviously in high dudgeon.

'Bloody little upstart!' the man was yelling. 'Who the hell does he think he is? How dare he!'

Whipple gasped as he recognized the man. The last time he'd seen him was in a photographic book about the Victorians, standing next to his grieving mother. 'No, it's impossible,' he breathed. But there could be no mistaking that portly figure. Unbelievable as it seemed, the future King Edward VII was stalking the small balcony, bellowing oaths.

As Whipple watched, yet another figure appeared out of the darkness on the prince's left side, and started speaking in a low and calming tone. At first the furious royal ignored him, angrily smacking his fist into his hand and uttering the occasional, 'No, blast him!' and 'I'll be damned if I do!' But eventually he calmed down. After several minutes, during which the mysterious figure continued to pour balm into the royal ear, Edward, chuckling now, lit up a cigar and strolled happily back inside.

Pausing for a few moments outside, the figure who'd been doing all the placatory talking stepped forward into the light spilling from the ballroom's tall windows.

'No!' Whipple's jaw dropped open in shock. The family resemblance was unmistakable, he could have been Sir Percival's brother. He was, in fact, the baronet's great-grandfather. Mortimer Trenchard looked out into the darkness at the estate which, come the next day, would be his, then smiled and followed his royal patron back inside.

'Oh, Flossie, not now, I've got a busy day tomorr . . . Oh!' General Raffin lifted his eye-mask to find it was not his first wife who was trying to stir him, but a tall and rather perturbed looking butler. 'Whipple? Is that you?'

'There's a masked ball going on in the West Wing,' Whipple whispered urgently.

'Thanks all the same but I'm not much of a one for parties.' The general readjusted his eye-mask and snuggled back down into his fruit-pallet cot.

'No!' said Whipple hoarsely, ripping off the general's tea-cosy blanket. 'I want to know what's going on!'

Suddenly wide awake, the General leapt up. 'Have you taken leave of your senses, man? What in God's name's happening?'

'You tell me,' said Whipple, his eyes bulging ominously. 'We seem to be entertaining a future King of England.'

'You should be honoured.'

'He's been dead for over a hundred years!'

'Ah, I see,' said the general, immediately comprehending Whipple's anxiety. 'Dead monarchs turning up must be a bit of shock.'

'I'll say,' Whipple agreed.

'Hmm . . .' General Raffin stretched and perched on the side of his cot. 'Did I mention the vortex effect – or space-time flux?'

'No, but you're about to.' Whipple narrowed his eyes, determined to follow the General's explanation, however complex.

'Ah, bit remiss of me,' said Glaak, yawning and scratching the fur on his belly. 'Now then. You see, when a wormhole gets a lot of use, strange things can start happening in its vicinity, a bit like eddies around a whirlpool.'

'Why didn't you tell me this before?'

'Sorry, old chap, must have forgotten in all the excitement. What you mustn't forget is that a wormhole exists in four dimensions.'

'*Four?*'

'Height, width, depth and time.'

'Oh yes?' said Whipple, treading water frantically.

'You see a wormhole is just like a doorway,' the general continued. 'But as stepping into one can involve traversing vast distances, one is also, in essence, travelling through time. The universe is continually expanding – whizzing out in all directions. Look into its deepest recesses and you can see planets that have long since disappeared, suns that eons ago exploded and are no more.'

'Um . . .?' said Whipple, waves of incomprehension beginning to close over his head.

'Think of a wormhole as an intergalactic bus stop,' the general continued, 'the difference being that your destination comes to you. In theory, if you were to pick a still point in space and wait there several million years, because of the movement of the universe, where you want to go will eventually fetch up at your stop. Do you see?'

'Um . . .?' Whipple repeated.

'Because wormholes inhabit a different dimension, they allow you instant access to just about anywhere. Unfortunately, the vast amounts of energy generated whenever a wormhole is used can, in some instances, create a vortex, warping space-time and shifting the temporal location of its immediate vicinity. Lucky you've only got a masked ball in your house; it could have been a party of dinosaurs.'

Whipple could just imagine Lady Trenchard's reaction to a herd of diplodocus making their way sedately down the avenue of beech trees, grazing on their succulent tops. He suddenly seized the general in his fist and spluttered urgently into his face. 'But what are we going to do about it?'

Glaak wiped his face with a forepaw. 'I say, steady on, old man.'

'Sorry, sorry,' said Whipple, gently replacing the general in his cot. 'It's been a bit of a day.'

'Look,' said the general, 'why don't you go to bed and sleep on it, hmm?'

'Sleep on it? The stables are full of spaceships, there's a dead king in the ballroom, and the fish pond is full of rutting nymphs!'

'Do nymphs rut? I thought it was only satyrs who did the rutting.'

'It doesn't matter! The fact is that the West Wing is full of dead people, and they're all going to need somewhere to sleep!'

The veins in Whipple's forehead were bulging ominously, his eyes were wild, and he was covering the general in spittle. It was obvious he was near breaking point. Glaak smiled gently in a placatory kind of way and laid a small paw on the butler's finger.

'My dear Whipple, what you have to understand about time past is that it's just that – *past*. Time future is another thing entirely, but we needn't go into that now. You see, what went on in the ballroom all those years ago is over. It's done. What you saw tonight was a window on history: a rare glimpse into the past, nothing more. So relax. Believe me, things will look better in the morning.'

But things did not look better in the morning. Glaak was rudely awoken at dawn by Whipple and marched downstairs into the kitchen where a young, rosy-cheeked woman, covered in flour, was beating a lump of dough into submission on the kitchen table.

'She says her name is Mary,' Whipple informed the general.

'Er, that's nice,' said Glaak, unsure of Whipple's point.

'She says she's the Prince of Wales's cook.'

'That's all your catering problems solved then.'

'She's from the nineteenth century!' Whipple growled.

'Oh, I see,' said the general, comprehension dawning. 'And you think she's here because of the wormhole?'

'No, no, no,' said Whipple in a worryingly normal voice. 'Victorian cooks often appear in the kitchen. Only last week we found three hiding in the scullery.'

'Really?'

'No! Of course she's here because of the wormhole, you . . . rat! I want her, the royal party and all your weird and wonderful friends out of here, now!'

Chapter 14

Matt and Mariella were bundled into the back of a police sweeper and driven at high speed out of the security compound and through the Park gates.

'Ah,' said Matt as the vehicle left behind the neat and tidy streets of Loomis Land and entered the dark and sprawling scruffiness of Twilight World.

'What does "Ah" mean?' Mariella asked.

'It looks like we've been invited to Rhinn's home. He won't live in Loomis Land – he's worried it might make him soft – so he lives in downtown Twilight World, which is definitely *not* a Neighbourhood Watch area.'

'How cosy. Why didn't he just kill us?'

'He's playing with us.'

'Why?'

'He must *know*,' Matt said quietly to himself.

Mariella looked at him suspiciously. 'Know *what*?'

'It's like this . . .' Matt began, but before he could finish, the sweeper came to an abrupt halt and the back doors were yanked open.

Granite-Face was standing there. 'Out,' he said, simply, waving his gun.

'Well, seeing as you put it so nicely,' said Mariella, stepping down from the vehicle. Matt climbed out behind her.

In front of them stood a four-storey hacienda with balconies on every floor protected with curls of razor wire. Although, strictly speaking, Rhinn's house was outside the Park perimeter, he had had the electric fence that kept the spooks out of Loomis Land diverted in a long loop around his habitation. He may not have liked sharing Loomis Land with tourists, but he wasn't stupid when it came to his personal safety. The house was also well guarded, surrounded on three sides by high concrete walls topped with yet more razor wire; the back wall of the house itself forming the final side of the large square compound and set right up against the crackling twelve-foot tall electric fence. Atop each corner were machine-gun posts manned by security guards and, sprouting from the walls, low pressure sodium lights cast an eerie yellow glow over the scene. The compound was covered with a vast white umbrella of tarpaulin, held aloft by a metal framework that resembled a clawed hand. Beneath this, fixed into the top of the walls, were rows of large, whirring air-conditioning units and air-scrubbers – essential for good health beyond the neat-and-tidy limits of Loomis Land.

Mariella grimaced. 'Nice place he's got.' She felt a dig in the back as Granite-Face urged them towards the front door.

'The boss is waiting.'

They were ushered inside and found themselves in an elaborate confection almost completely covered with filigree plasterwork and gold leaf. In the middle of the atrium, between a pair of ornately curved staircases, the doors of a lift slid open.

'Ah, welcome, welcome!' Rhinn Sloane was wearing a black silk kimono which hung awkwardly from his broad shoulders, not least because of the four arms that had been tailored into it. Thick black curls sprouted from around the garment's neck and, dangling from a thin gold chain, a pendant of a dragon with a red shining eye glinted on Sloane's barrel chest. Approaching his guests with terrifying speed, Rhinn stopped suddenly in front of Mariella and, taking her hand, caressed it with his mouthparts.

'What do you think of my humble abode, my dear?'

Fighting nausea, Mariella replied, 'I've always wanted to know what a wedding cake looks like from the inside.'

Rhinn smiled grimly. 'Such a treat to have you here. It's not often I get the chance to entertain people of quality these days.'

'Yeah, quality's in short supply everywhere. I'd have your decorator shot.'

Standing next to her, Matt silently willed her to stop talking.

'Now I know why Gulgus tired of you.'

Mariella flinched.

'Oh yes, I know who you are.' Stroking his pony-tail, Rhinn leaned in close – so close she could hear the sound of his mouth-parts clacking. 'Don't fuck with me, my dear: I've got techniques that will make Glitch McGilvray's efforts seem like a rather pleasant way to pass the time.'

Mariella cast her eyes down and resolved to keep her mouth shut. Rhinn moved on to Matt.

'Matt, Matt, how long's it been? Do you have any idea how much I've looked forward to this moment? You know, you've caused me and my associates no end of trouble. Let's hope you can make amends. I trust you haven't lost your way with the cards?' Rhinn smiled – his mouthparts opening wide to reveal a set of tiny, shark-like teeth. 'Please follow me into the games room, and bring your . . . friend.' He turned and marched back towards the lift positioned between the two imposing staircases.

'You shouldn't have insulted his taste – he's very house proud,' Matt hissed.

'He's an oily, eight-eyed creep,' Mariella replied.

'Move!' snarled Granite-Face, and they were propelled towards the waiting lift. Rhinn's natural animal scent was almost over-powering in the close confines of the wood-panelled lift, and Mariella was very relieved when the doors at last rolled open again.

They were ushered into a large room which took up the entire third floor of the house. Around its edge were small tables bear-ing trays of drinks and canapés, and right in the centre stood a big, round gaming table. Two other guests were already seated:

a Bwellburbian and a Swampfoot – a being from Athol N'Ath with a face like a gas mask and covered almost entirely in fur.

'So . . .' Rhinn hovered at the drinks table, 'what'll you have?'

'Plymmian whisky – no ice,' Mariella said immediately.

'At least she knows her liquor,' Rhinn smiled, picking up a bottle and pouring an evil-looking spirit into a heavy tumbler. 'And for you, Matt? Oh, but I'm forgetting, when it comes to cards Matt is the consummate professional.'

'Er, I'll have the same. A large one,' Matt replied.

Rhinn raised three of his eyebrows. 'Hmm, that's not like the Matt I used to know. I remember you always wanting to keep a clear head, especially when playing for such high stakes.'

'High stakes?' Mariella queried as Rhinn handed her the glass.

'Please be seated,' said Rhinn. Matt and Mariella were pushed forcefully into their seats by Granite-Face, and Matt's drink was placed in front of him. 'Now then,' Rhinn too took his seat at the table, 'what shall we play?'

'Unfortunately,' said Matt, 'you find me somewhat financially embarrassed at present.'

'You're among friends,' said Rhinn. 'I'm sure nobody would object to extending a line of credit to a man with an item of such rare value in his possession.'

Matt tried to laugh it off. 'Rare value? I don't know what you mean.'

'Come, come,' said Rhinn, 'you can do better than that.' He signalled to Granite-Face, who put his gun to Mariella's head.

'Matt, what's going on?'

'Sorry, Rhinn, I really don't have any idea what you could be referring to.'

'Oh, Matt.' Granite-Face cocked the gun and placed his finger lightly on the trigger.

'OK, OK,' said Matt. 'Can we all just calm down?'

'Well?' Rhinn smiled.

'I suppose you're talking about this.' Matt unzipped his fly.

'Whoah!' said Mariella. 'I didn't know you could bet on that kind of thing.'

Matt retrieved the Cartogram from his trousers and placed it on the table.

Rhinn touched the tips of his fingers lightly together. 'So it's true,' he smiled, his eight eyes wide with desire. Granite-Face removed the gun from Mariella's head.

She looked sideways at Matt. 'What is that?'

'That, my dear,' said Rhinn, 'is the key to the universe. Whoever holds it holds mastery over all things. It is the Helian Cartogram.'

Mariella gasped. 'You had this thing all the time? You jerk! Why didn't you take it to the general?'

'Because I came straight to rescue *you*!'

'I'm sorry,' Mariella stood and snatched up the Cartogram, 'but my friend here has made a mistake. We're not gambling with this.'

Granite-Face pushed her down into her chair and, wrenching the Cartogram out of her hand, placed it back on the table.

'Shall we get on with the game?' said Rhinn, impatiently.

'Why not?' said Matt. Feeling Mariella tense beside him, he placed a restraining hand on her arm. 'One hand, N'thoolian stud.'

'Agreed.' Rhinn signalled to Granite-Face, who handed him an unopened pack of cards. Grasping the small tear strip with his mouthparts, Rhinn pulled off the wrapper. He was about to open the pack itself when Matt reached across the table and grabbed one of his wrists. Rhinn looked up at him sharply.

'No, Rhinn,' said Matt. 'At these stakes, *he* deals.' Matt nodded towards the Swampfoot.

Furious, Rhinn held his gaze. Granite-Face raised the butt of his pistol above the back of Matt's head. But after a moment Rhinn gently shook his head and the thug relaxed. At length Rhinn smiled. 'As you wish.' He handed the pack of cards to the big, hairy monster. 'One hand, N'thoolian stud poker. If I win, you die and I keep the Cartogram.'

'And if *I* win?'

Rhinn looked at Matt across the table. 'Unlikely in the circumstances, don't you think?' Rhinn's mouthparts clacked stickily as he smiled at Mariella. She shivered and looked down.

The Swampfoot opened the pack, shuffled it, then passed it across to Matt. Matt tapped the deck and the monster dealt him and Rhinn five cards each.

Matt picked up his hand. It didn't look good: all he had was a paltry pair of N'ung N'ungs, and Rhinn was about to show.

'The pot looks a little light to me,' Matt said suddenly, stalling for time.

'I'm sorry?'

'The only thing I can see on the table is the Cartogram. Where's your stake?'

Rhinn looked across at him steadily. 'Stake?'

'Yeah, put in or fold.'

'Very well,' Rhinn sighed. 'Mere money could not hope to match the value of the Cartogram, so . . .' reaching into his pocket, he produced a set of keys '. . . these are the keys to my new toy: a Manganeutron Mark 3 Hyperturbo S. It's the top of the range model with bound-free transition drive, anti-clemester and walnut dash. It's very fast and very beautiful.' Rhinn laid the keys in the middle of the table alongside the Cartogram.

'OK, I accept.'

'Shall we continue?'

'Why not? Let's see what you've got.'

Rhinn laid down a royal flush.

'Very good,' said Matt, 'but I think you're in for a surprise.'

Mariella's eyes swivelled questioningly in Matt's direction.

'Really?' queried Rhinn.

'Oh yes,' said Matt, 'you're going to be pretty amazed once you set eyes on what I've got.'

Rhinn drummed his fingers on the table top. 'And is that likely to happen any time in the foreseeable future?'

'Oh, right, yeah,' said Matt. 'Catch a load of these babies.' He laid down his cards face up. Rhinn leaned forward to study them.

'A pair of N'ung N'ungs?' he asked, puzzled. 'Is that all?'

'No,' said Matt. 'There's also this!' He threw his whisky straight into Rhinn's face. Taking her cue from Matt, Mariella kicked back from the table and her chair connected with Granite-Face, who doubled over. Leaping up and grabbing the henchman's gun, Matt hit him across the back of the head with it and the thug collapsed on to the floor.

'Now then, gentlemen,' said Matt, covering the remaining players seated at the table with the gun, while stuffing the Cartogram and the keys to Rhinn's spaceship into his trousers. 'If you'd be so good as to put all your weapons on the table where we can see them, my assistant here will gather them up.'

After a lot of angry but ineffectual posturing, the Swampfoot pulled a bazooka tube and five rounds of ammunition out of his thick fur and laid them on the table, while Rhinn deposited a small silver blast pistol. The Bwellburbian held up his hands and shook his head.

'Assistant – please?'

Mariella scowled at him and moved slowly round the table. As she got level with the Bwellburbian, Matt caught a brief glimpse of something shiny in the little man's fist. 'Mariella, he's got a knife!' She reacted quickly, gripping the dwarf's arm and slamming his hand down on the table. The knife flew through the air and skittered across the floor, but the momentary confusion allowed Rhinn to pick up his own gun, and a shot whistled past Matt's left ear. Matt fired back, hitting Sloane in one of his four arms.

Yelping in agony, Rhinn threw himself to the floor and, reaching for the pendant hanging around his neck, pressed the dragon's small red eye. Matt saw it, but too late. As Sloane raised his gun to fire again, Matt kicked over the table and dived behind it, landing in a pool of Plymmian whisky. Rhinn then swung his gun on to Mariella, who was still holding the Bwellburbian around the neck. Spinning round, she dropped to her knees and hurled the dwarf backwards over her head. The small, airborne man's scream was cut short as his head collided with Rhinn's, and both slid to the floor, out cold.

But now the Swampfoot was making a move on Mariella.

'Behind you!' Matt warned.

She didn't even turn round. Throwing up a fist she caught the lumbering Swampfoot in the balls. As the poor thing doubled up in agony, Mariella straightened her arm and her knuckles connected with its face. The big creature toppled sideways and lay still.

Mariella stood up sharply. 'Assistant?' she snapped.

Matt smiled at her. 'It's tradition: the glamorous female always takes that role.' Matt staggered to his feet. 'We'd better make a speedy exit. Rhinn pressed his panic button, so his goons will be here any second.'

The lift indicator was already moving. Mariella looked desperately around the room – but the lift seemed to be the only way out. 'Where?'

Matt pointed to the window. 'There.'

'Are you out of your mind? We're on the third floor!'

'Do we have a choice? But we'll need to take a run at it if we want to clear the electric fence.'

Mariella looked long and hard at him. Then, with a yell, she ran straight at the window and smashed through it, sending glass and wood flying.

Matt watched her go. 'I was going to suggest opening it first.'

There was a *ting!* and the lift doors began to open.

Time to go.

Picking up the Swampfoot's bazooka tube and ammo, Matt ran at the shattered window and also dived through. 'Look out below!'

Flying blind through the dark night air, Matt couldn't see the ground as he raced towards it, but braced himself for the impact, certain that he was going to break a leg at least. However, the anticipated bone-jarring crunch of flesh on concrete never materialized. He landed with a squelch on something soft and gooey, and was immediately engulfed in an unpleasant and strangely familiar smell.

'Mariella!' he called softly. 'Mariella, are you OK?'

'Mmf,' came the reply out of the darkness.

'See, I told you we'd be all right. Hooee! This place stinks. What did we land on?'

'Mmf,' Mariella repeated, thickly.

They were caught in the beam of a high-powered torch, and from above them sounded an amplified voice. 'If you want to remain alive, stay exactly where you are!'

In the sudden light Matt could now see what it was that had broken their fall. They had managed to clear the electric fence and were now on an old broken pathway, sitting on the flattened remains of several Klaproths. Matt was immediately sick.

'Do not move. Put your hands above your head!'

Mariella turned to Matt. 'Can we go now?' she asked weakly.

'Yup,' he said, trying to get to his feet and putting his hand in something slimy. 'Just a minute.' He was sick again. 'OK, I'm ready now. On three. One . . . two . . . three!' Ducking out of the pool of light in opposite directions, they disappeared into the surrounding darkness. The torch beam wavered uncertainly, swinging ineffectually up and down the path – totally missing both targets, but illuminating small sections of potholed tarmac with absolute clarity. Frustrated, Sloane's heavies fired blind, lighting up the night with the flare from their weapons. While energy bolts bounced off the ground and whistled round their heads, Matt and Mariella regrouped and ran out into the untamed wilderness of Twilight World.

Chapter 15

Worried by Whipple's increasingly fragile state of mind, Glaak convened an emergency meeting of the Council before breakfast.

'Order, order!' he yelled over the blustering delegates, who were all extremely irritated at having been woken so early. 'We have a problem,' Glaak announced. 'It seems we may already have outstayed our welcome here.'

There was more huffing and blowing from the delegates.

'It appears that we are placing an almost intolerable burden upon Whipple. If we're not very careful the poor chap's going to crack. May I suggest that we all pull our weight and try and help out a little bit more.'

'And how do you propose we do that – tidy our own rooms?' asked the Glubbus, pompously.

'Yes,' Glaak replied, 'that would be a start.'

There was uproar in the chamber.

Glaak ducked as the Mufflet's head came bouncing over the table. 'Order! Order, please gentlemen!' The hubbub gradually subsided. 'Thank you. Now, if we cannot show our host here a little courtesy, how do we expect to bring tolerance and understanding to the rest of the galaxy?'

A shapeless mass of jelly seated at the far end of the table suddenly resolved itself into an exact copy of Glaak. 'Mr Chairman, are you really proposing that we become our own chambermaids?'

'That is exactly what I am proposing,' Glaak replied. 'And in future I would be obliged if the delegate from Q'tark would refrain from imitating other council members!'

'And what about breakfast?' enquired the Glubbus.

'I, for one, am more than happy to prepare my own breakfast and morning tea,' declared the Duppy.

'And who's going to make my coffee?' said its other head.

'I demand toast and jam!' said one of the Florea.

'Marmalade!' said the second.

'We demand jam *and* marmalade!' said the third.

'Biscuits! Biscuits! Biscuits!' said the Mufflet's head as it bounced around the room.

Glaak waited until everyone had finished. 'The fact is,' he continued, 'until Major Fripp arrives with the Cartogram—'

'*If* he arrives,' interrupted the Glubbus.

'*Until* Major Fripp arrives,' the general persisted, 'there is little we can do to put our plans into action. So, while we wait, in the interests of good inter-planetary relations, may I suggest that we extend to Whipple the goodwill and courtesy he might expect to receive from any other guest in this house? After all he has done for the cause, does he not deserve our thanks? I move that from now on we prepare our own meals and do our own laundry.'

At the conclusion of Glaak's speech there was stunned silence. At which point, leaving the delegates to mull things over, Glaak scampered out of the conference chamber to the sound of his own footsteps.

From that time onward relations between Whipple and his 'guests' became much more harmonious. The humanoids in the delegation made themselves discreetly useful around the house, while the more outlandish creatures crept about at night, tidying rooms and doing the washing up.

Whipple even began to appreciate that there were certain advantages to the vortex effect's time distortion. Mary was an excellent cook, despite the fact that – because of the nature of this particular vortex – she repeatedly made only steak and venison pie. When one pie was finished, time would loop back on itself and she would start all over again. This process would go on all day, from dawn till dusk, until, at last, she would dust the flour off her hands with a 'There, that's that, then', hang up her apron and walk out of the scullery door and disappear, only to reappear the next morning and start all over again. This particular kind of vortex, so Glaak informed Whipple, was known as an *episodic repeater*: the sequence repeating itself a number of times, then pausing for a space, then starting up again. Perfectly harmless, and something that would eventually fade away so long as the sequence was left well alone and remained uninterrupted. Needless to say, Whipple grasped Glaak's explanation about as successfully as a blind man might follow the Yellow Brick Road. He was, however, extremely relieved that this phenomenon actually produced something useful, and for a short while the Trenchards dined magnificently on steak and venison pie prepared by the Prince of Wales's personal cook.

Even the masked ball at which the future Edward VII was present had its uses. This too was a closed time-loop on a constantly repeating cycle. Whipple watched and learned when the bottles of claret and fine old crusted port were produced from the cellars, pouncing on the young footmen as they emerged with the wine and relieving them of their precious burden. He even managed to snaffle a couple of trays of canapés, which were a welcome supplement to the Trenchard's monotonous diet of steak and venison pie. In this manner he was able to keep the housekeeping budget to a minimum.

But it was not all plain sailing, and disasters did occasionally happen. Indeed, if it had not been for the quick thinking of Ing Thraat, the delegate from Sproog, Devon – and indeed the entire universe – might have been consumed in a doughnut-shaped void.

Because of the parlous state of the Trenchards' finances,

Sir Percival had pursued the only course of action open to him: he had taken to the bottle. And, to escape the disapproving looks of his wife, he had recently got into the habit of drinking alone, creeping down into the kitchen at night and having a quick snifter in the company of his ancient dog. One night, however, things went badly wrong.

Having said his customary goodnight to Lady Trenchard, the baronet retired to his bedroom and waited. Hearing the lavatory flush, he listened for the sound of his wife's footsteps as she made her way along the landing and into her bedroom. Once he heard her door close, he counted to two hundred before creeping stealthily out of his own room.

Halfway down the stairs he thought he could hear someone humming. But the house seemed to be alive with odd noises at the moment, and Sir Percival put it down to his imperfect hearing and the fact that his ancient family seat was slowly decaying around him.

Reaching the bottom of the grand staircase, he was greeted by Napoleon, his faithful, aged springer spaniel.

'Shh, Nappy,' Sir Percival cooed as the animal whined softly, excitedly wagging his tail until it seemed he might shake his large, flabby body to pieces. 'We don't want her waking up and discovering our little secret, now do we? Come on.' He led the way to the kitchen and Nappy followed eagerly, his nails clattering on the polished wooden floor of the hall.

Ing Thraat, a multi-armed disc with a single, central eye above his sucker-like mouth, had just finished washing the dinner things and was in the middle of drying up when he heard footsteps on the stairs. Hurriedly slithering to the floor and slipping into the gap between the larder and the china cupboard, he watched and waited. Suddenly the light snapped on and Sir Percival and Napoleon entered.

'Now then, Nappy. I've got something for you.'

Ing slithered further into his hiding place as the squire crossed to the larder and opened the door. A moment later he emerged clutching a chocolate doggie-chew. Crouching, Sir Percival held it out to the spaniel. The animal waddled eagerly across to him, seizing the doggie-chew hungrily in its few remaining teeth and dribbling chocolate saliva all over the kitchen tiles.

'Tch, my nice clean floor,' Ing grumbled to himself.

Then, something terrifying and completely unexpected happened. Sir Percival went back into the larder and emerged with a box of Bath Olivers and a large Stilton cheese – the temporary home of the Grushkin delegation.

'I think I'll join you in a little something,' he said to Napoleon, placing the cheese and biscuits on the kitchen table and fetching a knife from the drawer.

'No!' Ing gasped. He watched, helpless, as Sir Percival plunged the knife into the centre of the cheese, scooping up the Grushkins and spreading them on a Bath Oliver. In two bites, he had consumed the entire delegation.

Satisfied that he'd now lined his stomach, Sir Percival took down a small key from its hiding place above the scullery door and opened the drinks cupboard. Pulling out a half-empty bottle of supermarket brandy, he sighed and shook his head sadly. 'Ahh, Nappy, hard times. The good stuff's long gone. Oh well, no sense in complaining.'

Pouring a large tot into a balloon glass, he knocked it back. 'Filthy stuff,' he groaned. His spaniel, still busily gumming the doggie-chew on the floor, looked up briefly, then went back to work. 'Maybe a drop of soda will help.' Pouring himself another full measure, Sir Percival topped it up from an almost flat, half-empty bottle from the back of the cupboard. 'Well, here goes,' and he poured that one, too, swiftly down his throat. 'Not a great improvement. I think what we need is ice.' Pouring himself yet another large one, he moved across to the fridge and opened the freezer compartment. But, to his surprise, instead of being greeted by a view of its ice-encrusted interior, scattered with escaped frozen peas and the odd broad bean, he found himself staring into the aching void of space.

Sir Percival had discovered one of Glaak Raffin's space-time vortices, linking Hambledon Hall with a spot in deep space four billion light years away. Moderately confused at this turn of events, Sir Percy then found himself being drawn inexorably into it. Indeed, most of the contents of the kitchen seemed to be being pulled towards the freezer compartment. Kitchen utensils, bottles of herbs and spices, even quite large jars began whistling past his ears and out into the vacuum of space as Sir Percival reluctantly let go of his glass and clung to the sides of the fridge, trying desperately not to be sucked in himself.

Ing, still recovering from the shock of the awful massacre he'd just witnessed, did not at first realize what was happening. Then, as he too found himself being drawn out from his hiding place by the vacuum of deep space, the penny dropped. If he didn't do something soon, the entire kitchen – followed by Devon, the world, the galaxy and, finally, the universe itself – would end up being sucked into the void.

Napoleon watched open mouthed as a large, multi-limbed alien slithered out from beside the china cupboard and on to the kitchen floor. Clambering up the fridge and anchoring his body to one side of the open door with his mouth sucker, Ing wrapped several of his arms around Sir Percival's head, and pulled. At length he managed to wrestle the baronet out of the path of the dreadful sucking emptiness. Then, with a free arm, he quickly reached across and grabbed the fridge door. Unfortunately, as it was about to close, one of the kitchen chairs flew across the room and wedged itself in the opening.

For a long moment Sir Percival stared at the single-eyed thing that had just saved his life; Ing stared back. A kitchen knife whizzed off the sideboard and zinged out into the nothingness. 'Right,' Sir Percival shouted over the noise of the wind whistling into the open freezer compartment. 'We'll have to pull the chair out. Ready?'

Ing nodded and wrapped an arm or two around one leg of the pine chair while Sir Percival himself grasped another. 'On three! One, two, three!' Ing and Sir Percival heaved. The tug-of-war ended when the chair disintegrated, its seat and finely worked 'sunburst' back shooting off into space, and the freezer door slammed shut behind it.

Ing and his host were left breathless on the kitchen floor, each of them still grasping a chair leg. 'Well done, well done,' said Sir Percival. Getting up without another word, he went back to the drinks cabinet and, picking up the bottle of brandy, took it over to the sink and emptied it down the plug hole. Then he turned out the light and went back upstairs, his terrified and astonished spaniel trotting closely behind him. At the head of the stairs a small blue ball came flying towards him with a grin on its face, then bounced, giggling, down the stairs.

Sir Percival shook his head, 'From now on I'm sticking to claret.'

Chapter 16

As Matt and Mariella made their way deeper into the wilderness, away from the bright lights of Rhinn's compound, it grew unutterably dark. Strange animal sounds came to them out of the blackness.

'Spooks,' Matt explained, 'but not that close, thank God. We should be OK as long as we don't make too much noise.'

'You're a fucking idiot!' Mariella suddenly exploded.

'I'm sorry?'

'You had the Cartogram all this time? *And* you flew into Cullorum with it? Do you realize what would have happened if they'd found it?'

Matt unhitched the bazooka from his shoulder and leaned nonchalantly on it. 'Yes, I am aware of what would have happened if they'd found it. But may I draw your attention to the fact that they did *not* find it.'

'That's not the point! You disobeyed a direct order and put the mission in danger. No, not just the mission, the whole fucking universe!'

'Oh, I'm sorry. I must have misread the situation back there. I hadn't realized that you were having fun strapped into Glitch's dental chair.'

'My life is not worth the safety of the universe!'

'Well that's very altruistic of you, I'm sure. But I'm afraid I can't be all military and stiff-upper-lipped about the fate of a fellow agent, especially one *I'd* got into trouble. Call me sentimental but I didn't want your death on my conscience. And maybe shooting all over the galaxy with the Cartogram *was* a mistake, but I got away with it! So can we just focus on the positive and stop dwelling on what *might* have happened?'

Out of the darkness came a 'Squawk!'

Matt froze. 'Was that you?'

'No, it was *not!*' said Mariella.

'Lovely evening for a stroll,' came a strange voice. A match was struck, revealing in its flickering light a thin humanoid of about sixteen wearing nothing but a loincloth. His skin was green, with here and there a patch of purple, and his feet were covered with brown, bushy fur. His eyes peered out from beneath a fringe of spiky blond hair, and his mouth, down-turned in a permanent scowl, added to the youth's general air of adolescent seriousness. He clapped his hands, and torches flickered on in the darkness all around. With a shock Matt and Mariella saw that they were surrounded by a crowd of horribly disfigured creatures: some googlie-eyed, some with strange, puckered skin, some covered with hair, others completely bald.

'Hello, everybody,' said Matt in as friendly a voice as he could manage.

Having circled the two strangers, eyeing them up and down in brooding silence, the youth spoke again. 'Now, then, what's this?'

At his side a small feathery creature with a long neck, hooked beak and a bright red crest on its head squawked again and shook its head. 'No, no,' it said. 'What are *these* – plural.'

The boy waved his hand irritably in the creature's direction. 'What does they want here?'

'What *do* they want,' the creature sighed.

The youth ignored it and instead focused his attention on the bazooka that Matt was attempting, unsuccessfully to hide behind him.

'This might have a use,' said the youth, stroking the large weapon.

'Ah, yes, now then . . .' Matt fumbled. 'Um, this, I'm afraid, is an old family heirloom and is . . .' A hand darted out of the night and seized it. 'Now absolutely in the right hands,' he finished, unconvincingly.

The youth stopped in front of Mariella and looked deep into her eyes. 'Don't worry,' the youth said after a while, 'we's not going to eat you. We don't do that no more.'

'*Any* more. We don't do that *any* more,' corrected the small feathery creature. 'How many times— Gak!'

The youth had shot out a hand and grabbed the creature by the throat. 'Will you shut up, Mother!'

He put the creature down on the ground and it bustled away, squawking and muttering. 'I don't know, try to teach your child good grammar and this is the thanks you get . . .'

The youth moved on to Matt and studied him closely. 'So, what happen, then? Spend all your money and cash in your ticket?'

'Er, no, not exactly. Look,' said Matt, 'if you'll just let me explain—'

'No need,' said the youth, moving in even closer, 'I *know*. You be safarists, come out here for a bit of fun. Come to bag a few of us with your big gun, then scoot back to the Park before the atmosphere get to you. What larks, eh?'

The other creatures began closing around threateningly.

'No, no. We mean you no harm – really. We escaped from Sloane's compound. We're on the run. We're on your side.'

The thin youth made a small gesture with his hand, and the pack crowding eagerly around Matt backed off a little. 'What was you doing at Sloane's?'

'Losing at cards,' Mariella volunteered.

'Let me handle this,' said Matt, *sotto voce*.

'Yeah, you've done a great job so far,' Mariella replied.

The youth's hand closed around Matt's windpipe. 'You was playing cards, nice and cosy-like, with that eight-eyed murderer?'

'Good work, Mariella,' Matt said, hoarsely. 'No, no, it wasn't like that, honestly. Please, let me explain.'

The youth regarded Matt suspiciously. 'All right. Tell me all about yourself. And make it special – I likes a good story.' The youth released his grip and sat cross-legged on the floor. The other creatures did likewise, all looking expectantly up at their two guests in the flickering torchlight.

'Oh,' said Matt, rather surprised at this turn of events. 'Well . . . I . . . *we* . . . hijacked a spaceliner,' Matt began. 'I should probably tell you first that I'm a major with the Galactic Alliance. My name is Matt Fripp.'

The creatures burst out laughing.

'No, really. I *am*. Listen . . .' Matt told them the story right from their escape from Cullorum up to the flight from Sloane's compound, adding a few entertaining, swashbuckling elements on the way, but carefully avoiding any mention of the Cartogram. When he'd finished, the whole company applauded.

'We haven't had a story like that in a good long while,' the youth smiled. 'What's your names?'

'I've already told you, I'm Matt Fripp, and this is Mariella Sprungg.'

The youth laughed again. 'Matt Fripp, yeah, that's a good one. Mariella, how do you do? My name is . . .' He looked thoughtful for a moment, then smiled. 'Yeah, yeah,' he muttered. 'OK, my name is Falco Nemesis.'

'Oh no, it's not!' came a voice from the crowd. The press of creatures parted, and Falco's small, feathery mother came clucking and hopping through the throng. 'His name's Eggluth Snoggs, and it always has been!' She looked up at her son, 'Falco Nemesis? Balls!'

The youth caught his mother full on the beak with a backhander and she flew backwards, squawking, into the darkness.

'How do you do, er . . . Falco Nemesis,' said Matt. He was sure he knew the name from somewhere, but for the moment couldn't place it. They shook hands and Matt began to relax. But, at a click of Falco's fingers, Matt and Mariella found

173

themselves being bound tightly with rough twine. 'What are you doing?' Matt protested.

'Well, we liked your story, didn't we peoples?' The crowd of creatures roared their approval. 'But we still ain't sure of you, is we?'

The crowd shook their heads. 'No,' they chorused.

'So, we're keeping you "on appro", sort of thing. You keep us amused, we may even let you live.'

Chapter 17

Armani Banks, so called because of his fondness for fine clothes, was tonight wearing a fetching little all-black outfit with matching balaclava. One of Armani's many talents was fire starting, and he prided himself on his workmanship; forensics could sift through the wreckage of one of his 'jobs' and never find a single thing that suggested arson.

Creeping up the drive of Hambledon Hall, he was there to 'put the frighteners' on the Trenchards – do some little bit of mischief which, although in itself neither very harmful nor especially dangerous, would give an unmistakable signal to the occupants that they'd be wise not to thwart the wishes of a certain Harry Huxley.

Armed with a screwdriver and a Zippo, Armani was planning to start up a small blaze in the stable block. An electrical fault perhaps – ancient wiring was prone to causing problems. Under cover of the moonless night, Armani stole silently into the stable yard and lifted the latch of the stable door. Inside it was pitch-black. Flicking open his Zippo, he struck the wheel with his thumb and the wick took flame. Holding the flickering light aloft, he was about to search for the fuse box when something caught his eye. In the stall in front of him was . . . well, it was the right size and seemed to be made out of metal, but if it was a car, it was like no car he'd ever seen before. Raising the lighter higher, he explored further. There were dozens of them. Every stall was packed with the things: all shapes, sizes and colours, stacked up on top of one another. Some of them looked just like those spaceships that Dan Dare used to fly around in.

Spaceships? Armani scratched his head. This evening wasn't going to plan at all. Hearing a rustle behind him, he turned suddenly and found himself face to face with . . . what? It looked just like a large, loose, upside-down sack with strange misshapen growths coming off it, but this 'sack' had eyes. And there was more than one of them. For a moment, human and Wuboobians stared at each other. Then the frightened Wuboobians all started talking at once, whistling and farting for all they were worth. The huge amount of methane this generated made Armani's Zippo flare up so savagely that it set fire to his balaclava. Screaming in terror, and tugging desperately at his flaming wool and polyester head covering, Armani ran from the building, the acrid aroma of singed hair following him all the way down the drive.

The Wuboobians, delicate, sensitive creatures that they are, didn't sleep a wink all night.

There was uproar in the council chamber when Ing told the story of how the Grushkin delegation had met their end.

'They must be avenged!' roared the Glubbus.

'Seize the earthling and cut off his antennae!' yelled a stalk-eyed being.

'No, let the punishment fit the crime. He must be consumed!' bellowed the Grimley.

'Gentlemen! Gentlemen!' Glaak rapped his pipe on the table. 'We are not barbarians! Our aim is galactic harmony. Seeking revenge will only sow the seeds of discord. A terrible thing has happened, it's true, but we must remain true to our purpose. To alienate those who should be our friends will only make matters worse, and I'm sure, if they were still here, the Grushkin delegates would agree.'

An uneasy calm settled over the remaining delegates.

'Now,' Glaak continued. 'To ensure nothing like this awful

tragedy happens again, from now on, the kitchen is off-limits to anyone who might be perceived to be edible. Therefore, I'm moving the Grublins from the refrigerator to new quarters on top of the cold water tank in the attic.'

There was angry muttering from the Grublins.

'I'm sorry, I know it's a little warmer there than you're used to, but far better that you sweat than end up as somebody's breakfast. Now, to further business. It has come to my attention that last night the Wuboobians were disturbed by a strange earthling with a completely black head. They've been in shock ever since.'

The Wuboobian delegates all shook their heads and farted nervously.

'Yes, yes.' Glaak muttered sympathetically, then turned to a small Mingus at his side. 'Jak-ling,' he said in a confidential tone, 'could you open a window?'

The creature nodded and scurried off.

'This is a worrying development,' Glaak continued, 'and we should take care to minimize the risk of it ever happening again. Our discovery here would cause widespread panic among the people of Earth, which could seriously compromise our ability to operate.'

Armani Banks's eyebrows had been seriously compromised by the events of the previous evening. The right one had completely disappeared and the left one was nothing more than a sooty smudge. His hair too was badly singed, great chunks of it were missing, revealing a sore and reddened scalp, and what was left was matted with globs of melted balaclava. He looked, and felt, very sorry for himself as he stood in front of Harry Huxley's desk.

'Sacks? With eyes?' Opening a drawer, Huxley took out a cigar and bit off its end. 'You sure you're feeling all right in the cranial department, my old son?'

'Straight up, Harry. There must have been five or six of them.'

'Yeah, yeah, yeah.' Harry struck a match and held it to his cigar.

'They seemed to be guarding the spaceships.'

'Oh yeah, the spaceships. We mustn't forget the spaceships.' Harry took a long draw on his Havana before exhaling a choking, and extremely expensive, cloud of blue smoke. 'Now look, you and me, we've always had an understanding, right? I don't know what happened at the Trenchards' last night. All I know is that the job you were contracted to perform was not executed as per your usual high standards. Why you were prevented from completing your task God only knows. But it's all right, you fucked up – that's allowed.' He suddenly leaned forward and growled menacingly. 'What's not allowed is treating me like an imbecile and telling me stories about farting fucking sacks!'

'But it's the truth! It frightened the life out of me! I wouldn't lie to you, Harry,' Armani insisted.

'All right, all right, keep your hair on – what's left of it.' Harry took another draw on his cigar and settled back in his chair. 'New plan,' he said after a small pause for thought. 'I've had another idea. Perform this little task for me and I am willing to overlook your, to be honest, frankly worrying failure last night.'

Armani looked nervous. 'What do you want me to do, Harry?'

'The only bit of Hambledon Hall that is habitable at the moment is the East Wing, and the Trenchards sleep on the top floor. It's a terrible indictment on society today, but there are a lot of lead thieves about.' Harry gave Armani a knowing look. 'Know what I mean?'

Armani looked blank.

'Do I have to spell it out for you?'

Armani nodded.

'Strip the lead off the roof! The next time it rains Lord and Lady Muck are going to find themselves having a horizontal

Mariella settled back and watched the Spooks making preparations for the feast. 'Why do they all look so weird?' she asked.

'Pollution. Everything in the Park is made from highly volatile plastics which give off toxic fumes,' Matt replied. 'Inside Loomis Land the air's kept pure and fragrant by half a million air-scrubbers and conditioners. All the shit gets pumped out here.'

'Nice.'

'You want to know the bad news?'

'I've *had* the good news?'

'If we stay out here much longer, that's how *we're* going to end up looking.'

Mariella shivered. 'You really take me to the nicest places.'

'The green skin and purple blotches happen after a week or so,' Matt carried on, matter-of-factly, 'but that's reversible. After about six months the poisons start re-coding your DNA, and that's permanent. You might end up with an extra limb, or a tail, or you could find yourself going down the road of complete evolutionary reversion – look at Falco's mother and her magnificent plumage. Of course, the younger the body the longer it's able to hold out.'

Mariella had a sinking feeling. Their luck, if you could call it that, had got them this far, but seemed to have finally run out. 'You know,' she said, 'I've imagined my own death countless times, but never had I seen myself dying as a chicken.' She leaned her head against the bars of her cage. 'Matt,' she said softly, 'I know I've been a pain. I'm sorry I got so angry. I *am* grateful that you came back for me, even though it was your fault I was in that position in the first place. But that aside, in spite of myself, I've really . . . enjoyed is probably too strong a word to use under the circumstances, but . . . are you listening to me?'

Matt was deep in thought, watching the Spooks intently as they bustled busily about. 'You know, it could work. If we mounted a coordinated attack we could really do some damage. Especially with the bazooka.'

'Have you heard anything I've said?'

'Sorry?'

'Forget it.'

'No, listen,' Matt was suddenly animated. 'How many Spooks do you think there are here? There've got to be at least a few hundred, and this is only one encampment. There are probably thousands more out there. If we could get them organized, Sloane's guys wouldn't stand a chance.'

'Why didn't I think of that?'

'But first we'd have to disarm the electric fence.'

'And how would we do that?'

'We'd have to get to Zach.'

'Easy-peasy.'

'It's possible, if we can convince the Spooks to work together.'

'You think Falco Numbnuts will listen to you?'

'Do you have an alternative?'

Mariella shook her head and sighed. 'No.'

Now the preparations for the feast seemed to go up a gear. The fire, stoked with anything combustible that came to hand, was blazing brightly, sending sparks shooting up towards the roof and throwing monstrous shadows of the Spooks on the walls of the cave as they danced around the fire, moving in time to the boom of a large drum. Over this, the women sang in a high, wailing screech. The atmosphere was charged with electricity; you could almost taste the excitement in the air. Matt had the distinct feeling that anything could happen and that, whatever it was, it would probably hurt.

Falco came back and joined the captives. 'Good 'ere innit?' he said, handing Matt a singed and skewered, six-legged rat.

'I'm a vegetarian,' said Matt, declining his host's gift.

'Oh,' said Falco, taking it back and offering it to Mariella.

'I'm with him,' she said.

'OK.' Falco took it himself and, ripping it apart, started eating it with the same delicacy that a guest at a suburban barbecue might devour a chicken leg.

Matt tried not to watch. 'Um, Falco,' he said, looking at the ground. 'I've had an idea.'

'Mmhmm,' said Falco, his mouth full.

'Has anyone ever tried to escape?'

Falco finished his mouthful and swallowed before replying. 'From Twilight World?'

Matt nodded.

'Yeah, some have tried. But no one's actually managed it. Not *alive* that is. There be some who got fried on the fence, and some who got shot by the guards. It's only those who's gone soft in the head that tries.'

'And there can't be many of those out here,' Mariella observed, wryly.

'So,' said Matt, quickly. 'You've never actually made a concerted effort – all got together and planned some sort of mass escape?'

Falco snorted with derision. 'With this lot? It'd be easier to organize a karaoke party in a morgue.'

'How many other encampments are there?' Matt asked.

Falco shook his head. 'Dunno. Used to be loads. Prob'ly still are. But all we did was fight one another, so now we tries to keep out of each other's way.'

'Look, how would you like to break out of here – go home and lead a normal life again?'

Falco looked at him as if he was mad. 'Break out of here?' He leaned in close to the bars of Matt's cage. 'Is the air getting to you already?'

'No, no, listen, it's possible. I have experience in this sort of thing. Let me talk to your people and—'

But Matt was interrupted by the arrival of several other Spooks who began jostling the cages excitedly. 'It's time! It's time!' they shouted eagerly.

'Sorry, Matt,' said Falco, 'but it looks like you're on.'

'Please,' said Matt, as the cages were lifted up, 'Falco, you have to believe me. I can help, really I can!'

'Falco, listen to him!' Mariella pleaded. But their cries were drowned out by the swelling rhythm of the drums and the singers' high banshee wail as the two cages were manhandled through the excited crowd towards a small wooden stage, especially erected for the proceedings.

The cages were lifted on to the stage and their doors opened. Matt and Mariella crawled out and were grateful at least to be able to straighten their limbs once again. But they were still in deep trouble, as they could ascertain from the sea of crazy, leering faces looking up at them.

Mariella turned to Matt, 'Know any good jokes?'

'OK, everybody!' Matt held up his hands and tried to silence the noise. But this had little effect. The music continued, and the audience carried on moving in time to it, staring up at their two guests with big, vacant grins.

Matt tried again. 'Can I have your attention, please!' Still nothing. Then, as if by magic, there was an extra loud *Ker-thump!* from the big drum, and the crowd fell silent.

'Ah!' said Matt. 'That's better.' He glanced across at Mariella, who glanced blankly back. 'So!' Matt continued. 'My colleague and I are here to entertain you.'

The crowd roared their approval. Mariella shot him a questioning look.

'We'd like to begin with a little idea we've been formulating called: "The Great Escape!"'

'Ooh!' went the crowd.

'And it goes like this . . .'

'This better be good,' Mariella muttered.

'. . . Everybody dreams of a better life, with clean air, fresh water, fragrant flowers . . .'

'You sound like a commercial for fabric conditioner,' Mariella whispered.

'You're not helping!' Matt hissed. He turned back to his audience. 'All these things are now within your grasp, all you have to do is reach out and grab them. I . . . *we* can help you do that.

With a little foresight and planning, great things are possible. Now, first we have to get organized. Split up into teams of maybe eight or nine, and—'

'Is this the audience participation bit?' someone shouted from the crowd.

'No,' said Matt, 'this is the "how we are going to break into Loomis Land and then go home" bit.'

After a moment's silence the crowd started jeering and cat-calling.

'Nice going,' said Mariella. 'You've got 'em in the palm of your hand.'

'Please!' Matt shouted over the din. 'We can do it. We can help you get out of here!'

The jeering grew even louder.

'You're rubbish!' somebody shouted.

'Where are the jokes?' yelled someone else.

'Tell us a *story*!'

Matt waved his arms frantically. 'Listen, please!'

'Can you tap?' Mariella asked.

'You could at least *try* to help!' Matt threw back at her.

Then things took a decided turn for the worse. Someone started a chant of 'Burn them! Burn them! Burn them!' which was soon taken up by the entire audience.

'In the old days they used to just gong you off,' said Mariella.

Suddenly the stage was full of bodies as Spooks poured on to the apron. Matt and Mariella, their protestations drowned out by the howling of the mob, were engulfed in the violent, sweaty press, and felt rough cords being tied around their wrists.

Someone had brought over one of the long ladders that ran up to the high sleeping cots lining the walls and, placing its feet on the edge of the stage, let it tip over into the fire, creating a bridge between the wooden platform and the heart of the blazing inferno.

Now the crowd took up a new chant of 'Walk! Walk! Walk!' and Matt found his feet on the first rung of the ladder, being urged along it by a Spook who repeatedly jabbed a long-pointed stick into his kidneys. It was hard to balance on the narrow rungs, and the end of the ladder in the fire was already burning and settling into the flames in small jerks, which served to unsteady him further.

Jab! Matt took another small step. The heat of the fire was intense: he could feel it searing his eyeballs, and smell the sharp tang of burning rubber as the soles of his boots began to melt. *Jab!* Matt was forced to take another step, and then another. Now he was almost halfway across. Below him the flames leapt and crackled, while the ladder, burning fiercely, settled further into the fire. Matt wobbled unsteadily; his head was swimming and he didn't know how much longer he could keep his balance.

The chanting of the mob rose in pitch. 'Burn him! Burn him! Burn him!'

Jab! The stick dug into his flesh once again, but he could go no further; his legs had turned to jelly – he couldn't move them now if he wanted to. One more jab would have him in the fire . . .

Boom! Boom! Boom! The sudden sound of the drum cut across the frenzied screaming, and the mob fell silent. All eyes swivelled to the spot from where the noise had come. Falco was standing beside the drum, stick in hand, a copy of the *Galactic Informer* tucked under his arm.

'Wait!' he yelled. 'Looksee!' He opened the paper and showed it to the silent crowd.

'Ooh!' they went as they saw the photograph inside. It was above an article about Major Matt Fripp.

'He was telling the truth! He really is Matt Fripp!'

At that moment, the fire-weakened ladder, on which Matt was dazedly teetering, cracked and sent him plunging, head first, towards the leaping tongues of flame.

'Matt!' Mariella screamed.

But just as it seemed inevitable that he was destined for a fiery death, the laces of his left boot snagged on one of the ladder's splintered rungs. Matt's descent came to an abrupt halt and he hung limply over the flames.

'Quick!' Falco yelled. Many hands grabbed the smouldering ladder and hauled it back on the stage. Matt, his hair smoking slightly, was fortunately still conscious. Hastily untying him, the Spooks picked him up and carried him off the wooden platform, laying him gently on a soft pallet of straw.

Mariella kneeled beside him and touched his scorched face tenderly. 'Matt . . . Matt, are you OK?'

He looked up at her and smiled. 'Lucky boots,' he croaked, just before he passed out.

Matt awoke and looked groggily around. Gradually Mariella's face came into focus.

'Hi,' he said.

'Hello, stranger,' she said.

For a few moments he wondered where he was and what he was doing there. Then he remembered in a rush and his mind was filled with images of leaping tongues of fire and the con-torted, angry faces of the Spooks. 'I'm alive.'

'I've still got to be convinced,' Mariella replied.

'How long have I been out?'

'Nearly forty-eight hours.'

'Shit! We've got to move.' He tried to get up, but his skin seemed to be much tighter than it had felt before. Everything ached. 'Ow! Ow! Ow!'

Mariella pushed him gently back down on to his bed. 'Relax. Glaak can wait a little longer.'

Matt's hands had been wrapped in none-too-clean ban-dages, and the now faintly green skin of his face and legs was beginning to peel – he looked like he had a bad case of sunburn. Suddenly he grabbed his crotch.

'It's OK,' said Mariella. 'The Cartogram is still there.'

'You looked?'

'Don't worry, everything is where it should be,' she said with a sly smile.

Matt suddenly noticed that his feet were bare. 'My boots! Where are my boots?'

'Take it easy.' Mariella reached behind her and produced them, laying them on the floor by his head. They were even more ragged-looking than before, the suede having been scorched down to the leather in places.

Matt smiled at them. 'Thanks again, guys.' Then he turned back to Mariella. 'Now what do we do?'

'I got Falco to send messages to all the other Spook encampments, calling a meeting tomorrow night.'

'You've been busy.'

'I had to do something to keep myself amused while you were having your beauty sleep. You know, everyone's terribly excited about having the famous Major Fripp in their midst.'

'Yeah, not so long ago they wanted to kill me.'

'They're convinced you can do wonders, so you'd better not disappoint them.'

'How's it going, Major?' It was Falco. 'I brought you something to read.' He handed Matt his copy of the *Galactic Informer*. 'It's almost a week old now, but that's bang up to date for out here. We found it by the perimeter fence in the north quadrant. You're on page eight.'

'I didn't even make the front page?' Matt clumsily turned the pages with his bandaged fingers. Beneath the headline: 'Rebel's Death Crash into Green Planet', was a small image of Gweeb and, next to this, a rather old but still recognizable photograph of young Major Fripp. 'Lousy picture,' he growled.

'Let me see.' Mariella took the paper from him. 'Hmm, you used to be quite a looker.'

Matt grunted.

'You want me to read it to you?'

'All right.'

'"The glorious Crusader army has inflicted yet another defeat on the Infidel. The rebel Fripp and his bloodthirsty crew landed on planet Argus – secret fortress of the Helian Cartogram – with murder in mind . . ."'

Matt raised an eyebrow. 'Crew?'

'". . . After slaughtering hundreds of innocent, peace-loving Helians . . ."'

'That's not true!'

'". . . they threatened to destroy the planet and everything on it unless the Cartogram was handed over to them."'

'This is all lies.'

'"After getting what they had come for, the rebels murdered the Deputy Custodian in cold blood, then departed singing rebel songs."'

'I don't know any rebel songs!'

Mariella looked up. 'Do you want me to go on?'

'No,' Matt said irritably.

Mariella scanned the rest of the article in silence. 'That's about it anyway. The rest is just archive stuff about your career, along with a bit of government propaganda about the forces of the Crusade triumphing over the Infidel. Although they do grudgingly admit that you were a pretty good pilot.'

Matt shook his head in disbelief. 'Fucking journalists!'

'They're only printing the story the Crusaders told them to.'

'You really are Matt Fripp then?' Falco said.

'*Now* you believe me,' said Matt. A thought suddenly occurred to him. 'Wait a minute.' He grabbed the paper out of Mariella's hands and turned the pages until he found the cartoon section. 'If I'm not mistaken . . .' His eyes flicked down the page, stopping at an illustrated strip near the bottom. 'Yup, here we are: "Captain Nemesis, Space Pilot – the adventures of Falco Nemesis and his valiant crew".' He looked at Falco knowingly. 'So, you're the famous Captain Nemesis, huh?'

Falco half-smiled and looked down, his fringe covering his eyes. 'Yeah, well . . . it's just that his name's much sexier than mine. Besides, I always wanted to be a pilot,' he mumbled. 'But

Mum would never . . . 'course, that was before she . . . you know, the feathers and that.' He looked up, his big round eyes sorrowful and deadly serious. 'Sorry 'bout what happened.'

Matt looked up at him. 'That's OK. But next time you have a barbecue I think I might be washing my hair.'

The next evening, representatives of nearly all the Spook clans presented themselves warily in the great hall and sat beside the fire to hear what Falco had to say.

From his bunk, high up on the wall of the large main chamber, Falco rose and addressed the assembled throng. 'Peoples! Lis' up!' Beside him sat Matt, Mariella and his mother, an old sock knotted around her beak. 'We's got a plan!' Falco announced. He looked sideways at Matt and winked. 'We's gonna escape!'

A buzz went round the Spooks down below. 'And just how do you propose that we do that?' one of the clan representatives shouted.

Falco smirked. 'We's got a secret weapon. We's got us a Matt Fripp!' He indicated Matt, who stood up and raised his hands. There was excited murmuring from the Spooks.

'Good evening,' Matt began. He was hoping this was going to be a better audience than the last one he'd faced. 'I know a lot of you have been here a long time and that most of you have probably given up hope of ever seeing your homes again. But if we work together, I believe we have a chance of getting out of here.'

The crowd muttered animatedly, but one voice struck a note of caution: 'Sloane and his men have got powerful weapons and are surrounded by an impenetrable fence. All we've got are sticks and our bare hands.'

'But just think how many of us there are compared with Sloane's forces,' Matt replied. 'The odds are in our favour. Besides, we aren't completely unarmed.' Reaching behind him, he picked up the bazooka and held it aloft.

There was an 'Oooh!' from the crowd below.

But again the lone dissenter spoke. 'One bazooka – that's it? We're going to take on the whole of Sloane's army with just one bazooka? We might as well hang ourselves off the electric fence right now!'

The crowd erupted. The air was filled with a cacophony of angry shouts and recriminations.

'I've got a plan!' Matt shouted over the noise.

Falco tried to bring order. 'Peoples!' he yelled, waving his hands. 'Peoples, lis' to the plan!'

Gradually the noise subsided, and Matt carried on. 'Now, the last speaker had a valid point about our lack of weaponry, but we're going to rectify that. Every night gangs of safarists come out here on hunting sprees – we're going to take their guns.'

There was a questioning silence from the Spooks.

'Think about it, one vehicle could yield four weapons, and on an average night there are four or five cruising out here beyond the safety of the fence. That's a maximum of twenty weapons from just one night's work. And we can achieve this *if* we organize.'

The crowd bellowed their disbelief.

'Or,' Matt yelled, 'we carry on squabbling like children and stay here for ever!'

Eventually a sullen silence fell over the assembly.

'Thank you,' Matt continued. 'Now, phase one of the plan is weapons collecting. I'm going to split you up into units which will be spread out across the safarists' usual stalking area. When we have amassed sufficient weaponry, then we shall move on to phase two – getting to Zach Loomis and shutting down the power supply to the fence.'

*

The Spooks, motivated by the fact that they had nothing to lose, were eventually persuaded to accept Matt's plan and, after a prolonged briefing, the next evening at nightfall, small units were scattered all over the Twilight World, waiting for the arrival of the first safarists. They didn't have to wait long . . .

Matt tested the tension of the rope stretched between the two trees. 'A little tighter,' he whispered to the group of Spooks securing the line around the gnarled and knotted trunk of a pollution-blasted tree. The Spooks heaved one last time, then tied it off. The rope was in fact made from sinew – Matt didn't care to ask where or how they'd acquired it – and, as thin and strong as wire, would take the head off anyone travelling at speed in an open-topped 4x4. It hummed tautly in the gentle breeze.

Suddenly, there was a whistle from a thicket of scrub a little way off. They had their first customers.

'Hide!' Matt hissed, and his team quickly secreted themselves in the undergrowth. After a little while, the growl of the vehicle's engine grew louder, its lights jaggedly sweeping the dark brush as it approached over the uneven ground. Matt turned to Maloo, a young, lithe humanoid who as yet showed no disfiguring changes to his body.

'Ready?' Matt asked him.

Maloo nodded.

'Off you go.'

Maloo trotted out of the shielding brush and into the clearing, right in front of the two trees. Almost immediately the approaching vehicle's headlights picked him up.

'He's mine!' yelled someone from the hunting party in the 4x4, and a shot zipped past Maloo's head.

'Run, Maloo, run!' Matt urged.

The youth ducked under the rope, then dashed off, making sure those in the 4x4 could see which way he'd gone.

'Faster, faster,' the hunter shouted, 'we're going to lose him!'

The driver of the vehicle slammed his foot on the accelerator and the engine note rose to a scream.

Matt daren't breathe as he watched the speeding vehicle come ever closer, bouncing over the rutted ground.

His eyes flicked between the rope and the rapidly approaching 4x4. *Fuck*, he thought, *the rope's too high, we've put the rope too high!* Then, having resigned himself to spending the rest of his life among the Spooks, Matt watched as the vehicle hit a bump in front of the two trees and lurched into the air. The thin rope of sinew caught the driver and front passenger in the Adam's apple, and both lost their heads simultaneously. The back-seat passengers died moments later, when the now driverless vehicle slammed into a nearby tree.

A cheer went up from the Spooks, and they raced to the wreck to relieve the unprotesting occupants of their hunting weapons. Matt breathed a huge sigh of relief.

It was a busy night. The traffic out in Twilight World was particularly heavy due to the two runaways, since Sloane was eager to recover them and had sent out several search parties. In the space of an evening the Spooks managed to wreck twelve vehicles and gather thirty-nine weapons – the remaining nine having been rendered non-serviceable in the subsequent collisions.

Unfortunately, though, two hunting parties managed to make it back to the safety of the Park. This was bad news because it would alert Sloane's guards to this new and organized resistance from the Spooks. Recriminations would swiftly follow – Matt would have to act quickly.

Deciding to put phase two of his plan into action immediately, Matt curtailed the celebrations that had begun to break out among the triumphant Spooks, and instead organized his ad-hoc army into a long line just below the Park fence. As soon as the power was off, the Spooks would pour into the Park and it would all be over – at least that was the theory. But first, Matt had to get to Zach.

Mariella was already setting up a command post as close as she dared to the main gate when Matt arrived with his unit.

'O, mighty commander,' she greeted him, 'all ready for the assault on Zach's highly fortified, closely guarded secret chamber?'

'I'm making this up as I go,' Matt muttered.

'I know that,' she replied. 'Let's just hope you're better at improvising than you are at cards.'

'Major Matt!' It was Falco, dragging the bazooka behind him. 'We's ready when you are.'

'You know what you've got to do?'

Falco nodded eagerly. 'We's going to fire off the big bazooka, *Boom!* into the gates, while you scoot in to get Mr Loomis.'

'OK.' Matt turned to Mariella. 'In precisely ten minutes I want you to start firing that thing. Once I get inside it might take me a little while to get to Zach. But when the lights in the Park go down, that'll mean the fence is off: that's your cue. Wish me luck.'

'You're going to need more than luck.'

'I love the way you're always so supportive.'

With two Spooks, a ladder and a length of plank, Matt headed off along the line of the fence, keeping low to avoid the ever-sweeping searchlights – the guards in the watchtowers were just as trigger happy as the safarists. At intervals along the perimeter there were large ventilation units just behind the electric barrier, their squat, chrome towers blowing the noxious fumes from the Park out into Twilight World. But right at the edge of Kiddies Kingdom® there was one shaft a little taller and narrower than the rest. This was the main vent from Zach's underground bunker. Once inside its miles of underground ducting, Matt would be able to sneak past alarms, sentries and steel blast doors, and hopefully reach Zach's chamber. But first he had to get to the shaft and, just to make his job a little more interesting, it was situated right beside a watchtower bristling with Sloane's men.

Matt looked at his watch. He had less than three minutes before the bazooka started blasting the Park gates. He turned to the two Spooks who were carrying the plank and the ladder

– they were twin brothers and, although eager and cheerful, it had to be said none too bright.

'Now,' Matt whispered, 'we'll go through it again. Do you understand the principle?'

The twins nodded.

'OK, so what we have to do first is find something to act as a fulcrum.' They all looked around. 'There.' Matt pointed to a dead tree. 'Let's haul that over here.' Dodging the searchlights, they struggled with the rotting bole, dragging it as close as was safe to the Park's perimeter. Then, keeping a nervous eye on the watchtower which brooded menacingly above them, they placed the tree parallel to the fence and balanced the plank across it, pointing directly towards Zach's ventilation shaft.

'Get ready.' Matt looked at his watch: fifteen seconds to go. The three of them waited in tense silence as the second hand of Matt's watch ticked round its face.

Boom! Suddenly all attention in the watchtower was focused towards the direction from which the explosion had come.

'Now!'

Hastily assembling the ladder at the end of the plank nearest the fence, the twin Spooks climbed up to the top.

'No!' Matt said. 'Wrong end!'

The Spooks quickly climbed down and reassembled the ladder at the other end of the plank.

Boom! There was another explosion. The dummy attack on the gates seemed to be having the desired effect – Sloane's men were all crowding at the far side of the tower, trying to see what was happening.

As the twins remounted the ladder, Matt braced himself. 'Now!' he ordered. The Spooks jumped, and a second later Matt found himself flying through the air – in the wrong direction. He sailed over the twins' heads and landed heavily in a gorse bush.

'Ow, ow, ow! Fucking ow!'

Someone in the watchtower must have heard something,

because suddenly a searchlight lit up the darkness around them. However, after a few seconds' fruitless search, while the Spooks hit the dirt and Matt gritted his teeth, the light swung back towards where all the real action was.

It's not going to work, Matt thought, getting up and picking thorns from his still sore and seared flesh.

Boom! Now there were only two bazooka shells left, and he was running out of time.

He looked up at the fence, then down at the plank. *How the fuck do they do it in the circus?* He tried to picture in his mind the many times he'd seen this stunt performed.

Closing his eyes, he imagined the scene: in a pool of light in the middle of the ring, a man in a spangled Lycra suit perched on one end of a see-saw. In front of him towered a human pyramid of his colleagues and, behind him, at the top of a ladder, two more acrobats stood poised. There was a drum roll, and with a 'Hey-ya!' the two on the ladder launched themselves into space. As they hit the end of the see-saw, the flyer threw himself forwards, sailing upwards and performing a somersault in mid-air before making a perfect landing on top of the pyramid. The crowd went wild.

'Um, hello?'

Matt opened his eyes and looked down. One of the young Spooks was tugging anxiously at his shirt.

'Sorry,' Matt whispered. 'I'm ready now. Let's do it again.'

Both Spooks glanced at each other, then nodded uncertainly.

Matt eased the Cartogram to a slightly more comfortable position in the crotch of his lurid Bwellburbian trousers. *Well, at least I look the part*, he thought. Trying not to think of the consequences of getting caught on the electric fence, he took up his position on the plank, curling his toes over its very end.

Boom!

Matt waved to the Spooks and they jumped. As they hit the plank, Matt threw himself forward with all his might and flew high into the air. In the brooding shadow of the watchtower, he sailed over the fence towards the ventilation shaft, performing an unplanned somersault on the way. Unfortunately, Matt's imagination hadn't taken him as far as how he was going to land on a large, upright, steel tube without hurting himself and, with mounting horror, he realized that he was heading straight for the open mouth of the ventilation shaft head first. With a clang, he slammed into it and found himself falling.

'Now, let's have a look.'

The hand that had set the galaxies spinning pushed aside the stack of Daily Telegraphs and Galactic Informers that lay in a tottering pile on the table. Then, unrolling a map of the heavens, God's eye fell on the region of empty space between the Virgo and Coma clusters. 'Hmm, another galaxy would fit quite snugly in there. But what shape should it be?' He mused, His hand reaching across the table to the plate of Jaffa Cakes. Picking up one of the orange jelly-filled biscuits between finger and thumb, He was just about to take a bite when He stopped and examined it closely. His eyes moved over the small snack as He studied it from every angle, admiring its smooth, curved underside and the luscious, chocolate-covered top with that characteristic raised centre. 'Yes. That's not bad, not bad at all.' He turned back to the star chart. 'Good, good, then all we need is the . . . Goodness Me, now where did I put it?'

Scratching his head, God looked around His kitchen. He peered into cupboards, yanked out drawers and looked behind ornaments that hadn't been moved for years. He searched beneath the sink, under the table and in the fluff behind the Aga. Nowhere could He find what He was looking for. Finally He reached for His mobile phone and punched in a number.

'Gabriel, hello, it's . . . Damn, he's on voicemail.' God waited for the beep. 'Yes, hello, Gabe, God speaking. I was wondering if you could give me a ring back; it's rather urgent. Thanks.' He put down the phone and stroked His chin thoughtfully. 'Hmm, when did I have it last?' Closing His eyes, God cast His mind back several million years.

'That's right, I was just finshing off the Spiral Galaxy, putting the final touches to the planets of the Outer Rim, when Gabriel dropped by to ask if I could help with a nearby nebula which was refusing to fire up. I remember going with him, so I must have put it down, intending to come back and pick it up later. But where exactly was I? Think now.' Then He remembered. 'Helios! I was on Helios. Of course! Right, well, if that's where I left the Cartogram, that's where it'll be now. I'd better go and get it.'

Chapter 19

The captain of Gulgus's vast flagship turned and addressed his commander as the planet came into view. 'Objective in sight, sir.'

Gulgus growled his acknowledgement.

The helmsman felt the controls of the ship go light in his hands. 'They have control, Captain,' he announced.

A message suddenly crackled over the loudspeaker. 'This is Loomis Tower to Gologa 1, we have you now. Just sit back and relax, folks. You're in for the ride of your lives.'

'I'm not a fucking tourist,' Gulgus snapped back over the intercom.

'Oh, er, sorry, sir – force of habit. We'll try and make your landing as smooth and as comfortable as possible.'

'These Loomis Land controllers better be good. If they damage my ship, I'm going to snip off Rhinn Sloane's legs with a wire cutter.' Gulgus eased back into his chair. 'Glitch,' he said to the indistinct figure poised at his side.

'Master,' the Dastorian replied.

'You said she was a tough nut? What's the likelihood of her giving up the names of her colleagues?'

'Ooh, she'll never crack,' Glitch lied. 'But the major, now he may be persuaded to talk.'

'How?'

'Excuse my indelicacy, sir, but if he has *feelings* for the girl, then those feelings make him vulnerable. They would lead him to want to protect her, to prevent her from coming to harm. Do you follow?'

'You're going to use her to make him talk,' Gulgus said, bluntly.

'Succinctly put, sir.'

'And this time I don't want you running off mid-session to go and lay a bet.'

Glitch bowed his head deferentially. 'Rest assured, sir, I shall pursue my investigation with rigour.' Gulgus thought he detected Glitch give a little quiver of pleasure as he uttered the word *rigour*. Gulgus shivered, and leaned well away from him.

After hurtling vertically down the stainless-steel tube of the ventilator shaft for some minutes, Matt began to feel it curve slowly to the horizontal. Suddenly . . .

'Oooof!' Matt slammed into a grille put in place for the express purpose of preventing anyone doing what he was now attempting. 'Oh, shit, bollocks, fuck – ow!' he groaned. Taking stock of his bruised and battered body, he was pleasantly surprised to find that he hadn't broken anything.

What little light there had been outside did not penetrate this far underground, so it was pitch-black. Clicking on his watch light, he studied the grille. It was pretty sturdy: eight two-inch steel bars welded in position. *Let's get to work.* Unspooling the laser from his watch, he trained it near the top of one of the bars. In half an hour he was part-way through the third. *One more should do it.* Removing the fourth bar, he could just manage to squeeze through to the other side. *Now what?* In the dim light from his watch, he crawled on along the ducting, hoping that somehow he'd stumble upon the right direction; this time he had no carefully mapped out plan from Glaak. If he was lucky this shaft would take him directly to Zach; if not he could end up almost anywhere in the large underground complex. He just hoped that it wouldn't be one of the dormitories used by the guards that watched this place around the clock.

*

Zach Loomis was the key to the whole Park. He was like the central processing unit in a vast computer network. He turned on the lights when it got dark, regulated the temperature, issued maintenance schedules, even received bookings for tables in the restaurants of Gallowan Aight. There was not one piece of the Park in which he was not involved. Without him the system would collapse, which is why Rhinn had kept him going – and why no one was allowed to get near him.

Zach's brain rested in a fluid-filled beaker. Synthetic arteries kept it supplied with blood, endlessly recycled through an artificial kidney powered by a tiny cold-fusion reactor, and there were remote probes attached to the lobes of his cortex through which he could receive and transmit information to a bank of nearby computers. Originally his brain had been hard-wired into the system, but all it would have taken was for someone to trip over the cables, and he'd have ended up as blancmange on the floor. The wireless layout was much safer.

Now Zach was sleeping. On the computer screens strange images from the depths of his unconscious danced and twirled. There was a picture of a small boy on a toboggan, a frozen lake covered in penguins eating ice cream, and a swirling shower of golden leaves whipped up by an autumn wind. Suddenly, terrifying winged monsters swept down out of the sky, grabbed the penguins with their talons and carried them off to their mountain eyrie, where they ripped off their heads and fed them to their young.

Over the loudspeakers came the sound of gentle chuckling. Zach seemed to be enjoying his dream.

'The Unit is sleeping,' announced one of the white-coated technicians. 'Park close down commencing.' Zach was always referred to as 'the Unit', to depersonalize him and stop his attendants becoming too emotionally attached. As he fell into his deep, dream-filled sleep, so too the Park slept. Only vital systems were kept 'live', like the fire alarms and street lighting, the power to the underground complex and the electric fence guarding the perimeter. These were managed from probes in Zach's brain stem, and so were effectively run by his sympathetic nervous system – they never got turned off.

The technicians at the banks of computers sighed and stretched as the massive steel doors in the wall of the chamber slid open and the night shift entered. This was a much smaller group, whose main function was to keep an eye on Zach's brain's vital signs. The departing technicians bade their takeover crew a pleasant night, and headed for their sleeping quarters as the heavy steel doors slid ponderously shut.

Matt was at a crossroads in the ventilation ducting, listening intently for something to help him get his bearings. In the silence, the gung-ho spirit in which he'd begun this enterprise was rapidly evaporating. His sore, scorched hands were now even more painful, and his knees, protected only by thin bandages below his short trousers, were red raw from crawling along miles of hard, unforgiving stainless steel. He was beginning to face the possibility of never being able to find a way out of this maze of tunnels again. Even if he did manage to get to Zach's chamber, he had no idea what he was going to do once he got there.

He turned his head and strained his ears for the slightest sound. Nothing. *Fuck!* Then, echoing along the ducting that led off to the right Matt could at last hear something: the deep hum of heavy-duty electric motors. He looked at his watch: 10:45. *Close-down time. That must be the chamber doors opening to let the night shift in.*

He turned towards the sound and followed it down the smooth steel pipe. As he progressed he felt a slight breeze and noticed that the temperature was rising. After another fifteen minutes of slow, painful crawling he came to a ventilation fan, blowing stale air from the underground complex up through the miles of ducting to the outside, far above.

This close to the fan, the wind it produced felt more like a typhoon than the gentle tropical breeze that Matt had first sensed. He would have to disable it to get past, but that might trigger an alarm. *Why can't things be straightforward just for once? Oh Glaak, what would you do? That's a point, what would you do? With your teeth you could simply gnaw a hole and scramble out. Wait a minute, why don't I do that?*

He set to work with the laser on the floor of the steel ducting. In a few minutes he had made a small spyhole but, sliding the video probe from his watch through it, the images he received were not at all comforting. He was right above one of the sleeping guards: a large, muscular Gologon with a neck as thick as a tree trunk, who looked like he'd even worked on the muscles of his forehead. *Oh no!* Moving carefully along, Matt excavated another spyhole in the ducting just in front of the fan. This revealed the corridor outside the main chamber itself. Matt's heartbeat quickened as he started to think that, just for once, luck might be on his side, then he noticed the armed guard stationed in front of the large steel chamber door. Easing his way back beyond the dormitory he discovered that the duct was embedded in solid rock. Uttering a painful sigh, he crawled back to the spot above the sleeping Gologon.

To prevent any splashes of molten metal from falling on the guard below and setting fire to his duvet, Matt lasered a large hole in the roof of the ducting, covering himself in red hot globs of steel instead. When he'd finished there was just enough space between the ducting and the ceiling for him to squeeze out. Lying on top of the steel ventilator tube to catch his breath after his exertions, he looked down on a scene from a nightmare. There must have been at least ten beds in the dormitory, each one occupied by a being that looked as if it had been carved out of granite.

Now, calm, he thought. *Just don't make a sound and you'll be fine.* Matt was about to jump down to the floor when the door opened and the guard who'd been stationed outside the chamber entered. He went straight to the bed in the corner, pulled back the bedclothes and kicked its occupant awake.

'You were supposed to have relieved me half an hour ago,' he growled.

The figure in the bed opened a bleary eye. Puzzled, the sleepy Gologon peered at his alarm clock. 'Oh, man,' he groaned, sitting up. 'Fucking thing didn't go off.'

'Yeah, yeah, yeah. Just get your ass outside that chamber door.'

'OK, OK.'

Matt watched as the guards changed over. The one who'd just been woken pulled on his clothes and shoulder holster while the one coming off shift disrobed, hanging his gun on the back of the chair. Then, as the relief guard went out and closed the door behind him, the other sank gratefully on to the bed.

Matt clung, statue-still, to the ventilation duct and waited for the guard's breathing to fall into a slow, regular rhythm. Lowering himself gradually until he was clinging on by nothing but his fingertips, Matt finally let go and dropped to the floor. Crouching there a moment, he held his breath. But all around him the guards continued to snore and gurgle contentedly. Matt felt like a stray mouse who'd blundered into a cats' convention.

Now what do I do? Wait a minute, I'm probably going to need a gun. Creeping over to the sleeping guard's bedside chair, Matt slid the Gologon's pistol out of its holster and made for the door. He was just congratulating himself on getting this far when the door opened and he was confronted by a seven and a half foot square of highly trained muscle.

'Ooh, ahh. You must be, um . . . very big. You see, I was just looking for . . .'

The guard made a move for his own pistol and Matt shot him in the chest.

'Sorry.'

The guard collapsed on to the floor, but unfortunately the shot had awoken the others in the dormitory who were now all fumbling sleepily for their weapons. Stepping over the body of the dead guard, Matt was out of the room and into the corridor before any of them could take aim with any accuracy. Now he faced his next problem: the guard stationed outside the chamber. Luckily for Matt this guard, having just woken up, was not fully on the ball. By the time he realized that he was under threat, Matt had fired first, killing him instantly.

But now the dormitory guards had shaken the sleep from their eyes and were beginning to crowd into the corridor, pistols blazing. Flattening himself against the wall, Matt returned fire and two more of the guards went down. The rest of them retreated to the cover offered by the dormitory doorway, giving Matt a precious breathing space. He desperately punched the button by the main chamber door, but nothing happened. Looking closely at the small console fixed on the wall, he saw that underneath it was a slot for an ID card.

'Come on, Matt, improvise, improvise!'

Crouching to frisk the dead chamber guard, Matt found a ribbon around his neck from which dangled a credit-card-sized security key.

'Bingo!'

An energy bolt screeched off the stainless-steel wall just above his head, and Matt fired off another shot in the direction of the dormitory. Then, ripping off the guard's key, he inserted it into the lock. The massive lock *ska-chunked* open and powerful electric motors began to slide back the door. Firing two more shots at the pursuing guards, Matt slipped through the slowly widening gap and into the chamber itself.

'Nobody move!' Matt yelled, then checked his pistol. It was empty. *Oh great, now what?* As the dormitory guards began to follow him into the chamber, in desperation he dived on to the central platform, picked up Zach's jar with its tiny dialysis unit attached, and lifted it above his head. 'Anybody does anything stupid, the Unit's going to be cream cheese on the floor!'

The white-coated technicians stood looking helplessly at the security guards. 'Back off!' someone said finally. 'He means it!'

'That's right,' Matt said. 'I'm a desperate bucket, er . . . I'm just desperate, OK?'

'The Unit is waking up!' warned one of the technicians.

On the view screens the strangely juxtaposed images of happily playing children and monsters from the black depths of Zach's unconscious flickered, and were replaced by views of the moonlit Park as the Unit gradually came to.

'What's going on?' it enquired over the loudspeakers.

'Hi, Zach, I need your help,' Matt said.

'I know that voice,' Zach replied. From the speakers came a strange gurgling noise, interspersed with an electronic humming and clicking as the Unit searched its memory banks. 'You're Matt Fripp. I enjoyed our last little chat. Why do you never visit me any more?'

'It's Matt Fripp,' one of the security staff echoed incredulously.

'I've missed you too, Zach,' Matt replied. 'Now then, listen very carefully. I need you to shut off the power to the lights and the perimeter fence.'

There was worried murmuring from the technicians and guards.

'Do you mind!' Matt snapped. 'This is between Zach and me.' He addressed the brain once more. 'Can you do that for me, Zach?'

There was more gurgling and humming as Zach considered the request.

'But, Matt, I'm not supposed to do that. If I turn off the fence it could let bad people into my Park and that wouldn't be good.'

'Yes, Zach, the fence *is* a wise precaution, and it's very sensible of you to want to keep it switched on. But if you don't do this for me, something really bad's going to happen, and that would be awful.'

'Matt, you're worrying me. What's going to happen? What's going to happen to my Park?'

It was obvious Zach was becoming agitated. The tranquil scenes of the sleeping Park were replaced by a torrent of jumbled images flickering across the video screens in quick succession: a kite in a blue sky, a palm tree, a woman weeping, an angry man, a Gologon wearing a dress . . .

What was that? Matt thought.

There was anxious murmuring from the technicians as they viewed the images and studied the readings they were getting on their monitors.

'What is it?' Matt barked.

'Um, sir?' said one, stepping forward. He kept his voice low, so as not to let the Unit hear what he had to say. 'Although these random images belong to a personal database, they are not usually accessible to the Unit. Indeed, because access to these files could seriously unbalance the Unit, some time ago we created a firewall between personal and procedural memory. For its own integrity and stability it's better if the information contained therein remains inaccessible. This current firewall breach could lead to worryingly irrational behaviour, and there is a serious and imminent danger of system crash.'

If Zach crashed while Matt was still underground it would be impossible to open the security doors or use the lift, and he'd be trapped here. Climbing back up miles of smooth steel ventilator shaft was not an option. Another problem was that Zach's brain was pretty heavy, and Matt's arms were getting tired.

'Now, Zach,' Matt soothed. 'Listen to me carefully. Nothing bad is going to happen to your Park. All we're going to do is make a few teensy-weensy adjustments.'

'Well, some of the name plaques in the Walk of Fame could do with a polish, and the peanut and jelly dispenser in Kiddies Kingdom needs a tweak – the mixture's a little jelly heavy at the moment.'

'That's great,' Matt agreed. 'But before we do any of those

things we're just going to turn off the power to the perimeter fence.'

The random images on the screen became even more animated: a fish pond, two people having an argument, a meat cleaver smacking down on a bloody carcass, a male Gologon putting on lipstick . . .

Was that Gulgus? Matt wondered.

'But I can't turn off the power. That would be a bad thing. I never do a bad thing. I only do lovely things. I like lovely things. I don't want bad things in my Park . . .'

The images on the screens were becoming more and more disturbing: terrified animals entering a slaughterhouse, a man in a Balaclava holding a gun to another man's head, someone having their naked grey behind whipped by a woman dressed in leather . . .

That is *Gulgus!*

The lights in the large room flickered.

'System instability critical,' a technician announced.

'Can't you switch to back-up?' Matt asked.

'There is no back-up. The Unit forbade it because it would compromise the Unit's control.'

Matt suddenly had another idea. 'OK, OK. Zach?'

'Is that you, Matt?'

'I'm still here, Zach. Now, we're going on a little journey.'

'Can we take Petey?'

'Petey?'

Matt looked around for enlightenment, but all the technicians looked blank.

'My little Graggle hound.'

'Oh, of course – Petey,' said Matt. 'Yes, Zach, we're going to go and find him right now.'

'Go and find Petey?'

'That's right, Zach. Let's go and find Petey.'

The technicians and guards reacted instinctively as Matt made a move towards the door.

'Back off!' he warned.

'I never go anywhere any more, Matt,' Zach burbled. 'Are we going somewhere nice? Will there be candy?'

'Lots and lots of candy,' Matt promised.

Zach seemed to be calming down. Current views of the Park returned to some of the monitors, while on others, images of sacks full of goodies appeared, with red-and-white-striped candy canes protruding from their tops. But on one of the screens was a picture of a cuddly toy, with soft spines and large white teeth.

'Is that Petey?' Matt asked.

'Uh huh. He's my favourite,' Zach purred.

'Then let's go and see if we can find him.'

With Zach's jar still raised high above his head, Matt was about to head for the door when a thought occurred to him. He turned to one of the technicians 'How will I communicate with the Unit once I get outside?'

The technician looked nervously at his colleagues.

'Come on, come on,' Matt snarled impatiently.

Another of the technicians stepped forward. 'You'll need this,' he said, pulling something out of the breast pocket of his lab coat. 'It's a two-way communication device. It fits in your ear.'

Matt nodded him closer. 'You put it in,' he instructed, then added, *sotto voce*, 'but one false move and you'll be scraping Unit off the lino!'

The quivering technician inserted the device in Matt's ear, then retreated back to join the ranks of his anxious colleagues.

As Matt and Zach moved towards the door, technicians and guards parted to let them through. All Matt needed to do now was keep Zach calm until he reached the top of the lift shaft.

Up on the surface, Gulgus's ship had already landed, to be met by heavy security who escorted Supreme Commander Filch and Commissioner Glitch to their state rooms in Loomis Towers®

resort. Rhinn Sloane, one of his arms in a sling, was waiting for them in Gulgus's suite.

'Gulgus, how nice to see you again.'

'Listen, you freak, you better have some good news for me.'

'You haven't changed, Gulg,' Rhinn smiled. 'And where's McGilvray?'

Glitch was flickering round the room like a nervous moth.

'Glitch, will you stop that!' Gulgus barked.

The Dastorian suddenly appeared. 'Sorry, I'm not good at hotels.'

'Ah, Glitch, always a pleasure.' Rhinn held out one of his numerous hands and Glitch grasped it in a cold and clammy embrace. It was like shaking hands with death.

Gulgus was anxious to get down to business, but the room was still full of hotel staff bustling about, turning down the bed, laying out fresh towels and filling up the mini-bar. 'Can we get rid of these insects?' Gulgus enquired impatiently.

Rhinn clapped his hands and the staff vanished at once.

The big Gologon sat himself down on a large green sofa. 'So, what's the news?' he demanded. 'Where are Fripp and the girl, and do you have the Cartogram yet?'

Rhinn took a seat opposite him in a matching green armchair. 'Where's the military back-up I asked for?'

'Don't be ridiculous. A man in my position can't get involved a private war. I have to be discreet.'

'Discreet? From what I've seen, discretion is hardly your style.'

Gulgus's eyes flicked to Glitch. 'Can we discuss this later?'

Rhinn pursed his mouthparts. 'Very well, but I need help – the natives are getting restless.'

'All right, all right. I'll see what I can do. But *after* I have the Cartogram.'

Rhinn settled back in his armchair. 'Well now. Remember when I got in touch with you to tell you that Fripp and your ah . . . presumably *ex*-girlfriend were here, enjoying our legendary hospitality?'

'Get to the point!'

'There's been a . . . development.'

'Development? What do you mean?'

Rhinn removed his arm from its sling and held it up – it was heavily bandaged. 'There was a fire-fight; I was wounded.'

'And?'

'Thank you for your concern, but I'm no longer in any pain.' Rhinn tucked his arm back into its sling.

Gulgus snorted impatiently.

'Not to put too fine a point on it,' Rhinn continued, 'they escaped, with the Cartogram.'

Gulgus got up in a rage. 'Escaped! Holy Valohem! I'm surrounded by idiots! You let them get away?'

'It's a rapidly developing situation. The outcome may have serious implications – for you.' Rhinn looked up at him meaningfully.

Gulgus was shaking with fury. 'I should have got rid of you long ago. All it would have taken was one word from me and my ships would have blasted this worthless planet to dust!'

'Ah, but you couldn't risk that, could you? Not once I'd found out about your little weakness,' Rhinn leered.

Gulgus glanced over at Glitch, standing by the mini-bar, who had suddenly become rather interested in the conversation.

'Get out!' Gulgus ordered.

'But, master,' Glitch protested.

'Get the fuck out!'

Glitch bowed low and flickered over to the door. Gulgus heard it open and close, but, just to make absolutely sure he was gone, made a quick search of the room, the bathroom, the wardrobes, even the drawers of the big, reproduction desk. Then he went back to confront Rhinn.

'They'd better be safe.'

'Oh, they're safe – for now.'

Gulgus took a firm grip on the lapels of Sloane's jacket. 'What do you mean, for now?'

'Please, Gulgus, can't we discuss this in a civilized manner? Besides, this is an expensive suit and you're going to ruin the drape.'

Gulgus reluctantly released him.

'I don't blame you for your little . . . indiscretions, Gulg,' Rhinn began, smoothing the creases out of his silk lapels. 'I see nothing wrong with you acting out your sexual fantasies, I really don't. But then, *I* don't have religion. You know, I have to hand it to you, this whole religious scam is very clever. Feed people a line, get them to believe in all this *holy* shit, promise them a better life – and here's the good bit – not now, but when they're dead! Then tell them they'll only get there if they follow the code, i.e., do what *you* want them to do. Very clever, *very* clever . . .' He nodded his head appreciatively. 'As far as I can see it's only got one drawback, but it's a big one. If you want to keep the trust, admiration and blind devotion of your followers, you've got to appear to be whiter than white yourself. Something tells me they wouldn't take too kindly to seeing you dressed up like a hooker, being spanked by a dominatrix.'

Gulgus turned on him, incandescent with rage. 'My religion is not a scam,' he snarled. 'I am faithful and true to my people and my god.'

'And that includes getting your first wife to beat your bare arse with a ping-pong paddle?'

Gulgus lunged towards him and gripped him around the throat, pulling him upright until his feet left the floor.

'Kill me . . .' Rhinn gurgled, 'and those photographs will be all over tomorrow's edition of the *Galactic Informer*.'

Gulgus dropped him back into his armchair.

'I see the anger management course was a waste of money, then,' Rhinn quipped, gently massaging his throat.

Gulgus paced the room, trying to calm himself. 'Why she came to you I have no idea,' he muttered.

'Mimi and I always had an understanding. When you were inside, it was me she turned to for a shoulder to cry on.'

Gulgus stopped pacing suddenly and swung round to face him, eyes blazing.

Rhinn threw up his hands. 'She used to confide in me, that's all. You never did understand women, Gulg.'

'And you do?'

'I know how to treat a lady. Mimi had waited faithfully for you all those years you were in prison, and then, when you came out spouting all that stuff Angmar Blatch had pumped you full of, she felt betrayed and confused, especially by the whole polygamy thing. And she was frightened too. So many of your old friends had disappeared, she was worried you were going to dispose of her as well. She needed a little insurance. After she'd taken the photographs she came to me here and told me what she'd done. Of course, for the plan to work you needed to know about them, but she couldn't bring herself to tell you. She was in a real state at the time. She was all for simply ripping them up there and then.'

'But you recognized a business opportunity when it presented itself.'

Rhinn regarded Gulgus coldly. 'You're such a cynic. All I did was tell her to take some time to think things over and give her a free pass to all the rides in the Park. Then she has to go and choose the Deserts of Monnd . . .' He put one of his hands dramatically to his forehead. 'I still live with that guilt. If only I'd warned her . . .'

'Where are the photographs now?' Gulgus interrupted. 'Are they secure?'

Rhinn's eight eyes swivelled to meet Gulgus's two. 'Well . . . yes and no.'

'What does that mean?'

'It means, old friend, that you could be in a little trouble.'

Gulgus went white. 'Trouble? What trouble?' He felt the floor shift beneath his feet.

'Oh, don't worry just yet. The *originals* are in a safe place.'

An awful possibility dawned on Gulgus. 'You made copies?' His knees turned to jelly and deposited him back on the sofa.

Rhinn nodded. 'For my own security. It's a dangerous old galaxy out there, and one never knows what's going to be lurking around the next star system. Now the real problem lies in where those copies are at this particular moment.'

Gulgus had broken out in a cold sweat. 'Where?' he asked, faintly.

'Zach.'

Gulgus looked incredulous. 'You . . .?'

'I scanned them into his personal memory banks. He has no access to them – we sealed up all his old memories long ago to stop him going ga-ga. Well, to stop him going any more ga-ga than he already was.'

Gulgus hardly dared ask the question, 'And Zach's still safe?'

'Here's the crunch, old buddy. Fripp is holding Zach hostage.'

Gulgus leapt off the sofa and wandered around the room, moaning. 'Oh, no, no, no. Oh no.'

'Oh yes. Can I get you a drink?'

'Where are they?'

'Zach's lift, heading upwards as we speak.' Rhinn looked at his watch. 'By now they should be about halfway. The whole journey takes around twenty-five minutes.'

'I want security stationed at the head of the lift. When they come out, kill them both.'

Rhinn shook his head. 'Can't do that, I'm afraid.'

'What?'

'Zach runs my Park. He's the centre of this little enterprise. He's irreplaceable. Without him, I don't have shit.'

'I don't care about your fucking Park. I want him destroyed.'

Rhinn stood and faced Gulgus, noses to nose. 'You touch one fold of his cerebellum and I'm going to release those pictures.

And by the way, doesn't your religion have some ruling on bad language?'

Zach was humming a little melody in Matt's ear as the lift sped upwards.

'That's a nice tune, Zach.'

'I wrote it myself. It's called: "Hooray, Daddy's Got Parole". I wrote lots of songs once. Did you know that, Matt?'

'No, Zach, I didn't.'

'Oh yeah. I even had some published. This is another one of mine, it's called: "Momma, Who's the Man in Daddy's Pyjamas?"'

As Zach began his slow, mournful tune, Matt's eyes flicked to the level indicator above the lift door.

Nearly at ground level, he thought. *There's bound to be a reception party, so I'm going to have to be careful. Just for once, Matt, let's plan ahead.*

In the small, secret lobby of Zach's personal lift, a phalanx of armed security guards stood in a semicircle facing the sliding doors, pistols and boson arcs drawn. Behind them hovered Gulgus and Rhinn.

'Now, boys, remember,' said Rhinn, 'we don't want to hurt the Unit. He's very fragile, so try not to do anything to upset him. Wait until Mr McGilvray here is in position, and when he's safely in possession of the Unit, then you can shoot the crap out of Fripp.'

Gulgus turned to Glitch. 'Don't let me down. Your life may depend on it.'

Glitch bowed silently and took up his position to one side of the lift doors. The indicator blinked from red to green.

'Showtime!' Rhinn announced. 'Places, everyone.'

With a *ting!* the lift doors slid open to reveal Zach's glass jar.

'Hold your fire!' Rhinn warned.

Hiding in the corner of the lift, Matt was holding Zach's jar at arm's length, right in the line of fire. 'Nobody do anything stupid and maybe we can all survive,' he warned, though he wasn't able to prevent a small note of desperation creeping into his voice – Zach was heavy and Matt couldn't hold him up for long.

'Nobody's going to hurt you, Matt,' said Rhinn. 'Just come out nice and slowly where we can see you.'

Matt peeped around the lift door at the artillery assembled in his honour. 'Rhinn, tell your boys to put down the hardware.'

'Matt, I can't do that.'

'My arms are getting tired, Rhinn. Whoops!' Matt pretended to lose his grip on the jar, sloshing Zach's life-supporting fluid.

'OK, OK!' yelled Rhinn. 'Everyone put down their guns!'

Gulgus growled his disapproval, but the guards obeyed Rhinn's instruction, their weaponry clattering on to the hardwood-effect concrete floor.

'That's much more friendly,' said Matt.

Zach's voice came through Matt's earpiece, 'What's going on, Matt? I'm feeling a little dizzy.'

'It's all right, Zach, we're just going through some turbulence, that's all.'

Matt stepped tentatively out of the lift. He wasn't at all surprised to see Gulgus. 'Hi, Gulg. Me and Mariella have been having lots of fun.'

Gulgus clenched and unclenched his fists in mute fury.

The CCTV above the lift door whirred, surveying the scene. 'Who are all these people, Matt? Where's Petey? I thought you said we were going to get Petey?'

'Don't worry about all the people, Zach. And we'll find Petey soon.' Matt addressed the ranks of security men. 'Now, we're all going to face the wall.'

Nobody moved.

Matt raised Zach above his head. 'Do any of you have any idea how difficult it would be to put Humpty-Dumpty back together again?'

'Do what he says!' Rhinn yelled. The guards began to shuffle sideways and line up against the wall of the small lobby.

'That's it. Good. Now, I'm just—'

Matt saw something move out of the corner of his eye, and an indistinct shadow was suddenly breathing down his neck. It took him a moment to figure it out, but by that time, Gitch's black-gloved hands were already around Zach's jar.

This was not something Matt had anticipated. Of course, he could simply have dropped the jar – the lights would go out and he'd be able to escape in the confusion. But the memory of those strange images he'd seen on the screens back in Zach's chamber stopped him. Something told him he was holding a very important key, and he had to get it to safety.

'Zach!' Matt screamed as Glitch tugged at the jar. 'Oh no!'

'What is it, Matt, what's happening?'

'They've got Petey!'

The lights in the lobby flickered. The lights all over the Park flickered. Glitch momentarily let go.

'Who's got Petey?'

'These men, they've got Petey and they say they're going to rip out his stuffing!' That did it. Through the earpiece, Matt heard a terrified, high-pitched scream. The lights flickered once more, then died completely.

Everything in the Park died. The huge ventilator fans slowed and stopped, the street lamps winked out, the refrigeration units in the all-night Zach Cola® dispensers stopped humming. The Park lay dark and silent under the artificial moon.

'Kill Fripp!' Gulgus yelled. 'Don't let him get away!'

In the sudden darkness, the guards all made a dash for their guns, tripping over each other in their haste as they groped around on the floor. Although they couldn't see with any certainty what they were firing at, they started loosing off their weapons in all directions.

'Don't shoot, don't shoot,' Rhinn implored. 'You might hit the Unit!'

In the ensuing confusion Matt felt his way to the door of the lobby and fled into the night, still cradling Zach in his arms.

From the direction of the main gate came a loud cheer and the sound of gunfire. With the fence power down, the Spooks were flooding into the Park.

Heading directly towards the noise of battle, Matt almost collided with a figure in the dark.

'What took you so long?'

Matt's heart quickened as he recognized her voice. 'Mariella.' He wanted to collapse, sobbing, into her arms, but the emergency wasn't over yet. 'What's the situation?'

'We're winning. The guards at the gate just fell over. There are teams dealing with all the watchtowers. Once those guns are down it'll just be a walk in the Park.'

'Good, we have to get out of here.'

'We're leaving so soon?'

Matt nodded. 'Gulgus is here.'

'You've seen him?'

'I've talked to him.'

'Why didn't you kill him?'

'I had my hands full at the time. Here, there's someone I'd like you to meet.' He illuminated Zach's jar with his watch light.

Mariella flinched at the sight of the brain. 'What's that?'

'Zach Loomis. He'd shake your hand, but . . .'

'Yeuch. Well, I suppose his mother loves him.'

'I wouldn't count on it. Come on, we've to get Mr Loomis out of here double quick.'

'He's coming with us?'

'Oh yes. There's some stuff in Zach's memory banks I think Gulgus would rather not be made public.'

'Do you still have the Cartogram?'

Matt grabbed his crotch. 'You want to see?'

Mariella pursed her lips. 'Maybe later.'

The Park was full of bemused tourists in pyjamas who, wandering out into the night because their air-conditioning had gone down and the phone lines were dead, had found themselves in the middle of a war. The sound of gunfire echoed off the plaster buildings of Old Maccabar, and the limp, bullet-ridden bodies of Sloane's security guards festooned the brightly coloured merry-go-rounds of Kiddies Kingdom® as the Spooks pushed further into the Park.

Matt and Mariella picked their way through hordes of their victorious green and pink allies as they headed towards the spacepark.

'I feel bad about not saying goodbye to Falco,' said Mariella.

'We'll send him a postcard. Come on, Gulgus will already have figured out where we're headed. We have to get airborne before he does.'

On reaching the spacepark, Mariella gazed up at the huge, ten-storey building where a vast array of interplanetary craft gleamed under the artificial moon. 'Look at the size of this place.'

'Another of Rhinn's little money-making schemes,' Matt explained. 'There's a very lucrative second-hand spacecraft market. Anyone arriving in their own ship is immediately given complimentary tickets for—'

'The Deserts of Monnd.' Mariella finished Matt's sentence.

'You've got it.'

Reaching the barrier by the main entrance, they were stopped by an 'Excuse me, have you paid?'

Matt turned to see a Gopchic leaning out of a small hatch in the side of a concrete booth. The Gopchic was thin with lank, greasy hair, and even in the darkness Matt could make out the scowl on his sour face.

'I'm sorry?' Matt said.

'For your parking. Have you paid? I can't let you out without an exit chit.'

'We must be your first customers, ever, and you're asking if we've paid? Aren't you just the teensiest bit curious as to why we're here?'

'I'm not paid to be curious, I'm paid to do a job, which is to collect parking fees – payable prior to vehicle removal. So, just in case you didn't understand my query, I'll repeat it: have you paid? It's a simple question, requiring a yes or no answer.'

Matt pulled out the keys to Rhinn's spaceship. 'Look, we're in a hurry. I need you to tell me where we can find a brand new Manganeutron Mark 3.'

'Oh, I can tell you where it is all right. It's fitted with an anti-clemester device, bound-free transition drive, hyperturbo, antimatter leap constraints, emergency escape pod, leather seats and a rear spoiler. I've always thought such modifications rather vulgar; I'm surprised it hasn't got fluffy dice on the mirror.'

Matt grabbed the creature around the throat. 'Where is it?'

'I refer you to my previous question: have you paid?'

'Having trouble?' Matt spun round to see Falco, a rifle balanced casually on his hip.

'Ah, Falco, look . . .' Mariella began. 'I'm sorry we didn't come and find you. I know this looks bad, but—'

'We were somewhat pressed for time,' Matt added.

''S okay,' Falco replied, 'we's coming with you.'

Out of the darkness by his side came a 'Squawk!'

'Shut up, Mother. Let me do the talking.' He turned to the Gopchic. 'Give these peoples their ship.'

The Gopchic sighed. 'Not another one,' he muttered. 'Look, son, the regulations clearly state that craft must be paid for before removal. Don't blame me, I don't make the rules, but somebody's got to keep standards up, otherwise there'd be anarchyarrgh—'

Falco had stuffed the barrel of the rifle up the Gopchic's nose.

'You's got two choices: you can either tell us where's the ship, or you can have your sinuses cleared, permanently.'

'Level six, section C, bay number 9007,' the Gopchic replied nasally.

'Thanks.' Falco looked back to Matt and Mariella. 'Shall we?'

'Now, hang on a minute,' Matt began. 'We can't take civilian passengers. We're rebel soldiers. We're in the middle of a war. It's dangerous; there's no way we can guarantee your safety.'

'Oh, and we's not used to danger? I mean, life's one glorious holiday here, isn't it, Mum?'

'Squawk!'

'But, Falco,' said Mariella, 'there is only a very, very slim chance that we'll survive.'

'Do you have to be quite so realistic?' Matt asked.

There was the sound of approaching vehicles.

'Shit!' said Matt. 'That'll probably be Gulgus. OK, you can come with us. Is there a lift?'

Falco shook his head. 'It won't work with the power down. This way.' He hurried off into the darkness, his mother trotting along at his side.

'Squawk!'

With Falco and his mother leading the way, the small group hurried across the concrete expanse of the ground-floor level until they reached an access ladder running up the outside of the building.

'Up here,' Falco pointed into the darkness.

'You're the boss,' Mariella said, swinging herself on to the rusting rungs.

Matt followed. Climbing the ladder one-handed, while cradling Zach's brain in the other, was slow and painful work.

Falco waited until Matt was well on his way, then he too swung out on to the ladder with his mother perched on his shoulder.

Mariella was breathing hard by the time she clambered over

the parapet and on to the concrete floor of level six. 'Fuck, fuck, fuck,' she muttered.

Matt followed and, placing Zach carefully on the ground, stood bent-double, his hands on his knees, gasping for air.

'You two's out of condition,' Falco observed with a smile, leaping nimbly down from the ladder. 'We's got no time for you oldies to catch your breath. Come on, section C's this way.'

With Matt, Zach and Mariella following limply behind, Falco scurried off towards the coordinates the Gopchic had given them.

'Nine thousand two . . . three . . . four . . . five . . . six . . . ah, here we are.' Falco stopped in front of a handsome piece of space machinery. Even in the dark it looked the business, with its swooping, elegant lines and deep metallic-blue paint job gleaming in the moonlight.

'Squawk!' said Falco's mother appreciatively.

'Well,' Matt gasped, joining them, 'Rhinn certainly knows his craft.'

From way down below, echoing up through the many levels of the spacepark, came the sound of raised voices and the furious revving of an engine.

'Very pretty,' Mariella observed, 'but I'd feel better if we were inside it – and going somewhere.'

Matt fumbled with the keys and pressed the remote-lock button. A door in the ship's side hummed open and an articulated boarding gantry unfolded and gently lowered itself to the ground. 'Neat,' he commented.

Once inside, they were able to admire the walnut-veneered dashboard and door cappings, the deep, soft leather upholstery, and the extremely useful hydraulically damped, foldaway cup holders. 'Cool!' said Falco.

After carefully strapping Zach into the rear-facing child seat in the capacious aft section, Matt hurried for'ard and settled himself into the pilot's seat. 'Grab a chair, everyone,' he said, checking dials and flicking switches on the instrument panel. 'We're in for a bumpy ride!'

Gulgus's party, having been momentarily delayed by an argument with the Gopchic, was approaching in Rhinn's own private, executive limousine. At Gulgus's insistence, Glitch was driving, screeching round the tight, twisting turns and scraping the car's sides on the rough concrete of the spacepark.

'Mind the paintwork!' Rhinn moaned from the back.

'Faster, faster,' Gulgus urged from the passenger seat.

'Why don't we just let my men deal with this?' Rhinn asked.

'You keep out of it!' Gulgus boomed. 'If we'd done it my way in the first place, Fripp would be dead and you might still be in control of your Park. What level is your ship on?'

'I thought you wanted me to keep out of it.' Rhinn replied petulantly.

Gulgus turned on him in a fury. 'Listen you hairy heap of shit! Tell us where they are or you're going to start losing legs!' Gulgus's hand tightened around one of Rhinn's knees. Rhinn looked up into Gulgus's eyes – the pupils were tiny and the whites etched with red. In the circumstances, he decided, it was probably safest to comply.

'Level six,' Rhinn replied. 'But they'll be heading for the roof.'

'Thank you,' Gulgus snarled, releasing his grip. He turned to Glitch. 'The roof!'

'I heard,' Glitch snapped testily.

'Don't you start!'

Rhinn sat back in the deeply upholstered seat and massaged his bruised knee as Glitch clipped yet another concrete bollard. *Ouch!* Rhinn grimaced in the dark.

Having powered up Rhinn's ship, Matt eased it off the ground and began to manoeuvre the gently bobbing craft slowly out of the parking bay.

'Take a right and head for the roof,' Falco advised from the back seat.

'Aye-aye, sir.' Matt switched on the navigation lights. As he swung round to starboard, the lights picked out a white arrow above the word 'ROOF' painted on the floor of the cavernous spacepark. 'Could you mean this way?'

Falco smiled and nodded as they moved slowly along between the rows of neatly parked spaceships. 'So how come you never stole one of these babies and got out?' Matt continued.

'A few tried, but they never managed to get through the space gate.'

'Space gate?'

'One way in, one way out. Miss it and you smash into the force field. 'S only opened to let the big cruisers in and out.'

'Now he tells us.'

'Don' worry. 'S okay now that power's down.'

Matt turned to Mariella in the co-pilot's seat. 'So far so good.'

'Please don't say that,' she complained.

The headlights of Rhinn's limo suddenly appeared around the corner and started heading straight for them. 'Now see what you've done,' Mariella added.

'Is there any other way up to the roof?' Matt asked Falco.

The youth shook his head. 'Nah.'

Mariella turned to Matt. 'What now?'

Matt gripped the controls a little tighter. 'Ever played chicken?' he asked, beginning to accelerate towards the approaching headlights.

'You can't be serious.' Mariella nervously tightened her seat-belt as the limousine's headlights approached at speed.

'You have a better suggestion?' Matt wound up the power even more and got an answering roar from the ship's engines.

Inside the limo, Rhinn's eyes widened as he saw the space-craft heading straight towards them. 'Oh no. Please, Gulgus, slow down.'

'Keep going,' Gulgus ordered, putting his foot over Glitch's on the accelerator pedal and pressing down hard.

'Ooh that hurts,' said Glitch with a slight smile.

'Please, you'll kill us all,' Rhinn moaned.

'Who's going to blink first, eh, Fripp?' Gulgus narrowed his eyes as the collision speed of the vehicles soared through merely terminal and approached complete annihilation.

'Matt,' Mariella warned as the limo's headlights grew ever larger, 'Gulgus is very, very stubborn.'

'So am I,' Matt replied, his jaw set.

'I was afraid of that.'

'Squawk!'

From the back seat of the limo, Rhinn watched in terror as the ship's lights filled the windscreen. He could stand it no longer. 'NO!' he yelled. Diving over the front seat he grabbed the wheel. The vehicle swerved violently towards a row of parked spacecraft. As the ship zipped by with only inches to spare, the limo was sent spinning in its wake like a toy, and Glitch had to fight to keep it clear of the stationary craft.

Without the limo's headlights blinding him, Matt could now see that they were heading, at some speed, towards a solid concrete wall.

As Matt applied full brakes and slammed the engines into reverse, Mariella closed her eyes and waited for the inevitable and sickening *kerrump* of metal against unyielding concrete. But, surprisingly, the banshee wail of the hyperturbo stopped suddenly, to be replaced by the low, kidney-trembling *thrrum* of the engines on idle. Opening her eyes tentatively, Mariella could see the spacepark wall, brightly illuminated by the ship's lights, about a foot in front of the windscreen. She turned to Matt. He was still gripping the control yoke. She shook his arm. 'Matt, Matt. You can open your eyes now.'

'Did we survive?'

'Just.'

''S fun riding with you two,' Falco piped up.

'Squawk!'

Matt was trembling all over. 'Yeah, yeah, we're a laugh a minute. But we can't hang around here all day,' he said, trying to sound businesslike. 'Onwards and upwind . . . er, wigwam . . . willow pattern . . . er . . .'

'It's happening again,' Mariella observed.

'I know,' Matt replied, swinging the ship round and heading for the ramp leading up to the next floor.

In the limo all was silence as the three occupants slowly came out of their reverie of death. Glitch was the first to speak. 'It would appear that we need back-up.'

'Er, yes, yes, you're right. Good idea,' Gulgus agreed, picking Rhinn out of the footwell and dumping him unceremoniously back in the rear seat. Gulgus clicked on his wrist-vid. 'This is Big Chief to Gologa One, repeat Big Chief to Gologa One,' he began.

The image of the captain of Gulgus's flagship appeared on the tiny screen. 'Gologa One to Big Chief, receiving.'

'Gologa One, bogey on roof of spacepark. Rendezvous and contain, nothing more. Do not destroy the target, repeat, do not destroy the target.'

'Understood, Big Chief. Containment only.'

'And take care where you're shooting. I'm going to be up there too.'

'Roger that, Big Chief.'

Rhinn, having endured a near-death experience, was full of fellow-feeling for his colleagues. 'Thank you, Gulgus,' he said, reaching out and touching Gulgus lightly on the shoulder. 'I appreciate your not giving orders to wipe out my Unit.'

Gulgus flicked Rhinn's hand away. 'I don't give a shit about your brain,' he growled. 'It's the Cartogram I care about.'

'Oh.' Disillusioned, Rhinn slumped sadly back into his seat.

Matt piloted the ship up through the levels of the spacepark until the grey, enclosing concrete gave way to twinkling night sky.

'Made it,' he breathed. 'Setting for space travel.' He checked the instruments. 'Anti-clemester device on, medium sensitivity. Bound-free transition drive fully charged. Plasma energy at seven-tenths, fuel good, engine manifold pressure good, and I think we can safely assume we're free from hyperturbo icing.' He turned to Mariella. 'Shall we?'

'Get us out of here,' she whispered, bracing herself for the sudden surge of power that would hurl them up into the sky, and beyond.

Matt smiled. 'Here we—'

There was an almighty explosion just in front of them, and simultaneously a message came over the radio:

'This is Gologa One to target craft. Remain where you are. Repeat, remain where you are. Any attempt to take off will be met with extreme force.'

Matt leaned forwards to look up through the sloping windscreen. Gulgus's huge flagship was above them, the thudding bass rhythm of its engines rattling the smaller ship's cup holders. There was no way out. 'Shit!'

'Squawk!'

Matt spun angrily round to Falco. 'Can't she say anything else?'

'Not any more. I think she's grown a few more feathers too.'

Mariella looked suddenly very tired. She turned to Matt and touched his hand. 'Well,' she said, 'we tried.'

But Matt was concentrating on something, trying to follow a line of thought through the still-disturbed passages of his mind. 'Wait,' he said. 'Rhinn knows we've got the Cartogram, right?'

Mariella nodded.

'So, presumably Gulgus knows that too. And although he's pretty pissed off with both of us, would he risk vaporizing the biggest prize in the universe, just for the joy of seeing us dead?'

Mariella looked at him wearily. 'Gulgus has already threatened to destroy the Cartogram if he can't get his hands on it.'

'But that was when it was locked up on Argus, and no use to him at all. He's never been this close to it before. I'll bet he's feeling pretty excited right now.'

Mariella shook her head and sighed. 'I don't know. I didn't like the way Gulgus's captain just referred to us as the "target craft".'

The headlights of Rhinn's limo came up the concrete ramp and on to the open expanse of the roof.

'The situation looks hopeless,' agreed Matt, 'but I have a plan,' he added thoughtfully.

'Oh God, we're going to die,' Mariella sighed, tightening her seat belt.

Matt turned to Falco. 'You game to try something?'

'You've got the Cartogram?' Falco beamed in response. 'Wow!'

Matt composed himself behind the controls. He cast an eye over the instrument panel. All systems were still go. 'OK, here's the plan.'

Mariella looked at him, one eyebrow raised sceptically.

'We head for Gweeb and the wormhole. Now, we don't have a hope in hell of outrunning that cruiser . . .'

'*Now* who's being depressingly realistic?'

Matt looked up at the big spaceship, still above them. 'They'll be monitoring our systems, making sure we're not about to run, by checking for a steadily rising engine boost rate. What they won't be expecting is the sudden engagement of the bound-free transition drive.'

The lights of the limo came to a standstill ahead of them and the doors began to open.

'You can do that?' Mariella asked.

'Well, you're not *supposed* to,' Matt replied. 'There's a danger of ripping the engines out of the fuselage.'

Mariella nodded, 'Uh huh.'

'And it's very heavy on fuel. If we use it, it'll be touch and go us making it to Gweeb. And even if it *does* work, mere flesh and bone can be compressed beyond endurance by the enormous forces involved.'

'We could be crushed to death,' Mariella translated.

'That's about it. But we have got anti-clemester, which is supposed to counter the effects of extreme G.'

'Supposed?'

'On a leisure craft this size it's not usually very effective. It's just there to flatten out the bumps.'

Three figures had now emerged from the limo and were making their way towards the ship, backlit by the vehicle's headlights. The sight of Gulgus and Glitch brought back to Mariella all the hideousness of her recent experience in 'deep cover'.

'Let's do it,' she said.

'Yee-hah!' Falco screeched.

'Hold on to your feathers.' Then Matt had a sudden thought. Unzipping his fly he extracted the Cartogram and passed it back to Falco. 'If we're going to be pulling upwards of twenty G, I don't want any extra weight in my trousers,' he said, in reply to Mariella's questioning look. 'Just lay it on the seat beside you, OK, Falco? Don't play with it.'

Turning the anti-clemester to maximum sensitivity, Matt reached for the transition drive toggle switch. 'This could hurt,' he said, more to himself than anyone else. He gritted his teeth. 'Good luck, team.'

Click.

There was no time to duck. One minute the small ship was there in front of them, the next it was five miles behind. The craft's extreme velocity split the air into its component parts and sent Glitch's eye spinning madly round his head. In the crackling, highly ionized atmosphere, Gulgus's scalp felt as if it had been sand-blasted, and all the hair on Rhinn's body stood on end, making him look like a sea urchin.

A lone voice broke the stunned silence. 'Er, Big Chief? Are you there, Big Chief?'

Gulgus looked dumbly down at his wrist-vid. The worried face of his captain looked anxiously back.

'Big Chief, this is Gologa One, come in please.'

'Hello,' said Gulgus faintly.

'What would you like us to do, sir? Shall we follow the target craft?'

'Um, oh . . .' Gulgus looked around uncertainly. He was trying to come to terms with what had just happened and not managing very well. Likewise, Glitch too was in difficulty, stumbling dizzily around, grabbing ineffectually at his roving eye to stop it whizzing round his head like a demented fly.

Rhinn, brought to his senses by the approaching sounds of cheering and gunfire as the Spooks began their raid on the spacepark, was the first to recover his wits. Racing over to Gulgus, he grabbed his arm and screamed into his wrist-vid, 'Pick us up, you idiot! Pick us up, now!'

'Er, aye-aye, sir.'

The effect was not unlike being sat on by an elephant in a lift travelling upwards at light speed. Unfortunately, in the heat of the moment, Matt had failed to set the parameters for bound-free transition drive shut-down and, as he was now pasted to his seat like tomato sauce to a linen shirt, there was no way he could reach the controls to turn it off. The ship would simply carry on forever increasing in speed until it ran out of fuel, or hit something.

Mariella somehow managed to swivel her eyeballs in Matt's direction in an enquiring sort of a way.

'Gwaank glaargh,' said Matt by way of explanation, his tongue pinned to the roof of his mouth.

Surprisingly, Falco's mother seemed fully apprised of the situation and, while everyone else was becoming intimately acquainted with the sumptuous leather upholstery of their seats, her light-weight, poultry-bone structure allowed her a certain degree of movement. Exerting every fibre of her body, she struggled against the massive G force, craning forwards inch by painful inch towards the transition drive toggle. With one last almighty push, straining her neck until the vertebrae creaked, the tip of her beak finally made contact.

Click.

The ship came to an immediate standstill. But while Matt, Mariella and Falco were held in place by the state-of-the-art, plasma-bonded webbing of their seat belts, Falco's mother, unrestrained, careened into the windscreen in a frenzy of feathers.

'Squawk!'

'Let's hear it for the chicken! Extra corn for you tonight,' said Matt, plucking Falco's mum off the dashboard and handing her back to her son.

'Well done, Mum. That was brilliant!'

'Squawk!'

'I swear I'll never eat barbecued wings again,' murmured Mariella.

'Now, where are we?' said Matt. He looked up into the blackness of space, then down towards where Loomis Land should have been – but it seemed to have disappeared altogether. 'At least we didn't hit anything.'

'Well, that's something,' said Mariella, easing the tension from her neck.

'The question is, which side of the planet are we on?' After briefly scrutinizing the instruments, Matt clicked the switch on the star chart module.

'Hi,' came a husky female voice. 'Where are we going today in your brand-new, Manganeutron Mark 3, the most advanced personal spacecraft on the market? You know, I don't care. I'd go anywhere with a man who owns a Manganeutron.'

'Um, oh, that's great,' Matt replied.

Mariella rolled her eyes.

'We need to get to Gweeb,' Matt continued. 'Could you work out a route, please?'

'Sure thing,' the voice gushed. 'Anything for a man with a brand new, powerful Manganeutron Mark 3. By the way, as a man with an eye for fine machinery, are you aware of other products made by Yakizomo Enterprises, manufacturer of the Manganeutron Mark 3?'

'Er, not just now, thanks,' Matt said.

'OK, remind me to tell you later about all the other fine products available, from simple upgrades to entire power-plant exchanges which will help you maximize your Manganeutron experience. Don't go away, big boy, I'll be right back.'

'Oh, right.'

'Is it getting a little hot in here, "big boy"?' Mariella asked.

'Er, it's just a . . . silly gadget,' said Matt, colouring slightly.

'Hi there, I'm back,' the star chart purred.

'Oh, hello,' Matt replied.

'I's been a bad girl,' the star chart continued, in a silly, baby-ish voice. 'I'll bet you're going to want to spank me.'

'OK, sister,' Mariella interrupted, 'let's cut to the chase. Have you got a course for us or not?'

'Who's your friend?' the star chart asked tartly.

'Just answer the question,' Mariella insisted, 'do you have a course for Gweeb?'

There was a slight pause before the machine replied. 'Why are you letting her speak to me like this?' it sobbed.

'Answer the question!' Mariella insisted. 'Do you have a course?'

The machine stopped crying. 'Gweeb not found in database,' it said, matter-of-factly.

'Oh, perfect!' Mariella fumed.

'And dump the bitch before you call me again,' the machine added as a parting shot.

'Well, that's just great,' said Mariella. 'I have green skin, we're totally lost and our bimbo of a navigational computer can't read a map!'

'And that's not the least of our problems.'

'What do you mean?'

'There's a large Crusader ship coming up fast on our tail.'

'Oh, shit. Get us out of here!'

'That's not as easy as it sounds. We've barely enough fuel to get to Gweeb, as it is. If we set off in the wrong direction, we'll never make it!'

Falco, who'd been quiet for some time, suddenly said, 'Will this help?'

Matt turned to look. In his hands Falco held the Helian Cartogram, and above it, turning slowly, there sparkled a three-dimensional image of the galaxy.

'How did you do that?' Matt asked.

'Jus' foolin' around,' Falco shrugged. 'The principle's pretty simple really.'

Matt and Mariella looked at each other. 'Can you find Gweeb?' they said, together.

'Sure, give me a moment.'

'You've got thirty seconds,' said Matt, studying the ever-growing smudge of Gulgus's ship on the sensors.

The image above the Cartogram flickered and changed as Falco scrolled through its memory. 'Um, this do?' he said, handing Matt the Cartogram.

Matt took it. To one side of a holographic representation of Loomis Land and adjacent planets, a green arrow pointed across the wastes of space towards a small red spot, with the legend GWEEB via ALBORG written above it.

'It's pointing us to the nearest wormhole,' explained Matt.

'What does "Gweeb via Alborg" mean?' Mariella asked.

'It means we have to change.'

'Change?'

'Switch wormholes when we get to Alborg. Right, setting course.' Matt set the coordinates for the wormhole into the ship's computer, this time remembering to set the transition drive's shut-down parameters. A pulsar torpedo exploded right in front of them and a message crackled over the intercom. 'This is Gologa One to target craft. Stay where you are. Repeat, stay where you are.'

'I don't think so,' Matt replied. 'How do I get a fix on the Gweeb wormhole?' he asked, handing Falco back the Cartogram.

'No problem.' Falco stroked the black slab with his long, elegant fingers, and in a matter of moments a representation of Gweeb and surrounding space was floating above it. 'Here you go,' he said, handing it back to Matt. The wormhole above Gweeb was labelled *EARTH*.

'OK.' Matt hurriedly made a few more adjustments to the instruments.

Mariella sensed something was up. 'What are you doing?' she asked.

'This is only going to work one way,' Matt replied.

'Which is?'

'Unless we persuade him to go somewhere else, Gulgus is going to follow us straight down the wormhole.' Matt undid his seat belt and stood up. 'I'm going to take the escape pod.'

'No!'

'Look, if I can get Gulgus to follow me instead of you, then you've got a chance to get through to Glaak.'

'But he'll kill you!'

'Thanks, I hadn't thought that far ahead.' Matt opened a large hatch in the roof. 'I've programmed the pod to separate just before the wormhole to Alborg. To anyone following it should look like we're just slowing down.'

Mariella looked round hopelessly. 'But I can't pilot this thing.'

'You don't have to, it's all programmed in. Just try not to upset the ship's computer too much.'

Another message crackled over the intercom. 'Target craft, stand by for interception.'

'Got to go,' Matt said. 'If they get close enough to put a tractor beam on us, it's all over.' Matt hauled himself through the hatch and into the escape pod. 'When you get to Glaak, give him Zach. What he's got in his memory banks is dynamite.'

'Good luck,' Falco waved.

'Squawk!'

Mariella looked up at Matt one last time. 'Matt?'

'Yeah?'

But she couldn't think of anything to say.

Matt understood. 'Let me get in the pod,' he said, 'Count to three, then flick the transition drive switch. I'll see you when it's all over.' He smiled then closed the hatch behind him.

Mariella, her eyes fogging with tears, counted to three.

Then, *Click.*

In the flick of a Nunguthian hummingbird's wing, the point in space previously occupied by the small craft was once more a total vacuum.

The captain of Gulgus's ship watched the small craft sear a trail across his instruments. But he wasn't that bothered. If they continued using the bound-free transition drive they would soon run out of fuel and he'd collect them easily. Besides, he had a good navigational lock and the powerful flagship was more than capable of keeping up with them. 'They've jumped to transition drive again, sir.'

'Don't lose them,' Gulgus snarled.

'No danger of that, sir,' the captain smiled and glanced across at his helmsman. If he'd been studying his instruments a little more closely he would have noticed a small flash and the single blip on his radar momentarily become two. But when he looked back again, there was just the single signal, which now seemed to be slowing. 'He's come out of transition drive now, sir. I think he's shot his bolt.'

'Haul him in.'

'Aye-aye, sir. Steady as she goes, helmsman.' In a matter of minutes the big craft was close enough to deploy its tractor beam.

The captain made some minor adjustments to his instruments, then pressed a button. 'Beam deployed. Target craft ensnared. Time to rendezvous . . .' he checked the digital read-out '. . . ten minutes.'

Gulgus turned to Glitch. 'Warm up your instruments.'

Glitch flickered with an anticipatory shiver.

But what Gulgus saw when he marched on to the hangar deck of the ship to welcome his rebel captives displeased him greatly.

Beside the open hatch of the small escape pod stood a smiling Matt Fripp. 'Hi, Gulg, how's it hanging?'

Chapter 20

As darkness fell, Armani Banks, wearing a brand new black Bala-clava, crept silently up the drive of Hambledon Hall and, giving the stable block a wide berth, moved around to the back of the big house. There was an old, rusting fire escape leading up to a small crenellated parapet running in front of three arched windows. From there it was only a small step up on to the roof. It looked as though this was going to be an easy job. His soft rubber soles made no sound on the cast iron steps, and he had reached the second of the fire escape's rickety and rotting land-ings when he heard music: a waltz. He gazed around, trying to work out where it was coming from. It seemed to be emanat-ing from the ballroom, but he'd just walked past that dark and derelict part of the Hall; all the windows were broken and the ceiling had fallen in. Telling himself that the elderly Trenchards were probably listening to 'Friday Night is Music Night' or some other bollocks, he shrugged and continued climbing.

On reaching the parapet high above the back entrance, he was surprised to see light coming from the top windows and hear the sound of voices. He crawled along the narrow ledge and peeped inside. What he saw filled him with abject terror. In the large attic room was an assortment of the weirdest creatures he'd ever seen. Among them was a monster with two heads that seemed to be arguing with itself; something resembling a starfish hanging from the ceiling; a bulbous blue thing playing catch with its own head; and those farting sacks he'd seen before. While in the middle, standing on a table and directing proceedings, stood a large brown rat smoking a pipe.

As Armani watched in disbelief, the Mufflet's head came winging in his direction and smacked into the glass. Armani had a momentary glimpse of the creature's face as it smiled and winked at him before bouncing back into the room. Armani stifled a scream. Several of the creatures immediately looked towards the window, but Armani ducked just in time and, in his panic, started scrabbling frantically backwards. Blind to all sense, he edged back until he found himself hanging by his fingertips from the stone guttering. He looked down at his feet, and beyond them at the dizzily swaying ground, far, far below. Eventually recovering his wits enough to realize he should probably do something about his extremely precarious position, he was about to clamber back up when the window above him was thrown open.

'Flange buttock whig meery,' Armani heard. This was followed by three sharp whistles and a sound like someone breaking wind. Harry was right, he *was* losing his mind. Then he was overwhelmed by an aroma of bad eggs and old fish and realized with a chill that, no, this was actually *happening*. It was as real as, well, as real as farting sacks.

The quickest way to the ground would have been simply to let go but, thankfully, the urge to do so was overruled by the shred of self-preservation Armani still possessed. Hearing the window above him close, he started to swing his feet over to the near edge of the fire escape. Getting a toe on the handrail, he edged along the gutter with his fingertips until he could jump down on to the rusting sheet of the fire escape's top landing. Sadly, the ancient iron was not up to the task and, as his feet touched down, they punched a large hole in it, through which Armani would have plummeted, were it not for the fact that the waistband of his trousers caught on a jagged piece of metal at the edge of the opening, and he found himself suspended by his French bearer.

Chapter 21

'Phoowee, is that my pits or yours?' Matt asked one of his escorting guards as he was led along a corridor, deep in the heart of Gulgus's enormous flagship. 'It's me, isn't it? Well, it's been a good few days since I've been anywhere near soap and water.' The door to the medical centre slid back to reveal Glitch and Gulgus. 'Hi, boys! Do you have a shower on this crate? I'd love to freshen up.' Matt was propelled rapidly into the room and the door closed behind him. 'Nice place you've got here. A little Spartan for my tastes, but then it must be a dream to keep clean.'

'Same old Matt, but I doubt you'll appear so flippant once Mr McGilvray here gets to work,' Gulgus retorted.

At a signal from Glitch, the guards led Matt towards a large chrome and steel chair in the middle of the room and forced him to sit, securing his arms and legs with reinforced straps. As Glitch made himself comfortable on a stool next to the chair, Matt's eyes flicked over an array of terrifying instruments nestling on a small table at his elbow.

'Gulgus,' he said, looking into the Gologon's eyes. 'How long has it been? You know, you've changed style since I saw you last, but I have to say that pastel print with the lace flounces really brought out your eyes.'

Gulgus flushed pink under his pale grey skin. 'Everybody out!' he shouted suddenly.

'Master?' Glitch looked questioningly up at him.

'Out!'

'But—?'

'I'll conduct this interrogation. Get out!'

'As you wish.' Glitch bowed and left the room in the company of the two guards. When the door was safely closed once more, Gulgus leaned over Matt threateningly.

'What's to stop me killing you right now?'

'I know you better than that. You're curious as to how much I know.'

Gulgus slammed his fist down on the arm of the chair. 'OK, so how much *do* you know?'

'I always wondered why you tolerated Rhinn's excesses, especially with all that righteous shit you spout. Well, now I know.'

Gulgus gripped him around the throat. 'Few remain alive who have mocked my religion.'

'This is not the way to get the best out of me,' Matt wheezed.

Gulgus relaxed his grip. 'You've got a fucking nerve. First you steal my fiancée, then you take my Cartogram.'

'Strictly speaking it's not *your* Cartogram,' Matt corrected.

'It may have escaped your notice,' Gulgus growled, 'but I happen to be the most powerful force in the galaxy. Correction, the *only* force in the galaxy. Your puny Alliance couldn't organize the lettuce in a club sandwich; its delegates spend all their time squabbling about who sits where at the conference table. When I have the Cartogram, and make no mistake I *shall* have it, I intend to start a universal crusade, a spiritual revolution that will roll over all in its path – and I shall be its head. It's *my* Cartogram, all right, so where is it?'

'Um, I really couldn't say.'

Gulgus picked up a shiny steel implement with a murderously sharp blade at one end. 'Where is it?' he repeated.

'It's safe,' Matt replied.

'Not good enough.' Pushing Matt's head firmly back against the chair, Gulgus drew the surgical steel slowly down the side of his victim's face. Matt felt a sharp pain, followed by the sensation of something trickling down his cheek.

'You know, Gulg, I never figured you for a sadist,' Matt gasped.

'I could always call in a professional.'

'Go ahead, get McGilvray in here. All I'd have to do is tell him to talk to Rhinn about a certain set of photographs, and it would all be over. You may not have the Cartogram, but are you really going to risk losing what you've already got?'

'You give me no choice.' Gulgus gripped the steel instrument with renewed intent, but Matt could feel a slight tremor in the hand wielding the blade. For all his aggression and violence Gulgus didn't have the stomach for the prolonged cruelty needed to extract a confession. Snarling, he threw the scalpel across the room.

Matt smiled. 'Speaking as a friend, Gulg, keeping a record of your little foibles was pretty dumb. Why couldn't you have done what most perverts do and simply watch yourself in the mirror?' Gulgus whacked him across the mouth. 'I see I've touched a nerve,' Matt mumbled through swelling lips.

For a while, Gulgus paced the room like a caged animal, muttering unintelligibly and occasionally smacking his hand into the wall. Then he threw back his head and yelled, 'Why?'

'It was Mimi, wasn't it?' said Matt.

Gulgus stared at him for a long moment. 'She knew I loved her. All the other wives, they were just political decisions.'

'I'll bet they were pretty cute political decisions.'

'All she needed to do was just talk to me. I could have re-assured her.'

Matt looked at him. 'You didn't know she'd done it?'

'Of course I didn't know,' Gulgus snapped. 'Do you think a man in my position would take that risk? She set up a two-way mirror in the wall of our bedroom without telling me; the camera was on auto-timer.'

'Where is she now?'

Gulgus sighed. 'She wandered into one of Sloane's assassination parks. He claims it was an accident.'

'A fortunate accident for him.'

Gulgus addressed the ceiling, 'Why didn't I listen to Angmar and remain celibate? Why do I always think I know best?'

'You've got me there.'

Matt's remark seemed to return Gulgus to his senses. Retreating back behind his usual brusque and businesslike exterior, he straightened his uniform and walked over to where Matt was strapped helplessly into the chair. 'Make no mistake, Fripp, I shall find the Cartogram with or without your help. My men are everywhere – so it won't take long. As for you, you're going to die, so it doesn't matter what you do or don't know. I'm keeping you in isolation until we get back to Cullorum, then I'm going to personally feed you to the stelions. Enjoy the rest of your short life. Goodbye.'

Gulgus turned on his heel and walked out of the room. The door slid shut behind him and Matt was left alone, bruised and bleeding, to ponder his fate.

Chapter 22

Once again, Armani stood nervously in front of Harry Huxley's desk. 'I ain't never going back up there again. You can do what you like, Harry, but that place ain't right.'

Harry regarded him levelly. 'You been seeing more alien spaceships?'

Armani looked down at his feet and shuffled uncomfortably.

''Cos if you have I'll be very disappointed. Very disappointed indeed.'

'It's not just that, Harry. There was other weird stuff going on – like the party in the ballroom.'

'Party in the ballroom? You're trying my patience, old son. That place has been derelict for years.'

'I know. That's what I'm telling you. When I passed it on the way to the fire escape it was a mess: the windows were broken and the ceiling was all over the floor. But when I came back I heard music, so I stuck my head round the corner into that bit, you know, with all them naughty statues . . .'

'The Italian garden, yes.'

'. . . and the place was fixed up like new. The lights were blazing and it was full of people dancing. It was like magic. And in front there was this man dressed up like a clown and this naked woman who were going at it like rabbits in the fish pond.'

'Rabbits in the fish pond?' Harry frowned. 'Hang on, is this the same "Party in the Derelict Ballroom" story or have you started another strand?'

'There *was* a party going on in the ballroom,' Armani insisted.

'A party,' Harry repeated flatly.

'A party!'

Harry couldn't quite get his head round it. 'How many people were there?'

'I don't know. A hundred, maybe more.'

Harry screwed up his small eyes and glared at the man standing on the other side of the desk – Armani felt them bore into him like laser beams. 'You're not winding me up, are you, Armani me old mate? 'Cos if this is another of your farting sacks stories . . .'

Armani thought it best not to mention what he'd seen at the top of the fire escape. 'Please, Harry, you got to believe me. I wouldn't make stuff like this up.'

Harry reached into a drawer and pulled out a thinking cigar. If what Armani said was true it was worrying news. If the Trenchards could host a lavish party for a hundred people or more it must mean they had somehow gained access to secret funds, which could be a serious setback for Harry's takeover plans.

Harry fished around in his pocket and pulled out a set of keys. 'Here,' he said, throwing them at Armani, 'bring the Roller round the front. We're going fishing.'

Most mornings, in order to supplement a by now rather tedious diet of steak and venison pie, Whipple cycled down to the greengrocer's in the village in search of some green stuff. This particular morning he was also supposed to be booking the entertainer for the annual Hambledon Hall children's party. George Slocombe, a retired local man who had inherited his grandfather's Punch and Judy theatre and moth-eaten puppets, was usually hired for the event, but this year he was unavailable owing to the fact that he was going into hospital to have a long-awaited hip replacement. George had offered his nephew Derek as a substitute, and Whipple was going to talk to him to sort out arrangements for the day.

The party itself was a tradition started by Sir Percival's grandfather to give local underprivileged children a bit of a treat. These days, of course, as the local children all lived in grade II listed houses bought by their parents with bonuses from their city jobs, this philanthropical gesture was rather redundant. The only time George's shows got exciting was when he swallowed his swozzle, which he did with predictable regularity, and the modern-day village children would have much preferred to stay at home with their Gameboys. Their parents too never really relished the occasion, with its customary offering of stale buns and curling sandwiches, but they turned up every year nonetheless, out of a sense of loyalty and community spirit, dragging their reluctant offspring behind them.

For the Trenchards, the occasion provided something to focus on, helping to keep their minds off their pressing financial problems.

As Whipple freewheeled out through the imposing entrance of the Hambledon Hall estate and on to the main road, a gold Rolls Royce drew level with him. The rear window slid down and Whipple heard a 'Psst! We need to talk.'

After glancing behind, Whipple applied the brakes of his Sturmey Archer gentleman's bicycle with optional wicker basket, and came to a slow and controlled stop. 'Mr Huxley,' he said, addressing the Rolls's open window, 'I believe Lady Trenchard made the situation perfectly clear when she last spoke to your accountant, Mr Smythe. Now, if you'll excuse me, I have business in the village.'

'Just tell me this, Whipple. I know Lord and Lady Bollocks haven't got a pot to piss in, so how come they're throwing lavish parties? What's going on? A little information would be well rewarded.' A podgy fist came out through the open window of the car, clutching a thick roll of banknotes. From a quick calculation of the amount being offered, Whipple reckoned he could feed the household for a month, have the curtains cleaned, get that annoying floor tile in the servant's kitchen fixed, replace the rotten guttering above the south terrace walkway and sort out that damp patch in the ceiling of the Gilt Room. But Whipple was far too loyal ever to stoop to accepting money from the enemy.

'I'm sorry, Mr Huxley, but neither I nor Hambledon Hall are for sale,' he replied haughtily. Gripping his handlebars firmly, and checking behind to see that the road was clear, he gave a crisp and unambiguous signal before moving off.

Harry relaxed back in the beige leather upholstery and brooded. 'Something's going on.' But what it was, he couldn't for the life of him work out.

From this strange encounter, Whipple now knew that it was Huxley, or at least one of his minions, that had been snooping around the Hall and frightening the Wuboobians. But that didn't really bother the butler; the visible spacecraft were now all safely under lock and key in the large double garage and the sneak, whoever he was, had probably been more frightened than the Wuboobians. Besides, who would ever believe his story? But Huxley's discovery of the ongoing party in the ball-room could prove problematic. If he found out precisely what was happening, there was no telling what mischief he might cause. Huxley's interference might somehow jeopardize the time anomaly itself and, despite his initial misgivings, Whipple was now finding it very useful. He had been busy every night transferring as much fine wine as he could carry from Elgin Huxley's nineteenth-century cellars to the Trenchards' empty and echoing twenty-first century vaults, supplementing their few sad bottles of Vins du Pays with fabulous first growths and unobtainable port vintages. And then there was the unstoppable Mary, churning out steak and venison pies for all she was worth. As long as the time anomaly remained in place the Trenchards could survive. Without it, they would be forced into liquidation sooner rather than later. No, Huxley must not be allowed to interfere.

Another effect of this meeting with Huxley was to drive the fact that he was supposed to be booking the Punch and Judy man right out of Whipple's mind.

Returning to Hambledon, Whipple was alarmed to see an ancient battered suitcase in the hall – the unmistakable property of Tom, the Trenchards' amiable, but none-too-bright, thirty-year-old son.

Tom Trenchard was a sports coach – a cricket coach to be precise – at a minor public school in Somerset. He'd started out teaching English and coaching part-time, but his shortcomings in the English department were soon uncovered when it came to light that he'd spent a whole term examining not Tennyson, but the lbw rule. The headmaster, himself a keen cricketer, sympathized with Tom's enthusiasm for the game and, instead of sacking him, kept him on as full-time coach and hired a new English teacher instead. Subsequently Tom more than repaid his headmaster's loyalty by pushing the first eleven to the top of the inter-school cricket league.

Tom was happy enough spending the summers doing what he loved most: playing and watching cricket. The rest of the year he spent tending the pitch: experimenting with different kinds of fertilizer on the wicket, trying to create the perfect hard but neutral surface on which to play England's gladiatorial summer game. For someone like Tom it was an almost perfect existence. But even cricket fanatics sometimes feel lonely, and for him the shine was beginning to wear off the new ball of bachelorhood. Unfortunately, none of the young girls he met in the pubs and clubs around the school showed the slightest interest in googlies and flippers. As each successive season drew to a close it became harder and harder for Tom to face the desolate loneliness of his life away from the wicket, and he longed for someone with whom to share his long, green summers.

Pulling up stumps at the end of term, the one thing that made the endless holiday stretching out before him seem almost bearable was the trip home to visit his parents, which he undertook every summer. A fact which, in all the recent excitement, Whipple had completely forgotten about.

'Damn!' Whipple muttered. Putting down the small bag of vegetables and picking up Tom's old leather suitcase, he was just about to tidy it away into an understairs cupboard when he heard voices coming from the kitchen.

Scampering down the stairs, he was horrified to see Tom in conversation with Mary who was, as usual, rolling pastry and chopping up chunks of raw meat.

'. . . Then, you see, Mary, when all the batsmen are out, the fielding side goes in and bats and the batting side goes out and, well, fields.'

Mary shook her head. 'It all sounds terribly complicated, sir.'

'That's a common misconception. It really is a most fascinating game.'

'You make it sound so, sir.'

Tom flushed slightly. 'I say, do I?'

Mary nodded, coyly.

'Well it helps to have such an attentive listener. And please, call me Tom.' He extended a hand.

'Step away!' Whipple yelled from the kitchen staircase.

Tom looked up, sharply. 'I say, Whipple, no need for that. I thought we'd done away with class barriers and all that sort of thing long ago.'

'No, Master Tom, you don't understand.'

'No, I don't think *you* understand. This fine young lady is highly versed in the almost vanished art of pie-making. Indeed, she has done me the honour of constructing me a steak and venison pie, and I, at least, intend to show her the respect and dignity her calling deserves.'

Whipple grabbed Tom by the elbow and pulled him clear of Mary, who, eyes cast down and cheeks pleasantly pink, carried on making her pies.

'What are you doing back here?' Whipple hissed.

'I live here,' Tom replied. 'Well, I used to. I know I'm more like Hambledon's twelfth man, but I still have a room, don't I?'

Whipple's manner softened slightly. 'Of course you do, Master Tom. It's just that things are a little . . . strained here at present.'

'Strained, how?'

Whipple looked into Tom's wide open blue eyes, at his tanned and almost completely unlined face, and wondered where to begin. With talking rats? Interstellar space travel? A wormhole connecting the estate with the other side of the galaxy? Whipple sighed. 'Have you seen your mother yet, Master Tom?'

For a moment Tom looked puzzled, as though Whipple had mentioned a member of the animal kingdom with which he was unfamiliar, then the penny dropped. 'Oh, *Mother*. Er, no, can't say I have. Why – are you looking for her?'

'No, Master Tom, but I'm sure she'd be delighted to find that you have arrived safely.'

'Oh, yes, good idea. I'll go and say hello and all that sort of thing.' Tom nodded enthusiastically, then added, unsurely, 'Is that what you mean?'

'That's precisely what I mean,' Whipple assured him, 'and please,' he added, indicating the area of his heart, 'try not to upset her, she's been through a lot lately. Best not to mention this little incident with the kitchen staff.'

Tom sighed. 'I suppose you're right. Mother always was a stickler for protocol. Off I go then.' Making his way up the kitchen staircase, Tom waved back to Mary. 'Very nice to have met you. We must get together again sometime and debate the legitimacy of the backward sweep.'

'I'd like that very much – Tom,' said Mary, provocatively.

Whipple threw her a furious look.

Tom grinned inanely. 'It's a date then,' he said. 'And by the way, I look forward to my pie. Oh, speaking of which,' he turned to Whipple, 'what time is luncheon these days?'

'One o'clock, Master Tom, as it always has been.'

Luncheon at Hambledon Hall was not the grand affair it had once been. Due to the fact that the great and very valuable Edwardian dining table had been sold long ago, and the Trenchards had been forced to replace it with something rather smaller that looked lost in the large and elegant dining room, meals were now served in the decidedly cosier confines of the drawing room. But, covered with a slightly threadbare damask tablecloth and laid with what remained of the silver, the mass-produced pine table really didn't look too bad.

'We weren't expecting you, Tom,' said Sir Percy, eyeing his son suspiciously across the table.

'Nonsense, dear,' said Lady Trenchard, 'Tom is always home at this time, to help with the children's party.'

'Party?'

Lady Trenchard rolled her eyes. 'The party for the village children. We hold it every year.'

Sir Percy looked confused. 'Do we?'

'Yes, Father,' said Tom. 'And a fine old tradition it is too.'

As Whipple entered the room carrying a serving dish covered with a silver dome, Lady Trenchard sniffed the air. 'Don't tell me,' she said, 'steak and venison pie.'

'That's remarkable,' said Tom. 'For a woman of your age, your olfactory senses are remarkably acute.'

Lady Trenchard bridled. 'A woman of my age?'

'Er, just an expression, Mother.'

Whipple laid the serving dish on the table in front of an expectant Sir Percy and uncovered it with a flourish. 'Steak and venison pie avec pommes de terres frites.'

Sir Percy peered at what had just been unveiled. 'Oh,' he said, crestfallen, 'it's pie and chips again, Pamela.'

Lady Trenchard looked up at Whipple, a pained expression on her face. 'Is Cook quite herself? It seems she's got rather stuck in a rut.'

'I think she is merely perfecting her technique, ma'am,'

'I think it looks splendid,' Tom enthused.

Gliding over to the sideboard, Whipple picked up a bottle of wine. 'I hope you don't mind, sir, but I took it upon myself to open one of the better bottles in honour of Master Tom's homecoming.' Whipple poured a small taste into Sir Percival's glass.

As the elder Hambledon sniffed the bouquet, he raised an eyebrow and shot Whipple a questioning glance. And when he tasted it, his palate went into paroxysms of delight. 'Good God, man, what's this?' Whipple revealed the label. 'Château Lafite 1882? Since when have we had nineteenth-century first-growth claret in our cellars?'

'I, er, stumbled across it just the other day, sir. I was doing a spot of tidying up and there, behind an old sewing table stacked with boxes, I found a forgotten bin.'

'You mean there's more?'

'Oh, there are . . . several bottles, sir.'

In fact, Hambledon's once draughty, echoing vaults were beginning to resemble the cellar of a top-class restaurant.

Over the next few days, despite Whipple's best efforts to keep them apart, Tom and Mary saw more and more of each other. When Whipple was otherwise safely engaged, Tom would sneak down into the kitchen with a copy of *Wisden* and extol the steady virtues of Bradman, sing the praises of the elegant Sobers and enthuse about the energies of Botham. Not once did Mary blench, nor request to be excused and never return: something that often happened to Tom on first dates. Instead, Mary listened intently to everything he had to say – she even seemed to be interested. For Tom it was like an epiphany and, over the marble pastry-table, through a haze of flour, he fell head over heels in love.

Chapter 23

Had Armani read the weather forecast earlier and known the state of the ancient lead flashing between the chimney stack and the roof above the Trenchard's living quarters, he might have saved himself a lot of trouble and stayed at home. For, twenty-four hours after his daring roof-top escapade, a band of heavy rain swept in from the Atlantic, and Tom Trenchard was awoken by a drip landing on the end of his nose. He sat up and looked around. Another drip hit him on the top of the head. Finally he looked up at the ceiling and got hit in the eye.

'Water,' he concluded. Getting up, he threw on his old tartan dressing-gown and trotted downstairs. Opening the back door, Tom peeked outside. The rain was bucketing down. Deciding it was too wet to go looking for the source of the leak, he was just about to duck back inside when he thought he heard music. Music? On a night like this? He looked at his watch. At two o'clock in the morning? This demanded further investigation. Pulling on a pair of wellingtons and unfurling an umbrella from the stand by the door, Tom ventured out into the dripping night.

'Fucking weather,' Harry Huxley muttered, standing under one of the beech trees lining the drive. He was dressed in a black, all-in-one catsuit, which cut uncomfortably into his crotch and made him look a bit like an anti-shipping mine.

'Maybe we better leave it,' Armani said nervously, making as if to go.

'No way,' Harry grabbed the back of his companion's cashmere polo-neck.

'Careful, Harry, this is new.'

'Show me the stables,' Harry growled.

Armani led the way up the drive and, with trembling hands, cautiously lifted the latch of the stable door. Pushing him aside, Harry yanked it open and clicked on a torch. In the bright, narrow beam it became quite clear that all the stalls were empty.

'Just as I thought,' he sneered. 'Farting sacks and fucking spaceships.'

'But they were here, Harry, honest. You got to believe me,' Armani protested.

'You better not be pulling my plonker, Armani. If there wasn't a ball going on here last night, it could have very serious consequences – for you.'

'Come and have a look. They won't have had time to clear up yet. You'll see.'

As they left the stables and crossed the yard in the pouring rain, Harry stopped. 'Hang on,' he said, 'what's that?'

Armani cocked an ear. Over the noise of rain hitting the cobbles, the sound of a waltz could just be heard. 'That's the same tune they were playing last night.'

Harry wrinkled his large forehead. 'Two balls – two nights running?'

The pair of them raced towards the Italian garden and, pulling on his Balaclava, Armani cautiously peeped through the hedge. 'It's happening again,' he said in amazement. 'Just like it did last night!'

'Get out of the way.' Harry pushed him roughly aside and peered through the neatly clipped box hedge. There, beyond a man dressed as a Pierrot and a near-naked woman going at it hammer-and-tongs in the small fish pond, the previously derelict ballroom was now flooded with light and thronged with people. But what was even stranger was the fact that in the Italian garden it wasn't raining. Harry pulled his head out of the hedge and looked up at the sky. On this side it was chucking it down, but on the other it was as dry as a bone.

Just then, a portly man appeared on the small balcony outside the brightly lit ballroom and started shouting at the top of his voice. The fat man bore a striking resemblance to King Edward VII . . . but that didn't make sense. Nothing about the scene made any sense at all.

Huxley turned back to Armani. 'Give us your Balaclava.'

'Why?'

'Just give us your Balaclava!' Ripping it roughly off Armani's cranium, Harry pulled it over his own head. 'Stay here and wait for me.'

'You're not going in there?'

'Yeah, it's been years since I had a good bop.'

Striding purposefully up the stone steps and into the great hall, Harry stepped into the nineteenth century. But, strangely attired as he was, he did not arouse any undue interest. After all this was a masked ball, and the guests were dressed in all manner of disguises. Except, of course, for the Prince and his entourage, who felt that such frivolous behaviour was beneath them.

Whipple, as was his wont of late, had set his alarm clock to rouse him at one a.m. and was now once again busy siphoning off the precious jewels of the nineteenth-century Huxley cellars and decanting them into modern-day Hambledon Hall's. So often had he performed this operation that he was beginning to feel quite at home among the upper crust of Victorian society – but tonight was destined to be different. On one of his trips between centuries, he happened to glance in at the study where the game of baccarat was taking place, and was alarmed to see an extra player at the table: the dressing-gowned Tom Trenchard. But before he could do anything about it, Whipple felt a heavy hand on his shoulder and spun round to face a fat man dressed all in black, wearing a Balaclava.

Harry Huxley raised his head covering and addressed the astonished butler. 'What's happening, Whipple? Where'd the Trenchards get the money for this bash?'

'You!' Whipple replied.

'Yeah. Come on, I want some answers.'

'Answers?'

'Or else the Inland Revenue is going to get a tip-off that they should take a closer look at the Trenchards' declared earnings – know what I mean? Come on, the truth.'

Whipple couldn't help smiling. 'The truth?' he said. In other circumstances he would have laughed in the man's face but, after his conversations with Glaak Raffin concerning the strange behaviour of wormholes and their attendant phenomena, he realized only too well the danger posed by Tom Trenchard or Harry Huxley interfering with the delicate web of space-time. Putting down the phenomenally rare bottle of Dow's 1845 vintage that he had just liberated from a passing footman, Whipple grabbed Huxley's elbow and shoved his nose into the crack between the wall and the just-open study door. 'Look, for a moment suspend your disbelief and just say that it's 1894. Queen Victoria is on the throne and her son, the future Edward VII, is still behaving like Jack the Lad. In fact, he's in that room now, watching a rather important game of baccarat.' Whipple felt the big man start. Taking his nose from the door, Harry looked at Whipple with incomprehension. 'I know, I know,' Whipple continued, 'but, trust me, it's happening. I have seen the Trenchards' bank statements and I can assure you they do not have the funds for this sort of do. Unbelievable as it seems, *you*, my friend, have just stepped into the nineteenth century.'

Harry looked back into the study and at the game of cards that was taking place there. The man smoking a cigar over by the window could have been an actor – stick a moustache and pointy beard on any fat man and he was almost guaranteed to win an Edward VII look-alike contest. Tom Trenchard, of course, incongruous in his tartan dressing-gown, looked exactly like Tom Trenchard. It was the sight of the other men seated at the table that made Harry jump, one of them in particular. The man dealing the cards bore more than a passing resemblance to someone in a portrait that his father had once shown him, but the face of the man opposite him – dressed in a waistcoat and breeches – was disturbingly familiar. That squashy, unshaped nose, the high forehead above small blue eyes set into an almost completely round face. Harry knew that face well – he'd seen it in his mirror only that morning.

'Yes,' announced Whipple, 'it's your great-grandfather, Elgin.'

Harry had the strangest sensation that he was no longer standing on the earth. Or, if he still was, it had suddenly developed the consistency of curd cheese. It seemed impossible that what he was seeing was true. But then, it all made sense: the lack of rain outside, the overnight restoration of a derelict building – the liveried footmen, the dancing . . . He turned back to Whipple, his eyes wide with fear.

'Please,' said Whipple, 'you have to believe.'

After several attempts to speak, a word finally made its way on to Harry's lips, 'How?' he said.

Whipple shook his head. 'We can't go into all that now. We have an emergency on our hands and we have to rescue the situation. We must get Tom out of there before he does any damage – or changes anything.'

'Changes,' Harry repeated slowly. The word hit one of his less overloaded synapses and stuck. After being hurled around his neural pathways like a pinball, firing neuron after neuron, several of his brain cells eventually got together into something approaching a coherent thought. A faint smile began to play around his lips. 'Changes,' he said a little more confidently. Now the immense possibilities inherent in the situation were beginning to dawn on his twisted mind. 'My great-grandfather hasn't lost the house yet, has he?'

'No,' said Whipple, as an alarm bell started ringing far off at the back of his own mind.

'Which means Trenchard hasn't won it yet. Which means there's still the possibility that he never even gets involved in the bet in the first place.'

The alarm bell in Whipple's imagination had now become a klaxon.

'I think,' said Harry, 'that we should just see what develops.'

Whipple considered the possible consequences. If Mortimer Trenchard never won Hambledon Hall, it meant that the house never came back into the Trenchard family, which meant that Elgin Huxley remained its owner, which meant that Percy Trenchard never inherited it, which meant that he and Lady Trenchard could very well have ended up inhabiting nothing more prepossessing than a semi in Tavistock.

'No!' Whipple said at last.

'Oh yes,' Harry smiled.

This was an appalling situation. Whipple watched as Master Tom won yet another trick. But something was wrong with Harry's logic. Whipple racked his brains for the answer and, after several agonizing moments, it came to him. 'Aha!' he exclaimed, making Harry jump.

'What's up with you now?'

Whipple pointed a finger at Harry's chest. 'You,' he said, 'cannot exist!'

Harry's brow crumpled. 'Eh?'

'If Elgin never loses the house, he never meets your great-grandmother in Plymouth, they never have a brief but fruitful liaison in the backroom of the Jolly Tar, she never gives birth to your grandfather and you are never born!'

As Whipple spoke these words, Mortimer Trenchard, after losing yet another hand to Tom, looked up at the Prince, who shook his head; it was pointless carrying on – Mortimer's scheme had backfired. Trenchard pushed his chair back from the table. 'Gentlemen, it's been a pleasure, but I must be off.'

Harry looked at his hand resting on the door frame and was seized by a quivering fear – he was fading! Even now his flesh was becoming transparent around the edges, like smoke around a bonfire. He gaped at Whipple in a panic. 'Look at me,' he said, 'I'm melting!'

Back in the twenty-first century, the downpour continued. What had started off as a small drip from the ceiling above Tom's bed had, as the storm continued, turned into a steady stream, and then a raging torrent. Lady Trenchard, in the adjacent room, was awoken by the crash of Tom's bedroom ceiling collapsing. Running next door to investigate, she was greeted by a scene of total devastation. Bits of sodden wood and plaster littered the floor and the counterpane and, looking up through the hole where the ceiling should have been, she could see the night sky above. Their buildings insurance was dependent on the roof being kept in a good state of repair which, of course, it had not. It was the end; there was no way they would be able to afford to patch things up after this latest disaster. Pamela Trenchard broke down in tears.

Assuming that her son had retired to one of the guest bedrooms, she herself sought refuge in her husband's bed, where she wept copiously on Percy's shoulder, while he stroked her hair and cooed, 'There, there, Pamela old girl. There, there.' The rest of the night the two of them snuggled together, reminiscing about all the good times they'd shared in the house. So many memories were locked up in that rambling, draughty old Hall. Now, perhaps, it was time to let them rest, and move on.

'I'll phone Huxley in the morning,' Pamela Trenchard sniffed, 'and tell him we're ready to sell.'

Harry and Whipple watched in dismay as Mortimer Trenchard and the Prince of Wales both left the study and walked past them into the great hall. As they passed, Whipple heard the Prince say to Trenchard: 'Tell everyone that we're leaving.'

'What're we going to do now?' Harry panicked.

'Think, got to think,' Whipple muttered.

'Well, hurry up. If you don't get a move on, they'll be down the stairs and away and I'll disappear in a puff of smoke!'

Whipple looked up. 'Down the stairs? Of course! Brilliant!'

'Eh?'

'Stay here, keep your Balaclava on, I'll be right back.'

'What about the Prince?'

'Stall him.'

'Stall him?'

'Tell him a story!' Whipple shouted back, as he raced away towards the kitchen stairs.

'A story,' Harry repeated. 'All right, I'll tell him a story.' He pulled down his Balaclava. 'Oi, hold up your highness!' Running across the great hall, Harry grabbed the future King Edward VII by the arm. 'You see, this drunk goes into a bar . . .'

Whipple had planned to nip down to the kitchen and pick up one of Mary's succulent pies to tempt the Prince to stay but, reaching the top step of the kitchen stairs, he had a thought which made him pause. Mary had only ever appeared in the kitchen during the day, and now it was the middle of the night. What if he went down there and found himself back in modern times? At the moment, Hambledon Hall was still in the hands of the Huxley family; its future undecided. If Whipple stepped back into the twenty-first century leaving things as they were, what would he find? Where would he emerge? If Percival Trenchard had never inherited the Hall, it was unlikely that Whipple could ever have been employed by him.

He studied the possibilities. Even when he left butling school the prospects for a man of his calling had been limited. The number of families up and down the country who felt the need of, or could even afford, a butler were precious few. Whipple might therefore step back into a very different future from the one he'd left. What if he'd ended up as desk manager of a hotel? The thought was too hideous to contemplate. He stared down into the well of the kitchen stairs, not knowing what to do.

But then again, thinking logically, hadn't he seen, this very evening, servants emerging from the kitchen carrying plates of food? Perhaps by staying within the time anomaly he too could remain in the nineteenth century. There was only one way to find out. He ran down the stairs, two at a time.

The kitchen was almost unrecognizable. It was packed with people, and great copper vats steamed on the large open range.

Well, that's one question answered, Whipple thought with relief. He searched the unfamiliar faces in the bustling kitchen until he saw her, removing a tray of freshly baked pies from one of the large ovens.

'Mary!' he called. 'Thank God. Give me one of your pies.'

Mary looked puzzled as the strange man ran towards her and grabbed one of her steaming-hot pies. For once, Whipple wasn't thinking straight. Too late he realized his mistake and dropped the searingly hot ceramic dish which fell to the floor with a crash.

'Ow, ow, ow!' Whipple danced around, trying to soothe his blistered fingers by tucking them in his armpits.

The noise had attracted the attention of a sinister-looking figure, his pale face contrasting starkly with his black butler's uniform. He glided across the stone flags as silently malevolent as a viper. 'What are you doing in my kitchen?' he asked.

'Sorry,' Whipple said, 'but I've no time to explain.' Gritting his teeth against the pain, he snatched a tea towel from a rail above the range and wrapped it around another of Mary's pies. Picking it up carefully, he was just about to dash back upstairs when the evil-looking butler stepped in his way.

'Where are you going with that?' he said.

'It's really none of your business,' Whipple replied. There was a sharp intake of breath from the other servants in the kitchen.

The sinister butler's brow darkened. 'I beg to differ. What

happens in my kitchen is absolutely my business. Now, put down that pie and tell me who you are, or face the consequences.'

The other servants had by now stopped what they were doing and were crowding round, waiting to see what would happen next.

Whipple considered his options. As he saw it he had two choices: a lengthy exposition concerning the strange phenomena accompanying wormholes and space travel in general – or violence. He chose the latter. Putting down Mary's pie with a smile, Whipple hit the man full on the jaw. Then, picking up the pie once more, he stepped over the fallen butler and headed back upstairs.

By the time he reached the grand hall, the Prince was backing down the front steps towards his waiting carriage, still being relentlessly pursued by Harry. '. . . so then the drunk says: "Well, if your lemons haven't got legs, I've just squeezed your canary into my drink." Get it? Here, I've got another one. This horse goes into a pub—'

'Your royal highness!' Whipple shouted.

The Prince looked up. 'Oh God, now what?' he muttered.

'Forgive me, sir,' said Whipple, running down the great stone steps and elbowing Harry out of the way, 'but Mary baked this especially for you. She didn't want you going on such a long journey without having something hot inside you.'

The Prince looked at him questioningly. 'Mary made this?'

'Oh yes, sir.' Whipple wafted the pie under the Prince's nose. The aroma of fresh-baked pastry mingling with the dark gamey scents of the underlying meat and rich gravy took a direct route to the royal's pleasure centres, and the Prince's salivary system went into overdrive. Whipple could tell he was wavering. 'May I suggest a bottle of Comtesse de Pichon Lalande to accompany it?'

That was the clincher.

'Very well,' the Prince drooled, 'perhaps Mary's right. Long journey and all that. Makes sense to line one's stomach for the road.'

'Absolutely, sir. If you'd care to follow me this way?' And Whipple led the Prince of Wales back into Hambledon Hall – by his nose.

Chapter 24

Just as they thought the bone-jarring ride was never going to end, the small spaceship shot out of the end of the wormhole, and once again Mariella, Falco and his poultry parent found themselves floating smoothly through open space. Ahead of them loomed a large planet with wispy white clouds floating above acres of sun-baked desert.

'That must be Alborg,' said Mariella.

'The wormhole to Gweeb is on the far side,' Falco informed her.

'Let's just hope that Matt was together enough to input the right coordinates.' But as she spoke the engines cut back in and the ship made a long, looping turn to avoid the planet's gravity field. Reaching the other side of Alborg, the main engines stopped and the occupants of the small ship heard the hiss of the thrusters as it made small course and altitude corrections. Then, startlingly, the blank area of space in front of them suddenly opened up, and once more they were hurtling down a long tunnel.

In stationary orbit around Alborg, Drikk Digit was just checking his route in his Planetary A to Z before diving down to Mrs Clunn's Home for Foundlings. 'Now then, Orion City . . . Orion City . . .' he muttered to himself, turning to the detailed maps of towns and cities in the back of the book. 'Ah, here we are. I always get this bit wrong. It's *left* at the Great Sea, continue straight on over the salt flats, bear right at the Hippian Desert, then it's first on the left by the uranium fields.'

Deep in his galactic atlas, Drikk was unaware of the small vortex opening up in the fabric of space-time right in front of him. The use of the wormhole in the near vicinity had stirred up all kinds of strange, whirling vortices in this region of space, and Drikk was about to get sucked right into one.

When he looked up again it was not to see the surface of a small, dusty planet. He found himself instead looking down a long, sparkling tube. *I don't remember this bit*, he mused. As he checked his A to Z once more, his old Drill-Scoter was drawn into the wormhole like fluff down a plughole.

After another jolting fun-fair ride through the neon-flashing tube, for a few moments, Mariella and the Nemesis family had the fleeting impression of scooting at tree-top height over a green and densely forested planet, then they were swallowed by yet another wormhole and their roller-coaster ride continued.

Circling high above Gweeb on his lonely mission, the bored pilot of the Crusader reconnaissance vehicle was surprised to see a blip suddenly appear on his radar screen and then, just as quickly, disappear again. 'What was that?' he said to himself. He checked his other instruments, but everything looked normal. 'It must have been a neutrino spike. Looks like the shielding on the plasma generator's ruptured – again.' He sighed and shook his head. 'The equipment we have to work with. Ah well, at least it'll give me something to do.' Pushing back his chair, he sat on the floor and undid the wing-nuts that held the inspection panel in place. Delving deep into the dense forest of wires, he located the plasma generator and, laboriously undoing the eighteen bolts that secured it to the bulkhead, slid it carefully out on to the floor where he proceeded to take it apart, piece by piece.

*

Whipple, having installed the Prince in the dining room with one of Mary's pies and a bottle of wine, then went in search of Harry. He found him nervously pacing the small balcony out- side the ballroom.

'There you are. I've been looking all over for you.'

'It's no wonder you couldn't see me. I'm disappearing fast.'

It was true. Harry Huxley's normally robust figure was becom- ing rather indistinct around the edges.

Whipple tried to calm him. 'We mustn't panic,' he said. 'The Prince at this moment is enjoying one of his favourite meals. As long as he remains here at the Hall, there is hope.'

'And how are we going to keep him here? Even *his* appetite must have a limit.'

Whipple hadn't quite worked out how exactly he was going to prevent the future king of England from leaving, let alone engineer things so that Hambledon Hall fell into Mortimer Trenchard's hands. But there had to be a way.

Tom suddenly appeared on the balcony. 'I say, isn't this fun!'

Huxley made a lunge for him, grabbing him around the throat. 'This is all your fault, you berk!'

'Who's your friend, Whipple?' asked Tom, with some diffi- culty.

After separating the two men, Whipple turned to Master Tom. 'We need to talk.'

'Absolutely, and then you can tell me what all this is in aid of. Mother and Father never mentioned they were having a party. Where are they, by the way?'

Whipple glanced at Huxley. 'I believe they went to bed early, Master Tom.'

'Shame, I wanted to show them this.' He pulled a sheaf of banknotes and IOUs from his dressing-gown pocket.

'What's that?' Harry asked.

'Beginner's luck. Baccarat's a wonderful game, you know.'

A lightbulb clicked on in Whipple's mind. 'You won that from Elgin Huxley?'

'Chap with a big face, squashy nose?'

Whipple nodded.

'Oh, so that's his name. Yes, there was another fellow, but he dropped a packet and left, so me and Elgin carried on for a bit. I'm afraid I left him sobbing into his port.'

'How much have you got there?' Whipple asked.

'No idea,' Tom said brightly. 'Poor chap got rather desperate towards the end and was asking all and sundry to lend him the necessary funds. Sad to say they weren't forthcoming; he's obviously blotted his copy-book around here, so I told him he could owe me the money.'

'Would you mind if I counted it?'

'Rather you than me, Whipple old man. You know what my maths is like.'

Whipple took the bundle from Tom's hand and began counting out the notes on the balcony balustrade. There was twenty thousand pounds in cash, and another fifteen thousand in IOUs.

'Thirty-five thousand pounds.' Whipple looked up at Harry. 'I do believe I've got it.'

'Got what?'

Whipple waved the sheaf of notes under Harry's nose. 'This is a huge amount of money to a Victorian. Now, we know for a fact that Elgin is already thousands in debt. He can't possibly hope to pay off his creditors and honour these IOUs in his lifetime, but what if we offer him a way out?'

Huxley screwed his eyes up tight, like he always did when figuring out a particularly vicious property deal. 'Carry on,' he said.

'We waive the IOUs and, with the cash offer to pay off all his debts, put him in the clear. All he would have to do is play one more hand at baccarat.'

'Oh, I don't think that's on,' said Tom. 'Chap's not got a brass farthing to his name.'

'No,' said Harry, catching on, 'but he has got rather a nice Hall.'

Tom looked confused.

'Master Tom,' said Whipple, 'I ask you to trust me now like you have never trusted me before.'

Tom smiled lopsidedly. 'You know I trust you Whipple. I always have.'

'And I am extremely grateful for that, sir. Unfortunately there is no time to explain everything now, but the whole future depends on this one hand of cards.'

Tom frowned. 'I'm not sure I follow.'

'It is rather a complex situation. What we need to do is to borrow your winnings.'

'Oh, I see. Well, I don't see but . . .'

'It's called "baiting the hook",' Harry added.

'Quite so,' Whipple said.

Tom shrugged. 'Very well. Bait away.'

'Thank you, sir.'

With the Prince still completely immersed in his epicurean task, Whipple went straight to Mortimer Trenchard and put the scheme to him. Trenchard was hugely attracted by the idea, if a little curious as to why a man he had never met before wanted to help him win the Hall.

'Let's just put it down to professional reasons,' Whipple told him.

While Whipple and Trenchard went in search of Elgin, Harry slipped into the study. To make sure that things went according to plan, he was going to 'fix' the deck of cards to favour Trenchard. In the process he dropped some and, stooping to pick them up, noticed several more cards stuck into small cracks in the underside of the table on the side where Elgin had been seated. 'He couldn't even cheat well,' Harry sighed.

It pained Harry deeply that he should be a party to removing Hambledon Hall from his own family's grasp, but he cast all doubt aside about this when he noticed that he could now dimly make out the cards through the flesh of his hands. Having completed his little job, he went in search of Whipple to tell him that everything was set.

Elgin jumped at the slim chance of being able get out from under his crushing burden of debt. To make sure that everyone understood what was at stake a solicitor was found – the damp Pierrot from the fish pond – and instructed to draw up a document that stated clearly the terms of the game, so that there could be no reneging on the deal. For this one hand of cards it had been agreed that there would be no 'bank' and that the best hand would be the instant winner. To keep matters absolutely above board, a 'disinterested party', in the shape of Harry Huxley, was chosen to deal the cards. Once everything was in place, the two men took their seats around the green baize.

The tension in the room was palpable. The solicitor placed the document he had hastily drawn up in the middle of the table, alongside the pile of banknotes and IOUs.

'Gentlemen,' he said, 'do you agree to be bound by the terms of this contract, as witnessed by those here present?'

'Aye!' nodded Mortimer Trenchard with a smile.

Elgin downed the last of his port and reached for the bottle, only to find that it was empty. 'Snagge!' he called. A tall, thin butler with a bruise spreading across his chin appeared at his side. 'Bring me another.'

Snagge lowered his head and whispered something in Elgin's ear.

'The entire cellar?'

Snagge nodded.

'Dash it all, man! There's nothing left?'

Snagge shook his head.

'Hah!' Elgin laughed grimly. 'Very well. I accept the terms.'

Everyone, with the exception of the Prince, who was still finishing off his pie, had crowded into the small room to watch.

Elgin, exploring the underside of the table with his fingers, discovered that all his cards had been removed. He glanced up in terror into the eyes of Harry, who shook his Balaclava-covered head in gentle remonstration as he pretended to shuffle the cards.

Four cards were dealt. Trenchard was the first to reveal: a five and a four – a 'natural'. With trembling fingers Elgin turned over his cards: a six and a three – another natural. It was a tie. Whipple looked sharply at Harry, who stared dumbly back; he seemed to be on the verge of tears. What had gone wrong? Then Whipple caught sight of the smugly smiling Tom, and guessed immediately. Pushing through the crush of spectators, Whipple grabbed hold of the lapels of Tom's dressing-gown. 'What have you done?' he spluttered.

'Your friend was in here earlier,' Tom whispered, 'I peeped in and saw him doing something fishy with the deck. I didn't think it was cricket, that's all, so I shuffled the cards.'

Whipple could hardly watch as the next hand was dealt, and now it wasn't only Elgin who was trembling; Harry too was visibly shaking. Mortimer, as steely as ever, turned over his cards . . .

Chapter 25

Finally the bright flashes of the inside of the wormhole were replaced by blue sky and the sturdy trunk of a tree dead ahead. The thruster brakes cut in automatically and the ship thumped down into the bottom of the ha-ha, coming to rest a few feet from the large horse-chestnut.

'Looks like we're here,' Mariella announced.

'Squawk!'

'Calm down, Mum, you'll soon be free-range.'

Mariella hit the door release. It opened with a *hiss* and the soft and subtle scents of the English countryside filled the ship's cockpit. Falco was the first to scramble out.

''S different,' he said, surveying the acres of green grass and the crowded clumps of tall, elegant trees.

Falco's mother jumped down next and began scratching and pecking contentedly at the ground.

'Well at least *she* seems happy,' Mariella observed, getting out and joining them. She looked around. 'Now I've got to find Glaak.'

She didn't have to wait long. Soon, scurrying eagerly towards her, came the Chief Custodian of Argus and chairman of the Galactic Alliance Council. 'Mariella!' he squealed excitedly. 'You're alive!'

She crouched to greet him. 'Am I glad to see you.' She tickled Glaak tenderly behind the ears and he closed his eyes and nuzzled her wrist.

'Where's Matt?' he asked eventually.

The sudden tears in Mariella's eyes told him the whole story.

'Oh dear . . . Oh dear, oh dear.' He laid a small paw gently on her finger. 'I am sorry.'

'Squawk!'

Glaak looked up at the chicken that loomed over him, eyeing him suspiciously. 'I don't think we've been introduced,' he said.

Mariella wiped her eyes. 'Oh, er, this is Falco's mum.'

'How do you do?' Glaak said uncertainly.

'And I'm Falco.' The youth knelt down to say hello and Glaak's eyes went immediately to the black rectangle he held in his hand.

'The Cartogram, you've got it!' Leaping excitedly in the air, Glaak ran to Falco and seized it, gratefully.

'Without Falco we wouldn't be here,' Mariella explained.

'Really?' said Glaak vaguely, all his attention focused on the Cartogram.

'Yes, he can read the Cartogram.'

Glaak looked up sharply. '*Read* the Cartogram?'

Falco smiled.

Glaak regarded the youth with renewed interest. 'How do you know how to read the Cartogram?'

Falco shrugged. 'Dunno, just do.'

'Show me.' Glaak handed the smooth black rectangle back to Falco, who took it and immediately began to stroke it with his long fingers.

'Good God,' Glaak gasped as a representation of the solar system flickered into life above the youth's hands. 'Extraordinary.'

''S not that difficult, really,' Falco said, modestly.

'Really? It took me years to get to grips with it,' Glaak said faintly. 'Oh well, come on, no time to stand about. I must call a meeting of the Council. We have to get to work: organize; plan; make strategies.'

'There's one more thing.' Mariella stood and went back into

the spaceship. A moment later she reappeared cradling Zach in her arms.

'What's that?' Glaak asked.

'Zach E. Loomis.'

'What in God's name are you doing with Zach Loomis?'

'It's a long story, but the point is, Matt said there was something lodged in Zach's memory that would blow you away.'

Glaak was puzzled. 'I thought his memory was scrambled long ago.'

'Matt seemed to think it was really important,' Mariella insisted.

'Oh, very well. I'll get our technical team to look at it.' He tapped the Cartogram gently with his claws and hugged it to his chest. 'But *this* . . . what a relief.'

Towed along in Mariella and Falco's wake, Drikk had been pulled through a parallel wormhole vortex which had dumped him in the compost heap at the back of Hambledon Hall. Emerging from his Drill-Scoter, white-faced and shaken after his ordeal, he looked around. Although he only made one trip a year to Alborg, this wasn't how he remembered it. Alborg was dust-dry and hot as hell, whereas this place was cool and green and pleasant. And the orphanage – he recalled it as a small wooden shack in a dust bowl of a yard, not a large, stone building with a columned portico standing in acres of lush parkland. As he was pondering this strangeness, a tall woman he'd never seen before came out of the house and walked towards him.

'Can I help you?' Lady Trenchard enquired.

'Ah,' said Drikk, 'I'm—'

'Oh, of course, forgive me. You must be Derek, George's nephew. How do you do.' Lady Trenchard extended her hand. Drikk took it automatically.

'Your uncle has told me all about you,' Lady Trenchard continued. 'George's show is very popular with the children; I hope you're as good as he is. Come along, I'll show you where to set up.'

Drikk, still confused from his recent experience, but hearing a couple of words that seemed to make sense: *show* and *children*, assumed, against all evidence to the contrary, that he was in the right place, that somehow the orphanage had been completely transformed and that this lady, whoever she was, had taken over the running of it. Wrestling his trunk from the boot of the Drill-Scoter, he followed her meekly inside.

Once the delegates of the Galactic Alliance were assembled, Zach was handed to a technician – a young Gleek called Coyle O'Flexx – and Mariella, Falco and his feathery parent were introduced in turn to the Council. Of course Glaak had first to seek the Council's permission by formally proposing a motion that the 'strangers' be allowed to enter the hallowed space of the Council chamber.

The Grublins had no objections, but then they never objected to anything: they hated warmth and just wanted to get the meeting over as soon as possible so that they could retire to the relative cool of their cold water tank.

Unfortunately the Galazion delegation protested in the strongest terms to the admittance of the outsiders, and a heated debate ensued.

'I move we allow them to watch, but afterwards cut off their heads,' said the Mufflet, bouncing his own head off the ceiling.

'I agree with my colleague,' said the Glubbus. 'I see no reason why they shouldn't watch as long as they cannot later divulge Council secrets. I move we allow them to stay and afterwards cut out their tongues.'

'Pluck out their eyes!' said the first Florean.

'Pluck their eyebrows!' said the second.

'Give them a full facial!' said the third.

'The admittance of strangers,' said the Duppy, looking slyly sideways at its other head, 'might tempt certain delegates to "play to the gallery" and thus deflect them from the seriousness of our business here.'

'Are you talking about me?' said its other head.

'Yes,' the first head snapped. 'You'd show off shamelessly.'

'I object. Withdraw that immediately!'

'I stand by what I said.'

'Oh, do you?'

'Yes!'

'Then stand by this!' With that, the Duppy head-butted itself and fell over.

Eventually, after more tedious and pointless discussion, the motion was carried and the newcomers were allowed to stay *and* remain intact.

At last, the Council settled down to the main business of the day: the implementation of Glaak's plan, but not before the Ning Thong delegate had proposed a motion to debate exactly what form the debate itself should take.

Glaak vetoed the motion. 'It seems to me, gentlemen,' he said, wearily, 'that the only question we should be addressing is where, initially, we attack Filch's empire.' Immediately all the delegates started shouting at once, each one loudly promoting his own planet as the ideal spot to launch a first strike. As the room erupted with self-interest, Falco wandered over to the corner where Coyle O'Flexx was connecting up Zach to a laptop computer.

'How's it going?' Falco asked.

'Nuffin' yet. Look.'

The laptop's screen looked like a blizzard, and white noise emanated from the small speakers.

'And that's an improvement,' said Coyle. 'I just got a blank screen from the remote broadcastin' probes, but after solderin' a couple of leads to 'em it looks like there might be somfin' there. I think his batteries are low.'

'What's all them numbers on the bottom of the screen?' Falco asked.

'Frequency modulator,' Coyle replied. 'I been through 'em all though, and got nuffin'.'

Falco sat down next to him. 'D'you mind if I have a go?'

'Be my guest.'

Falco stroked the computer mouse tenderly with his sensitive fingers. Under Falco's gentle persuasion, the pointer at the bottom of the screen moved slowly along the line of numbers like a needle along a radio tuning dial. Suddenly, over the speakers there came a sort of a click and something blipped across the screen.

'What was that?' exclaimed Coyle. 'Go back.'

Again Falco stroked the mouse, gently, gently, ever so gently . . . The blizzard began to coalesce into a picture and the white noise became focused into a single tone. The picture too suddenly came into sharp focus – it was an image of a young girl, holding a rag doll, playing noughts and crosses on a toy blackboard.

'That's it!' yelled Coyle. 'We've got it. We're in! Whee-hoo!'

One by one, the delegates around the table ceased exercising their vocal chords and looked towards the corner where Coyle was whooping excitedly. Eventually, Glaak got down off the table and scurried over to him.

'What the hell are you doing?' he asked, outwardly furious that they were not giving the Council the respect it deserved, but secretly relieved that they'd managed to temporarily silence the argumentative delegates.

'Sorry, General,' said Coyle, 'but look, we've got a picture.'

Glaak looked at the picture of the young girl. 'That's it? That's what all the excitement is about?'

'Nah,' said Coyle, 'but now we know what frequency he's broadcastin' at we can start stimulatin' his ganglia with all kinds of shit: short waves, long waves, microwaves, you name it.'

'Very well, carry on,' Glaak replied. 'But try and keep it quiet,' he added with a wink.

'We will, General, sorry,' Coyle replied.

'Yeah, sorry,' echoed Falco.

Chapter 26

Bound and gagged, Matt was escorted from the newly landed flagship, bundled into a waiting armoured personnel carrier and driven at high speed into the centre of Cullorum City. He knew where he was going: the arena. *Oh well*, he thought, as the vehicle bounced over the cracked and rutted streets of the capital, *at least I'll make it spectacular. I'll go down in a blaze of organza . . . or something. And maybe I'll take a few stelions with me.*

There were no windows in the back of the personnel carrier but, from the steadily rising volume of the sound of the baying arena crowd, he could tell they must be getting near. It was an awful, inhuman noise and, although he was now resigned to his fate, Matt couldn't stop his heart rate rising rapidly.

At last the vehicle stopped and there was the clatter of boots on tarmac. The door opened and sunlight flooded into the back of the vehicle, making Matt squint. Rough hands grabbed him and hauled him out into the bright day, and he was led through the quiet midday streets towards the huge hulk of the arena which dominated the centre of the city. The cheers and shouts of the crowd echoed down deserted avenues and alleyways, reverberating with a strange electric resonance, the sound doubled and redoubled by the bare brick walls of the surrounding houses. Looking up, Matt saw the great vault of the heavens arching overhead, clear and serene, with not a cloud in sight. *What a day to die*, he thought. Then the bright-blue of the sky was abruptly replaced by the dull, rough concrete roof of the arena stage-door entrance.

'Name?' the stage-door keeper enquired.

'Mmf,' Matt mumbled into his gag. Neither of his guards made any attempt to remove it.

The stage-door keeper, an old, wrinkled Sinesian whose movements were slow and measured, stuck his head out of the small hatch in his glass booth and cupped a hand to his ear. 'I'm sorry, you'll have to speak up. Name?'

'Mmf,' Matt repeated, a little louder.

'Nah, still can't get it,' the stage-door keeper's head withdrew back into his booth like a tortoise's retreating into its shell. 'Tell you what,' he said, picking up a battered clipboard, 'I'll put you down as a guest artiste.'

One of the guards thrust a letter at him. The Sinesian took it and studied it carefully.

'Ooh, you're the special,' he said, raising an eyebrow. 'We know all about you. We've had a command from himself, no less, to make sure you get exceptional treatment.' Clearing his throat, he bent his head towards a small microphone, and his voice reverberated around the miles of backstage corridors: 'Could someone from Wardrobe come to the stage door immediately, please. That's someone from Wardrobe, please. Thank you.' Removing a key from a board behind him, the Sinesian offered it through the hatch. 'The number two dressing room,' he said, as if handing Matt the key to Paradise. 'I can't give you the number one; that's reserved for visiting clerics of unapproved faiths.'

Matt took the key in his bound hands.

'Now it's just been redecorated, so it might smell a bit of paint. They've done a lovely job though: all silk hangings and draperies. Just a couple of things: the shower's not plumbed in yet, and they haven't quite sorted out the air-conditioning. But you can always open the window. And will you be taking any fruit?'

'Mmf?'

'Fruit,' the Sinesian repeated. 'You see, there's a basket of fruit provided, but there's a charge per piece if you want to eat any of it.'

Matt shook his head.

'Very well. I think that's about it. If you've got any worries at all, just give me a shout. My name's Paul, but everybody calls me Eric. Oh, and one more thing: please don't pee in the sink. Nothing personal, but we had a load of Bwellburbians in last week and they pulled the bloody thing off the wall.'

'Mmf,' Matt said again.

'Don't mention it.' The stage-door keeper pressed a button under his desk and the door alongside his booth hummed open. 'Now, if you go through there and wait over by the coffee machine at the foot of the stairs, someone will be along in a minute to look after you.' He turned back to Matt's guards. 'It's all right, you can leave him with us now.'

They nodded and left, their duty done.

Matt went through the door and entered the backstage world of the arena. As he'd been bidden, he took up his position over by the coffee machine. There was a Post-It note stuck to the front of it: OUT OF ORDER. On one side of the machine a concrete staircase curved away upwards, and on the other was a set of double doors bearing the sign: STAGE ONLY. NO ACCESS TO OTHER SIDE OF ARENA. Beyond this was a corridor leading off into the gloom. The two-tone brown and white walls were slightly damp to the touch, and the place had a peculiar smell: fear and make-up.

As Matt waited, people came and went along the corridor and *thumpa-thumpa-thumped* through the double doors, while high up above his head a tannoy relayed an audio feed of the action in the arena. There was the growling of a great beast followed by the sudden, sharp, desperate cries of its opponent who, Matt guessed, had just lost this particular 'bout'. The cheering of the crowd was so loud it distorted the sound from the small speaker.

Lost in terrifying visions of life-and-death struggles with fearsome monsters, Matt never even heard the scuffing of shoes on concrete as someone descended the stairs.

'Hello, my name's Alasteer.' Brought suddenly back to earth, Matt looked up into a pock-marked face under short bleached-blond hair.

'Hmm mmf!' Matt said.

'Oh, hasn't he taken that off?' Alasteer glanced over at the stage-door keeper. 'He's a bit of an old fart,' he said, *sotto voce*.

The Sinesian looked up, 'I heard that.'

Alasteer removed the gag and Matt was once again able to move his jaw.

'Thank you,' he said, relieved. 'I'm Matt.' He offered up his bound hands.

'I know who you are, silly.' Pulling an outsize pair of shears out of his back pocket, Alasteer cut through the binding.

Matt massaged the blood back into his fingers.

Alasteer led the way up the stairs. 'Come along then. Now, Sylv's pulled out a few things for you to try but, I mean, they're only suggestions. Anything you don't like we can always change. You've probably got your own ideas. I mean, it's you that's got to perform. Here we are.'

They were on a half-landing outside a door that had on it a five-pointed gold star above a brass nameplate which read: *Fllingg Pillich*.

'He was useless,' said Alasteer. 'Didn't last five minutes.'

Matt gave him a wan smile.

'Should be your name up there now, though. I'll have a word.' He knocked at the half-open door. 'Are you ready for us, Sylv?'

The reply was a fit of coughing, followed by a rasping, 'Come in, come in.'

The room was small and, although it stank of paint, still looked shabby and in need of redecoration. The once lush red carpet was worn to the backing in places, and the 'silk hangings and draperies' were no more than bits of old material stapled around the functional dressing-table, and a fringe of soiled lace above the full-length mirror. The walls were bare and a naked lightbulb hung limply from the ceiling. The only other decoration in the room was a gilded basket of fruit on the window-sill, its contents quietly decaying beneath a cellophane wrapper.

In the centre of the room, surrounded by an assortment of armour, cloaks and leather accessories, stood the wardrobe mistress: thin, middle-aged, in skin-tight jeans, her black hair streaked with grey and a lit cigarette dangling from her lip.

'Hello, I'm Sylveenia. Call me Sylv,' she announced huskily.

'Er, how do you do?' Matt replied. 'Matt Fripp.' He held out his hand and she grabbed it and pulled him to her, kissing him on the cheek and depositing cigarette ash in his ear.

'Now then, how had you seen your character? Noble slave?' Sylv held up a worn cloth garment and a pair of old sandals. 'Or rebel with a cause?' Stooping, she scooped up a leather breast-plate, short sword and bronze greaves.

'Rebel with a cause, definitely,' said Matt.

'That's what I thought,' she agreed. 'Pop these on then, love. Now, do you think you'll be wearing your helmet, or just carrying it on with you for the look of the thing?'

'Er, well, I think I'll need as much protection as I can get.'

'That's what Alasteer's always telling me,' she chuckled wheezily.

Alasteer went beetroot red. 'She's terrible. And it's not true. I'm a good boy. Sometimes.' They both dissolved in fits of laughter.

Alasteer scrabbled around at his feet and started strapping on the greaves, and Matt pulled the breastplate over his head, admiring his reflection in the full-length mirror. The leather armour gave him wide shoulders and made him look strong and muscular, and the one bronze greave that Alasteer had already fitted accentuated the bulge of his calf. Even the small wound that Gulgus had inflicted on his cheek added to the picture, and immediately Matt began holding himself erect and proud – like he imagined a warrior would stand.

'Stop there, Ali,' said Sylv. 'I like that. What do you think?' she asked Matt.

'Sorry?'

'Just the one greave. I think it gives you a purposeful air, you know? Sort of stripped down and ready for action.'

Alasteer stood to take in the effect. 'Mmh, yes, I see what you mean. It's much more, well . . .' he hesitated.

'Go on, say it,' Sylv urged.

'More butch.' They both looked at each other and giggled like schoolgirls.

Turning back to Matt, Sylv took another drag on her cigarette. 'Sorry, dear,' she coughed. 'It's up to you, of course, but bear in mind you have to balance the protection another greave would give you against the extra weight. You're going to be doing an awful lot of running around.'

The stark simplicity of the phrase brought home to Matt the hideousness of his coming ordeal. 'Yes, yes, I suppose I am,' he muttered.

'The same goes for helmets,' Sylv continued. 'This one' – she heaved a great metal bucket with a full-face visor off the floor – 'can easily withstand the crushing jaws of an enraged stelion, but it weighs a ton.' Returning it gratefully to the floor, she picked up another. 'Whereas this, although it won't help you a lot if you get stuck in the stelion's jaws – I mean, to be honest, your skull would be crushed like a grape – it *will* deflect a glancing blow from a talon, *and* it's as light as a feather. It's up to you.'

Looking at himself in the mirror, Matt noticed that he'd turned rather pale. 'Do you, um, mind if I think about it?'

'No, love, not at all. I'll leave them both here and let you decide. Now then, as for *below the waist*, we can give you a simple leather jock-strap, but I rather like those shorty trousers of yours. Do you have any objection to wearing your own stuff?'

Matt shook his head.

'Good. Can I just try something?' She bent and pinned the excess material of his Bwellburbian trousers, so that they fitted close around his thighs. 'That's better. But those boots' – she indicated Matt's 'lucky' footwear – 'will have to go.'

Alasteer shook his head. 'Can't mix suede and leather, dear me no.'

'I think that's it, then,' said Sylv. She pursed her lips and studied Matt for a long time. 'Can I make a suggestion, dear?' she said in a confidential tone. 'A little bit of body make-up wouldn't go amiss. What do you think, Ali?'

Alasteer nodded. 'Hmm, and maybe a spray of glycerine to catch the lights.'

'Yes! I'll drop by later and sort you out. When are you on? I don't think it's until the second half.' She picked up an itinerary from the dressing-table and, holding it at arm's length, squinted at it. 'Here we are. The second half kicks off with Crusaders versus Infidels, then it's mass slaughter of the innocents; ensemble dance number; execution; execution; execution . . . Ooh, you're the grand finale. Well, we'll have to make you look a bit special, then. Don't worry, dear, there's plenty of time.' She started gathering up discarded costumes and handing them to Alasteer. 'There's a pile of sandals over in the corner. Choose whichever feel comfortable. I must dash, I've got to dress a troupe of sacrificial virgins: they're closing the first half.'

'What's a virgin, Mummy?' Alasteer asked in a baby voice.

'There are very few of us left,' Sylv replied, mock serious.

They both giggled again.

'Come on,' said Sylv, 'back to work.' Pausing in the doorway, she turned back to Matt. 'Don't worry, you'll be marvellous, darling.'

Alasteer winked. 'Break a leg.' And then they were gone.

Matt stared at his reflection in the mirror and suddenly thought how foolish he looked.

Chapter 27

The mood in the Council chamber was growing even more confrontational. The debate had been going on for nearly three hours now, and the only thing they'd decided was what time they should break for tea.

'Gentlemen,' Glaak pleaded, 'if we can't reach some sort of a decision soon I'm going to be forced to dissolve the Council. Then it'll be every man for himself. Is that what you want?'

There was dark muttering from the delegates.

'Do I have to remind *you*, General Raffin,' said the Glubbus, 'that your powers, such as they are, are bestowed upon you by the Council, which, I might add, retains the right to strip you of them at any time. After due process, of course.'

'Hear, hear!'

'Strip him of his powers!'

'Strip him of his rank!'

'Strip him of his trousers!'

Mariella could stand it no longer. She rose to her feet in a fury. 'A good man died just so we could bring you the Cartogram!' she snarled.

The delegates all stared at her in shock. Glaak looked up and gently shook his head, but she was in no mood to stop now.

'Don't you cretins understand what's going on? Safe and smug here in your little chamber in what may be the last safe house in the galaxy, you seem to have forgotten that there's a war on! People are dying out there. You've got the Cartogram, so come on, make a fucking decision! Start your offensive.

What's at stake here is far more important than your precious little careers. We're talking about the universe! We have to act. We may fail, but if we sit and do nothing it's an absolute certainty that we're all going to die. I know Filch and what he's capable of. Once he's conquered the galaxy, he won't stop there. He'll go on until he has *everything*. The time for discussion is over, so put aside your petty differences and be guided by those who have your best interests at heart. Glaak Raffin is one of the finest generals in the business. Listen to him, I beg of you.'

Mariella sat, handing the floor back to Glaak, who raised his eyebrows appreciatively towards her. But before he could speak, the Glubbus piped up yet again.

'I move that the testimony of that woman be struck from the record. Why should we listen to someone who has been sleeping with the enemy for the past six months?'

The chamber erupted yet again. Mariella was on her feet in a flash, and the Glubbus's life was saved only by a strange noise emanating from the corner of the room.

'Whee-hah! Yahoo! Yippee! Yes! Yes! Yes!' Coyle and Falco were on their feet, jumping up and down excitedly. The delegates stopped shouting at each other, and all turned to look. Glaak scampered over to the pair.

'What is it?'

'We're in!' said Coyle. 'We've cracked it. Look, he's operational.'

Glaak stared at the screen of the laptop wired into Zach's brain. The image of the small girl by the blackboard had been replaced by that of a gawky, awkward boy cuddling a toy Graggle hound. As Glaak watched, the picture changed again: to that of a big, angry man behind prison bars. Then came a torrent of images cascading on to the screen one after another: strange, nightmarish visions of death and monsters. But suddenly, among all the chaos, there was a crystal-sharp image of a large Gologon wearing make-up and a floral print dress. Although he only got a fleeting glimpse of it, Glaak knew immediately what it was. 'Good God,' he breathed. He turned to Coyle. 'Will you be able to access these images again?'

'Oh yeah. It's all a bit of a mess at the moment, but once we've de-fragged his hard drive we'll be able to call any of this up anytime we want.'

For the first time in years, Glaak's spirits began to rise. Now he had something he could work with. 'Mariella, come quick!'

Mariella reluctantly dropped the Glubbus back in his chair and joined Glaak at the laptop.

'Look at this,' Glaak, pointed at the screen.

It was a bit like watching a surreal art-house animation film; none of it made sense, except for the occasional image that seemed to linger on the retina just that little bit longer. Especially one of a large Gologon being paddled by a woman in black leather. 'Wow!'

'We've got him,' crowed Glaak. He looked back at the delegates and a slow smile spread across his face. 'Watch this.' Clambering back up on to the Council table, Glaak reared up on his hind legs. 'Gentlemen, I hereby dissolve the Council.' The delegates looked at each other in stunned silence for a moment. The Mufflet even put his head back on. Then a worried-looking Mingley nervously tabled a motion questioning General Raffin's authority to dissolve the Council, and the delegates happily settled into another debate.

Glaak hopped down off the table and scuttled back over to the small group in the corner. 'Let's leave them to it.' He turned to Mariella, 'That ship you arrived in, will it get us to Cullorum?'

'Doubtful. Matt said we had barely enough power to get here.'

'Never mind, we'll take the Glubbus's – he won't miss it for a while. Come on, and bring Mr Loomis.' And he led Mariella, Falco and his mum, Coyle and Zach out of the chamber.

Lady Trenchard, her face drawn, led Drikk into the formal dining room. 'This is usually where we do it,' she said, waving a hand around the large, empty room. 'We haven't had cause to use this room for years. It's not ideal, I know, but at least it's dry.' She bit her lip, stifling a sob, and produced a handkerchief from the sleeve of her cardigan. 'Sorry,' she said, dabbing her eyes, 'but we had a bit of an accident last night and I'm afraid I didn't sleep awfully well.'

'Oh,' said Drikk, at a loss. 'Well, that's . . . hmm.' They both stared at the floor for some moments.

Lady Trenchard broke the deadlock by walking over to the French windows opening on to the gardens. 'These let in rather a lot of light, I'm afraid. I don't know if that's going to be a problem?'

'No, that's where I'll build the Thrringg wall. If I set up opposite, it'll make a great place for the entrance of the wolf – right behind the audience.'

Lady Trenchard had no idea what he was talking about. 'Yes, quite so,' she nodded. Moving back into the centre of the room she looked earnestly into Drikk's face. 'We must think of the children. They look forward to this all year, you know. You won't disappoint them, will you? You see, it's very important that this show should be absolutely tip-top.' Tears welled up in her eyes again. 'I'm sorry,' she said, 'will you excuse me a moment?' and she made a hasty exit.

Left alone, Drikk looked around at his unfamiliar surroundings, and even *his* slow mental processes were now beginning to suspect that perhaps he wasn't on Alborg, the dust bowl of the Andromeda system. But wherever he was, it was obvious that he was expected and that children were on their way. The performer in him wasn't about to disappoint his audience and, opening his trunk, he began to set up.

Matt waited, shivering, in the wings. He knew what was coming. For the past hour he'd watched the previous 'acts', which consisted either of men hacking each other to pieces with swords and pitchforks, or helpless souls trying to escape from monstrous creatures against which they had no chance. Now the long show was reaching its conclusion, the bright day had turned to starlit night and, once the present fight was over, it would be his turn.

Just before he'd been brought down to arena level, he'd had a meeting with the director. 'Whatever you do, keep moving,' he'd been told. 'The whole thing falls terribly flat if you just stand there. The audience wants to see fighting spirit; that's what they've paid for. We need to at least create the *illusion* that you stand a chance. So give them a bit of a show. Let's have lots of ducking and weaving. This is theatre, remember, they want action, drama, conflict! Go out there and give 'em hell. And above all, smile.'

Matt rated the odds of his survival at around two hundred to one against. *I hope Glitch has got a bet on the stelion*, he thought. But, even if Matt did the impossible and succeeded in killing the creature, there were trained gladiators stationed at every exit with strict instructions not to let him leave the arena alive. He'd often wondered how a condemned prisoner on the scaffold felt as the rope was placed around his neck. Now he knew. In his fantasies, facing such a moment, he'd always been full of bravado, cracking jokes with the crowd, laughing in the face of death. The truth, he now realized, was somewhat less romantic; knowing the hour and manner of one's death was truly terrifying.

Through a small window in the massive wooden door set in the wall of the arena, Matt watched the drama reach its climax on the bloodstained sand beyond. The two gladiators who'd been slugging it out for the past ten minutes were both tiring. One of them, dripping blood from a thousand cuts, looked ready to drop. His rival, sensing victory, reached down into his last reserves of strength and slashed out with his long pikestaff, catching the other one under the chin and knocking him to the ground. Standing over him, the soon-to-be-victorious gladiator raised his pikestaff high.

The crowd went wild. 'Kill him! Kill him!' they chanted. 'Kill! Kill! Kill! Kill!' The gladiator, covered in sweat and gore, heart pounding, chest heaving, stood poised. He glanced up towards Gulgus's box, and the Gologon smiled and gave a slight nod of his head. Looking around the vast arena at the baying crowd, the gladiator prolonged the moment, heightening the drama. Then, with sudden, shocking violence, he plunged his pikestaff into the man's chest. The crowd roared its approval.

Matt had seen death before, but never in such a cold, calculated fashion. This was simply murder. Convulsed by a spasm of fear, he dropped his sword and it clanged to the ground.

'Shh,' the stage manager warned, 'you'll ruin his exit.'

'Sorry,' Matt mouthed, stooping to pick up the blade.

He stood aside as the door leading on to the stage was opened and the fallen combatant was hauled into the wings by stage hands. The victor, enjoying his moment of triumph, remained in the centre of the arena, taking the applause.

'Tch!' The stage manager shook his head. 'Milking it again.' He looked at his watch. 'We'll be here all night at this rate.'

Eventually the victorious gladiator clattered into the wings, flushed with success. 'How's about that then?' He beamed at the stage manager.

'Go on, bugger off to the bar. Some of us still have a show to do.' He nodded in Matt's direction.

The gladiator turned to Matt and put a hand on his shoulder. 'They're a great crowd – you'll have a ball.'

'Mmhmm,' Matt mumbled. He felt as though his knees were about to give way.

'Knock 'em dead!' the gladiator added, slapping Matt cheerfully on the back. He walked off into the backstage darkness, undoing his breastplate as he went.

'You're on next,' the stage manager said. 'Wait to be announced, then on you go.' He turned and spoke into a small microphone. 'Cue smoke machine. Stand by: limes; LX cue 307; and stelion holding area.'

Matt felt a tap on the shoulder. Swinging round, he was confronted by a man in evening dress holding a script. 'How do you want to be announced?' he asked.

'Eh?'

'Is it plain Matt Fripp; Major Matt Fripp; Matt Fripp the Rebel? What do you want?'

'Um, oh, just plain Matt Fripp will do.'

'OK.' The man smiled and took up his position at a backstage microphone. On a cue from the stage manager, and reading his script in the light spill from the arena, the man announced the next act. 'Ladies and gentlemen, we now come to the grand finale of this, our three hundred and fifteenth Colon-Eze Games. Do you wake up in the mornings wondering where your get-up-and-go got up and went? Are you troubled by trapped wind; bloating? Is the visit to the smallest room in the house not the easygoing event it used to be? Take Colon-Eze – it removes blockages faster than a charging stelion. (*Consult your doctor if pregnant or suffering from a heart condition. May cause drowsiness; do not drive or operate heavy machinery if affected. Colon-Eze may contain traces of nuts.*)'

'Stand by,' the stage manager warned.

The announcer looked up at Matt and winked. 'And now the moment you've all been waiting for . . .' The arena was suddenly plunged into darkness and a fanfare of trumpets sounded. '. . . The highlight of our show. You've read about him in the papers; you've pored over his exploits in the magazines. Now, here he is in the flesh. For one night only we give you the darling of the tabloids – Matt Fripp!'

The darling of the tabloids? Matt wondered. But there was no time to think. He felt a hand in the small of his back. 'Go limes,' was the last thing he heard before being thrust out of the wings and on to the vast stage of the arena. The wooden door slammed shut behind him and spotlights snapped on, picking him out of the darkness. He was blinded by the sudden light and deafened by the cheering of the crowd. To add atmosphere, the arena had been filled with smoke, swirling eerily around up to the level of Matt's waist. It was a bit like being caught in fog with a growth deficiency.

As his eyes gradually became accustomed to the light, Matt peered around. The crowd was on its feet. Remembering the director's instruction to 'give the audience what they've paid for', Matt responded by parading through the waist-high smoke, his sword held high. *Well, at least they seem to be on my side*, he thought.

But the moment the gate of the stelion holding pen crashed open and the huge creature made its bellowing entrance, it became obvious where the crowd's loyalties really lay. They went wild, throwing their seat cushions in the air, whistling and stamping.

I see, Matt thought.

Looking up at the huge beast towering above him, he had a strange feeling of looseness in the rectal area and began to shake violently, dropping his sword once again. 'Oh fuck.' Stooping to retrieve it, he realized for the first time that he had an unexpected ally: the smoke now hid him from the stelion's view. Appreciating suddenly that the contest might not be so completely one-sided, Matt's courage returned and he began to plan some sort of strategy.

If I can get close enough to do it some damage, I might still be in with a chance.

Peering up through the shielding smoke, Matt kept his eye on the hideous creature and worked his way around behind it. As the puzzled stelion scoured the white and seemingly empty arena for its prey, Matt got down on all fours and crawled right underneath its vast bulk until he was in striking distance of the soft, unarmoured tissues of its belly. The stelion, meanwhile, remained blissfully unaware of the extreme danger it was in.

Lying beneath the awesome animal, Matt was caught once

again by an attack of trembling fear. *Oh fuck, oh fuck.* Willing his muscles to work, he gripped the hilt of the sword with both hands and with a supreme effort thrust upwards. The stelion answered with a deafening roar, its half-digested lunch of vanquished gladiator falling out of the newly-opened gash in its stomach and landing sludgily on Matt's head. *Ach, shit, bugger!* Matt rolled away across the smoke-shrouded sand and knelt to wipe gladiator guts out of his eyes.

The audience, their vision of the bloodshed obscured by smoke, booed their disapproval. The stelion slumped to its knees, head drooping, to survey the damage Matt had inflicted upon it. Licking the wound gently for some moments with its rasping tongue, the enraged animal then uncoiled its long neck and hungrily searched the arena with wild, bloodshot eyes, looking for the creature that had dared to do such a thing.

Although he was now some way distant, unhappily for Matt the smoke was thinning and, as he cleared the last of the entrails from his eyes, he looked up to see the stelion fix earnestly on him. *Now we're in trouble.* The wounded stelion, moving at a speed Matt thought impossible, was suddenly on top of him, lunging at him with steak-knife claws. Matt got out of the way just in time and the audience cheered at the resurgence of their favourite.

Yeah, great fucking audience, Matt thought, *if you happen to be covered in spines. Well, fuck 'em. I'll give them a show to remember.*

Matt stood and faced his opponent. 'Come on then!' he yelled. 'Let's see what you're made of! How do you feel about getting another length of cold steel up your insides, eh?'

The stelion regarded him with its mean, evil eyes. It was obvious this new turn of events was not to its liking – *it* usually called the shots.

'Come on!' Matt stamped his feet and slapped his sword against his small shield.

Realizing that it had no alternative but to play along, the stelion lowered its head and charged.

As the huge beast thundered towards him, the ground beneath Matt's feet began to shake. At the last moment Matt dived out of the way and the stelion passed by harmlessly. But reaching the far side of the arena, it turned and came in again without a pause. *That thing's got stamina*, Matt thought with dismay.

As the stelion was almost on top of him a second time, Matt dodged left and extended his sword arm, slashing sideways at the creature's head. The animal roared in pain and pulled up sharply: Matt's blade had sliced through its eye. Sitting on the sand, the stelion rubbed fretfully at its bleeding orb with a front foot, giving Matt some much-needed thinking time. *Good. If I can stay on its blind side I may actually be able to survive this encounter. The guards at the exits I'll think about later.*

The stelion, now severely annoyed, stood up slowly and turned back towards its opponent. With its sightless eye and blood-smeared face, it looked uglier than ever. Seeing the intense hostility burning in the creature's one surviving eye, Matt began to appreciate that the battle wasn't over yet. The stelion lowered its bloody head and charged again. Matt waited, feinting from side to side, but the stelion, ever watchful, kept his image right in the middle of what was left of its vision – it wasn't going to be caught out again.

The stelion was almost upon him now. Raising his sword, at the last second, Matt stepped to the creature's left, planning to slash down on its neck, but the beast swept its head sideways and its nose horn connected with the blade. Matt watched as the sword flew out of his hand and landed with a soft thud on the sand, thirty yards away.

Oh bugger!

The stelion came to a sudden standstill and turned to face its adversary. It was breathing hard and in pain, losing blood rapidly from its stomach wound. But soon it would have its revenge, and it seemed to be relishing the moment.

Everyone's a fucking performer, Matt thought. *Well it's not over till the fat lady sings*. He glanced sideways towards where his sword lay. The stelion followed his gaze then looked back at him. It seemed to be daring him to try for it. *OK, if that's what you want. Let's make this a great finale.*

The combatants faced each other for some moments. Any small movement that Matt made, the stelion echoed. Then, in an explosive burst of energy, Matt raced away across the sand. The stelion fixed him with its good eye and took off after him at terrifying speed.

It was like a nightmare: Matt was running but didn't seem to be getting anywhere. He felt as though he was moving through mud, the sword remaining impossibly out of reach. Meanwhile, the stelion was closing fast. 'Shit! Shit! Shit!' Matt could feel its hot, snorting breath on his neck. He wasn't going to make it.

In preparation for the *coup de grâce*, the thrust with its nose horn that would put an end to this annoying insect, the stelion pulled back its head.

Straining every sinew, his thigh muscles aching with the effort, Matt sprinted for his still-distant blade as the stelion uncoiled its neck and lunged.

Craning desperately forwards, Matt stumbled and fell. The stelion's great horn flashed in the artificial light as it scythed through the insubstantial air. It had missed!

Spitting sand out of his mouth, Matt looked down at his feet. The laces of his boots had come undone and tripped him up. *Way to go, guys!* But, glancing quickly around the arena, he saw that his sword still lay far out of reach. The stelion, however, was standing right over it and, as Matt watched, the creature stepped deliberately on the blade, snapping it in two. *Now* it was over. The wounded animal roared in triumph, then lowered its head and charged in for the kill. Closing his eyes, Matt braced himself for the lethal impact. This time his boots couldn't save him.

But the final death shock never came. Eventually registering that the arena was no longer trembling in time to the pounding feet of two tons of highly mobile cutlery, Matt opened an eye. The previously wildly cheering crowd was now mutedly muttering, nudging each other and pointing up at the large vid-screens dotted around the seating tiers, which relayed the action down in the arena in graphic close-up. The stelion stood over Matt, looking bemusedly up into the crowded tiers of seats, somehow aware that its fans were no longer engaged in the contest, and unwilling to continue the bout until he had their full attention.

What was going on? Searching for the answer, Matt's eyes eventually came to rest on one of the vid-screens and, with heart-opening gratitude, at last he understood.

There, for all to see, was the unmistakable form of Gulgus Filch, wearing a floral print dress and putting on lipstick like a fourteen-year-old girl.

More images followed: Gulgus's large grey behind being soundly spanked by someone dressed head to foot in black leather; Gulgus wearing a bikini; Gulgus being led on a chain like a dog; Gulgus tied to a bed . . .

After a burst of feedback, Glaak Raffin's voice boomed over the arena's PA system. 'Ladies and gentlemen. What you see on the vid-screens is real. These images have not been tampered with in any way; what they show actually happened. While you were on your knees in prayer, or your husbands, sons and daughters were laying down their lives in battle for this man, this is how he repaid your devotion, by flouting every religious stricture he has ever imposed upon you!'

As more and more uncharacteristically secular pictures of their devoutly spiritual leader flashed up on the screens, the mood of the crowd became noticeably more hostile. A few began to laugh, but they were soon silenced by their fellows.

'Be oppressed by this hypocrite no longer,' Glaak continued, his voice echoing around the hushed arena. 'The time is ripe – rise up and overthrow this tyrant!

Matt looked towards Gulgus's private box. The Gologon was on his feet, dodging flying seat cushions while shouting at the audience. 'It's a trick! I would never behave in such an ungodly manner! This is a vile plot by our enemies!' But the crowd clearly wasn't buying it, and Gulgus was beginning to panic. Now they were throwing more than cushions – an egg suddenly hit Gulgus on the forehead. He screamed at his personal guard to find the culprit, but even they had turned their backs on him. Laying down their arms, they regarded him with disgust. It was over. In a matter of moments Gulgus had lost not only the trust of his people, but also his entire empire.

Got you!

Now other figures began to file into the leader's box – one was a figure Matt knew well, though it took him a little while to work out who it was. But eventually wonderful, warm realization dawned, and he jumped up and down, yelling, 'Mariella! Mariella!'

She returned his greeting, smiling and waving. She even blew him a kiss. Then . . . it all seemed to happen in slow motion. Even as Matt watched, Gulgus's grey arm slid around Mariella's neck and in his other raised hand something glinted in the light – the blade of a knife.

'No!'

Completely ignoring the stelion, which now lay on the sand, dazed and confused from blood loss, Matt ran across the arena and stood beneath the tyrant's box.

'Gulgus! Let her go!' he screamed.

Gulgus looked down at him and growled, 'Fripp, this is all your fault.'

'Damn right!'

'And now she will suffer the consequences of your actions!' Gulgus took a firmer grip on Mariella's neck and placed the tip of the knife to her breast.

'Wait!' Matt yelled. 'Killing an unarmed woman is the act of a coward, not a galactic ruler. Let her go, Gulgus. You know this isn't your style.'

But Gulgus had a wild look in his eye.

'Come on, Gulgus, it's over! Wake up to the facts! Put down the knife and let her go.'

The others in the box – Gulgus's ex-personal guard and a small force of rebel soldiers gathered hastily together by Glaak – all stood around helplessly. But Glaak himself, unseen on the floor, was working his way around behind Gulgus, planning to jump him – or at least create a diversion.

'What will killing Mariella prove? It certainly won't save your skin,' Matt persisted. 'Use that knife and you're dead. Let her go and I guarantee you a fair trial. The worse that could happen is exile to Delta-Origon 15. Would that really be so bad?'

'I have no wish to waste away on a glorified asteroid. I'll die right here, and I'm taking her with me.'

'No!'

As Gulgus's hand tightened around the hilt of the knife, Mariella struggled desperately, throwing him slightly off balance. Stepping back involuntarily, Gulgus trod on Glaak's tail.

The general let out an anguished scream. 'OOWW!'

Startled, Gulgus momentarily looked down. It was all Mariella needed. Powering her elbow into his stomach, she grabbed the arm wrapped around her neck and pulled hard, simultaneously dropping to her knees. Gulgus went flying through the air and tumbled over the rim of the box.

He landed heavily in a shower of sand at Matt's feet. Slightly dazed by the fall, Gulgus looked up into Matt's triumphant face.

'Hi,' said Matt.

'OK,' Gulgus mumbled, reaching out towards him. 'You win. Give me a hand up.'

'Oh no,' said Matt, 'I'm not falling for that one. I'll watch you from here.'

Gulgus struggled to raise himself up, but it seemed that his right arm was useless; he kept falling back, grimacing in agony.

Matt couldn't help himself. 'What's up, old buddy? Hurt yourself?' But as he leaned forwards to help, Gulgus struck out with his 'bad' arm. Matt felt a thump in his side, and looked dumbly down at the hilt of the knife protruding from the fake musculature of his breastplate. 'Oops,' he said.

'Matt!' Mariella leaned anxiously over the edge of the balcony.

Sinking to his knees, Matt grasped the knife and pulled, slowly withdrawing it from the thick leather of the breastplate. It came out clean. He held it up for Gulgus to see.

'Hey, Gulg. You missed me.'

To the jeers of the crowd, Gulgus rose to his feet and began running away across the sand. 'It's over, Gulgus!' Matt called after him. 'Give up!'

Seeing every exit blocked by a well-armed gladiator who had just swapped sides, Gulgus turned back to Matt defiantly. 'I'm not finished yet, Fripp. I will rise again! Elron *will* one day unite the universe, I promise you that! You have merely postponed the event, for what Valohem wills *must* come to pass!'

But now the stelion, roused by all the racket, was beginning to take an interest in the noisy grey thing standing right in front of it. Raising its large head it gazed down at Gulgus, ranting on the sand.

'Gulgus, behind you!'

The Gologon smiled and shook his head. 'You can't catch *me* like that, Fripp. Unlike you, I'm not stupid.'

They were the last words he ever uttered. For, craning forwards, the stelion neatly nipped off his head as if picking a grape from a bunch, then threw it high in the air, opened its huge mouth wide and swallowed. Gulgus's head rolled down the creature's oesophagus – only to reappear through the gash in its stomach and thump on to the sand.

The creature looked confused. It had just eaten, and yet wasn't experiencing that usual, comforting feeling of satiety. Baffled, and tired now because of the gallons of blood it had haemorrhaged on to the arena, the creature lay down and closed its eyes.

Matt looked down at Gulgus's head lying, sightless, on the damp red sand. 'Somewhere along the line, you must have really pissed Valohem off,' he muttered.

'Matt!'

He turned and was greeted by the most beautiful thing he had ever seen. Mariella stood, arms outstretched towards him, a slight breeze ruffling her hair.

Wordlessly, he stumbled towards her and fell into her arms. There, on the bloody killing field of the Cullorum arena, they kissed. Matt felt like he'd come home. The war was over. Of course, it would be some time before things were back to normal. There were bound to be groups of fanatical Elron terrorists roving the galaxy who couldn't accept that they'd lost. But it was a new beginning, not only for Matt and Mariella, but for the galaxy, the universe itself.

Mariella looked up into Matt's eyes. 'Come on, let's go somewhere a little less public. I need to . . . debrief you.'

Matt smiled. 'That could take some time.'

'Hmm, I hope so.' She ran her hand appreciatively over the fake muscles of his breastplate. 'And you can keep this on.' She grabbed his arm and led him out of the brilliance of the arena into the backstage darkness.

The crowd meanwhile, in an ugly, revengeful mood, was scouring the arena for members of Gulgus's inner circle. But in the confusion following the sudden and unexpected dissolution of the empire, two figures escaped the attention of the angry mob. One, indeed, was almost impossible to make out with any clarity, and the other, though a distinctive dark form with more than his fair share of limbs, was at present unknown to the vast majority of the populace.

'Through here,' Glitch hissed.

Rhinn Sloane, a satin cape wrapped tightly around him, was trying to follow the Dastorian down a service passage leading under one of the arena's seating blocks, but it wasn't easy; Glitch was flickering like a candle flame in a hurricane.

'Where are you?' Rhinn demanded.

'I'm still here,' Glitch replied testily. 'Keep up!'

'I'll keep up if you stay visible. It's like following mist.'

'Shh!'

They had come to a door marked: ARENA STAFF CHANGING. Glitch opened it carefully.

'What's that?' Mariella put her hand to Matt's mouth as the door to their hiding place opened and two figures crept into its dimly lit interior.

'What are we doing *here?*' Rhinn asked.

Glitch unhooked two sets of overalls from a row of pegs on the wall and handed one to Rhinn.

Rhinn stared at it. The back of the garment was emblazoned with the message: *Colon-Eze is proud to support the Cullorum Arena* in large, luminous orange letters. 'Oh no,' said Rhinn, 'I never wear off-the-peg.'

'Put it on,' Glitch urged, stepping into his.

'But it won't fit me.'

'Just drape it over your shoulders and tie the legs around your waist. So long as the logo's visible, people will accept you as a member of staff. No one ever looks closely at the cleaners.'

Rhinn didn't like it, but did as he was instructed.

'Come on,' Glitch urged once Rhinn had wrestled the garment on. But as the two fugitives prepared to leave the small changing-room, they found their way barred by the form of a gladiator. 'Well, well, well,' said Matt, placing the tip of his sword against Rhinn's belly, 'who have we here?'

Glitch spun round and found himself looking into Mariella's eyes. Flickering madly, he appeared to dissolve, but Mariella was quick. Darting out a hand, she grabbed a handful of his overall and pulled him to her, placing the barrel of a pistol to his neck.

'You and I are going to have a nice little chat, McGilvray.'

The Dastorian swallowed hard.

Having handed Rhinn and Glitch over to the tender care of Glaak's rapidly growing force of Galactic Alliance soldiers, Matt and Mariella then went in search of Glaak himself. They found him overseeing operations from Gulgus's private box. He was perched on the back of an ornate gilt chair, instructing one of Gulgus's erstwhile personal guards.

'Very well, Lieutenant, I think our first priority has to be public order. If you can get the men together and calm every-one down that would be a great help.'

The lieutenant saluted crisply and marched out of the box.

Glaak looked up as Matt and Mariella entered. 'Ah, there you are. What have you two been up to?'

They looked at each other and smiled.

'Oh, silly question,' said Glaak. 'Now look, there's loads to do here, but I left Earth in rather a hurry, and I'd like to pop back there to make sure everything's all right. I should really return the Glubbus's spaceship and, besides, I never said good-bye to Whipple.'

'What did you do with Zach?' asked Matt. 'I'd like to pay my respects.'

'Ah,' said Glaak.

'He's not the man he once was,' Mariella warned him.

Falco and Coyle were in the projection room unhooking Zach from the arena's video system. To enable them to interface more easily with him, the two youths had rigged up a portable audio communication system which allowed them to converse freely with the long-lived creator of Loomis Land.

'Where are we?' Zach asked.

'Um, it's a sort of theatre,' Coyle informed him.

'Theatre? What's the show? Is it a musical? I love musicals.'

Falco and Coyle looked at each other.

'Not exactly,' Falco replied. 'It's more a kind of . . . improvisational thing.'

'Oh,' Zach sighed. 'I never was a fan of experimental theatre. When's the interval? Is there going to be ice cream? Once my mom took me to see the Alvorg Bunny show. In the interval we had caramel tutti-frutti with white chocolate and cinder toffee. Do you know the Alvorg Bunny tune?'

Coyle and Falco had a feeling that they soon would. 'Er, no,' they admitted.

'It goes like this: "Oh, here comes the Bunny, the Bunny, the Bunny . . ."' It was obvious that Zach's three-hundred-year-old circuits had become even more confused by recent events, and he was now deep into his second childhood – although at his age it could easily have been his third, or fourth.

'"He's Alvorg the Bunny, the Bunny, the Bunny.

Is he a monkey, a monkey, a monkey?

NO! He's Alvorg the Bunny, the Bunny, the Bunny . . ."'

Falco and Coyle were just beginning to wonder if it had been such a good idea to rig Zach up with speakers when Matt, Mariella and Glaak came into the room.

'Good job, boys,' said Matt. 'Hi, Zach.'

'"Is he an ostrich, an ostrich, an ostrich?

NO! He's Alvorg the Bunny, the Bunny, the Bunny . . ."'

'Um,' said Falco, looking pained. 'What do you want to do with him?'

'Glaak,' said Matt, 'didn't you say you needed to nip back to Earth?'

'Yes.'

'I've got an idea.'

Chapter 28

By the time the children started to arrive, Lady Trenchard was in a much better frame of mind, although feeling slightly concerned about the whereabouts of Tom and Whipple. She hadn't seen either of them all morning and, when breakfast hadn't materialized with its usual punctuality, she stepped into the kitchen to discover not her butler but a young, flour-covered maid who introduced herself as Mary. Confused, and having to make do with yet another steak and venison pie for breakfast, she hoped that Whipple hadn't suddenly decided he'd had enough and jumped ship. She wouldn't blame him, of course. But where could Tom have got to?

When Whipple still hadn't turned up half an hour before the party was due to begin, she concluded that he wasn't coming back. Distressing as this knowledge was, she still had a party to host, and focused her mind instead on the rather large amount of cash that Harry Huxley had offered for the Hall, and the possibilities that would open up. Although Huxley too seemed to have disappeared – she'd been calling him all morning without success.

After instructing the equally confused Mary to make a pot of tea, Lady Trenchard went to greet her guests. The children were a mixed bunch, ranging in age from three to nine, but what united them all was a tremendous desire to be somewhere else – which they shared with their parents. Seating the grown-ups on a row of chairs at the back of the room, Lady Trenchard organized the children into a rough semicircle in front of where Drikk had set up his equipment.

Drikk's set consisted of a backdrop of stars and moons, a table on which were several boxes full of assorted balloons, and in front of this a small wooden chest with an elaborate gilt keyhole and hinges. On either side were two miniature speakers and in front again, a three-legged stool, below which lay a small mat, which Drikk had given Lady Trenchard strict instructions not to let the children go anywhere near, as this hid the control panel for all his 'magic' stunts.

'Now then,' said Lady Trenchard once they were all seated. 'Can everyone see?'

'Yes,' the children chorused unenthusiastically. Under strict instructions from their parents not to misbehave, they sat sullenly on the floor, desperate for the ordeal to be over.

'Good. Well, first I'd like to welcome you to Hambledon's annual children's party. As you all know, this event has a long history, but I'm afraid, due to circumstances beyond our control, this will have to be the very last one.'

'Awww,' went the children, secretly relieved. Likewise, the adults adopted attitudes of concern and shook their heads in feigned disappointment.

'I know, it's very sad, but a large country house like this demands a lot, both in physical and financial terms and, at our advanced age, I'm afraid my husband and I no longer feel up to the challenge. So we have decided to bow to the inevitable and move on. We would like to thank all of you for the many kindnesses you have shown us over the years, but don't think you'll be getting rid of us completely. This has always been our home, and so it is our wish to remain in the area. We hope to find somewhere nearby, but of more modest proportions. It will be a wrench, but all things must pass, progress marches on and we must keep in step.' Her eyes were glistening. 'But I've wittered on long enough.' She looked down at the children. 'I expect you're all eager for the show to begin.'

The children stared up at her blankly.

'Unfortunately, George wasn't able to make it this year and so, fittingly perhaps, we've got something a bit different for this, our final party. And now, without further ado, I'm going to hand over to Digit the Clown!'

As Lady Trenchard left the 'stage', the lights dimmed and strange music began to emanate from the small speakers. This particular number was currently top of the hit parade back on Drikk's home planet, and sounded a bit like someone being hit over the head with an iron bar while a cat wailed in the distance. Digit entered, wearing his threadbare clown's costume and ancient wig. 'Hello kiddies,' he waved. 'My name's Digit!'

'Hello, Digit,' the children dutifully answered.

That's a first, Drikk thought, seating himself on his stool and placing his feet gently on the mat hiding the electronic controls. 'Now, I'm going to make something for you. See if you can tell me what it is.'

Taking two long balloons, Drikk inflated them, twisted them together in the middle and made a little bulb on each of the four ends. He held the resulting construction up for all to see. 'Any ideas?'

The children shook their heads.

'It's a flying moothon from Sneeal, of course!'

There were a few knitted brows and questioning glances among the audience, but when Drikk set the moothon spinning and it took off and flew around the room, few remained unimpressed.

The children were immediately entranced. This wasn't the usual boring old Punch and Judy show. 'Wow!' they went.

'Did you like that?' Digit asked.

'Yes!'

This is a great audience, Drikk thought.

'Would you like to see something else?'

'Yes!' they chorused.

'OK.'

Next, Drikk transformed four long balloons into an alien landscape complete with palm trees, sparkling water and animals. 'The oasis on Sprulle!' he announced. Throwing a small round balloon up into the air, he clicked his fingers. The balloon lit up and hovered over the strange scene. 'By moonlight!' The trees began to wave and the animals moved down to the water hole to drink. It was startling. The adults sat, mouths agape, while their children looked on, spellbound.

Upstairs in the servants' quarters, the newly dissolved Galactic Alliance Council had slipped into a bemused silence. With Glaak not there to orchestrate proceedings things had become very confused indeed, and now none of the delegates had the slightest idea which of the many motions that had been put forward they were supposed to be debating.

'Um . . .' began the Mingley, nervously, 'Shouldn't morning coffee have been served by now?'

'Custard creams!' said a Florean.

'Jammy dodgers!' said another.

'Custard creams *and* jammy dodgers,' said the third.

'I move,' said the Glubbus, 'that we adjourn the meeting and go in search of sustenance!'

'Hear, hear!'

For once, the other delegates agreed without argument, and rose as one.

As Whipple, Tom and Harry all emerged, blinking, into the daylight, and stumbled down the stone stairs of the Hall into the Italian garden, they looked back at the elegant Victorian soirée they had just left. The ballroom was once more deserted and derelict; the gilded ceiling under which couples had glided to the latest waltzes was now scattered damply across its dull and worm-eaten floor. Needless to say, the second round of cards that Harry had dealt favoured Martimer Trenchard, to the great relief of everyone, with the exception, of course, of poor, dispossessed Elgin.

Tom, his brow crumpled into a frown, looked up at Whipple in confusion. 'Um . . .?' he began.

Whipple merely shook his head and smiled.

'Right,' Tom nodded.

Turning to the rotund form of Harry Huxley, Whipple looked him in the eye. 'That was very noble of you, Huxley.'

'Bollocks,' Harry replied sadly, removing his Balaclava. 'I didn't have a choice, did I?'

'Nevertheless, it took courage to do what you did.'

'Whatever.'

Whipple glanced at his watch. 'Good lord!' he exclaimed. 'Will you excuse me, gentlemen, but I have a rather important meeting.' And he hurried off, mysteriously.

Tom took Harry by the hand and pumped his arm vigorously. 'A great pleasure to meet you. Do please drop in if ever you're passing this way again.'

'That's doubtful,' Harry muttered.

'Must be getting along.' Tom hurried off after Whipple, eager to find out if Mary was still around.

Wandering out of the Italian garden Harry found Armani fast asleep where he had left him, under the box hedge. Harry nudged him with his foot.

Armani was instantly awake. 'Where have you been?' he asked blearily.

'Hell and back. Get the Roller, we're leaving.' Harry slumped down beside him and stared glumly at the ground.

'You all right, Harry?' Armani said softly.

'Just get the car. I'll stay here.'

'Oh, right.' Getting up, Armani dusted down his linen and silk mix trousers, and set off down the drive.

Harry looked up at the nobly rotting hulk of Hambledon

Hall with tears in his eyes. 'I gave it away,' he sobbed. 'I just gave it away.'

Drikk had been a little worried about the size of the room and the range of his now ageing electronics set-up. But, so far, the transmitters and holographic projectors seemed to be working all right.

'Now then,' said Digit, 'would someone like to help me?'

Drikk searched the eager young faces through the forest of raised hands. Girls were best; they did what they were told, unlike boys who had a tendency to get their fingers into things they weren't supposed to.

'How about you?'

She was a small, timid-looking child with glasses.

'Come on, come up here.' She got up slowly and squeezed her way through the other children. 'Stand there, dear – and don't move.' Drikk grabbed her and stood her beside him, making sure her feet were just clear of his mat. 'Now then, tell us your name.'

'Amy,' she said, shyly.

'That's a very pretty name,' said Digit. 'And because you've got such a pretty name, I'm going to give you something very pretty, to tell people who you are.' Reaching behind him, he pulled something out of a small sack and, after fiddling with it for a few seconds, placed it on Amy's head. It was a hairband with the word 'Amy' on it in flashing lights. She was delighted.

Next, Digit inflated a balloon and handed it to her. 'You hold that a second, Amy, because I'm just going to get another one so I can make something.' As Drikk turned round and pretended to look for another balloon, he pressed lightly on the mat with his left foot. The balloon Amy was holding immediately transformed itself into a Lappett snake from Tarmidian 4. Amy shrieked, and the other children all called out.

'Look! Look!'

Digit spun back round. 'What is it, what is it?'

'There, there!' They all pointed at the now very ordinary and innocent-looking balloon in Amy's hand.

Digit laughed and rolled his eyes. 'Oh, you're awful. You're having me on.' He picked up another two balloons and blew them up. 'Now, see if you can guess what this is.' Turning his back on Amy again, he began twisting them together. Of course the moment he did, the balloon in Amy's hand became the Lappett snake once more and the children went wild. *It hasn't gone this well since Ormidia in '76*, Drikk thought with satisfaction as he picked up yet another balloon and started constructing the Graggle hound. 'Have you guessed what it is yet?' he asked the children.

'Snake! Snake!' they all cried.

'Snake?' He held up the partially completed Graggle hound. 'This isn't a snake.' He regarded his audience suspiciously. 'I think you're teasing me.'

'NO!'

'Oh yes, you are.'

'Oh no, we're not!'

'Oh yes, you are!'

'Oh no, we're not!'

'Oh well, I can see what I'm going to have to do. This calls for drastic measures. Any more messing about and I'll set the Suture Monster on you.' Drikk went back to his Graggle hound and Amy found herself holding a snake once again.

'SNAAAKE!' the children called.

Digit almost fell off his stool. 'Snake?' he asked, looking around. Then he turned on his audience. 'Right,' he said, putting down the half-completed Graggle hound. 'I did warn you. I'll have to get the Suture Monster out.' Drikk adjusted the position of his feet on the mat, and from the speakers boomed a series of ominous, dramatic chords. Reaching into his pocket in an exaggeratedly theatrical way, Digit pulled out a large iron key and inserted it into the lock of the small chest in front of the table. From inside the box came a terrifying CAW! And as Digit slowly raised the lid, a monstrous creature began to emerge. Its beak was long and armed with teeth, its head adorned with an elaborate crest festooned with sharp spines, and its eyes were bloodshot and angry. Its long wings sprouted murderous claws, and on its feet it had talons like knives. How it had fitted inside the box was a mystery – it was at least five times its size. After clambering out, it stood towering over Amy, fixing her with its malevolent eye.

Amy, who was terrified, immediately peed her pants and, as Drikk feigned disinterest and carried on making the Graggle hound, the Suture Monster snapped her up in its beak, and with a flap of its great wings took off, circling the room over the heads of the children. Amy, wriggling between its jaws, screamed at a pitch audible to bats, and was then violently sick, covering the children below with regurgitated Frosties.

Bugger! Drikk thought. *I knew it was going too well.* 'Don't struggle,' he called to Amy. 'The teeth won't hurt if you don't struggle! Hang on, dear, I'll soon have you down.' But, pressing the control button beneath the mat with his right foot, nothing happened. Amy's urine had seeped into the electronics and shorted the system. The Suture Monster was out of Drikk's control.

'Get my child down!'

Drikk looked up to see a short, angry woman.

'I'm sorry, madam, but I'm having a bit of trouble with my remote servos.'

'You'll have more than trouble with your remote servos if you don't get my Amy down this instant!'

'Just give me a moment.' Putting the Graggle hound down beside him, Drikk lifted the sopping wet mat. Everything underneath was soaked. 'Oh dear.' As he spoke these words, the Graggle hound, sparks flashing from its ears, started growling and strutting around the room, slavering all over the watching children. The adults were instantly on their feet, gathering up their offspring and making for the door. But, to their surprise, the false wall Drikk had constructed in front of the French windows suddenly exploded and they found themselves faced with a terrifying creature the size of a bear: the Thrringg wolf was loose. Now the grown-ups were screaming too, and everyone was rushing around in terror while Drikk frantically tried to dry out the electronics, using his wig as a mop.

'Please,' he called out, 'don't panic. They won't hurt you.' But the inaccuracy of this statement was amply demonstrated by the Thrringg wolf, which now had one of the children between its jaws and was thrashing it violently from side to side. The child's mother looked on in horror. 'Oh shit, oh shit,' Drikk murmured, mopping frantically.

It took two of the other parents to free the child from the jaws of the Thrringg wolf, after which the terrified mother wrenched open the French windows and escaped, clutching her bawling child under her arm. Others followed, only to run straight into a phalanx of strange creatures straight out of a nightmare. There was a thing with two heads, a blue monster with no head, a group of glass-like beings and a clump of sacks with eyes. This induced even greater terror in adults and children alike, and they ran around in panic, not knowing which way to turn, menaced by the Thrringg wolf from behind and harried from above by the Suture Monster, swooping low over their heads.

Armani, driving Harry's gold Rolls Royce up the drive, was suddenly faced with a troupe of panic-stricken children and adults, all running around in circles. But Armani was getting used to strange things happening at Hambledon and, after all the other weirdness he'd witnessed, wasn't much surprised at the large prehistoric-looking bird with a small child in its beak, which was repeatedly dive-bombing the panicking people.

'Tch, this place,' he muttered.

Piloting the car through the terrified crowd, he pulled into the turning circle at the top of the drive outside the Hall itself and wound down the window. 'Harry!' he called. A white-faced Huxley emerged from around the corner of the building and climbed wordlessly into the back seat of the Rolls.

'You all right, Harry?' Armani asked.

'Just drive,' said Harry, wide-eyed with fear.

'Oh, right.' But, as Armani was about to move off, a small army of strange creatures, led by a large slug-like being, suddenly appeared and surrounded the car, while a gaggle of what looked like large, loose sacks, who seemed to be breaking wind and whistling simultaneously, nervously brought up the rear.

'See – farting sacks,' Armani crowed.

'I know,' Harry whispered.

The large slug tapped on Harry's window and, obediently, he wound it down.

'Excuse me,' enquired the Glubbus, 'but we're looking for Whipple. Do you happen to know where he's organized refreshments?'

Harry simply shook his head.

'Oh,' said the Glubbus, disappointed. 'Well, thanks anyway.' The slug turned back to its companions. 'He doesn't know. Maybe we should look in the kitchen.' The creatures trooped back around the corner of the Hall.

Armani swivelled round in his seat to address his employer. 'I told you this place wasn't right.'

Harry sat dumbly in the back – he'd gone rather a strange colour.

After a few moments of absolute silence, someone else appeared at Harry's window. It was Lady Trenchard.

'There you are,' she said to Harry, 'I've been trying to get hold of you all morning. We've decided to accept your offer.'

Harry, ashen-faced, remained silent.

'I said we want to sell. We'll accept your offer,' Lady Trenchard repeated.

'Offer?' Harry replied in a small whisper. 'For this place? You must be joking.'

Lady Trenchard looked confused. 'Oh, but I thought—'

'The offer's withdrawn. Get us out of here, Armani.'

'With pleasure.' Armani clunked the Rolls into gear and the big car moved sedately off down the drive.

Lady Trenchard was left alone and feeling rather lost. Turning back towards the Hall, she suddenly felt icy cold fingers close around her heart and she clutched at her cardigan as the world began to spin. 'Oh dear!'

'Pamela! Pamela old girl!'

Sir Percival was racing towards her, ahead of Whipple and another man she didn't recognize. Her strength failing, blackness ringed her vision and her knees buckled.

Drikk, who was slumped despondently on the floor of the silent dining room, surveyed the ruins of yet another failure. *This is it*, he thought, *the end of the road. Who am I trying to kid? I'm just not very good. Dad was right; I should have stayed in insurance.*

'Excuse me.'

Drikk looked up to see a man, covered in plaster from the Thrringg wolf's exploding wall, beaming down at him. 'Yes?'

'I love your act.'

'I'm sorry?'

'I've never seen anything quite like it. It's very unusual, very *now*.'

'Now?'

'I think you've really got something.'

'Me?' Drikk queried.

'Sorry, I'm Richie Darling.' The man offered his hand.

'How do you do?' said Drikk. 'Digit the Clown.' He gave a sad little shake of his head.

'I should explain,' Richie said. 'I'm a producer for Channel 5. I'm developing a new late night comedy show and we're looking for unusual speciality acts. I'd say yours fits that description. I'm only here by chance because I'm staying with friends down in the village. Serendipity, eh?'

Drikk gave him a wan smile.

'I nearly didn't come at all,' said Richie. 'Kids' parties aren't really my thing. Look, I'd better go. That was my friend's child your creature was trying to eat.'

'Sorry,' said Drikk.

'Don't mention it – she's a little monster.' Richie handed Drikk a business card. 'Why don't you come and see me next week? Good to have met you, cheerio.' He paused in the doorway. 'You really are very talented, you know.' Richie walked out through the French doors into the gardens, leaving Drikk alone, confused, but basking in the afterglow of the first praise he'd ever received.

The delegates, being unable to find Whipple, or indeed any sign of refreshments, at last began to realize that they'd been abandoned. Deciding to call it a day and go home, they headed up towards the field at the back of the Hall where their spaceships were parked, and walked straight into Richie Darling as he was coming out of the dining room.

'Guys,' said Richie. 'I think you're fantastic.' He handed his business card to the Mufflet, who was carelessly tossing his head back and forth between his hands. 'Love it!'

Taking the card, the Mufflet proceeded to eat it. Richie laughed. 'Great act,' he said. 'Really *great* act.'

On the grass verge at the side of the drive, Lady Trenchard came round to the smell of an amyl nitrate capsule that Whipple was wafting under her nose, and looked up at the three men surrounding her.

'Oh, Percy,' she sobbed. 'We're done for.'

'Nonsense,' Percy replied, gently stroking the back of her hand.

'No, you don't understand. Huxley doesn't want the Hall.'

'No, Pamela old girl, *you* don't understand. May I introduce Mr Lockwood Stiles, Christies' wine expert.'

'How do you do, Lady Trenchard. Please don't get up.'

The man was immaculate in an expensively tailored dark-grey suit.

'Delighted,' replied Lady Trenchard, offering her hand.

'Whipple invited him down to have a look at our cellar,' Sir Percy continued. 'Apparently we've got stuff in there that's worth a packet!'

Lady Trenchard wasn't sure if the amyl nitrate had befuddled her thinking. 'But—'

'I know,' said Percy, 'we thought there was nothing down there but Blue Nun and three-year-old Beaujolais Nouveau. But Lockwood here's found some dynamite stuff, haven't you?'

'It really is most exciting,' Lockwood said. 'A double magnum of 1865 Château Lafite-Rothschild sold for over £27,000 at a recent auction, and you have several dozen. And that's not all. Your case of Dow's 1896 vintage is alone worth a small fortune. I don't think I'm sticking my neck out by saying that your entire collection, should you wish to sell, would easily make seven figures.'

The Suture Monster, its batteries at last running out, swooped low overhead, landing softly on the smooth green lawn, and Lady Trenchard watched blankly as Amy was reunited with her relieved mother. But, seeing several strange-looking craft scooting low over the greensward, only to disappear with a *whoosh* into the rhododendron at the end of the ha-ha, was too much for Pamela Trenchard. She lapsed into unconsciousness once again.

*

As the Glubbus's borrowed spaceship approached Gweeb, Matt cut the engines.

'What are we doing here?' Mariella asked.

'Visiting a friend,' Matt replied enigmatically, landing the ship in a small clearing. Unbuckling his seat belt, he opened the hatch. 'Falco, grab Zach and follow me.' Matt looked back at Mariella and Glaak. 'Keep her warm – we're going to need to get out of here fast.'

Stepping out into the jungle, all Matt's senses were on high alert. 'OK, Falco, put him down and get back in the ship.' Zach's life-sustaining fluid sloshed about in the jar as he was laid gently down on the jungle floor. Falco looked up at Matt questioningly. 'Go on, get out of here!' Matt ordered. Falco shrugged, then turned and ran back to the ship.

'Where are we, Matt?'

'Journey's end, Zach. You'll enjoy it here. There's no Park to worry about; you're absolutely free to be who you are. And there's someone here you're going to love – someone more your own age. You know that song you were singing earlier?'

'"The Alvorg Bunny" song?'

'Yeah, that's the one. Will you do me a favour?'

'Sure, Matt. What do you want?'

'Count slowly to fifty, then start singing it, will you?'

'Oh, is this a game? I love games. OK, one . . . two . . .'

Matt cupped his hands to his mouth. 'Hey! Planet!' he yelled into the surrounding jungle. 'I've got something for you! Come and get it!'

At the very edge of his consciousness, Matt felt something stir. Time to go.

''Bye, Zach, have fun now.' Matt ran back to the ship. He found Glaak standing on the gangplank, the Cartogram in his hands. 'Come on, Glaak, we've got to leave.'

'You know,' Glaak replied thoughtfully, tapping the Cartogram with a small claw, 'this thing has caused nothing but trouble.'

'You're telling me. But we have to get out of here. Now.'

'Perhaps it would be better for us all if it were to get . . . lost.'

'Excuse me?'

'What if it were to fall into that tangle of razor-thorn there, never to be seen again?'

'Glaak, are you serious? I've nursed that thing all over the galaxy. I've risked my life to get it to you – I've got the bruises to prove it – and now you're just going to throw it away?'

'As long the Cartogram exists there will be people hungry for it and the power that it wields. Think about it: if it vanishes as if it had never existed, it would be one less temptation for the megalomaniacs; one less problem for the rest of us. The Cartogram is a heavy load; believe me, I know. I myself have suffered under the crushing weight of responsibility that comes with the office of its Chief Custodian, and I'm not going to pass that burden on to anyone else.'

'But what if someone finds it?'

'Who, apart from us, is going to know it's here? Gweeb has a big "Keep Out" sign written right across it. The Cartogram is safer here than anywhere else in the galaxy.'

Matt could feel the planet's consciousness rising up from the depths of sleep. 'But what about the Helians? I thought the Cartogram was sacred to you?'

'We're used to making sacrifices, so one more will make little difference, especially if it's for the good of the entire universe.'

Now the planet was wide awake – Matt could feel it all around. 'We've got to go! Glaak, I've always trusted you. It's your call.'

'Thank you, Matt.' Glaak walked to the edge of the gangplank. Looking down one last time at the black rectangle he was carrying, he bade it farewell. 'Goodbye.' Then, opening his paws, he let it fall. The Cartogram hit the ground and tumbled, end over end, finally coming to rest among the tangled tendrils of a razor-thorn.

Scooping Glaak into his arms, Matt ran up the gangplank

and into the ship. 'OK, next stop, Earth.' The door closed with a *hiss* and, seconds later, the craft was shooting away across the sky.

Well, well, well, what do we have here? The planet's probing psychic fingers began to explore its latest visitor.

'. . . forty-five . . . forty-six . . . forty-seven . . .'

My word, what a vast range of experiences there seem to be packed into one so small. Oh, I can see we're going to have fun, you and I . . .

'. . . forty-nine . . . fifty! Ready or not, here it comes!' Zach broke into song. '"Oh, Here comes the Bunny, the Bunny, the Bunny . . ."'

Ah, music! I can't tell you how one has been starved of culture out here. No one appreciates the Arts any more. But let me enjoy your song . . .

'"Is he a monkey, a monkey, a monkey?

NO! He's Alvorg the Bunny . . ."'

Whipple was in the kitchen making a pot of tea when he heard the familiar scuffling of rodent feet. 'General,' he said as he saw Glaak Raffin scurrying across the floor towards him, 'would you care for a cup of tea?'

Glaak held up a front foot. 'It's tempting, but no time I'm afraid. I've come to say goodbye.'

Whipple put a cosy over the steaming teapot. 'You're leaving?'

'Well, there's nothing left to do here. And, may I say, we couldn't have done it without you.'

'You've saved the universe?'

'Let's not be too hasty, but I believe we have a good chance, a very good chance. I just wanted to thank you for all your help, and to apologize for my rather ill-behaved colleagues, talking of which, you don't happen to have seen them, do you? They seem to have disappeared.'

'I did see the Glubbus,' Whipple replied. 'He was wandering around looking rather lost.'

'Ah,' said Glaak, 'I'd better go and find him.' He extended a front foot and Whipple knelt and took it.

'It's been a pleasure,' said the butler. 'I can't say it's been easy, but it's certainly been . . . different.'

Glaak rolled his eyes. 'It's been that, all right. I'm just sorry I couldn't do more to help. I hate leaving you like this, what with the house falling down around your ears and all.'

'Oh, you've helped more than you know, General. And don't worry about Hambledon. I have a feeling that everything's going to be just fine.'

'Glad to hear it. Oh well, must be off. Can't keep everyone waiting.'

'If ever you're in this neck of the woods again, don't pass us by,' said Whipple.

'And miss the best cup of tea in the known universe? Try and keep me away. Cheerio, old friend.'

'Cheerio,' Whipple echoed.

Glaak hurried out of the kitchen and Whipple watched through the window as the fat brown rat raced across the lawn and almost collided with the large form of the Glubbus, who was mooching around looking very sorry for himself. After a short exchange, both creatures disappeared into the ha-ha.

Seeing the spacecraft rise out of the ditch and hover slowly towards the rhododendron, Whipple was surprised at the depth of emotion he felt.

'Good luck and God speed,' he said, wiping his eyes.

As the small craft reached the end of the ha-ha it disappeared into the flowering shrub with a *whoosh*.

Lady Trenchard, much recovered, was seated on the drawing-room sofa between Sir Percy and Lockwood Stiles, Christies' leading wine expert.

As Whipple entered, carrying a large silver tray laden with tea things, Lady Trenchard looked up. 'Ah, Whipple,' she said, 'we were just wondering how it was that we could have remained unaware of our extensive wine collection for all these years. Do you have a theory?' she said with a searching look.

Whipple placed the tea-tray down on the dining-table before replying. 'I'm sure I don't need to tell you, ma'am, that this house has many little secrets. One could live here a lifetime and never uncover half of them. It's as much a mystery to me as it is to you how those bottles conspired to avoid discovery – a mystery, indeed, we may never get to the bottom of.'

'No,' said Lady Trenchard, 'I don't suppose we ever will.' And she stared hard at Whipple's usually implacable visage, where she thought she detected just a hint of smugness. But Whipple reckoned he was allowed to indulge himself in a little self-satisfaction: after all, one didn't help save the universe *and* rescue one's family from ruin every day.

'Ah, tea, good.' Sir Percival stood and eyed the tea-tray eagerly. 'Um, is there any cake?'

'I believe we have some rich tea biscuits in the larder, sir. And, of course, there is pie.'

The baronet grimaced. 'Erm, just bring the biscuits, there's a good chap.'

'Certainly, sir.'

As Whipple was about to leave, Tom entered the room, arm in arm with Mary.

'Ahem,' he cleared his throat nervously. 'Mother, Father, Mary here . . .' He looked lovingly at the young woman, and she blushed. 'Mary,' he repeated, 'has graciously consented to be my wife.'

'Hoorah! About bloody time, Tom,' said Sir Percival, gleefully.

'Percy, *language*,' admonished Lady Trenchard. 'Congratulations, Tom. Welcome to the family, Mary.' She stood and embraced her prospective daughter-in-law.

Sir Percival gave Mary a peck on the cheek. 'We were despairing of ever getting rid of him.' He thumped his son playfully on the arm. 'Well done, son. Well done.'

Lockwood rose and applauded the happy couple. 'Congratulations, Tom. You'll make an elegant bride, Mary.'

'This calls for something special,' said Sir Percy. 'Whipple!'

Whipple was still standing in the doorway. 'Sir?'

'What would you suggest to celebrate such an occasion?'

'May I suggest the 1873 Malmsey, sir?'

'Perfect!'

Lockwood's eyes widened. 'You're not going to *drink* it?'

'Well, we're not going to polish the bloody furniture with it. Whipple, crack open a bottle! On second thoughts, crack open the whole case!'

Whipple bowed. 'Certainly, sir.'

Parking His asteroid in orbit, God descended to the surface of planet Gweeb. Almost immediately He felt a presence. He also became aware of someone singing:

'". . . Is he a zebra, a zebra, a zebra?

'"NO! He's Alvorg the Bunny, the Bunny, the Bunny . . ."'

Help! went another voice in His mind. It seemed to be clawing at Him in desperation. *You've got to make it stop . . . Ouch!*

God had slapped the planet down and was metaphorically standing on its neck. *Behave!* He warned.

Sorry, said the planet miserably.

'*I need your help*,' said God. '*I'm looking for . . . ah!*'

Something had caught His eye. There, in a tangle of vicious razor-thorn lay the greatest prize in the universe: the Helian Cartogram. '*There you are*,' said God, bending down and picking it up.

'"Is he a turkey, a turkey, a turkey?

'"NO! He's Alvorg the Bunny, the Bunny, the Bunny . . ."'

'*Who's your friend?*' God asked the planet.

He's not my friend – he's a living hell.
'I thought you were always complaining that you were lonely?'
Believe me, my solitude was paradise compared to this.
'Well, he seems happy enough. I think it's very nice that you've got someone to play with after all these years.'
' "Is he a camel, a camel, a camel?
' "NO! He's Alvorg the Bunny, the Bunny, the Bunny . . ." '
'Quite catchy, this tune, isn't it?'
You have no idea.

God straightened up and prepared to leave. *Right then, must be getting on: people to see, galaxies to build . . .*

No! pleaded the planet. *You can't leave me like this!*

'Why don't you let him teach it to you? Then you could sing a duet. Cheerio!' And God left the planet in a puff of fragrant smoke.

' "Is he a . . ." ' Zach paused for a moment. 'You know, Matt was right, I'm really having fun. No one has ever allowed me to sing all the verses of "The Alvorg Bunny" song before.'

How many verses are there?

'Nine thousand, two hundred and seventy-three. ' "Oh! Is he a Klingon, a Klingon, a Klingon?

' "NO! He's Alvorg the Bunny, the Bunny, the Bunny . . ." '
AAAARRRGGHHH!

'The Alvorg Bunny' song and the anguished cries of the planet rang out across the empty deafness of space – and would do for some time.

News of the fall of the Crusader Empire slowly filtered through to even the most far-flung of the old Alliance planets, and those who had remained loyal to the rebel cause finally came out of hiding and began flocking to Cullorum. Even the delegates of the old Rebel Council eventually worked it out for themselves and began to head for the reconquered Alliance base.

Under Glaak's guidance, Cullorum City was gradually restored to its former glory. The arena was demolished and the old government building completely refurbished – with a little help from Falco and Coyle, whose newly opened computer business had won the lucrative contract to supply the Alliance Council with computers and peripherals. They also had a little sideline selling free-range eggs.

Finally, in a grand ceremony to celebrate the reopening of Government House, Glaak, Matt and Mariella were awarded the highest honour any serving officer can receive: the Galactic Cross. Falco and Coyle were awarded lesser honours, and even Falco's mum received a shiny gold medal for gallantry, which she pecked at happily.

In an unprecedented move by the new Council, Glaak was offered the premiership of the galaxy, but he declined, saying that no one person should ever again be allowed to wield such power. He did, however, momentarily take up the premier's right to perform certain ceremonies, and married Matt and Mariella in the Great Hall.

After the ceremony, the newlyweds stepped out through the doors of Government House to be met by cheering crowds, who lifted them on to their shoulders and carried them to the recently opened Raffin Square, a large open area in the centre of the city where the arena had once stood, and where their spaceship was waiting, festooned with ribbons and balloons, boots and cans tied to its bumpers.

They were seen off by Glaak, Coyle, Falco and his mum.

'Have a good one,' Coyle grinned.

'Wish I was coming with you,' said Falco.

'Squawk!'

'No, Mum's probably right. Have a good time.'

Glaak wished them goodbye with tears in his eyes. 'The very best of luck,' he sniffed.

Mariella crouched and tickled the rat under the chin. 'You know where we are if you need us.'

'I think I can probably manage things from here. Besides, you're not going to want to be disturbed for a while.'

'What are you going to do now?' Matt asked.

Glaak shrugged. 'Someone's got to play nursemaid to the infant parliament, and it looks like I picked the short straw. But as soon as it can stand on its own two feet, I'm retiring. I've had enough of politics. Do you know, we've had reports that Helios is alive and habitable once more – it's a miracle! So, once I'm through here, I'm going back to Argus to lead what's left of us Helians back home.'

'Enjoy your retirement,' said Matt. 'You've earned it,'

Glaak smiled and nodded his head. 'I have indeed.'

'We'll come and visit,' said Mariella.

'Do, and I want you to promise to bring your first-born to meet me.'

'We'll name him after you,' said Matt.

Mariella turned to him. 'Will we?'

'Of course.'

'But what if he doesn't look like a Glaak? What if he looks more like a Hal, or a Jeff? He may even be a she.'

'So?'

'You can't call a girl "Glaak".'

'Why not?'

'Children, children,' Glaak interrupted, 'don't let *me* be the cause of your first marital row.'

'We're not having a row,' said Matt.

'Well, that's what it seemed like to me,' Mariella snapped. 'You started it.'

'I did not!'

'Go, just go!' Glaak urged them into the spaceship.

Matt and Mariella turned and waved to the crowd as they walked up the gangplank. 'I can't get over the fact you want to call our boy Jeff,' muttered Matt as the door of the small craft closed behind them.

Moments later, to a great cheer, the spaceship rose ponderously into the air, did a slow circuit of the square, then soared off into space.

Glaak watched the craft until it was a distant speck. 'Go in peace, my friends.'

A Mingus pushed through the crowd and bustled up to him, clutching a piece of parchment. 'Sir, I have the draft of the amended constitution. Would you like to go through it now?'

'Oh, yes, Jak-Ling, yes of course. Ah well,' Glaak sighed, wiping his eyes, 'back to work.' And he allowed himself to be led through the cheering crowd and back into the airy vastness of the parliament building.

Glitch and Rhinn, having been found guilty of war crimes, crimes against humanity, and just about every other crime in the book, were banished for life to the penal colony on Alkan 5. Once there, for their own safety, they were put immediately into joint solitary confinement. Over the years both of them had made numerous enemies, and many of the other inmates were anxious to settle old scores.

Rhinn suffered terribly; the clothes he'd been given were made of the coarse wool of the Drugget sheep, which brought him out in an itchy rash. Likewise, Glitch too was far from happy. During his interrogation, the arm of his revolving eye had become twisted, and now pointed heavenwards. All day long his unblinking eye was forced to stare at the sun which beat mercilessly down upon the scorched prison planet.

The two convicts spent all their mealtimes together, miserably bemoaning their fate and fruitlessly planning revenge on those who had put them there.

Back at Hambledon, things are very different these days. With the money the wine made at auction, the Trenchards have been able to fix up the Hall, pay Whipple his back-salary as well as give him a generous raise, and employ more staff to help out around the place. Their unexpected windfall also enables them to take several holidays a year, and Lady Trenchard has discovered golf, with subsequent benefits to her health. Sir Percival, however, does not share his spouse's enthusiasm for the game, preferring instead the more sedentary delights of the club house.

Sadly, the Hambledon annual children's party is no more, the Trenchards choosing instead the safer option of donating a lump sum to the village, which now has a brand-new adventure play-ground, built on a plot of wasteland behind the pub.

As for Harry and Armani, they haven't been seen ever since driving out of the gates of Hambledon Hall, but are rumoured to have joined a small farming community in the Solomon Islands.

Tom and Mary married in the spring and soon after, having found something more interesting to do with his time, Tom gave up his cricket coaching job, and he and his new wife moved into a small house in the village to be near his parents. With a bit of financial help from mum and dad, Tom bought Harry Huxley's suddenly vacant offices and converted them into Trenchard's Hot Pie Shop, serving pies made to a traditional, but secret, old English recipe. Business is booming and the love-birds are blissfully happy, although Tom has put on a little weight.

Drikk, having had great success in his Channel 5 slot, now regularly features on programmes such as *Celebrity Haircut* and *I'm an Alien, Get Me Out of Here!*

Something else that's been making the headlines recently is the discovery of a new galaxy between the Virgo and Coma clusters. Because of its particular shape – a deep smooth base with, on top, a strange raised section right in the middle – it has been nicknamed: *The Jaffa Cake Galaxy*.